**W9-DIW-550**

## ALSO BY HIDEO YOKOYAMA

*Six Four*

# SEVENTEEN

MCD ⬡ FARRAR, STRAUS AND GIROUX   NEW YORK

# SEVENTEEN

## HIDEO YOKOYAMA

*Translated from the Japanese by*
*Louise Heal Kawai*

MCD
Farrar, Straus and Giroux
175 Varick Street, New York 10014

Printed in the United States of America
Originally published in Japanese in 2003 by Bungeishunju Ltd., Tokyo, as *Kuraimāzu hai*
  (Climber's High)
English translation originally published in 2018 by Quercus Editions Limited, Great Britain
English translation published in the United States by MCD / Farrar, Straus and Giroux
First American edition, 2018

Library of Congress Cataloging-in-Publication Data
Names: Yokoyama, Hideo, 1957– author. | Kawai, Louise Heal, translator.
Title: Seventeen / Hideo Yokoyama ; translated from the Japanese by Louise Heal Kawai.
Other titles: Kuraimāzu hai. Engish
Description: First American edition. | New York : Farrar, Straus and Giroux, 2018. | "Originally
  published in Japanese in 2003 by Bungeishunju Ltd., Tokyo, as Kuraimāzu hai (Climber's
  High)"
Identifiers: LCCN 2018006845 | ISBN 9780374261245 (hardcover)
Subjects: LCSH: Suspense fiction.
Classification: LCC PL877.5.O369 K8713 2018 | DDC 895.63/6—dc23
LC record available at https://lccn.loc.gov/2018006845

Designed by Abby Kagan

10  9  8  7  6  5  4  3  2  1

## PREFACE

Five hundred twenty dead, four survivors.

The plot of *Seventeen* combines the real-life 1985 crash of a Japanese passenger plane with the fictional struggles of a local newspaper reporter.

The scene of this crash of unprecedented proportions was a remote mountain range in Gunma Prefecture. At the time, I was working as an investigative/police beat reporter at a local Gunma newspaper. I arrived at the crash site after trekking for more than eight hours up a mountain with no routes or climbing trails. The terrain was steep and unimaginably narrow, and it was the rare lucky reporter who didn't inadvertently step on a corpse. After sundown, I spent the night on the mountain, surrounded by body parts that no longer resembled anything human.

For an extended period of time a huge volume of information was relayed from the ridge of Mount Osutaka by a huge number of reporters. And yet, despite the enormity of the accident, as time passed the interest of the public waned. The kind of information we call news will always eventually evaporate, fade from memory. That hollow sense of loss was one of the reasons I quit the newspaper industry, and turned my hand instead to writing fiction.

News fades away, but stories stand the test of time. But in my case, even after my debut as a novelist, my mind was still possessed by that one shocking experience. My plan had been to write perfectly ordinary novels that relied on neither documented facts nor personal memory, but my fixation on the crash site got in the way of those ideals. Finally, seventeen years after the crash, the writing of this book enabled me to escape its curse . . . It took this novel's main character the same length of time to be ready to revisit the events of August 1985. By finally letting go of the memories you cling to, you allow new doors to open. In *Seventeen*, in distancing the action from the crash site and allowing the drama to be played out in the newsroom, far from the immediate tragedy, a whole new story has come to life. I believe that by detailing every psychological shift the editorial team undergoes as they are inundated by one problem after another, I have shed some light on the workings of the Japanese media. I'm also confident that the reader will witness both the positive and the negative essence of human nature.

—HIDEO YOKOYAMA

# CAST OF CHARACTERS

**Kyoichiro Anzai**: Key member of the Circulation Department at the *North Kanto Times* (NKT), who has been in the job for just under ten years. In his mid-forties, three or four years older than Kazumasa Yuuki. An extremely enthusiastic character: fond of drink, laughter, talking, and shaking people heartily by the shoulder. A fanatical rock climber, who single-handedly started the *NKT*'s hiking club.

**Rintaro Anzai**: Thirteen-year-old son of Kyoichiro and Sayuri Anzai. A shy boy by nature. (*Rintaro is thirty years old when he climbs Tsuitate with Yuuki in 2002.*)

**Sayuri Anzai**: Anzai's wife and Rintaro's mother. A genuine and unassuming person.

**Aoki**: Political correspondent at the *North Kanto Times*. Is away on an assignment in Tokyo at the time of the Japan Airlines (JAL) crash.

**Mitsugu Endo**: Anzai's previous climbing partner, who lost his life climbing Tsuitate in 1972.

**Kanae Fujinami**: Head of the Ministry of Transport's Aircraft Accident Investigation Committee, otherwise known as the JAL "crash investigation team."

**Prime Minister Takeo Fukuda**: A former Japanese prime minister, who left office in December 1978.

**Gunji**: Works in the *North Kanto Times*'s General Affairs/Facilities Department. Has often recommended that its reporters upgrade to using word processors, but in vain. Joined the company at the same time as Yuuki. Loyal to Chairman Shirakawa, but also an advocate of neutrality in the workplace.

**Hanazawa**: Junior police beat reporter at the *North Kanto Times*, and third in line at police headquarters behind Sayama and Wajima. A twenty-six-year-old with delicate features; has three years' experience as a reporter. Accompanies Sayama up Mount Osutaka to the crash site on the first day.

**Harasawa**: One of the members of the Ministry of Transport's crash investigation team, who it transpires is a good friend of Tamaki's university engineering professor. He implies that the cause of the JAL crash was likely the rear bulkhead.

**Iikura**: Managing director of the *North Kanto Times*, and the second most powerful figure at the company. Reportedly consolidating his support base in Circulation, ahead of making a play for the chairman's position. His subtle politicking has earned him the nickname "the Clever Yakuza." He is former Japanese Prime Minister Fukuda's closest ally at the *NKT*.

**Inaoka**: Veteran member of the *North Kanto Times*'s Editorial Department, in charge of the readers' letters page, Heartfelt. Worked for the paper's Arts and Culture page for many years. Is due to retire the following year.

**Yasuo Ito**: Head of the Circulation Department at the *North Kanto Times*. Has a distinctively oily voice, a hooked nose, and a mustache. He is Anzai's boss, and is politically sided with managing director Iikura.

**Jinbo**: Member of the copy team at the *North Kanto Times*. Responsible for the second local news page. Up until the previous year he had been a reporter at the paper's branch office in Tatebayashi City. He is viewed by senior management as a failed reporter. Between twenty-five and twenty-six years old, he often has a flushed expression on his face.

**Kaizuka**: Deputy chief of the *NKT*'s Book Publishing Division. Prior to this post he worked in the paper's Editorial Department. Yuuki contacts him to sound out the idea of a potential JAL crash book.

**Kamejima**: Chief copy editor at the *North Kanto Times*. Has a round moon face, and a habitually cheerful disposition. Nicknamed "Kaku-san" by his colleagues.

**Kasuya**: Editor in chief at the *North Kanto Times*. Has a very large physical frame. Is nonconfrontational, and as such has the nickname "the Conciliator." Not politically aligned to either the chairman or the managing director.

**Kishi**: Sub-editor on the *NKT*'s Political News Desk. Joined the company the same time as Yuuki. Has a long, narrow face. Has two daughters, named Kaz and Fumiko, who—despite having adored him as infants—now treat him, in his own words, like "some kind of germ."

**Kudo**: The *North Kanto Times*'s Maebashi branch chief. He is about to turn fifty; has a professional reputation for panicking and a personal one for gambling. Is often found at the *keirin* cycle track.

**Kurasaka**: General manager of the *North Kanto Times*'s Advertising Department. Is a couple of years older than Yuuki and was previously a member of the Editorial Department. Described as having a square face, and falls out with Yuuki when his shopping mall ad is dropped without notice.

**Mina Kuroda**: Previously personal assistant to Chairman Shirakawa, though she left her position three weeks prior to the JAL crash under a cloud of controversy.

**Miyata**: A staff member in the *North Kanto Times*'s Advertising Department. Also member of the company's hiking club and an enthusiastic rock climber. Is heavily tanned, and wears glasses.

**Ayako Mochizuki**: The female cousin of Ryota Mochizuki. Twenty years old and a second-year media studies and history of journalism student at Gunma Prefectural University.

**Ryota Mochizuki**: Junior *NKT* reporter who died in August 1980, six days into his assignment with Yuuki. Death was classified as a traffic accident, though is widely believed to have been a suicide, driven by shame.

**Moriwaki**: A first-year reporter at the *North Kanto Times* who only started going on assignments in the few months before the JAL crash.

**Moriya**: Chief political news editor at the *North Kanto Times*, and Kishi's and Aoki's senior.

**Moro**: Chief of the *NKT*'s Book Publishing Division. Has longish hair that falls below his ears. A smug, know-it-all type.

**Prime Minister Yasuhiro Nakasone**: Japan's prime minister at the time of the JAL crash. When the story breaks, he is preparing to visit the controversial Yasukuni Shrine to coincide with the fortieth anniversary of the end of the Second World War.

**Nozawa**: Copy editor for the *North Kanto Times*'s local news section. Started at the paper the same time as Yuuki, but rarely talks to him, due to a grudge held about a joint murder case scoop in 1970, for which Yuuki alone received the Editor in Chief's Award.

**Oimura**: Managing editor at the *North Kanto Times*. Nicknamed "the Firecracker," owing to his short fuse. Is loyal to Chairman Shirakawa, and was one of the main beneficiaries of the paper's golden Okubo/Red Army era.

**Sayama**: The chief police beat reporter at the *North Kanto Times*. Thirty-three years old, with ten years' reporting experience. Orphaned young: his father committed suicide when he was a child, and his mother died in a traffic accident. Like a younger brother to Yuuki, and saved Yuuki's career by coming to his rescue over the Ryota Mochizuki incident in 1980.

**Shimagawa**: Detective within the prefectural police department, and currently head of its Forensics Division. An elegant dresser, with the outward appearance of a salaryman. Two or three years older than Yuuki, he and Yuuki have not seen one another for roughly five years prior to the JAL crash.

**Shirakawa**: Chairman of the *North Kanto Times*, and holder of the most powerful position in the company. Was previously editor in chief at the paper. Is wheelchair-bound, having damaged his spinal cord in a traffic accident six months prior to the JAL crash. Has a notorious temper, which has earned him the nickname "the H-Bomb."

**Suetsugu**: An old climbing acquaintance of Anzai's. In his mid-forties, and around the same age as Anzai. Deeply suntanned, with a wide, friendly face. His small shoes are a result of his losing his toes to frostbite.

**Suzumoto**: Assistant manager of the Photography Department at the *North Kanto Times*. He points out his junior colleague Tono to Yuuki when Yuuki comes looking for him.

**Manami Takagi**: Personal assistant to Chairman Shirakawa. Described as stunningly beautiful. Started in the role three weeks before the JAL crash.

**Tamaki**: A reporter in his third year at the *North Kanto Times*, currently covering the Maebashi City Mayor's Office. It transpires he is the only reporter at the company with a degree in engineering, and so is subsequently reassigned to follow the Ministry of Transport's Aircraft Accident Investigation Committee. Has an earnest face, and wears his hair in a neat side-parting.

**Todoroki**: Chief local news editor at the *North Kanto Times*. Wears gold-rimmed spectacles with dark lenses. Along with managing editor Oimura, he has profited most from the paper's Okubo/Red Army era—to the extent that he still carries clippings from the period in his pocket diary.

**Tono**: A young member of the *North Kanto Times's* Photography Department, in his fourth year at the company. Sports a neat crew cut, and his wife is pregnant at the time of the JAL crash. Is the only *NKT* staff member to witness Hanazawa's punching Kurasaka on Mount Osutaka.

**Totsuka**: A reporter based remotely at the *NKT's* Fujioka City branch office. In his fifth year with the company.

**Ukita**: Chief of the Advertising Department at the *North Kanto Times*. The superior of Kurasaka and Miyata, who cameos when calling Yuuki's bosses to register his indignation about the dropping of the mall opening advertisement.

**Wajima**: Deputy police beat reporter at the *North Kanto Times*. Considered too timid to hold this role. Is first to reply to Yuuki once the JAL crash site is confirmed, but then fails to make it up Mount Osutaka.

**Yamada**: Reporter working on the regional news desk at the *North Kanto Times*. His trademark is his tousled hair.

**Chizuko Yorita**: Provides administrative support to the Editorial Department at the *North Kanto Times*. Treated like a tea lady by the reporters. Twenty-seven years old, she aspires to be the paper's first female reporter.

**Yoshii**: A veteran copy editor at the *North Kanto Times*. Although he's in his mid-thirties, his slight build and childlike face give him a much younger appearance. Almost always seen with a ruler in his hand.

**Jun Yuuki**: Teenage son of Kazumasa and Yumiko Yuuki. A gloomy thirteen-year-old who largely ignores his father.

**Kazumasa Yuuki**: The novel's main character, and a roving reporter at the *North Kanto Times*. Yuuki is forty years old, and the paper's longest-serving reporter. Only staff member to hold the unusual title of "roving reporter," having shunned managerial career development since the issue with Ryota Mochizuki five years previously. Made JAL crash desk chief when the crash is confirmed to be in Gunma Prefecture. (*Yuuki is fifty-seven years old when he climbs Tsuitate with Rintaro Anzai in 2002.*)

**Yuka Yuuki**: The daughter and youngest child of Kazumasa and Yumiko Yuuki. An energetic, sweet-natured girl.

**Yumiko Yuuki**: Wife of Kazumasa Yuuki, and mother of Jun and Yuka.

# SEVENTEEN

**1** The wheels on the old-fashioned train clanked to a stop.

Doai Station on the Japan Railways Joetsu Line was in the far north tip of Gunma Prefecture. The platform was in a deep underground tunnel, with 486 steps to climb to reach daylight. Perhaps "scale" would have been a better word than "climb," given how much his legs were having to work. It was fair to say that the ascent of Mount Tanigawa began right here.

Kazumasa Yuuki began to feel pain as the tips of his toes pressed against his climbing boots. Pain-free, it would have been enough of a challenge to get to the top of the steps in one go. He reached the landing at the three hundredth step (the number was painted on it) and took a breather. He was struck by the same thought he'd had all those years before. He was being tested; maybe this was what separated the men from the boys. But if climbing stairs was enough to leave him out of breath, perhaps he didn't have what it took to make an assault on Devil's Mountain. Seventeen years ago, the excesses of a newspaper reporter's lifestyle had left him struggling for breath; now, his fifty-seven years on this earth were taking their toll on his heart rate.

He was going to climb the Tsuitate rock face.

He felt his determination beginning to waver, but Kyoichiro Anzai's twinkling eyes were still there in the back of his mind. He could still hear him, too—particularly one phrase that the veteran rock climber had casually dropped into conversation: "I climb up to step down."

Yuuki raised his head and began once again to climb the stairs.

*"I climb up to step down."* He had always wondered about the meaning of

this riddle. He believed he had the solution, but the only person who knew the definitive answer wasn't around anymore to ask.

Ground level at last. He stood a moment, bathed in the gentle early autumn sunshine. It had just turned two in the afternoon, and the wind felt a little cold on his cheek. Takasaki City, farther south in Gunma Prefecture, where Yuuki had lived most of his life, was nothing like this. The temperature and the way the air smelled were completely different here.

He set off walking north along Route 291, leaving the red, pointed roof of the station building behind him. He passed over a level crossing, through a snow-break tunnel, and then, on his right, was a large swath of lawn. Doai Cemetery.

He glanced at the monument put up by the local people of the village of Minakami. It bore the names of all 779 climbers who had lost their lives on Mount Tanigawa. The nickname Devil's Mountain only began to convey its gruesome history. Other popular nicknames were Gravestone Mountain or Man-Eating Mountain. It was part of a two-thousand-meter mountain range, and nowhere on earth was there a deadlier peak. One reason was its location. It marked the border between two prefectures, and the weather there was notorious for changing with no warning; the results were often fatal. But the real reasons for Mount Tanigawa's reputation were its infamous vertical rock faces.

It was all about being the first to conquer an unclimbed rock face, and rivalry was fierce. In the early days, the most extreme climbers poured into this area like a tsunami, craving the challenge and the kudos. When the underground station was first built, they used to run at full speed up all 486 steps. Every minute—every second—counted in the competition to scale the rock walls. They climbed with abandon, and fell with the same abandon. The more the word went around that Tanigawa was a treacherously difficult mountain, the more adrenaline-pumped these young, passionate climbers became, and the list of names on the monument grew longer.

But one of the Ichinokurasawa rock faces, Tsuitate, remained unconquered; for years it had been among rock climbers a synonym for "impossible" or "the ultimate challenge." As time passed, equipment was improved, climbing skills became more sophisticated, and a dozen or so climbing routes were marked out on the Tsuitate face. Needless to say, it took the sacrifice of many more lives to accomplish this.

The Worst of the Worst—the nickname given to Tsuitate.

"Hey, Yuu. Let's take a shot at Tsuitate!"

Anzai had brought Yuuki to check out the Tsuitate face. It was Anzai, too, who had taught Yuuki everything he knew about climbing. Seventeen years ago, Yuuki and Anzai were supposed to have attached their climbing ropes and made their assault on the mountain.

But their plans had been thwarted. The night before they were due to set out, a Japan Airlines jumbo jet had crashed into the mountains near Uenomura, Gunma Prefecture. In an instant, 520 lives were lost. Yuuki had been put in charge of coverage of the crash at the local *North Kanto Times*, so, as it turned out, he'd done battle with a completely different "Gravestone Mountain."

And Anzai— Sensing activity ahead, Yuuki looked up to see that he had almost reached the Doaiguchi ropeway terminal. The square in front of the station and the nearby parking lot were bustling with day-trippers. Ignoring the souvenir stalls, he continued along the old road until he spotted the Climbing Information Center. He glanced at his watch. It wasn't quite three o'clock. He had a little time to wait, so he sat down on one of the benches inside. He was approached by a cheerful-looking man wearing an armband that identified him as a guide.

"Hello there. Which route are you planning to take?"

"We're going to set up camp at Ichinokurasawa, then climb the Tsuitate face tomorrow."

As he spoke, Yuuki unzipped his waist pouch and produced his climbing permit. He'd submitted his application by mail about ten days previously, and it had been returned to him approved and stamped.

"Tsuitate, huh?" the guide muttered, looking down at the permit. The first thing he must have spotted was Yuuki's age. Then the section giving details of his experience raised an eyebrow. In preparation for this ascent, Yuuki had been rock climbing many times at the Haruna and Myogi ski resorts, but he had no serious climbing experience under his belt. The guide was finding it increasingly difficult to maintain his cheerful expression, but just as he was about to say something, a tall young man walked through the door and greeted Yuuki with a bow.

"I'm sorry I'm late."

"What, you're young Anzai's climbing buddy?" said the guide, his tone softening. Any trace of his earlier anxiety vanished, and he stood up and left.

"Thanks."

Yuuki gave a wry smile, and the young ace of the local mountaineering club flashed him a grin in return.

When Rintaro Anzai smiled, he was the embodiment of youth. It was hard to believe he had already turned thirty. He'd inherited his father's large, twinkling eyes, but his shyness and modesty had come from his mother. Anzai senior had once confided in Yuuki that his son was supposed to have been named Rentaro, not Rintaro. If you'd put his family name and the first part of his given name together (Anzai Ren) it would have sounded like the German *anseilen*, which, in the climbing world, means tying on the rope.

"But the wife saw through that one right away," he'd said wistfully.

"Yuuki-san, any news of Jun?" Rintaro asked.

"I haven't managed to get in touch with him."

Yuuki couldn't look Rintaro in the eyes. His son, Jun, had an apartment in Tokyo. Yuuki had left a message on his voice mail to let him know about today's plan, but Jun hadn't called back.

"So it'll be just the two of us. That was the plan in the first place, anyway."

"All right. So how shall we do this? We could stay the night here, if you like?"

"No, I'd prefer to get up to where the rivers meet at Ichinokurasawa and pitch the tents. It's been so long. I'm looking forward to seeing it again."

Rintaro nodded, clearly pleased by Yuuki's enthusiastic response, and started to check the equipment.

Yuuki watched him in admiration. He'd known Rintaro since he was thirteen years old. The boy had grown up into a sturdy young man, both physically and mentally. Most important, he'd been raised to be kind and honest.

Two months ago, Rintaro had been standing alone in the parking lot of a funeral hall in Maebashi. He was silently watching the trail of smoke rising from the square chimney of the crematorium. His eyes were wet but he didn't let himself cry. Yuuki had come up and patted him on the shoulder.

"Looks like Dad headed north after all," Rintaro had mumbled, still looking up at the sky.

"Ready."

"Great. Let's go."

They left the information center and set out along the shaded, zigzagging trail. The slope was still gentle. The tall beech woods that lined the route made the air seem dense. There was a noise in the undergrowth, and a wild monkey warily crossed the trail ahead of them.

Rintaro walked ahead in silence and Yuuki simply followed. After a while, they arrived at the Ichinokurasawa intersection. Immediately Yuuki realized that his memory had failed him. Back then the rock face had taken him by surprise, appearing out of nowhere. All that had stuck in his mind was the impact of that moment.

He was caught off guard again today. Rintaro, walking in the middle of the track, suddenly moved over to the right, opening up the view for Yuuki. He caught his breath and stopped dead.

A fortress of rock towered darkly before him. It was still quite far off, but overwhelming, looming over everything else in his field of vision. The ridge cut a straight line through the air, leaving nothing but a narrow sliver of sky above. It wasn't what he'd call a magnificent view; it was too oppressive for that. Ichinokurasawa wouldn't let mere mortals in. Yuuki was struck by the thought that Nature had constructed this rampart for that very purpose.

Tsuitate. It stood there, the main gate protecting these giant castle walls. A painfully sharp vertical rock face like a hanging screen or a wall. It looked as if it had been folded vertically over and over, producing a series of overhangs, or "roofs." The rock itself had a brutal countenance, worthy of its nickname the Worst of the Worst.

Yuuki gave voice to his misgivings. "I don't know if I can do this."

Rintaro's response was brief. "Sure you can."

The younger man set off down toward the dry riverbed, presumably searching for a good location to pitch their tents. But Yuuki couldn't move. His body was seized by the fear he'd felt almost two decades before.

And that time they'd only been checking out the climbing route. This time they were actually doing it.

The two Gravestone Mountains merged in his mind. He felt the same excitement as seventeen years ago rush through him.

It had been a plane crash of unprecedented proportions. An out-of-control Japan Airlines plane, Flight 123, had strayed into Gunma Prefecture. Yuuki had also changed course that day. He'd been drifting along, leading a life that was not healthy for him, not making any effort to improve it. But the monotony of his daily routine had been turned completely upside down by that accident. Those seven days on the newsroom floor, dealing with something huge. Every agonizing minute that ticked by had brought a new self-awareness and, consequently, his life had veered off on another course.

Yuuki looked up at the Tsuitate face defiantly.

*Elevation: 330 meters—I'm going to haul myself up a vertical cliff face the height of Tokyo Tower.*

*"I climb up to step down."*

He could see the look in Anzai's eyes. Months before, even with his body covered in tubes, held captive in a bed, his eyes had twinkled.

He'd climbed this, Kyoichiro Anzai. Suddenly Yuuki's vision blurred. He took a deep breath, closed his eyes, and slowly exhaled. He listened once again to Anzai's voice in his head. Yuuki had to climb the mountain. He needed to know what these last seventeen years had been about.

August 12, 1985. That was the day it had all started.

**2** Even early in the morning, the heat was oppressive.

Yuuki had spent the start of his working day at the home of an ex-soldier in the outskirts of Takasaki City. He was gathering material for a ten-part series the paper was running: "Forty Years after the War: Stories from Gunma." It had been published daily since August 6, and the final installment was due to appear on the fifteenth, the anniversary of the end of the Second World War. However, Aoki, the political correspondent assigned to write the final article, had suddenly been called away to the Tokyo office, and the job of collecting the material for the story had fallen to Yuuki.

In the provinces, the rush to get out of the city to visit family homes for the Obon holidays was supposedly under way, but in Nagatacho, where the central government buildings were located, it was business as usual. Japan's prime minister, Yasuhiro Nakasone, had decided to pay an official visit to Yasukuni Shrine, which honored Japan's war dead. Such visits had become controversial, ever since 1979, when it had come to light that Yasukuni Shrine held the ashes of fourteen Class A Second World War criminals. It looked as if the format of the visit was going to be decided today, the twelfth. Calling from Tokyo the previous night, Aoki had sounded excited about being in the capital, competing with journalists from the whole of Japan. He'd forgotten to thank the senior reporter for covering for him.

Yuuki drove toward Maebashi City. It was the monthly commemoration of the death of Ryota Mochizuki, who had been a junior reporter at the newspaper, and after paying his respects at Mochizuki's grave, he headed back to work. It was lunchtime when he arrived, but he didn't feel hungry.

He decided to forgo the basement cafeteria and go directly to the main office of the second-floor Editorial Department, the newsroom. The *North Kanto Times* didn't produce an evening edition, so there were few people there this time of day. Fortunately, it seemed that the air conditioner had been on full blast since the morning. The heat outside now was beyond description. In the short time it had taken him to hurry from the parking lot on the other side of the street into the office, his shirt was soaked with sweat and sticking to his back.

"Hello. *NKT* here."

The first thing he heard was the cheerful tone of Yoshii in the copy team, from the farthest desk. The call was from a reporter covering this year's Koshien—the national senior high school baseball tournament— and they seemed to be having a lively chat about it. Yuuki had always worked on local news and didn't know much about sports, but it sounded as if the team representing Gunma Prefecture, Nodai Niko High, was doing well. They'd won the first-round game in the bottom of the ninth with a walk-off home run, and the paper had just dispatched an extra reporter and photographer to cover their second-round match.

Turning his face full-on to the chilled breeze of the air conditioner, Yuuki reflected on what had just happened at the cemetery. As he was leaving, he had run into Mochizuki's parents, carrying flowers, which of course was unsurprising. They had bowed politely to one another and continued in their separate directions, but the young woman accompanying them had turned up her nose and glared defiantly at Yuuki. She looked to be in her late teens, and Yuuki had the vague feeling he had seen her before. If it was the girl in the school uniform he'd seen at the funeral five years earlier, it would be Mochizuki's cousin. He wasn't sure if her own memories of the events had caused her to react to him that way, or if perhaps the parents, who had lost their only son, had expressed their resentment of Yuuki to other members of the family. Yuuki had wondered about this the whole drive back.

"Morning."

It was the laid-back voice of Kamejima, the chief copy editor, coming over to take advantage of the cool breeze, too. His round moon face was sweating heavily. Everyone called him Kaku-san, but not because of his resemblance to the anime character of the same name, or because his name began with the sound "ka." It was a play on the word for "write": in kanji, the characters of his name had the most strokes, and therefore took the longest to write, of anyone's in the office. It went without saying that the creator of this nickname was a member of the proofreading team.

"It's fucking sweltering!" Kamejima pulled his shirt collar away from his neck and leaned forward to let in the cool air from the unit. The toothpick he was chewing told Yuuki that he hadn't just arrived at the office. He'd been in early and had just returned from the cafeteria.

"Kaku-san, anything happen today?"

"Yeah. Early this morning there was a development in the Glico Morinaga case."

Yuuki had asked only as part of a perfunctory greeting, so this was a complete surprise.

Kamejima talked for a while about the story, which had come to them through the Kyodo News Service. In the midst of the summer slow season, this was A-grade material. The article that would appear in tomorrow morning's national news would have been put together in a hurry and already passed to the copy team, so Kamejima knew what he was talking about.

Having cooled off sufficiently, Yuuki took a pad of writing paper over to the desk by the window and sat down. The desk didn't really belong to him, but he'd been monopolizing it for years. The desk phone had an outside line, so it was useful for gathering information. He had membership in the press clubs attached to both the prefectural government office and the prefectural police headquarters, but he rarely went to them. The newspaper had its assigned representatives at each of these pressrooms and, if Yuuki turned up, as a senior reporter, he would just be in the way.

He'd turned forty last month and was the longest-serving reporter at the paper. "Roving reporter," "relief reporter"—there were many names for what he did—but, put simply, he had no people working under him and he was given a free hand to report on whatever he wanted. There were plenty who envied him, and many who pitied him. His contemporaries— the reporters who had joined the company at the same time—had long since been assigned to positions at specific news desks. And recently, junior staff members had started to be promoted to branch offices in major cities like Takasaki or Ota. There were rumors that Yuuki had been subjected to a five-year disciplinary action, gossip that had reached even Yuuki's ears.

Had it really been five years? Ryota Mochizuki had been a junior staff member in his first year as a reporter, and assigned to Yuuki. It had been back when Yuuki had been the *North Kanto Times*'s lead police beat reporter, attached to the prefectural police headquarters. Mochizuki had been promising, but he had passed away before he got the chance to prove himself.

It had been only the sixth day of his assignment to Yuuki. There had been a fatal traffic accident in Ogomachi, the neighboring town to Maebashi City. A thirty-eight-year-old surveyor riding a motorbike had been hit by a car and died of a cerebral contusion. Yuuki had sent Mochizuki to get a photo of the deceased. It was usual practice to send the rookie reporter to hunt down a photo of the victim in a criminal case or an accident. Mochizuki had cheerfully accepted the task and set out. However, less than an hour later he was back in the pressroom, utterly dejected. He'd found the surveyor's home, but an official of the local residents' association who was helping the family prepare for the deceased's wake had chased him away, asking him what the hell he was playing at, "showing up and demanding a photo at a time like this."

Yuuki ordered him to go back again. This time he was to try to talk to a relative or ex-classmate of the deceased. But Mochizuki didn't budge. When Yuuki got angry and raised his voice he became defiant. Why was it so important to print a photo of the victim in the newspaper? Yuuki was taken aback. It was true that, every year, reporters seemed to be getting more and more gutless, but it was the first time he had had a confrontation with one who was like that from the get-go. His response was brutal. "You fucking idiot. That's our business. The product is better when it has a photo." He had used a whole load of other choice expressions, too. He'd been furious.

Mochizuki had bitten his lip and fled from the pressroom. And that was the last time Yuuki had ever seen him. An hour later, he had a car accident. On the Route 17 bypass in Takasaki City he had run a red light, crashed into a ten-ton truck, and died instantly. In a terrible irony, the following morning's edition carried no head shot of the surveyor but featured the serious-looking face of Mochizuki, taken from his employee ID card.

Mochizuki's parents didn't make any fuss. They didn't look up when Yuuki explained the circumstances of their son's death; they never spoke a single bitter word; they simply stood side by side, staring at the floor.

The reaction within the company was mostly sympathetic toward Yuuki. The argument with Mochizuki had been overheard by the *North Kanto Times*'s number two at the police headquarters, a reporter by the name of Sayama, and the details had spread around the company. It was generally agreed that "anyone would have been angry under the circumstances." Yuuki had hated having to listen to this and similar phrases, and being patted on the shoulder each time. Still, Sayama had defended Yuuki one hundred percent. He had given up his day off to look into the surveyor's personal circumstances. He had discovered that the man had no relatives or ex-classmates in the Takasaki City area and so, rather than being in the process of hunting down the victim's photo when he had had the traffic accident, Mochizuki had been heading toward his own parents' house. Sayama used the rather harsh expression "desertion in the line of duty" in his report. With that, the last smoldering embers of sympathy for Mochizuki at the company were extinguished.

Sayama's father had committed suicide and his mother had died in a traffic accident, and this had caused him much suffering over the years. These experiences had led him to go all out to defend Yuuki.

*No further action to be taken.* That was the company's decision regarding Yuuki's conduct. However, this didn't mean that Yuuki's conscience was clear. On the contrary, the heavy, leaden feeling in his heart only got heavier. Mochizuki had been an inexperienced first-year reporter. In retrospect, Yuuki believed he should have stayed calm and patiently explained to him that the impact of a newspaper article is increased by the addition of a photograph. That it gives the story more weight. And his patience would have prevented another tragic traffic accident. Through the Mochizuki incident, Yuuki had come to realize that, with his lack of self-control, he should never be put in a position where he could exercise control over others.

Yuuki had suspected for a while that he was able to love only people who loved him. And even when he was sure he had their love, he couldn't forgive them if they were ever cool or indifferent toward him. He expected absolute, unconditional love, and when he realized how elusive that was, he would fall into utter despair. So, instead, he kept his distance from people. He was wary of anyone who showed him kindness and never let anyone see his private side. He was afraid of being hurt.

When his son, Jun, became old enough to think for himself, Yuuki found himself unable to relax. He was perplexed by this innocent little thing who would fling himself at his father with complete confidence. He was delighted by his son, but maybe too delighted. Perhaps he got too close to Jun. As a father, he was unable to take a step back. He was always closely observing his son's expressions. And instead of worrying about how to raise him, he was concerned with how Jun felt about him: Would he always respect his father? Would Jun ever stop loving him?

As time went by, he found himself desperate to make Jun like him. "Wow, that's amazing!" "Great job!" "Really good try!" He'd shower him with flattering phrases that he didn't really mean, all the while checking out his son's reaction. Whenever Jun was in a good mood, Yuuki felt easy in himself, but if the boy showed the slightest sign of defiance, the love that overflowed in his heart would turn in an instant to bottomless hatred. Mostly, on these occasions, he would simply treat his son coldly; sometimes he would raise a hand to him. But if he felt seriously disappointed or let down by him, he would fly into a blind rage.

It might have been because he'd never known his own father. When he was a child, his tearful mother explained that his father had vanished. Yuuki was terrified by this word: "vanished." He could neither swallow nor digest the information, and it vaguely, uneasily haunted him. Vanished— where to? How? He had no idea whether his father was dead or alive. Why had he gone? He couldn't ask his mother. There wasn't a single photograph of his father in the house. He was even envious of his friends whose fathers had been killed in the war. The absence of a father left a vacuum in his life and made him ask himself if his own existence was really that insignificant to someone. He felt miserable every time he thought about having been abandoned. At times he would curse his father, and then there'd been another period when he'd held out a faint hope that the man would suddenly reappear. Right before he started primary school he used to sit in front of his mirror at night and practice shouting out, "Dad!"

Yuuki felt he'd missed out on his chance to become a real dad.

Jun had grown into a gloomy thirteen-year-old. As a father, what should he have taught him? What lesson could he have given him? The damage was probably irreparable by this point. But Yuuki had no idea of the kinds of things a father was supposed to tell his son.

The incident with Mochizuki had been forgiven, but Yuuki had offered his resignation to the editor in chief at the time. It wasn't out of any sentimentality over Mochizuki's death. It was because he had realized he didn't have the talents or the qualifications to be a supervisor.

He believed that Mochizuki's death was pretty much a suicide. He didn't buy into the theory that Mochizuki, preoccupied and dispirited, had failed to notice the red light. Mochizuki probably had a personality similar to his own; he overreacted to everyday setbacks and had, on impulse, wanted to end it all. That was why Yuuki couldn't really grieve Mochizuki's death as such.

But back at the cemetery—the look the young woman had given him and the lifeless faces of the parents—these did weigh heavily on him.

The newsroom was getting busier.

Yuuki had written around thirty lines on his notepad. He clipped the pages together and stood up, craning his neck to look across the newsroom at the central island of desks. He spotted the long, thin face of Kishi at the political news desk. He was a good-natured type who had joined the company at the same time as Yuuki. He dropped the draft on his colleague's desk.

"I've got the supplementary story here. Can you tag it onto the end of Aoki's article?"

Kishi looked grateful.

"Must have been boring. Sorry you ended up having to do that."

"Don't worry about it. I wasn't busy."

Just as Yuuki turned to leave, Kishi spoke again.

"Are you going to the meeting this evening?"

"What meeting?"

"That wireless thing again."

"Huh." Yuuki nodded without any real interest.

Last year, two trains had collided head-on on the single-track Joshin Dentetsu railway line. There had been only one building, a private home, close to the accident site. A reporter from the *Asahi Shimbun* newspaper had made it to the house a few moments before the *North Kanto Times* reporter, and had proceeded to monopolize the house's telephone line. The *NKT* reporter had been forced to run for fifteen minutes to the nearest public phone booth and he'd had to make this round-trip five times in total. *If wireless transmitters were too expensive, then how about carrier pigeons?* The young reporter's rage had finally gotten a reaction from the General Affairs Department. Kishi held out a catalogue of wireless transmitters.

"Looks like we're going to get the Motorola model."

"If we're going to spend the money, then wouldn't it be better to get cell phones? Nippon Television's Sanada is always flashing his around."

"Oh, that great big thing? No way. We can't use that. It's really heavy to cart around, and the battery only lasts about two or three hours at most."

"If you insist on the wireless, you may end up getting turned down. Last month, General Affairs were going on about how circulation was down. Readers have been switching to the *Yomiuri* and the *Jomo*."

"You may be right. Anyway, are you coming?"

"I'll pass. I have plans this evening."

Kishi suddenly remembered, and laughed.

"Yes, I heard. You're going climbing. Anzai dropped by yesterday and told me about it."

Yuuki had been planning to invite Anzai to go for something to eat that evening.

"You're going to climb the Tsuitate rock face? I'm pretty sure that's the place where that big incident happened. You know, when the Self-Defense Forces guys shot down that climbing rope."

Kishi turned his head. Someone was calling his name. It was the managing editor, Oimura, nicknamed the Firecracker. He was beckoning urgently to Kishi.

"Be careful, won't you?"

But as he hurried off, Kishi's expression was doubtful, as if he couldn't believe Yuuki was going to make it up a mountain like that.

Yuuki returned to his desk by the window, picked up the telephone, and pressed the button for the Circulation Department. It was after 2:00 p.m. and he still wasn't hungry. It was partly the heat, partly what had happened at the cemetery, that had killed his appetite. But more than anything it was probably the fear of climbing Tsuitate. As he listened to the ringtone, he felt a slight tensing of the muscles throughout his body.

**3**  The cafeteria wasn't completely underground but in a semibasement. The glaring midsummer sunlight poured in through the high windows, throwing shadows of the window frames on the tiled floor. Given the late hour, the only people eating lunch were Yuuki and two men from the Business Department. The noise of dishes being washed drowned out their voices.

No one from the Circulation Department had picked up the phone. It was hard to believe that there was nobody in the office in the middle of the day, but Yuuki didn't really have much idea what went on in that team. He knew that their primary job was to cultivate good relationships with the many newsdealers around Gunma Prefecture, but if someone were to ask him what exactly it was that they did, the first thing that came to mind was a vision of them wining and dining and playing games of mah-jongg with the shop owners. Nevertheless, in-house they were considered a vital cog, as they helped to keep home delivery of the newspaper going. It was rumored that their entertainments expense account was unlimited. However, this whole "department" was in fact a small family of fewer than ten employees in a dim little office. Yuuki was one of the many who referred to the room as the "Black Box."

The other two men got up, leaving Yuuki alone in the cafeteria. He decided that he might manage some cold noodles in broth, but after about half a bowl he gave up.

The Tsuitate rock face . . . He let out a nervous sigh.

A couple of weeks earlier, when they'd gone to check it out, he'd been afraid that Anzai would notice the alarm bell clanging in his chest. But back then at least he'd been able to reassure himself that he still had two weeks' leeway. And now the two weeks had suddenly become tomorrow.

He had heard of Tsuitate long before Anzai had mentioned it. Every resident of Gunma over a certain age, even those without any interest in climbing, like Kishi from political news, knew about it because of the Self-Defense Forces shooting.

It was in 1960—so Yuuki had been fifteen at the time. The news had been sensational. Two members of a mountaineering club who had been climbing the rock face had fallen and ended up hanging from their climbing rope. By the time they were spotted it was too late; they were already dead. All this was verified by the use of binoculars, but the problem remained how to retrieve the bodies. The first-ever ascent of the Tsuitate face had been made only the previous year, and even the most accomplished mountaineers now hesitated to go near the scene of the accident. Especially as the bodies were suspended in midair. Everyone was convinced it would be impossible to carry the bodies down, so the unprecedented decision was made to employ the Self-Defense Forces to shoot through the rope.

It was six days after the accident. At the request of the governor of Gunma Prefecture, the headquarters of the First Division of the Japan Ground Self-Defense Forces issued the order to the troops at the Somaga-hara military camp to mobilize. The top eleven marksmen from the First Reconnaissance Unit were chosen, and opened fire from a crag around 150 meters away. Their target was a piece of rope a mere twelve millimeters thick, buffeted by the wind. They had great difficulty hitting it. They tried rifles, carbines, machine guns. They fired a total of 1,238 rounds before the rope was finally severed.

Yuuki had been sent to interview a former Self-Defense Forces marksman who had been assigned to retrieve the bodies. After the rope was cut, the bodies had dropped like dolls and bounced off the rock face four or five times before skidding down the steep slope. Even though the marksmen knew the two men were already dead, it wasn't pleasant to witness the bodies and rucksacks being smashed into pieces. The retired soldier told the story with a distant look in his eyes.

And Yuuki was going to climb that same rock face.

How had he gotten himself into this situation? But he knew there was only one reason: he had allowed Kyoichiro Anzai to sweet-talk him into it. It had all started three years ago when Yuuki had shown up for drinks at a get-together of the hiking club Anzai had started at the paper. As the name suggested, it was not a group for serious climbers; they hiked in the hills or along mountain streams, and the attraction was an after-hike beer or a barbecue. It was all about the social side. The club had both male and female members from various departments, around thirty in total.

Anzai had been at the *North Kanto Times* fewer than ten years, but he was three or four years older than Yuuki. The first time they'd exchanged greetings, Anzai had said, "Let's call it even, then." This was his way of rejecting the traditional age-based hierarchy and an invitation to become friends. He had put one hairy arm around Yuuki's shoulder in an over-familiar manner and shaken him enthusiastically. The adjectives "easy-going" and "openhearted" came to Yuuki's mind, but the man just came on too strong. The amount of goodwill in his heart exceeded common sense. It made Yuuki wary, and he made a point of not getting too close to him.

Despite that, three years ago he had finally been tempted to go to one of these get-togethers. It was probably because of the Ryota Mochizuki business. Things weren't going well at home, either, and he was feeling depressed. He had just wanted to have a quick drink and listen to a few hikers' anecdotes and tall tales.

The get-together had been boring. It turned out that, as well as hiking and mountain climbing, Anzai was obsessed with the poetry of Byron and the fantasy writings of Michael Ende, with the boxing manga *Ashita no Joe* and the pop idol Momoe Yamaguchi.

Still, Yuuki continued to go to these gatherings, but it wasn't until he joined the group on a hike along the mountain ridge of Mount Myogi that things changed for him. He'd only reluctantly agreed to join them, but the whole experience was beyond any of his expectations. He'd set off to go for a simple hike in the mountains. His legs began to feel heavy, but at the same time he became more relaxed. He was walking in a group, but he could have been alone, all his senses reaching to the sky. He was confused by this brand-new feeling, but he wasn't imagining it. The cloud of depression that had enveloped his heart ever since childhood wafted away on the mountain breeze.

Hoping to recapture this feeling, Yuuki went hiking every chance he got, usually with Anzai's group. He wasn't able to express to Anzai exactly what it was that attracted him to the mountains, but Anzai was delighted, and every time Yuuki joined him for a hike he put his hairy arm around his shoulder and shook him heartily.

Before long the two of them would meet to go rock climbing together. It was Yuuki who first suggested it. He had a feeling it might be really good for him. Mostly, they climbed in the Kuroiwa area of Mount Haruna, at around thirty or forty meters' altitude. Anzai claimed to have honed his skills on these rocks in his youth. At Kuroiwa there was a huge variety of climbing routes: the west ridge, gully number nineteen, the pyramid face, the great slab . . .

The rock gave Yuuki a chance to be alone. His feeling proved to be right. His mind emptied of all thoughts. And that was the moment he felt the fog lift. Clinging to a rock in midair, he savored the sensation.

A "late-blooming rock jock": that was what Anzai had jokingly called him, after observing the way Yuuki became utterly engrossed while he was climbing. Although there was definitely a budding friendship there, they weren't completely open with each other. In a way, Yuuki was using Anzai to gain some solitude. He benefited from Anzai's lack of sensitivity; because he knew Anzai wouldn't be able to see into his heart, Yuuki could spend as much time in quiet reflection as he liked.

Over the course of these three years, Yuuki's impression of Anzai had never changed. He was just as he'd seemed at their first meeting: fond of drink, laughter, talking, and slapping people heartily on the shoulder. They were colleagues at the *North Kanto Times*, but they never discussed work. Anzai belonged to the Circulation Department, so Yuuki unkindly assumed there was nothing to ask about beyond all the client entertaining; in turn, Anzai never asked a single thing about Yuuki's work as a reporter. Yuuki supposed he had no interest in what went on in the Editorial Department. Just one time, a little drunk, Yuuki tried to bring up the newspaper. Anzai immediately shut him down with a neatly employed quotation from Michael Ende's most famous novel: "But that is another story, and shall be told another time." To sum up, Anzai was an expert at enjoying life. He came across as happy-go-lucky, a bon vivant, a frivolous party animal.

But that same Anzai became a completely different person when he was climbing. There was no laughing or joking around. There was an odd glint in his eyes. He knew everything there was to know about each rock face, but he never let it show. He behaved with respect and humility toward the mountain. Occasionally this could even come across as cowardice.

It was Anzai who'd suggested they should climb the Tsuitate face. It had been about three months earlier and, without thinking about it too much, Yuuki had agreed. Now he realized he really hadn't been thinking at all.

"There he is!" The familiar booming voice bounced off the walls of the cafeteria and assaulted Yuuki's ears from all directions at once.

Anzai came stomping in. To Yuuki's surprise, he was wearing a red T-shirt.

"Been looking for you, Yuu. Thought you were hiding from me."

"Hiding?"

Anzai exploded with laughter at Yuuki's serious expression and plunked himself down in the seat opposite.

"Just kidding."

He was soaked in sweat. Even his mustache and goatee were glistening. There was a huge wet patch on the front of his T-shirt that made him look like he was wearing a baby's bib.

"So, we're going as planned, then? We'd better get the seven thirty-six out of Gunma-Soja Station."

It was possible to get as far as Ichinokurasawa on Mount Tanigawa by car, but Anzai didn't think they would get the full experience that way. His plan was to take the Joetsu Line to Doai Station, then walk as far as the Climbing Information Center, where they would spend the night. First thing the next day, they would set out for Ichinokurasawa and begin the assault on that sheer wall of rock known as Tsuitate.

Yuuki glanced up at the clock. It was already past 2:30, which meant that they'd be leaving in under five hours. So many thoughts and feelings came bubbling up. Perhaps they should abandon it because of the heat? But it didn't look as if Anzai were about to announce a cancellation or a postponement.

"What are you looking so gloomy about? You afraid?"

"No, that's not it."

"There's nothing to worry about. I'll be with you the whole time."

Yuuki really couldn't bear to look at such a carefree, smiling face today.

"I'm not worried, really."

"I get it. I get it. I was the same the first time. My body wanted to climb—it was raring to go—but in my mind it was a different story. Just like when I lost my virginity."

As usual, Anzai's story had taken a bizarre turn.

"Wonder if women feel the same way the first time. Momoe Yamaguchi?"

"No idea."

"But there are plenty of guys like you who do it."

Yuuki clicked his tongue. "What do you mean, 'do it'?"

"Climb."

They were back to talking about mountains.

"There are guys who are normally perfectly calm and composed but who set off climbing as fast as they can, utterly focused on what they're doing. They get a massive adrenaline rush and start clambering up at crazy speeds."

"Is that true?"

"Climber's high."

Yuuki shrugged. "Climber's high?"

"I didn't tell you about it?"

"First I've heard of it."

"It's when the body gets overstimulated, reaches a level of extreme excitement. The fear makes them numb."

"Numb? You mean they don't feel afraid anymore?"

"Right. They climb in a mad frenzy and, before they know it, they're at the peak of Tsuitate. An incredible feat."

Anzai grinned. He seemed to be telling the story to make Yuuki feel less nervous.

"Okay, then, Yuu. It's quiz time."

"Eh? Not again!"

"Okay, here's your question. How many times has Kyoichiro Anzai climbed Tsuitate?"

Yuuki gave a snort of derision, but Anzai wasn't giving up that easily.

"*Beep, beep, beep*—you've got three more seconds—*beep*—"

"Ten," Yuuki replied, with a look of irritation. He'd already been subjected to Anzai's boasts about climbing the rock face.

"Correct! And Kyoichiro Anzai is alive and well and here to tell the tale—"

"Yep. Unfortunately."

"Come on, loosen up. I need you to laugh with me. I'm counting on you."

With that, Anzai reached across the table and shook him heartily by the shoulder. Yuuki sighed.

"It was fifteen or twenty years ago that you climbed Tsuitate, right?"

Anzai curled his hand around his mouth to make a megaphone.

"Hey! Yuu!"

"Ow! That's loud!"

"You can still ride a bicycle after twenty years, can't you? I'm an old hand at this. It's in my DNA."

"Really?"

Yuuki was both amazed by Anzai's stubbornness and surprised at his own inability to know when to give up.

Yuuki moved his noodle bowl aside and leaned across the table.

"Hey, Anzai, why do you climb mountains?"

"To step down," Anzai responded lightly.

It felt to Yuuki as if he'd had a ladder pulled out from under him.

"To step down . . . ?"

"Yeah. I climb up to step down."

Yuuki was silent. Yep, as he'd predicted, he had no idea how to react. Nor what the appropriate response might be. He knew he probably looked completely dissatisfied with the explanation. Climb up a mountain to step down? Was this something to do with having the courage to turn back when things get too tough, something he'd heard about? But no—that hadn't been what he was asking. He didn't get it. Climb up to step down. What did it mean? Was this an attempt to stun him into silence?

But there was no gloating expression in Anzai's eyes. He had on his usual face. The harmless expression of someone who was looking for fun and had complete faith that he would find it right away.

Was this another quiz? Yuuki wondered. But if it was, he had no enthusiasm for it whatsoever. Yuuki had asked a serious question and, if Anzai were to laugh now and simply launch into another question, he knew he was going to despise the man sitting there across from him.

Yuuki got up.

"Gotta go?" Anzai was still drinking his iced coffee. "I'll see you on the train, then. If you miss it, at the information center. Okay?"

"Right."

"There's a fine if you back out."

"Right."

"Tsuitate's no big deal when you have middle-aged superpowers!"

Anzai punctuated his speech with fist jabs. He was imitating the boxing hero of *Ashita no Joe*.

Yuuki watched Anzai's excited expression. He was like a child with a birthday cake.

As Yuuki left the cafeteria, he still felt unsettled about the following day's climb.

**4**  By six o'clock that evening, all the editorial staff were in turmoil.

Yuuki was sitting at the political editor's desk, checking the draft of his article. As he'd refused to attend the wireless meeting, he was stuck filling in for Kishi instead.

The top story had been decided. The Sanko Steamship Company was in financial difficulties and was planning to file an application the next day for assistance under the Corporate Rehabilitation Law. The company had an aggregate debt of more than five hundred billion yen. It was the biggest financial collapse since the Second World War. Yuuki had been covering cases for the local news section for a long time, and rarely looked at the economics pages, but even he knew that the real owner of the Sanko Steamship Company was Kawamoto, a Cabinet minister. It was clear that bankruptcy would not be the end of the affair; the dynamics of political power would be affected. Sure enough, as soon as this thought ran through his head, a wire from Kyodo News Service was delivered to him with the heading "Kawamoto Tenders Resignation." Once again, Yuuki reached for his red pen.

To Yuuki's left sat Nozawa, copy editor for the local news section. He was puffing on a cigarette as he flicked through an album of clippings about the Glico Morinaga case. The two men had started at the newspaper at the same time, but Nozawa never spoke a word to Yuuki. He held a grudge, and the sheer doggedness with which he held on to it was impressive. It seemed he would never forgive Yuuki for what had happened fifteen years previously, when the two of them had worked together on a case where a husband had murdered his wife and children but it had been Yuuki alone who had received the Editor in Chief's Award for the story.

Today, even though Yuuki was just filling in for Kishi, it was clear that Nozawa didn't like him sitting at the desk of someone of a higher rank, and was demonstrating this by frequently clicking his tongue.

Yuuki had just sent his article on the steamship company off to press when the phone rang. It was the political correspondent Aoki, calling from Tokyo.

"Sorry about today. How did the interview and stuff go?"

"Ah, it was no big deal. I got it all finished."

"Cheers. I'll treat you to dinner when I get back."

"Don't worry about it. Anyway, what's up?"

"Yeah, about Yasukuni Shrine—it looks like it's been officially decided that Prime Minister Nakasone will visit it on the fifteenth."

Chief Cabinet Secretary Fujieda had apparently made the formal announcement at a meeting of the Liberal Democratic Party. The format of the visit and the exact sum of money that should be offered at the shrine had not been decided, and that would be the focus of any further talks. Clearly excited, Aoki explained the current state of affairs and got off the phone as soon as he could.

Yuuki looked at the wall clock. It was 6:40 p.m. The meeting was running over. As well as Kishi, the editor in chief, the managing editor, and the chief editor of the local news section were all away from their desks.

Yuuki began to calculate backward; it took less than three minutes to walk to Gunma-Soja Station but, as the train would leave at 7:36, it'd be safer to leave the office by 7:30. He planned to change into his climbing gear in the night duty room and slip out of the back exit. Allowing ten minutes to change, he'd need to get out of the Editorial Department by twenty past seven.

"High of eighty-nine degrees!" someone shouted. The temperature hadn't reached that of the human body today, so it must be the humidity that was making it so damn uncomfortable. Yuuki was just thinking this when the prominent beer belly of the editor in chief, Kasuya, appeared in the doorway. The meeting must be over.

"Suits you."

Kasuya made the remark as he passed behind Yuuki's chair on his way back to his office. His tone was ironic. Back in early spring, Kasuya had sounded out Yuuki about moving to the regional news desk. He'd have been in charge of all the reporters from the branch offices scattered around the prefecture. But Yuuki had quickly shut the conversation down by telling him he didn't want to be responsible for anyone. Kasuya had groaned and scowled at him.

"Don't keep on expecting special treatment," he spat out.

Yuuki understood his meaning well enough. It had been the previous editor in chief who had refused to accept his unofficial resignation and had set Yuuki up as a "lone wolf" reporter. Five years had gone by, and now Kasuya was editor in chief. Yuuki had still not been promoted to editor. The fact that he was still a reporter gave rise to all kinds of speculation. *No further action to be taken*—while that had been the company's official position following the incident with Mochizuki, in reality he'd been frozen in the same position ever since. However, in Yuuki's case, it just happened that this continuation of the status quo was exactly what he wanted. But from Kasuya's point of view, as the person who had to manage and unify the department, Yuuki was something of a headache. Kasuya most likely wanted to give Yuuki some kind of editorial position as soon as possible, just to stop the false rumors that he was trouble.

The other reason for assigning Yuuki a managerial role was that more and more of the younger reporters had begun to express a wish to be like Yuuki—a career reporter. This was not the usual vision of people in the profession. To turn one's back on a managerial post and dream of spending the rest of your days at crime scenes, pen in hand, was definitely proof of a healthy attitude toward reporting. But if you looked at the actual structure of the newspaper, the only people who remained reporters their whole lives were those who were deemed incompetent by management and packed off to some tiny branch office in the mountains. Yuuki's existence had disrupted this pattern. The forty-year-old roving reporter in the head office appealed to the younger staff members' sense of adventure.

Needless to say, Kasuya was not happy with this trend. It'd be different if they were a national newspaper company where reporters were a dime a dozen, but this was a small local paper with fewer players. If too many reporters tried to do their own thing, the situation could easily get out of hand. Kasuya was aiming to get rid of the bad example.

Yuuki had never expected to be allowed to continue as he was for so long. This spring he had somehow managed to get one more year's stay of execution. He had the impression that if he turned down an editorial post again in April, the beginning of the next fiscal year, he wouldn't be kept on at the main office. He suspected a transfer to the Business or Advertising Department, or perhaps even banishment to the Utsunomiya or Ashikaga branch office in neighboring Tochigi Prefecture. Ten years ago, the *North Kanto Times* had tried to increase its circulation outside the prefecture, but now the number of subscribers in Tochigi was pitifully low. The announcement of a transfer to one of these branch offices was essentially a recommendation to retire.

*Suits you.* Kasuya's words were still ringing in his ears. Yuuki sometimes felt like telling Kasuya to transfer him wherever he liked, but, as he'd known nothing but working as a reporter, it was difficult to imagine any other life.

He looked at the clock again. It was after seven. The meeting had definitely finished, but Kishi still hadn't returned.

He suddenly felt like calling home. He hadn't told Yumiko about tomorrow's trip to the mountains. She was used to being the wife of a reporter, and was never bothered by her husband staying out all night. However, tomorrow would be different. He wasn't off interviewing someone or covering an event. This was Tsuitate. Feeling, ridiculously, as if he were about to write his last will and testament, Yuuki picked up the phone.

No one answered. Jun was probably out at cram school. The bus ran only once an hour, so whenever Jun missed it Yumiko would drive him. That would explain their absence, but he wondered why his daughter, Yuka, wasn't home. She'd told him that her sports club practice finished by 6:00 p.m. in the summer.

There was no point trying to figure it out. Apart from the cram school and sports clubs, Yuuki knew very little about his children's schedules.

As he replaced the receiver, he noticed that managing editor Oimura was heading toward his desk. Yuuki hurried to catch up with him.

"Sir?"

Oimura turned around, revealing his usual disgruntled expression. "What?"

"Is Kishi still in the meeting room?"

"Yes. He's talking to General Affairs."

Yuuki was exasperated. It was now a quarter past seven.

"I hear you're off mountain climbing."

Yuuki turned his attention from the clock back to Oimura.

"That's right. I need to get going."

Oimura lowered his voice. "Best to stay away from that one."

There was a tiny explosion of anger in the managing editor's eyes. "That one . . . ?"

Then Yuuki realized that Oimura was talking about Anzai. He was completely taken aback, but didn't have time to ask Oimura what he'd meant. Kishi's long, thin face had appeared in the doorway. He was talking to Todoroki, the chief local news editor, the two of them moving at a snail's pace across the room.

Yuuki returned to the political editor's desk. He quickly tidied up his stuff and laid out the memos relating to the finished article that he'd sent to press for Kishi. The phone on the next desk began to ring. He ignored it, but it kept on ringing. He glanced up and saw that no one else was going to answer it. Nozawa must have taken a toilet break.

There was nothing for it but to pick up. On the other end was Sayama, the current chief reporter at police headquarters. He'd been promoted from second reporter after Yuuki was removed from the top post. Sayama sounded both surprised and pleased to hear Yuuki on the line, but then quickly lowered his voice.

"Yuuki-san, is everyone freaking out over there?"

"Why?"

Yuuki glanced around the room. The activity and noise level seemed about the same as usual.

"No, not especially."

"Really? Okay, well, the Jiji Press reports have been saying something strange."

He'd been listening in to the reports in the press club room.

Worried about the time, Yuuki spoke faster. "What were they saying?"

"A jumbo jet's gone missing. At least, that's what I thought I heard."

A *jumbo jet?* Yuuki looked into the distance. His gaze fell on the TV set perched on top of a bookcase. The NHK news was on.

"Oy!" Nozawa was back and trying to get Yuuki out of his seat. Yuuki moved, but his gaze was fixed on the news ticker running across the bottom of the screen.

*A Japan Airlines jumbo jet has vanished off the radar.*

"Hey! Look!" The loud voice was from the copy team. Suddenly a bunch of people were gathered around the TV.

"Does that mean it's crashed?"

"Jumbos don't crash."

"So the radar's broken?"

"Where did it go missing?"

"Well, it's not going to be around here. There are no flight paths over this area."

The crowd around the TV was two or three people deep now. There was still no follow-up report. Yuuki had crossed to the door and, half in, half out of the corridor, was watching the screen over the crowd. He had to leave now if he was going to make the train.

If a plane really had gone down somewhere, then the whole of tomorrow's newspaper would need to be rewritten. In other words, it meant a lot of work for the section that handled the Kyodo News reports, and particularly the Copy Department, who would have to rearrange the layout of the pages. Unless there were residents of Gunma Prefecture on the passenger list, there shouldn't be too much work for the reporters. But if the plane had gone down somewhere in the prefecture, it would be a different story.

Yuuki decided to wait to hear where the crash site was. But after several minutes had passed, there was still no update. He left the room. As someone had said, there were no jumbo-jet flight paths over Gunma Prefecture. If he missed the train because he was worrying about such a remote possibility, it'd seem like Anzai had been right—he was trying to get out of it.

However, just as he set off down the corridor, it happened. He heard the familiar *ping* from the speaker in the newsroom wall. The sound was to warn staff that a transmission from Kyodo News was about to start.

The announcer sounded agitated.

*Kyodo News Service report: A Japan Airlines jumbo jet has disappeared off the radar at a position tens of kilometers northwest of Yokota Air Base! Repeat: . . .*

Yuuki stopped dead. A crash site tens of kilometers northwest of Yokota? He couldn't immediately work out where that would be. But he did know it wasn't far away. He turned and hurried back to the newsroom. The place was in turmoil. People had grabbed maps and were spreading them out on their desks.

The NHK news updated their report.

*According to the Ministry of Transport, Japan Airlines Flight 123 disappeared off the radar along the border of Saitama and Nagano Prefectures.*

*It wasn't Gunma.* There was a slight sense of disappointment.

But just then a much louder chime rang out. It was different from the usual *ping*, and always preceded Kyodo's most serious announcements.

*It appears that Japan Airlines Flight 123 has crashed on the Nagano-Gunma prefectural border.*

Roars went up in the newsroom.

"Nooo! You've gotta be kidding!" someone yelled. It expressed perfectly what everyone was thinking at that moment.

As if to deal the final, devastating blow, the speaker then gave the number of passengers and crew aboard: 524.

The room fell silent.

It was impossible to conceive of such a number being dead. There were, in total, 511 people employed by the *North Kanto Times*. It was as if the whole company had been annihilated, plus another thirteen.

"Biggest-ever crash involving a single plane!"

This comment from a staff member in the reference room was the signal that brought the whole floor back to its senses.

"Page everyone who's out of the office!"

"And Tokyo! Get in touch with Haneda Airport!"

"Call Japan Airlines! Get the passenger list!"

Yuuki stood frozen by the door. But then it was as if a fire had been lit, and he was moving again.

*We've got to get to that crash site.*

What he felt wasn't a huge rush of flames, more a spark running along a fuse wire toward something that threatened eventually to explode.

But it still wasn't clear where to go. Was it Gunma? Nagano? Saitama? Where had that plane come down?

"Yuuki!"

He turned at the sound of his name. Editor in chief Kasuya was heading in his direction.

He had a bad feeling. How many different motives were concealed behind those eyes?

"You take this one."

There was no question of refusal. This was an order.

"JAL crash desk chief. You're in charge of seeing this story through to the end."

Yuuki stiffened.

He'd been put in charge of the story. And that meant telling other people what to do.

The Tsuitate rock face had gone from his mind. Ryota Mochizuki's nervous face had also been banished. But, for some reason, he could still hear Anzai's words.

*"There's a fine if you back out."*

**5**   War had broken out in the newsroom.

Someone had written in large letters on the blackboard: "JAL desk chief: Yuuki."

All the empty desks in the central island had been given over to reporters assigned to the story. Newly designated subeditor Nozawa slammed the Glico Morinaga file down on his desk, complaining bitterly that he "can't work like this."

Everyone was too busy to pay Nozawa any attention. Between eight and nine that evening, Yuuki had been leading the troops. From the speaker in the wall, fragments of information about the crash came raining down on him. There were raised voices coming at him from every direction. He felt battered from all sides, but he was eventually able to cobble together all the bits and pieces into what was known for certain.

The vanished plane was Japan Airlines Flight 123, a jumbo jet flying from Haneda Airport in Tokyo to the city of Osaka. It was an American-made Boeing 747S with 15 crew and 509 passengers on board. Most of the passengers were either on business trips or on their way to spend the Obon summer holidays with family, and the plane had been completely full.

Flight 123 took off from Haneda at 6:12 p.m. Around twenty minutes later, at 6:31 p.m., and approximately fifty-five kilometers west of Izu Oshima island, the aircraft sent out a distress signal. Another ten minutes later, at 6:41 p.m., Haneda Airport's Japan Airlines Operation Center received a radio broadcast from the pilot: "*Rear right-side door damaged. Loss of pressure in passenger cabin; initiating emergency descent.*" After that, two broadcasts of the phrase "out of control" before all communication with Flight 123 was lost.

At 6:54 p.m., the aircraft disappeared off the radars of both the Ministry of Transport's Tokyo Airports Bureau and the Yokota Air Base. It was concluded that the plane must have crashed. Immediately afterward, a resident of the village of Kawakami, in the Minamisaku District of Nagano Prefecture, contacted the police to tell them that a low-flying aircraft coming from the direction of Saitama had just crashed into the mountains on the border of Gunma and Nagano, and that bright red flames and black smoke could be seen rising from the southern part of Budotoge Ridge.

At 7:13 p.m., a U.S. military C-130 transport plane spotted a burning aircraft 54.4 kilometers west-northwest of Yokota Air Base. At 7:30 p.m., an RF-4 reconnaissance plane out of Hyakuri Air Base, belonging to the Japan Air Self-Defense Forces, confirmed the report. The crash site was a mountainous region between fifteen hundred and two thousand meters above sea level.

Yuuki scowled at the wall clock. It was exactly 9:30 now. Waving away five or six staff members who were leaning over his desk, Yuuki reached for the phone and paged Sayama. He should be at the Second Security Division of the prefectural police headquarters. Around eight that evening, an incident room devoted to the "missing JAL aircraft" had been set up.

Sayama called back right away.

"So which is it?"

Yuuki's question was blunt. He meant, was the crash site in Gunma or Nagano Prefecture? That was the biggest issue as far as the *North Kanto Times* was concerned. If it was Gunma, they would have to treat it as "our crash." The company would pour all its resources into the coverage.

"They're not sure yet. At the moment they think it's likely to be Nagano, but they haven't dismissed the possibility of us or Saitama."

Yuuki pressed the palm of his hand over his other ear. Right above him, someone from the copy team was having a loud argument with a guy from local news. And the Kyodo News chime must be broken, because it was ringing nonstop.

Yuuki was forced to raise his voice, too.

"How come they don't know? Both the U.S. military and the Self-Defense Forces released information about direction and distance."

"That's just it. At Yokota, they use this thing called tactical air navigation to measure the distances. Seems it's fairly rough in its estimates. Could be several kilometers off, apparently."

Yuuki let out a groan. He'd assumed that establishing the exact location of the crash would be a simple matter, but now it looked as if it was going to drag on for ages. It'd affect the deadline of the paper going to press.

"What are the police doing?"

"They're heading off to Budotoge Ridge in droves. The incident room here has been renamed the Plane Crash Emergency Task Force. And they're also setting up a local incident room tonight, at the village office in Uenomura."

Budotoge Ridge was right on the Gunma-Nagano border. Yuuki had already put together a team of four, plus a photographer, from the press club at police headquarters, added one member from each of the newspaper's branch offices in Takasaki and Fujioka, and dispatched them to the crash site. Anzai had always told him that for a person with no experience or knowledge to attempt to climb a mountain in the dark was tantamount to suicide. The six reporters and the photographer were to wait in their vehicles. Under no circumstances were they to set foot on the mountain. However, if the prefectural police were setting up a local incident room, it'd be wise to have them on standby there, where there were both telephones and information to be had. As for the Uenomura village office in the Tano District, Yuuki thought, that would serve as the NKT's news-gathering front line.

Just then Sayama's voice suddenly became excited.

"Yuuki-san, please let me go to the crash site, too."

"If you go, who's going to cover police headquarters?"

"I can ask the guy who covers the prefectural office business. Just let me go. Please."

"We still don't know if it's Gunma or not—"

Sayama went on the offensive.

"Yuuki-san! You know that's got nothing to do with it. The world's largest-ever plane crash has just happened right on our doorstep. It doesn't matter whether it's us or Nagano—reporters still need to be there."

Yuuki instructed him to be patient a while longer and hung up the phone.

He felt a little envious. To be there at the site of the world's biggest crash. Sayama was going to get that chance.

He looked around at the heaving newsroom and noticed something for the first time: there were about three times as many people as usual. The noise was about the level of a rock concert, but all the older men—and by "older," he meant those of his age or over—didn't have the same energy or excitement about them as the younger ones. Even if they were trying to hide it, they weren't succeeding. They were faced with the biggest accident this region had ever seen, but, somehow, they weren't on board; they wore expressions of utter indifference—as if it were someone else's problem. Even Kishi at the next desk was acting this way. And Nozawa's sulking wasn't just because he'd been made subeditor and he'd have to now take orders from Yuuki.

Yuuki understood because, in a way, he felt the same. The most famous incidents to date in Gunma Prefecture were the case of the serial killer Kiyoshi Okubo and the Japanese Red Army siege at Mount Asama, both back in the early seventies. Calling them "big stories" didn't come close to describing how important they were. For the local news reporters, these were unique incidents. Nothing like this had ever happened before, and nothing like it would ever happen again. In the Okubo case, eight women had been raped and murdered, then buried on Mount Haruna. The Red Army incident was even more gruesome. First, at their hideout on Mount Haruna, Red Army members had tortured and killed twelve of their comrades, then twenty-four-hour television coverage of the ensuing siege at a mountain lodge on the lower slopes of Mount Asama had shaken the whole country. The cases had happened in successive years, 1971 and 1972, meaning that reporters from that era had experienced two once-in-a-lifetime cases in quick succession.

They referred to it as the "Okubo/Red Army" period. Many of the reporters from those cases had seen their professional lives completely changed by the experience. To put it bluntly, their heads swelled. Okubo/ Red Army had been their meal ticket for the past thirteen years. They'd drunk expensive sake to the tale of Kiyoshi Okubo, stunned junior reporters into silence with their tales of the exploits of the Red Army, behaved with the arrogance of people who'd gone to battle with something huge and emerged the victors.

By sheer fluke, these reporters had scored themselves career gold medals. And despite failing to set any records, they would still be considered winners for the rest of their lives. The two with the worst superiority complexes were managing editor Oimura and chief local news editor Todoroki, who back then had been lead and number-two reporter at police headquarters, respectively. Their junior staff had consisted of Yuuki, Kishi, and Nozawa, all of whom had spent time at the crime scenes. To this day, all these men still relished the good fortune that had allowed them to set foot on such sacred ground.

Tonight, that golden age had come to an abrupt end. The biggest single aircraft disaster in history . . . In a matter of an instant, their medals' gold had lost its sheen. Or rather, now there was a medal that threatened to gleam even more brightly than gold.

Although there was a tinge of disappointment, it was mostly relief that Yuuki was feeling. It was as if he had been waiting for this day for the past thirteen years. Somewhere deep inside, he was ashamed of the lifestyle he'd been leading, exploiting his past Okubo/Red Army glories.

Kasuya would be having mixed feelings right about now. One reason he had rushed to put Yuuki in charge was strategic: he was laying the groundwork for Yuuki's probable transfer next spring. But there was another one. During Okubo/Red Army, Kasuya had been chief local news editor and had to remain in the office, missing out on going to the crime scenes. He'd had his hands full with Oimura and Todoroki, as they became ever more arrogant, so doubtless he was making sure not to repeat this mistake. He was afraid that if they got this case, too, they'd be even more out of control. And so he'd attached the chain to Yuuki's neck—or that was how Yuuki saw it.

It was all about the crash site.

Yuuki would be giving orders and directions, but he would not actually be working at the scene. A true dyed-in-the-wool reporter couldn't boast about working at a scene unless he'd personally experienced it.

Anzai's face flashed into his mind. For him, there was no other site besides Tsuitate. Yuuki hadn't contacted him, so he could only assume he'd taken the train by himself. Yuuki estimated that he would have reached Doai Station long ago. Humming the theme song from the anime version of *Ashita no Joe*, he was no doubt ambling his way to the Climbing Information Center.

He suddenly wished Anzai were here. He didn't mean to repeat what Sayama had just said, but even if the crash site turned out to be on the Nagano side, the *North Kanto Times* was based just over the mountain ridge in the neighboring prefecture. Tomorrow, as soon as the sun rose, he was going to have to send several reporters up the mountain. The crash site was at a similar elevation to the Tanigawa mountain range. If it was a mountain that people didn't usually climb, there wouldn't be any climbing courses marked out. And he was sending a group of reporters who had no experience of mountains beyond a bit of hiking. He shuddered to think of it. But if Anzai were to lead them, the danger would be considerably less. If every media company was racing to get to the scene of the accident first, then Anzai would be a valuable asset.

Yuuki decided he had nothing to lose by calling Anzai's home phone, just in case. It wasn't beyond the realm of possibility that Anzai had been disappointed at being stood up by his friend and had gone home.

"Hello, this is Anzai."

It was the voice of Anzai's wife, Sayuri. He'd been dragged into that house by Anzai so many times in the past that he knew Sayuri better than any other of his colleagues' wives.

"This is Yuuki. I'm sorry to be calling so late."

"Oh, Yuuki-san."

In her unassuming way, Sayuri sounded pleased to hear from him.

"Is he home?"

"What? I thought you were going up to the mountains tonight."

Yuuki was disappointed. Feeling bad about worrying Sayuri, he explained that he'd been unable to go because of the plane crash. Sayuri sounded surprised, but then soon made the connection between Yuuki's explanation and the TV screen before her. After asking her to get Anzai to contact him the minute he got back, Yuuki hung up.

Yuuki opened his pocket diary. He hadn't been able to get hold of Anzai, but he could do the next best thing—put together his own support team. There was still the hiking club. The group may have been all about having fun, but they weren't complete amateurs. Several of the members also dabbled in rock climbing. He could use them. He set about making a list of five candidates and immediately called the strongest climber of the group, Miyata in Advertising.

Miyata answered the phone right away and was instantly enthusiastic. It sounded as if he was ready to run right over. Yuuki called the other four and asked them to make any necessary preparations and be on standby.

As Yuuki replaced the receiver, Kishi, at the next desk, frowned at him.

"You're using the hiking club guys?"

"Yeah."

"But they're from other departments."

"Beggars can't be choosers. If our reporters get lost or injured in the mountains, they won't be covering anything."

"Hadn't you better check with management, just in case?"

"Forget about it. It's been over a year now and General Affairs still can't make up their minds whether to get wireless transmitters."

Yuuki couldn't help the cynicism in his tone. Up in the mountains, a lack of communication could be fatal. The North Kanto Times reporters were going to climb a mountain and put together a report on the crash, then it wouldn't be until the whole party had gotten down again that they'd be able to get their article to the newspaper. And if they met with some kind of accident on the way, they wouldn't even be able to achieve that much.

Yuuki snorted irritably. One of the reasons the introduction of the transmitters was dragging on so long was because nothing like that had been used in the Okubo/Red Army days. Back then the reporters had run around the mountains in below-freezing temperatures, jumping on bicycles and cycling for miles to get to the nearest telephone. That was what it meant to be a newspaper reporter—nothing easy about it, no time to think about being comfortable. This over-the-top idealism frequently got in the way of the modernization of the North Kanto Times.

Yuuki knew that he was one of these hardened "war criminals." He often felt guilty about it.

A shout went up from the team working on the passenger list.

"Look! I've found one! This guy!"

Five employees were working through the official manifest they'd got from Japan Airlines, trying to find anyone with a connection to Gunma Prefecture.

There was one—the father of one of the baseball players from Nodai Niko High School. He'd boarded Flight 123 to watch his son play his second-round match in the Koshien baseball tournament. He must have been feeling excited and proud . . .

There was a brief moment of silence, and then everyone was shouting at once.

"Photo and interview, ASAP!"

"The game's in Osaka. Call up the Osaka Koshien Committee!"

"Redo of the local news pages!"

The hands on the clock showed it was after 11:00 p.m.

It was agreed the deadline should be put back an hour, but that still meant they had less than two hours. The copy team began to work on the front page. The top headline would be JAL JUMBO IN FIERY CRASH. The subhead would be NO HOPE FOR 524 ON BOARD? But they still didn't have confirmation of the crash site.

"You don't know yet?" yelled Oimura, who had gone into full-on Firecracker mode. It sounded as if he blamed Yuuki for the lack of information.

"We're going to be down to the wire on this one. Please let Production know."

The phone rang, breaking up the confrontation. It was Sayama. His voice was brimming with excitement.

"Looks like it's our crash site."

Yuuki shuddered. He paused before asking, "What's your source?"

"The emergency task force just heard an eyewitness report. There was white smoke coming off Budotoge Ridge, apparently from the Gunma side. Nagano and Saitama police radio are reporting the same thing."

"Just a minute."

Yuuki put Sayama on hold and stood up, cupping one hand around his mouth to amplify his voice.

"Likely to be Gunma!"

Fifty heads turned to look at Yuuki, and a split second later the same number of voices reverberated loudly through the newsroom.

Yuuki put the receiver back to his ear, only to have Sayama's eager voice pierce his eardrum.

"So we're good, then? Let me go to the site."

Yuuki was at a loss for words. Sayama was a hunting dog that had caught the scent of its prey and was pawing impatiently at the ground. Yuuki could barely keep hold of his collar.

He really wanted to let Sayama go, but in his absence there would be no core team working with police headquarters. And if the plane really had gone down in Gunma Prefecture, Yuuki was going to have to assign twenty or thirty more reporters. He didn't know how he was going to supervise them all. A feeling close to a prayer came bubbling up.

*Let it be Nagano!*

He couldn't believe he was even thinking that. Now he felt even less confident of his abilities.

There was no other reporter who Yuuki was as close to or trusted as completely as Sayama. He was thirty-three years old, with ten years' experience at the newspaper. He was also highly regarded by all the young reporters. With Sayama next in the chain of command, Yuuki could get full cooperation. He couldn't see any other way of managing the coverage.

He knew he owed Sayama for the Ryota Mochizuki incident. Yuuki hadn't asked for Sayama's support—in fact, he'd tried to hold him back. But it was still the case that Sayama had saved him. If Sayama hadn't been so eloquent, Yuuki would have been at the mercy of the powers that be in the Editorial Department or General Affairs.

Sayama was the only one who liked him. That was what he secretly believed. And one thing that Yuuki and Sayama had in common was that Sayama had also had a hard time with his father. There were seven years between them and sometimes it felt as if Sayama were his little brother.

"Yuuki-san!"

"Okay, then." Yuuki said it knowing he was caving in to pressure. "Go.

But get there, gather your information, and get it back here as quickly as possible. And promise me you won't set foot on that mountain before sunrise."

"Got it. Thank you," Sayama replied briskly. "And can I take a photographer?"

"There aren't any. Apart from the one I already sent up to Budotoge, they're all covering the baseball games."

"I see. Then I'll take Hanazawa from the press club with me."

"Wait!" said Yuuki hurriedly. "There's one more thing. There's a guy in Advertising by the name of Miyata. Take him along, too."

"*What?*"

Sayama didn't sound pleased.

"You know him, don't you? The ad designer—"

"I know him," Sayama interrupted. "Heavily tanned, wears glasses. Why do we have to take him with us?"

"He knows his way around mountains. He'd definitely be useful."

"You must be kidding. This is the real thing here. There's no room for some flashy adman who gets his kicks from prancing around in the mountains."

What he meant was, *Don't diminish the value of our work.*

Yuuki felt his blood rise. It was on the tip of his tongue.

*Who are you to take that tone? You're little more than a junior reporter yourself!*

His savage side was stirring. Or rather, the side of Yuuki that, for the past thirteen years, he'd been denying existed. He knew he, too, had been carrying around a belief in his own self-importance ever since the Okubo/Red Army years.

But he replaced the receiver without saying a word.

Yuuki's left elbow was resting on his desk, and now he noticed it was being jiggled around. Nozawa was tapping his foot nervously, and the tip of his toe was rubbing against the leg of Yuuki's desk. Yuuki glared at him.

"Stop it."

It was at that moment that the announcement came. The chief copy editor, Kamejima, called from across the room, his circular face animated.

"Yuuki! Look at the TV!"

Yuuki stood up and looked at the screen. The announcer was just saying that they'd been able to determine the scene of the crash—the north face of Mount Ogura in Kitaaikimura, Minamisaku District, Nagano Prefecture . . .

"What the . . . ?"

Yuuki paged Sayama immediately, but there was no response. Ten minutes, fifteen, went by, but still he didn't call back. He must have decided not to get in contact again until he reached Uenomura.

He'd fooled Yuuki . . . No, he wouldn't have lied just to get to go to the crash site. He wasn't the sort of person to resort to something like that. News was always a tricky business. But still, it was true that Sayama had refused to follow Yuuki's instructions.

He felt uneasy and irritated. He was unable to control his one and only subordinate. He was forced to admit that he was completely powerless.

But never mind about that for now. The deadline was getting closer, and everyone was yelling and shouting.

Nagano being the crash site was still only a theory. The rest of the TV report had been very fuzzy on details. Mount Ogura? Kogurayama? Senpeizan? Mikuniyama? All the possible locations flashed through Yuuki's mind.

It was half past midnight—thirty minutes left until the deadline. The newsroom was at the peak of activity. Kamejima came toward him, his expression uncharacteristically stern.

"Which one are we going with?"

He laid out two versions of the headline side by side on Yuuki's desk.

MOUNTAINS ON THE NAGANO-GUNMA BORDER

MOUNTAINS ON THE GUNMA-NAGANO BORDER

By rights the final decision about headlines should go to the chief copy editor—in other words, Kamejima himself. But Yuuki had been given the role of supervisor, so this time Kamejima deferred to him. Instead, though, he'd put Yuuki in a difficult position.

He compared the two headlines. All around him, his colleagues were holding their breath. He reached out and, as if possessed, his hand went to the one on the right: MOUNTAINS ON THE NAGANO-GUNMA BORDER.

It wasn't so much a decision as a hope.

He suddenly felt like throwing up. But that visceral physical reaction that seemed to be telling him all hope was lost was just a hint of what was in store in that long, hot "JAL crash summer."

**6**   One after the other, delivery vans with the bold insignia NKT running along both sides sped out of the office gates.

Ever since the layout had been finalized and turned over to the Printing Department, information had gone backward and forward between Nagano and Gunma as the location of the crash site. According to the reporters camped up at Uenomura, a search party made up of police officers from both prefectures, along with the Self-Defense Forces and the local fire departments—more than a thousand people in total—had been working all night without a break. Not only did they have no precise information as to the location of the site, the mountainous terrain was treacherous. Until about a decade before, the area around Uenomura had been known as the Tibet of the Kanto region. The reality was that no one would know anything for sure until morning.

Around three hundred members of Japan's press corps had driven up to Budotoge Ridge by car, causing a huge traffic jam. The TV channels were endlessly repeating all 524 names on the manifest.

It was 3:00 a.m. The newsroom was as silent as a geriatric ward. More than a third of the staff had made the decision to stay all night, but now exhaustion showed on every face. People had collapsed on sofas or had their heads down on their desks. In about another hour it would start to get light, and bodies and voices were getting a little rest before the fight recommenced.

The TV sounded the first battle cry of the morning. Just after 5:00 a.m., all stations simultaneously began to broadcast footage taken from a helicopter circling the crash site. Shouts went up around the room. Like boxers after the one-minute break between rounds, everyone leapt to their feet and converged on the TV set.

What they saw was nothing like they'd imagined. There was no sign of anything resembling a jumbo jet. There were beautiful green hills— and then, in sharp relief, shredded remains. An L-shaped piece here, a V-shaped bit there, something resembling a boomerang . . . As the camera angle changed, their shapes shifted. White smoke rose. There was no sign of the wings. The letters JAL could be made out. But that was about it. There was nothing else left of the fuselage. Where on earth could the main body of the aircraft be? Had it fallen into a valley somewhere? The surface of the mountain glittered, just like a road covered with shards of glass from a car headlight after a traffic accident.

Startled, Yuuki looked away—down at the surface of his desk. A copy of the morning edition lay there, hot off the press, with a photo of a jumbo jet, the same model as Flight 123.

A shiver ran up his spine. The jet had been smashed into little pieces. Those glittering fragments reflecting the morning sun—a mere twelve hours ago, they had been a giant passenger plane, calmly flying along with more than five hundred human beings on board.

Yes, the people. The people on board had also been smashed into little pieces. He felt a hot wave of anger begin to build. Why had this plane come down? He began to wonder for the first time about the cause of the crash.

The TV journalist in the helicopter was doing his best to shout over the roar of the blades.

"This is Gunma. The crash site is most definitely inside Gunma Prefecture!"

*Ding-dong!* It was the Kyodo News chime.

*The crash site is Uenomura in the Tano District of Gunma Prefecture.*

There was no reaction. As if everybody in the newsroom had just realized that they were in it for the long haul, they sat and stared at the TV screen. Five hundred and twenty-four people had died on that mountain. That sparkling mountain.

In the still of the newsroom, muted voices started up like pattering raindrops. The drops grew to a shower, eventually becoming a full-on downpour. And, with that, the newsroom was back to normal.

Hearing the crash site was in Gunma, the three managers directly under editor in chief Kasuya, who had gone home in the early hours, came straight back to the office, their expressions shocked.

A little while later, the mountain was identified by name: Mount Osutaka. Osutaka had always had a formidable, almost spiritual reputation. Yuuki was shaken by the sound of its name. The previous night, of all the mountains he'd imagined, not once had that one occurred to him. But now that he heard it, it seemed to make sense that Osutaka, more than any other mountain, was the one to go down in history as the scene of a fatal accident.

In fact, there was nothing strange about it being Mount Osutaka. Several thousands of pairs of eyes were scouring the crash site right now. Right now, tens—no, hundreds—of thousands of pairs of eyes were focused on maps. How had Mount Osutaka managed to conceal itself so well until now?

*Because it was mourning the dead.*

It was something he recalled from a story his mother had told him. When he was a child, she would get drunk and tell him traditional folk stories. He closed his eyes.

His mind was awash with all sorts of shameful thoughts. He wanted more than anything just to get out of there. If it had been Nagano, he wouldn't have cared whether it was five hundred or a thousand people who had died. He opened his eyes again and looked at the TV images of Mount Osutaka.

And suddenly he was wide-awake.

"Bring me a map!" he yelled.

Along with around ten of his colleagues, he studied the routes up the mountain. Budotoge Ridge was in the wrong direction. If, instead, they went up the road toward Hamadaira Hot Springs, then followed the Kanna River through the forest until the path ended . . . then climbed up along the bed of a tiny mountain stream . . . Well, they couldn't tell if it was the best way, but according to this map it was definitely the shortest route up Mount Osutaka. They calculated that, if all went well, the party he had sent out could reach the crash site in three to four hours. Yuuki paged the reporters and the photographer. The first to respond was Wajima, the number-two reporter at police headquarters.

"Okay, you can start climbing. Follow the firefighters up. If you can't find them, follow the police rescue team or the Self-Defense Forces."

Yuuki had received word that the search party had grown to around four thousand people. The reporters were going to have to rely on them. As long as they didn't set off in completely the opposite direction, they'd be able to avoid the danger of climbing alone.

"If anything goes wrong, if you have an accident or something, get hold of a Kyodo News reporter. Get them to give you ten seconds of wireless time. Beg them to send a message to the Maebashi city office."

"Understood."

Wajima's voice was strained. Yuuki had heard rumors that he was rather timid for a reporter.

Yuuki lowered his voice.

"How's Sayama doing? Was he at the incident room?"

"Yes, they left earlier, saying they were going to take the route from Minamiaiki in Nagano. They heard from the Self-Defense Forces guys that was the quickest way."

The information was vague, but there was nothing he could do about it. If Sayama and Hanazawa had already crossed Budotoge Ridge, then their pagers must be out of range.

"Okay. You'd better set out now. Don't push it too much, okay? If it gets too difficult to continue, come back down right away."

At 6:00 a.m., Yuuki took part in a meeting of the top Editorial Department managers. How much space should they allocate to the story? Obviously the front page and the local section—a total of twelve pages, including photos—would be dedicated entirely to articles related to the crash. Stories about the Ministry of Transport and Japan Airlines, as well as the relatives of the victims in Tokyo or Osaka, would be put together mostly from Kyodo News wires, but everything that happened in Gunma Prefecture would be written by *North Kanto Times* staff. It was agreed that all crash-site eyewitness pieces would carry the bylines of the paper's own reporters.

For quite a while after the meeting, Yuuki was busy preparing the stories for publication. Around half past eight, he felt a tap on his shoulder. It was Miyata from Advertising. It seemed he'd taken the day off and had been on standby at home, expecting to be asked to climb. Yuuki began to apologize, but Miyata interrupted him. He looked worried. There was something more important he'd come to tell Yuuki.

"Anzai-san's been taken to the hospital."

*He must have fallen.* Yuuki began to tremble. In his imagination, all he could see was his friend slipping on the rock face . . . He swallowed.

"Tsuitate?"

"I'm sorry? What?"

Miyata had no idea that the two men had planned to climb Tsuitate that day. He'd been waiting since early morning for a call from Yuuki, and when none came he'd decided to call Anzai to find out what was going on.

"His kid answered. He wasn't very clear on the details, but it seems Anzai-san was taken to the hospital and his wife is there with him."

That must have been Anzai's son, Rintaro. He was the same age as Yuuki's boy, Jun. The first year of junior high school, but he still looked like a fourth- or fifth-year at primary school. He was painfully shy, and if you asked him a question he never really answered properly, just as Miyata had said. Still, according to both his parents, Rintaro was really fond of Yuuki. Yuuki would never have guessed.

"Thanks. I'll try to get some more information out of him."

Yuuki called Anzai's house right away. Rintaro must have gone out—to school or the hospital. Yuuki really wanted to know what had happened. Why had Anzai been taken to the hospital? Had he climbed Tsuitate alone? And then . . . No, Anzai would be the last person to attempt something that dangerous.

This made him think of Mount Osutaka. Was that dangerous, too? In the TV footage, the slope's gradient had looked fairly gentle overall, but here and there he'd seen much steeper parts. Was it going to be more difficult than anyone could have foreseen? No, really, it hadn't looked that bad. Perhaps the reporters and photographers would make it up there as planned . . . As he thought about this, the chime sounded again.

*Four survivors have been found at the scene.*

It was mind-blowing information. People had actually survived—a young girl, a mother and daughter, and a young woman. In all his time at the company, Yuuki thought he'd never witnessed scenes of such jubilation. The whole newsroom was rejoicing. It was a miracle.

"Fuji TV's showing it!"

It was the young girl being rescued. A member of the Self-Defense Forces held her little body in his arms as the two of them were hoisted into the air by a rope up into a helicopter.

Cheers went up in the newsroom. Applause. Even whistles. This was why he would never give up reporting. Because, sometimes, these things happened. So many smiling faces . . .

Four survivors. There was going to have to be a major reorganization of the local news pages. Yuuki chose four reporters to cover the hospital nearest the crash site and sent them to get ready to leave immediately.

But what had happened to the reporters at the crash site? It was past two in the afternoon now, coming up on three. Yuuki began to get agitated. He glanced at the TV screen and saw faces he recognized: a chief inspector, a detective, the riot police commander. The uniforms of the Self-Defense Forces and the fire department were also clearly visible. Among them were people who looked like media representatives. But his men were not there. He didn't spot a single face of a *North Kanto Times* reporter or photographer.

All in all, he had sent a total of twelve reporters and photographers to Mount Osutaka. Had not one of them made it to the crash site? What about the byline articles? Kyodo News Service had already sent eyewitness pieces. At this rate, the world's biggest air disaster would have happened on the *North Kanto Times*'s doorstep and the local paper was going to have to print eyewitness accounts written by someone else.

It was humiliating. Eyewitness pieces were different from straight news articles. There was a reporter's point of view, a *North Kanto Times* point of view. It was a place to observe, feel, and write your own thoughts. If reporters who were born and raised in Gunma wrote about cases and accidents that happened in Gunma, they brought a deeper knowledge and feeling to the text. In other words, a sense of pride. The *NKT* was in North Kanto, and its reporters should be the ones to write the feature stories, Yuuki believed. No question.

As the clock hands passed 4:00 p.m. the news wires on Yuuki's desk continued to pile up.

Fifty-two bodies recovered

Tailpiece found in sea off Miura Peninsula

Gunma Prefecture sets up own investigation team

Foreign leaders offer messages of sympathy

Nodai Niko baseball nine in shock

Originally on waiting list for flight

Unprecedented sum to be paid in compensation

Aeronautics specialists offer theories

Radioactive material in cargo

Boeing investigators arrive in Japan

JAL president Takagi hints at taking responsibility

Safety myth debunked

As soon as he read one, another landed on his desk. In brief breaks between working, Yuuki would take a moment to scan the TV images for his reporters. As he watched, he hit the redial button on his phone. The Anzais' home number—his concern about that situation was also growing by the minute.

"Anzai here . . ."

It was Rintaro's feeble voice.

"This is Yuuki. You remember me?"

"Um . . . yes."

"What's happened to your father?"

"He's in the hospital."

"Why?"

"I don't really know."

"Is he ill? Injured?"

"They said he collapsed . . ."

So he hadn't fallen from a cliff. But Yuuki didn't know if he should feel relieved or not. He gripped the receiver more firmly.

"Where was he when he collapsed? Do you know what caused it?"

"I don't know . . ."

Rintaro's voice began to break. He was probably in tears. Yuuki pictured his eyes—those big round eyes—the image of his father's.

"Did you go to the hospital to see him?" he asked, as gently as he could.

"Yes. I've come back to get some pajamas for him."

"I see. I'm sorry I'm disturbing you. So, how's your dad doing?"

There was silence on the other end.

"Can you hear me?"

"His eyes are open but he's asleep."

Yuuki was horror-struck. Asleep with his eyes open? The doctor's words, perhaps. He thought it was an awful way of putting it. He decided it would be cruel to try to make Rintaro say anything more. He asked for the name of the hospital and hung up.

He wanted to go and visit Anzai straightaway, but in those few minutes that he'd been on the phone the pile of wires on his desk had gotten out of control.

What did it mean, "His eyes are open but he's asleep"? He couldn't bear to sit around, not knowing. Anzai was at the prefectural hospital. If he just popped in to check on him, it'd take about an hour, round-trip. He could ask Nozawa to cover for him; surely even Nozawa wouldn't begrudge him that.

Nozawa was busy marking proofs of articles with a red pen, but his movements were out of the ordinary. His gaze was switching back and forth between the pile of papers in front of him and the TV screen. Yuuki saw it right away—Nozawa was checking on the crash scene and editing the articles at the same time. Yuuki began to pay closer attention to Nozawa's hand movements. It was just as he thought—Nozawa was using the latest TV coverage to correct a Kyodo News eyewitness report and transform it into an *NKT* article.

The blood rushed to Yuuki's head. He snatched the article out of Nozawa's hand, causing all the other papers on his desk to tumble to the floor. Nozawa stared at him in amazement.

"What the hell are you doing?" Nozawa demanded.

"I might ask you the same thing. Who told you to do this?"

"Todoroki-san. My boss! If you have a problem with it, you'd better talk to him!"

*What the . . .*

The chief local news editor had instigated this? More than anyone in the whole company, Todoroki had always boasted of his involvement in the Okubo/Red Army cases. Still, now, he carried newspaper clippings from that period in his pocket diary. That was the kind of man he was, but this time, for once, he was keeping a low profile, sneaking around giving people these kinds of directions behind Yuuki's back.

Yuuki got up and walked purposefully over to the chief local news editor's chair. Todoroki looked up. The thick dark lenses of his gold-rimmed spectacles concealed a sharp, glowering gaze. To this day, he had the look of a true police beat reporter.

"Sir?"

"What is it?"

"Can you please stop doing that?"

"Doing what?"

"The eyewitness articles."

"Can't be helped. None of our guys made it."

"We don't know that yet."

The tone of Yuuki's voice made his feelings very clear. Todoroki's reply was even clearer.

"They won't make it in time. Poor leadership on your part."

"That's not the point!"

Right as he spoke, he heard a voice behind him.

"There's Sayama!"

Yuuki spun around to look. There he was, in the TV footage from the crash site. It was definitely Sayama. And there was Hanazawa, standing just behind him. Clothes in tatters, their rain-soaked hair plastered to their foreheads, they looked exhausted. But they were there! Someone from the *North Kanto Times* was standing on Mount Osutaka.

Yuuki looked at the clock. It was 5:10 p.m. If Sayama were to head back now, he'd be climbing down the mountain in the dark. It was too dangerous, especially for someone without any climbing experience.

But he knew Sayama. Somehow, he would get back. There was no way that man would give up his chance to get his byline on an article. Whether it was the riot police or the Self-Defense Forces, he'd find someone to tag along with and get down that mountain. Seven hours until the deadline.

Or eight, in fact. Just like yesterday, they'd extend it by one hour. It looked like they'd just be able to get the article.

Yuuki turned his attention back to Todoroki.

"Sayama'll be writing the feature article."

"If he makes it in time."

There was a hint of amusement in Todoroki's eyes.

Yuuki went back to his desk. He swallowed his anger, for now. If he didn't, he'd never get his job done.

But time rushed by. 9:00 p.m. . . . 10:00 . . . 11:00 . . .

Just two hours left to the deadline. There'd been no contact from Sayama.

There was nothing to do but wait. The layout of the city news pages had been completed. It consisted entirely of the Kyodo articles Nozawa had been working on. The moment they received Sayama's draft, they would switch it around. The plan was in place, but still the phone didn't ring. Time was steadily creeping up on Yuuki.

Anxiety was stalking him, too. Since night had fallen, there had been one piece of bad news after the other. Mount Osutaka was a formidable mountain indeed. The reporters who'd struggled their way up to the top had been lucky to make it. Far more of them had gotten lost en route, found their path blocked by a cliff face, or collapsed from sheer exhaustion, the *NKT* party included. Out of the twelve staff members dispatched to the site, Sayama and Hanazawa were the only ones who'd made it.

It was almost midnight. Yuuki was silently praying: *It'll be all right. They'll make it back. Sayama knows what he's doing. He'll know we can put the deadline back an hour. He's taken that into consideration. As soon as he gets back to civilization, he'll find a phone and call in his story.*

"It's about time to send it down."

The voice of the editor in chief came out of nowhere. Yuuki didn't take in the meaning right away. *Send it down . . . Send the paper down . . .*

*Of course. Send it to press!*

Yuuki leapt from his seat. *What the hell?*

"It's going to press already?"

The staff of the newsroom were already swarming out the door and downstairs to the Production Department, where the galleys would undergo a final proofread before being handed over to the printers. Kasuya was also heading toward the door.

"Wait! There's still another hour!" Yuuki bellowed.

Kasuya turned around. He looked puzzled.

"There's no extension today."

"Why not?"

"I thought I'd said? The rotary press isn't working properly. We're going to have to use the old, slow one."

Yuuki thought he'd misheard. He'd been told nothing about this.

*No. Wait . . . This can't be happening. No one told me . . .*

Slowly, Yuuki turned around. He focused on the chief local news editor's desk. Todoroki sat there, no expression on his face, staring through his dark lenses into the distance.

*"If he makes it in time."*

He'd seen the ghost of the Okubo/Red Army era. That had to be it. Todoroki didn't want to publish an article on the world's biggest air disaster with a junior reporter's byline.

His whole body trembled. Jealousy? Could jealousy make a man sink so low?

In the lull that followed the exodus of all the newsroom staff, Todoroki stood up and headed toward the door. Yuuki let rip.

"And you call yourself a reporter?"

Todoroki faltered a moment, but he didn't turn around, and continued out the door. Yuuki slumped down into his chair. Sayama was going to call. He had to wait for him. No escape from the newsroom yet. He'd been awake now for forty hours straight, but not a bit of him felt sleepy.

It was half past midnight when the telephone on the JAL crash desk finally rang.

"We've got our article. *Sayama and Hanazawa reporting from Mount Osutaka . . .*"

It was a perfect feature piece, with punch and intensity. But it would never be printed. Yuuki couldn't bring himself to tell Sayama that part.

Sayama was still trying to catch his breath as he read his script. As Yuuki transcribed his words, he mentally prepared himself for the intense pressure that was going to weigh on the reporters of the new "JAL crash era."

**7**

It was three o'clock in the morning.

Yuuki left the newsroom and climbed the dark staircase. At the far end of the third-floor corridor was the on-call room, where the reporters on night duty could catch up on some sleep, or occasionally people stayed when they couldn't make it home. He turned on the air conditioner and flopped down on the bunk by the wall. He'd known he couldn't trust himself to drive home safely. It was more than just a headache he had; his brain felt swollen, as if it were trying to burst out of his skull. He'd felt this way for hours.

Five hundred and twenty dead. The world's biggest single-aircraft crash.

He hadn't expected the job of JAL crash desk chief to be this tough. It was a job that was far beyond his capabilities, he believed. And it had only just begun. It was now thirty-two hours since Japan Airlines Flight 123 had crashed into Mount Osutaka in Uenomura, Gunma Prefecture. And still, only two morning editions of his newspaper had been published since then.

He'd asked the night-duty reporters to wake him at six. There was an internal phone line by his bed. Yuuki pulled off his sweat-stained necktie with one hand and with the other dragged the pillow under his head. A sour smell enveloped him: the body odor of junior reporters. Yuuki, who had long since moved on from the night shift, felt a pang of nostalgia, along with a sense of loss. When he'd been constantly flitting about as a young reporter on the police beat, this bunk had been a kind of perch. In between chasing down news stories late at night and the next dawn attack, he'd rest his wings here for a while. However, his mind would never fully switch off, and he'd dream short, vivid dreams, tinged with ambition.

In the back of his mind, he could see Sayama's angular face.

Under the blazing hot sun in the middle of summer, Sayama had fought his way for twelve hours through a forest with no clear paths to get up Mount Osutaka. He'd come down the mountain in the dark, literally risking death to carry out the orders of a local newspaper, to relay by telephone his eyewitness account of the accident scene. And yet, at this very moment, the *North Kanto Times* was being delivered to households throughout the prefecture without that reporter's byline. All because Todoroki, the ex–star reporter of the Okubo/Red Army era, couldn't stand the idea of a new star being born.

Sayama had missed his opportunity to carve a name for himself in the history of the *North Kanto Times*.

How would he react? Yuuki wondered. Sayama was one of the best interviewers they had. He'd long established his reputation as a leading reporter at the *North Kanto Times*. And he was probably one of the strongest-willed people at the newspaper. Sayama's attitude could potentially cause problems with future coverage of the accident.

Sayama'd get his revenge, he thought vaguely. But as he turned on his side to sleep, the reporter's face faded from his head . . . It was Anzai who concerned him now. He could still hear Rintaro's feeble voice.

*"His eyes are open but he's asleep."*

At 7:00 a.m. they'd have the morning planning meeting. After that was over, he'd have a little spare time. He could probably rush home, then go straight from there to the hospital. He needed to hear what was going on directly from Anzai's wife. Probably it wasn't anything that serious, after all . . . Not Anzai—he was as strong as an ox . . .

He lay there thinking and, gradually, the sound of his own breathing took over.

Only a few seconds later—or that was how it seemed—something or someone was shaking him vigorously.

"Wake up!"

Yuuki sat up like a jack-in-the-box. He had difficulty opening his eyes right away, as his eyelids were still sticky with sleep. But he recognized the voice. It was the general manager from the Advertising Department, Kura-saka, a colleague of Miyata's.

He wiped his eyes with his shirtsleeve, and it was as he'd thought—he was looking into the bright red square face of Kurasaka.

"What the hell is this?" he roared, shoving a newspaper under Yuuki's nose. "What have you done?"

It was a folded copy of this morning's edition, with the second page of local news on top, on the right-hand side. Yuuki finally found words.

"What is it?"

He looked up at the clock. Six ten a.m. He'd been asleep for three hours.

"Are you stupid? The ad! Local news, second page, five full columns. It's missing!"

It came back to him. Last night one photo after another of the crash site had arrived from Kyodo News. He couldn't bear to discard any of them. He'd told the copy team to put them all in. After a while the copy people had come back to him to say there wasn't enough space for all the photos, and Yuuki had yelled at them to get rid of some of those damn ads if they had to.

He'd meant to ask senior management to let Advertising know that they were removing one of their pieces, but he'd forgotten. He'd been distracted by worries about Sayama's safety and Anzai being in the hospital, and it had completely slipped his mind.

Wide-awake now, Yuuki put his feet on the floor and sat up properly.

"I'm sorry. I took it out."

"Orders from the top?"

"No, it was my decision."

"What the hell were you thinking?"

"I had photos of the crash scene that I couldn't leave out."

"Do you realize what you've done?"

Threateningly, Kurasaka reached into his breast pocket and snatched out another piece of paper. He unfolded it roughly and threw it down on the bed. It was the proofs for an advertisement, the one that should have appeared in this morning's edition.

It was an ad for the opening of what was proudly touted as Takasaki City's biggest shopping center.

Yuuki felt faint all of a sudden. The announcement of the mall's opening had been left out of the paper on the very day it opened. He bowed his head deeply.

"It was a very careless mistake."

Kurasaka went on the attack.

"You think apologizing is going to solve the problem? It can't be fixed now. How exactly do you intend to take responsibility for this mess?"

"Their sales promotion people said they were only going to put it in the *Jomo*, so Ikeyama from our department did everything he could to talk them into going with us, too. And that took some doing. He had to go down on hands and knees and beg them. Do you have any idea how that feels?"

"I'm really sorry. The crash was such big news, I didn't stop and think."

"The crash was such big news? Are you kidding me? If something had happened to the emperor, maybe, but some plane going down? That kind of shit's not worth pulling an ad for!"

Yuuki stared Kurasaka in the face. *Some plane going down? That kind of shit?*

Kurasaka was a couple of years older than Yuuki, and had started out in the Editorial Department. He had spent a long time covering politics, but last spring he'd been lured away by the offer of promotion to manager. He'd moved down to the Advertising Department on the ground floor. Yuuki might have been able to forgive a man who had never been anything but an advertising guy. But not this ex-reporter.

Yuuki leaned toward Kurasaka.

"You're a manager. You get it. This was no ordinary crash."

Kurasaka clenched his jaw defiantly.

"Why? They never pulled an ad in the Okubo/Red Army days. Back then, they used to pull one or two articles, a photo or two, to make room for the ads. Because they understood that advertising's our bread and butter."

Yuuki's expression hardened.

"What's that face for? Look, Yuuki, you know how much a five-column ad's worth?"

Their newspaper was made of fifteen vertical columns per page, so a five-column advertisement would be a pretty big one, at a third of a page.

"I've no idea."

"One million and twenty-five thousand yen."

"Really?"

"Yes, really! You guys have no idea how hard we work. You all have it so easy."

"Easy?"

"You don't have to earn a single yen for the company. We're the ones who earn your living for you."

It was less than a year and a half since Kurasaka had been transferred to Advertising. This was hardly the way an ex-writer should speak. Yuuki couldn't believe his total turnaround in attitude. His blood began to boil.

"At a newspaper company, it's the newspaper itself that's the product. We writers are in the business of creating a newspaper. Don't you dare tell us we're not earning the company any income."

"That's nonsense. You're so ignorant. Subscription fees are insignificant. If you didn't have the advertising income, no matter how much you all go on about the state of the world, you wouldn't even be able to put out a single day's edition."

"If we didn't do a decent job with the real substance of the paper, do you think we'd attract a single advertiser?"

Kurasaka flinched for a moment as Yuuki raised his voice, but quickly covered himself by violently shaking the advertising proofs in Yuuki's face.

"Never mind all that! What are you going to do about this? How are you going to cover our loss?"

"I'll pay my debt. Kindly ask General Affairs to bill me in monthly installments. But you need to understand one thing—if any huge event like last night ever happens again, I won't hesitate for one moment to remove all the ads."

He'd given as good as he got.

"You what?"

"Have you forgotten, Kurasaka-san, what it's like to be in the Editorial

Department? You'll recall that the editorial staff has complete authority in the matter of page layout. Might I suggest that it's pointless to try to interfere?"

"You little prick!"

If the bedside phone hadn't started to ring right at that moment, the two men would definitely have come to blows. The call wasn't from the company night watch but from Totsuka, who had spent the night at the Uenomura village office. He was a reporter in his fifth year at the Fujioka City branch office.

"They've almost finished constructing the emergency heliport on Mount Osutaka."

"That means they're about to start airlifting the bodies out, then?"

"Right. They're aiming for an eight thirty a.m. start."

"Have the investigators got there yet?"

"I'm sorry. Who . . . ?"

"The members of the Ministry of Transport's Aircraft Accident Investigation Committee. When they get there, keep a watch on their movements."

He replaced the receiver and looked up. Kurasaka was standing in the doorway, looking subdued.

"And I'd heard you were a decent person," he spat out. "Someone you could talk to."

Yuuki was puzzled, but before he had a chance to ask Kurasaka to repeat what he'd said the advertising manager was already away down the corridor, leaving nothing behind but the irritated click of his footsteps.

*Someone you could talk to?* Yuuki thought it over while he was putting his tie back on. Who could have said something like that to Kurasaka?

He'd just stood up when his eye fell on the advertising proofs for the mall opening, still spread ostentatiously on the bed. He grabbed them, and tore them right through the middle. Then he turned and marched out of the on-call room, his head already switched into meeting mode.

**8** Seven in the morning.

There were three very sleepy faces in the editor in chief's office. Kasuya was at his desk, talking on the phone. Managing editor Oimura and chief local news editor Todoroki were sitting on sofas positioned across the table from each other, pointing at the stocks column on the financial pages of the morning edition.

JAL STOCKS HIT LOWEST LEVEL EVER . . .

"Of course. Even All Nippon Airways has made a loss, just by association."

As Yuuki sat down at the far end of the sofa, he was struck by something odd. At some point, he had searched for elements of a father figure in all three of these men. It had been shortly after he started at the company. His real father had disappeared when he was still a child, so he'd felt a kind of connection to these senior figures: Kasuya, who'd then been at the local news editor's desk, Oimura, and Todoroki, who were the lead police beat reporters. Although, considering their ages, they were all more likely to be older brothers than fathers to him, to him they'd seemed heroic figures and come to represent the father whose face he had never known. He saw them as tough and dependable; broad-minded. He believed that their whole existence as reporters was built on a firmness of conviction and purpose, and he had never suspected otherwise. Until—

Kasuya hung up. He looked as if he'd just swallowed some very bitter medicine.

"Yuuki, if you're going to drop an ad, then at least give us a heads-up first."

It had been Ukita on the phone. Ukita was the Advertising Department chief and Miyata and Kurasaka's superior. Apparently he'd been outraged to hear the story of the dropped ad from Kurasaka and had called to register his official indignation.

"I apologize. I'll be more careful in the future."

"Please do. Seriously. They all spend their whole time trying to catch our mistakes. They're giving me stomach ulcers doing it. Make sure you don't give them any way in."

Kasuya spoke with real distaste, then proceeded to swallow some actual stomach medicine. He couldn't bear even the slightest disagreement. The Conciliator and Chicken Liver were two of the names for him secretly used in the office. When his "tough boss" veneer had peeled away, it had affected Yuuki. His disappointment was deep, and it still affected him.

"Right. Let's get started."

Kasuya moved his large frame to the sofa, causing Oimura and Todoroki to sit up straighter.

"Today's layout. Yuuki, what do you think?"

Yuuki gave a quick nod of his head and began to speak.

"I believe we should run four headline stories."

"Four? That's a lot."

Yuuki opened his notebook.

"First, the airlifting of the bodies from the mountain. That's about to start right now. Next, we need to cover Fujioka Municipal Sports Center, where the bereaved families are being reunited with the bodies of their loved ones. Then there's the testimony of the survivors and, lastly, of course, the cause of the crash."

"We're not really qualified to go into the cause of the crash. And besides, they've already decided it was a broken rear door, haven't they?"

"No, they're saying it's more likely to have been tail damage. I don't know any more details, though."

"The tail, huh? Well, in any case, we'll just have to sit back and let Kyodo sort that one out."

Kasuya relaxed his almost two-hundred-twenty-pound frame back into the sofa. Yuuki tried to lure him into the conversation again.

"We can't just give up before we've started. The accident investigators arrive on site today. The lower-level ones are staying overnight, so I'm planning to assign Tamaki—he's an engineering graduate—to stick with them."

"I see. Okay, get him to do what he can."

"I will. Then, the removal of the bodies—"

He was just about to explain when Oimura chimed in.

"The reunions are more important than a bunch of airlifts. Sorrowful reunions—that's going to be the topic of today's section."

The Firecracker had started to sizzle already. As always, he was forcing through his own personal opinion with his aggressive way of speaking. He was a total contrast to Todoroki, who always kept his scheming secret.

"They're going to be lifting hundreds of bodies by helicopter," Yuuki retorted. "It's never been done before. It's history-making."

Oimura's eyes turned steely.

"That kind of thing can be covered by a photo or two. Give 'em something to make them cry. Get it?"

Yuuki kept quiet, so Kasuya the Conciliator stepped in.

"Well, let's not make any hasty decisions. What's more important is to ask Yuuki here whether he anticipates being able to get hold of any survivors' testimony."

"A direct interview is out of the question, of course, but I think today we may manage a short chat with some relatives. I've got staff on the hospitals. I've asked them to try to catch the family members on their way in or out."

"I see. It'll be quite a scoop if you can get them to tell you what state the plane was in at the time of the crash. And one of them was a stewardess, too. She'll be able to give a professional viewpoint."

One of the rescued passengers was a Japan Airlines assistant cabin crew manager. She hadn't been on duty but had happened to be traveling privately on Flight 123 that day.

Oimura butted in again.

"There's no way we'll be able to get a scoop on the other papers. The press are going to be all over the hospital. No point in wasting our time.

Get everyone down to that city sports hall and have them interview the families."

In an attempt to change the subject, Kasuya turned this time to Todoroki.

"How many foot soldiers do we have at our disposal today?"

The chief local news editor always had the say over allocation of personnel.

"About twenty, I think."

Immediately Yuuki replied, as firmly as he could, "I need thirty."

The gold-rimmed spectacles turned toward Yuuki. Behind the dark lenses were two sharp pinpoints of light. Yuuki glared right back. Since entering this room, he had been avoiding making eye contact with anyone, but if Todoroki wanted a staring match, then he wasn't going to hesitate. The anger he had felt the night before came rushing back. Todoroki hadn't told Yuuki that the rotary press was broken and that there would be no extension of the deadline. Because of that, Sayama's feature story had gone up in smoke. As for Todoroki, he surely wouldn't have forgotten what Yuuki had said to him: "And you call yourself a reporter?"

Todoroki was the first to break the silence.

"We're not a national newspaper. If we send thirty reporters out on this one, there'll be no one left to cover the rest of the news."

"Twenty-five, then. Can you spare that many?"

Yuuki compromised right away. He knew that, if the argument stretched on, Kasuya and Oimura would take Todoroki's side.

Todoroki picked up a file and began to flick through the pages.

"Twenty-five people . . . I suppose I could manage that."

"Then we'll go with that!" Kasuya announced.

He asked Yuuki how he intended to divide his forces.

"Ten to the sports hall, five to the hospital. I'm going to have the other ten climb Mount Osutaka."

"What?"

This time the Firecracker exploded.

"What the hell do you need ten people on the mountain for? Send more people for the interviews."

"The prefectural police have sent fourteen hundred people—half of their total force—to that crash site."

"They've got proper work to do. If we send ten people, what are they going to do up there? Go for a hike? You've been spending too much time around that damned Anzai."

For a split second Yuuki lost all ability to think. This was the second time Oimura had spoken ill of Anzai. Two days ago, he'd said, "Best to stay away from that one."

Intuition kicked in. He saw the connection between that phrase and the enigmatic words he'd heard first thing that morning from Kurasaka from Advertising. *Someone you could talk to.* It must have been Anzai who'd put that image of Yuuki into Kurasaka's head.

Yuuki regained his ability to think. Time to react to Oimura's pigheadedness. He took a deep breath and opened his mouth.

"What's the problem if it does just end up a hike?"

The three bosses looked at one another in astonishment. Oimura looked searchingly at Yuuki.

"What do you mean by that?"

"That there is merit enough in being able to set foot on the site of the world's largest accident. It's only been thirty-six hours since the plane came down. I think we should send as many people as we can, before it's too late."

"Huh, that's a bit conceited, isn't it? You're suggesting we should use a real accident scene as some kind of training ground for reporters? We don't have the manpower for something like that."

Yuuki had a ready response for that one.

"Of course, I'm giving them work to do."

He tore a page out of his notebook and scribbled something on it.

## SITE OF A TRAGEDY: MOUNT OSUTAKA

"I want a ten-day run."

"You mean a series?"

"Yes. I'm envisioning an expansion of the usual eyewitness accounts.

I want our reporters to focus on writing a different feature story under their own byline each day."

This speech was aimed at Todoroki. He guessed it had hit its mark, because a very unhappy voice now reverberated through the room.

"The mountain's going to be nothing but a repository for corpses and the monotony of them being airlifted away. There's not enough material for a ten-day series."

Yuuki fixed Todoroki with a stare.

"I don't think that's true. That mountain took the souls of five hundred and twenty living beings in a single moment. More likely to be too much material there."

"You can't just say whatever your feelings tell you to say."

"You're the one who's all about feelings."

"What?"

Yuuki psyched himself up for the attack.

"This isn't a site you can measure against Okubo or the Red Army."

Todoroki suddenly looked very severe indeed. Kasuya and Oimura's expressions also changed. Yuuki looked at each of them in turn.

"This crash site is beyond anything any of us could have imagined. Because we are sending people to cover something that is completely beyond comprehension, we have to make sure we get the highest caliber of reporting. That's why I think it's important for us to have an overwhelming force out there, outnumbering the rest of the press presence, keeping up the *North Kanto Times*'s proud eighty-year tradition."

The three managers stayed silent.

There was a knock at the door and Chizuko Yorita from the editorial administrative support team brought in tea. Reading the sensitive atmosphere in the room, she didn't offer her usual charming smile. Instead, she gave a quick bow, placed the teacups on the table, and left the room as quickly as possible.

Kasuya let out a tiny sigh, incongruous with his giant body.

"Understood. Let's do it."

It was Kasuya who had made Yuuki desk chief for this case. He clearly realized that it would be ridiculous to destroy him now, after setting him up.

Oimura tutted his frustration, but that was all. Todoroki was looking at the wall. Apparently he had nothing to say.

Yuuki suddenly felt as if a weight had been removed from his shoulders. It was the first time he had ever gone up against these three and been able to express his opinion so openly.

"However, are these reporters going to be able to make it to the crash site?" Kasuya asked. "Yesterday, only two made it, didn't they?"

"The Self-Defense Forces and the police have already started work on a cable ropeway from Sugenosawa to the summit. If our reporters use that, I believe they can make it up in two to three hours."

Oimura snorted at Kasuya and Yuuki's exchange.

"All this talk about feature stories and bylines! Let's just call a spade a spade. It'll end up being a load of froth, sucking up to the SDF and the police."

Oimura's allergy to the Self-Defense Forces was well-known at the newspaper. A while ago, there'd been a dispute over whether or not to publish an SDF recruitment ad in the newspaper. Following his vehement opposition, it had ended up being cut.

"Yuuki. I'm just going to say this—I think you should concentrate on the bereaved relatives. You shouldn't get too carried away. It'd be less shameful than a bunch of vague, unfocused pages."

With this parting shot, Oimura got to his feet. Todoroki followed suit. Throwing Yuuki a glance full of loathing, he followed Oimura out of the room.

"Well, try to get it done without too much fighting," Kasuya offered, a faint smile on his lips. His expression showed none of the tension or excitement that a journalist ought to feel on coming face-to-face with the biggest air disaster of all time.

**9** It was a little after 7:30 a.m. In the newsroom, the early morning sun lit the dancing dust particles that followed everyone around.

It was quiet this morning. Right now the world's biggest plane crash existed only on the TV news. Yuuki reflected that it wasn't only Kasuya and the rest of the senior management who didn't seem to grasp the full reality of the accident. Even he hadn't, and he was sure it was because he hadn't been to the crash site in person. If he took the Kan-Etsu Expressway, he could get there in around two hours. However, Mount Osutaka couldn't be measured in distance or time; it had become something more distant, far more complicated, than that.

Yuuki sat down to begin the process of selecting the twenty-five reporters for his news crew. He already had twelve out in the field, so he had thirteen more to choose from the various branches scattered throughout Gunma Prefecture. He was picking the ones who seemed to have a history of doing good legwork, but he also had to consider a balance of the regions and not take too many reporters away from either the east or the west of the prefecture. There was no way of knowing where and when the next big story might happen.

The young administrative assistant Chizuko Yorita had offered to page everyone for him, and he had just handed her the completed list when Kishi's narrow face appeared in the newsroom. He put his shoulder bag down on the political editor's desk.

"It's just as hot today!" he exclaimed.

Yuuki was momentarily surprised by Kishi's sweaty forehead. He himself hadn't set foot outside the office building for two days straight and, sitting there in the comfort of the air-conditioning, he'd forgotten about the midsummer heat.

"It's boiling out there. Hey, you don't look too good, Yuuki. Did you get any sleep?"

"Yeah, I slept. Anyway, you got a call this morning from Aoki in Tokyo."

"About Yasukuni Shrine, I guess."

"Yeah. Prime Minister Nakasone's going to visit the inner sanctuary, but he's going to keep it simple. Just a bow, apparently."

"And the offering?"

"Seems he's dispensing with that. The official announcement's going to be tonight. If only we had an evening edition."

"I'll let management know Aoki's got a story. Thanks."

"You're welcome."

"How's that going?" Kishi asked, indicating with a flick of his head the pile of proofs on Yuuki's desk.

"They're removing the bodies today."

"Already? Gunma police have really got their shit together."

"Seems the Self-Defense Forces have already managed to build a heliport."

"Aha! Yes, in an emergency, it's the SDF you want."

"Yeah, but they're not the ones who get to investigate it."

"What?"

"Late last night the prefectural police set up a special investigative unit."

Kishi looked amazed.

"Wow. Local police have to investigate *this* crash? You must be joking."

"It happened here, so they have jurisdiction."

"That's bad luck. This has got to be the worst accident the Gunma prefectural police have ever inherited." Kishi frowned. "Us, too."

Yuuki decided to ignore Kishi's gaffe.

*An inherited accident.*

Sooner or later there would be plenty of people within and outside the department saying the same thing, Yuuki guessed. It happened quite often with murder cases, too. Gunma, with all its mountains, was frequently used as a dumping ground for corpses. The killers would drive the bodies up from Tokyo. Every time, the prefectural police would mount a big investigation.

And so would the *North Kanto Times*. Scores of reporters would run around covering the case—all for someone from a different part of the country who had committed their crime far from Gunma.

"Some plane" had just happened to crash—that was how Kurasaka from Advertising had so dismissively put it. A plane connecting Tokyo and Osaka, with no ties or relationship with Gunma, had just happened to crash into their side of the border that divided them from Nagano. That was how Kurasaka saw it.

Deep down, Yuuki's own feelings were not all that different. Back when it had been difficult to get information and they hadn't been sure where the crash site was, he'd hoped it was in Nagano. And he still hadn't completely banished that thought. Why did it have to be Gunma, which wasn't even on any flight paths? Why did he have to be saddled with supervising this, of all cases?

Maybe it was just some inherited accident, after all. If someone high up at the paper were to say it loudly enough, then perhaps the whole thing would just fade away. *The world's biggest airline disaster.* Maybe the words would lose their magical power before too long. And if they did, would he breathe a long sigh of relief that this huge burden was off his shoulders? Or would he be overcome with regret? Right at this moment, Yuuki had no idea.

The newsroom was filling up.

The reporters who'd been paged began calling back, and Yuuki was busy explaining their assignments to each one. Wajima was the one person he didn't expect a fast response from, and he was indeed the last to call. He sounded worried.

"This is Wajima . . . Did you page me?"

The previous day, Yuuki had given the timorous reporter the order to climb Mount Osutaka, but he'd gotten lost and had been forced to turn back.

"Climb it again."

The line went silent.

"We're starting a series of feature stories. You'll be one of ten people climbing the mountain, and I want you to be in charge."

"You want me—?"

"You'll be fine. The Self-Defense Forces and the police are constructing a ropeway. It'll be completely different from yesterday."

He somehow managed to persuade him, but after hanging up the phone he still felt uneasy. Not only was Wajima cautious but since the previous day's failure he'd lost all his self-confidence. All Yuuki could do was offer words of encouragement. Wajima wasn't a novice. He'd been working as a reporter for seven years now and should be able to supervise the junior staff members. He was doing a good job as the number-two reporter at police headquarters. But the thought that he hadn't been able to climb Mount Osutaka had the potential to haunt his future as a reporter.

The next thing Yuuki did was page Sayama and Hanazawa. It wasn't to send them back to the crash site but to call them into the office. He wanted to thank them for their hard work the day before, and to reward them for it. He'd decided that Sayama would get to write the first feature story.

When the phone rang, Yuuki took a moment to gather himself before he picked up. But it wasn't Sayama or Hanazawa. It was an update from Totsuka, the young reporter from Fujioka.

"The heliport's finished. They're about to start removing the bodies."

"Got it. Thanks."

Yuuki replaced the receiver and paged the two men again.

Still no response.

They must have somehow gotten hold of a copy of today's paper and discovered that their eyewitness account wasn't in it. They'd be devastated, furious even. They'd probably turned off their pagers.

He tried to reach them one more time. Still, his desk phone stayed silent.

Yuuki let out a quick breath and looked up. It was ten past eight. From the afternoon on, he was sure to be buried again under a pile of papers. What if he quickly called in at home and then on Anzai in the hospital? If he was going to do it, it would have to be now.

"Kishi, can you cover for me for a couple of hours?"

Just as he spoke, he heard the beep of a pager right behind him. He turned and was blown away by what he saw.

Sayama and Hanazawa had just walked in. Yuuki was not alone in his reaction—everyone who'd seen them arrive had gasped in shock.

They were in a terrible state. Their once-white shirts were completely brown; not just dirty—there was absolutely no white left anywhere. It was as if they had been soaked in brown dye. In contrast, possibly from the two having sweated so much, their navy-blue trousers were now white with salt. Their sunburned arms were covered with cuts and gashes. Apparently they'd had to beat their way through heavy undergrowth. But it was Sayama's eyes that were the worst. Yuuki recoiled at the look in them. They were horrifyingly dark, the eyes of someone in deep distress.

They'd witnessed something unthinkable, Yuuki's instinct told him.

Sayama walked straight up to Yuuki.

"Did you page me?"

His voice was hoarse, like an old man's.

"Yes, I did. You did a great job out there."

"Why was my report dropped?"

Perhaps Sayama was already way past his anger. He was strangely calm. Yuuki looked him straight back in the eyes.

"The rotary press was broken. We had to use the old one and couldn't extend the deadline."

He didn't want to tell Sayama what Todoroki had done. As far as Sayama was concerned, he would just have to believe that Todoroki had notified Yuuki that there could be no extension. Yuuki knew there was no point in arguing any further; otherwise, it would never end.

Yuuki couldn't tell whether Sayama had understood what he'd said. He just nodded his head vaguely two or three times.

"Then why didn't you tell me when I was phoning in the story?"

"I couldn't bring myself to."

"I see."

Once again, Sayama nodded unsteadily. His mind was only half there. At least, that was how it looked.

But now it was Hanazawa, behind Sayama, who began to worry Yuuki. Standing there, looking like some kind of feral animal, he had begun to shake. From the moment they'd arrived in the newsroom, in contrast to Sayama, Hanazawa had been fixated on Yuuki's face, a peculiar gleam in his eyes. He was twenty-six years old, with three years' experience as a reporter. It was fair to say he was still just starting out. He had delicate features, didn't really say very much. Yuuki had always thought of him as someone who didn't stand out. This Hanazawa in front of him seemed to have appeared out of nowhere.

Yuuki led the two men out into the corridor and over to the area where people took their breaks—a small corner with vending machines and a couple of sofas. He bought three cans of iced coffee from one of the machines. Staff from other departments stared at the two reporters' tattered clothes as they walked by. Hanazawa scowled back menacingly at them all.

"What was it like at the crash site?"

At Yuuki's question, a visible chill passed through Sayama's whole body. But it was Hanazawa who spoke.

"Every single thing was in pieces. Heads, hands, feet . . ."

Yuuki sat and listened to their story for a full hour.

It was mostly Hanazawa who talked. They'd followed the Self-Defense Forces up the mountain from the Nagano side, but there turned out to be three separate mountain ridges, divided by steep, scree-covered valleys that they had to slide down. They'd had neither water nor food with them, so they scooped up puddle water with a small plastic film cylinder. They'd had to fight their way through thick bamboo grass taller than they were; then, after practically crawling up one last cliff face, they'd finally reached the crash site. Dead body parts were strewn everywhere. There was nowhere one could step without treading on something.

As Hanazawa talked, editorial staff began to gather around the sofas. People from other departments, too, paused on their way past and listened in from a distance.

The light in Hanazawa's eyes was far from normal; he sounded like some kind of lifeless robot as he recited the gruesome details of the crash site. In particular, his tone was flat as he described the state of the bodies in the minutest detail. It was as if the human part of him had been broken.

In contrast, Sayama just sat there lifelessly, his eyes on the floor. If he spoke, it was with great hesitation. He looked terrified of something, almost possessed. When he'd phoned in his article in the middle of the night, he'd been in high spirits. Turning over in his head what he'd seen up on that mountain, he must have suffered some kind of aftershock. They were both damaged, Sayama and Hanazawa, but in different ways.

Yuuki could tell more about the atrocity of the crash site from the reactions of the two men than from the details of Hanazawa's account.

Yuuki turned to Sayama.

"Please write one more eyewitness piece about the crash site."

He began to explain his plan for the feature series. Sayama merely folded his arms in silence. Instead, it was Hanazawa who responded.

"It's too late for that!" he snapped. "It might have meant something if it'd appeared in this morning's paper. We risked our lives to send that report, but you didn't even bother to use it!"

Yuuki turned to Hanazawa.

"It wasn't that I didn't bother to. I wasn't able to."

"For fuck's sake. The whole paper was filled with Kyodo articles. We were made to look like complete idiots!"

"That wasn't it at all," said Yuuki, his tone hardening. Hanazawa was getting angrier, criticizing the Editorial Department's decisions. He was playing to the gallery now, all the people around getting him far too worked up.

Yuuki turned back to Sayama.

"What do you think?"

After a long pause, Sayama replied.

"I feel the same as Hanazawa. I gave my report in the proper manner."

He'd spoken quietly, but his words oozed with the indignation and chagrin of a journalist who had been prevented from leaving his mark on the history of the *North Kanto Times*.

"I'm asking you personally."

"I already sent it."

Yuuki bit his lip. He was getting frustrated by this defiant attitude, and from a junior reporter. It was true that he'd been prevented from printing Sayama's report. But his new plan was a way of rewarding Sayama's hard work. He'd bulldozed the idea through at the meeting. He was not retreating now. Sayama was vital to his plan and, if he turned Yuuki down now, everything would have to be put on hold. Yuuki couldn't bear to imagine Oimura and Todoroki's sneering faces if that were to happen. He lowered his voice.

"That bullshit—is that what you call a feature article?"

Sayama's cheek twitched.

"That *bullshit*?"

"A measly thirty lines of copy delivered in the middle of the night?"

"It was all I could manage in the time."

"I understand. But NKT has its pride. That was no feature article."

It was a childish trick. But once an investigative reporter grew up and acted maturely, you couldn't call him an investigative reporter anymore.

"Write me eighty, a hundred lines. As much as you want. Let us read about what you've seen."

This was something he felt strongly about. What did it look like, this phenomenon that in one night had transformed a competent reporter in his prime into this despondent, gloomy man? Yuuki wanted to know.

Sayama thought it over for a while.

"Okay. I'll do it."

A little color had returned to his complexion.

Hanazawa was furious, but Sayama stayed firm.

When they returned to the newsroom, the TV screen was showing helicopters airlifting the dead bodies.

The pile of articles and memos on Yuuki's desk had grown.

*Thirteen members of Ministry of Transport's Aircraft Accident Investigation Committee arrive at crash site. Work under way to retrieve voice and flight recorders.*

*Interview with doctors from Tano General Hospital: "Survivors' blood pressure, breathing, back to normal. Transfer to regular wing in two/three days."*

*Patrol boat of the Third Regional Coast Guard finds piece of fuselage from crashed plane in Sagami Bay, 18 kilometers south of Enoshima.*

Every now and then, as he made his way through the heap of articles, Yuuki would throw a glance to the opposite end of the newsroom. In the corner desk sat Sayama, hunched over, his pen barely moving. Normally he was the fastest writer in the local news section.

Three hours went by. It was nearing the end of the lunch break by the time Sayama brought over his copy.

"Here you are."

The hardness in his face had softened a little.

"Thank you. I'll read it right away."

"I'm glad I wrote it. It helped me feel better."

With this very uncharacteristic comment, Sayama turned and headed for the door.

Yuuki pulled out a red pen and placed the sheets of copy in front of him. Sayama had written more than a hundred lines.

As soon as he started in on the lede, a shiver ran through his body. The words on the paper bore no resemblance to the ones he'd heard in that midnight call. This didn't sound like any newspaper lede he'd ever read.

### Report by Sayama on Mount Osutaka

*The young Self-Defense Forces soldier cut an impressive figure.*

*Clasped in his arms was a young girl with a red dragonfly-shaped barrette in her hair, and dressed in a blue polka-dot dress. Her tiny right hand, golden-tanned, dangled loosely down.*

*The soldier looked up at the sky. How could it be so blue? How could the clouds float so lightly? Birds were chirping. The wind blew gently across the mountain ridge.*

*The soldier looked down at the hell below him.*

*It must be around there somewhere . . . He really needed to find it—this little girl's left hand.*

Yuuki put down his red pen.

He reread the opening over and over. Then he went on to the main story. He waited until he'd regained control of his emotions, then stood up. Even then, he still felt he was looking directly at the crash scene. It was right there in front of his eyes.

He handed the article to the copy chief, Kamejima.

"Kaku-san, this is our front-page story."

"What's up? Your eyes look red."

Yuuki didn't reply. He walked toward the door, loosening his tie as he left.

# 10

The sun felt blistering on his skin, but he crossed the parking lot with a spring in his step. After two days shut up in the office, he felt free again. He'd escaped momentarily from the noise and chaos surrounding the plane crash. Above all, the opportunity to read Sayama's eyewitness account had given him a clear picture of what they were dealing with.

It was too hot to get into his car right away, so instead he opened all the windows and turned the air conditioner on full blast. From Sojacho, where the newspaper offices were located, it would take him about twenty minutes to drive home. After that he planned to return to work via the prefectural hospital in Maebashi City. He'd have to put the pedal down to make it.

His wife's little red car was in the drive. Yumiko wasn't a bit surprised when he turned up suddenly in the living room.

"Hi there. That plane crash is big news, eh? Did you go all the way to that mountain?"

"I had to run it all from the office."

"The whole time?"

"Yep."

"You must be pretty stressed, then."

She understood reporters better than they understood themselves. It came from fifteen years of living with one.

"Where's Jun?"

"Around somewhere."

His heart lurched a little. Why hadn't he come out to say hello?

"Yuka?"

"She's gone swimming with some friends."

"Sports club?"

"You've forgotten it's the summer holidays." She laughed.

He handed her his sweaty shirt and his necktie.

"So, are you going back to the office?"

"Yes, right after I take a shower. Could you pack me about three days' worth of clothes?"

"Rough time?"

"A bit, yes."

As Yuuki turned to get a bottle of cold barley tea out of the fridge, Jun walked by, dressed in pajamas. To his father's greeting of "Hi!" he replied with his usual grunt. He took a manga book off the bookshelf by the TV and lay down on the sofa to read. He'd grown a lot since starting junior high school that spring. He couldn't stretch out completely on the sofa anymore. From his ankle bone to the top of his head, he could no longer fit comfortably on the two-person sofa.

"Why's he still in his pajamas?" Yuuki whispered to Yumiko, who had just come back into the kitchen. Yumiko lowered her voice, too, as she always did.

"He's got a bit of a cold."

"Does he have a temperature?"

"I don't think so."

"Did you check?"

"No."

"Has he taken any medicine?"

"Try asking him yourself."

Yuuki hated the way Yumiko looked when she suggested something like this. There was a mixture of compassion and cruelty in her eyes. *You're his father, aren't you?* Three years ago, Yuuki had slapped her cheek when she had asked him that question out loud; now she just spoke it with her eyes.

They'd lived together ever since they were university students, so they pretty much knew everything there was to know about each other. Except for the disappearance of his father, which Yuuki had kept to himself. He'd told her that his father had died when he was in junior high. He hadn't lied out of an inferiority complex about his upbringing. He was afraid that talking about his father's disappearance might raise questions in Yumiko's mind as to how Yuuki's mother had managed to support her family.

When he was a kid, there had been a succession of male visitors to their home. Yuuki had spent many a sleepless night in the corner of the outdoor storage shed. When his mother had passed away of heart failure nine years ago, Yuuki had heaved a sigh of relief. For an independent working man, having a mother with a dark past had made him vulnerable.

Yuuki and Jun just weren't compatible. At least that was how Yumiko seemed to see it. She never took sides, but she served as a buffer between them. If they could continue to interact through Yumiko, then all would be well. He'd resigned himself to the situation. In about ten years, Jun would leave home. As long as things didn't get worse between them before then, it'd be better to let the distant father-son relationship continue.

"Jun?"

"Yeah?"

Jun looked up at his father, his eyes devoid of emotion.

"You've got a cold?"

"Yeah."

"Temperature?"

"No."

"Did you take it?"

"Hmm."

"It's not good to lie right under the air conditioner, you know."

"Hmm."

Yuuki went to take a shower.

He guessed that Jun's *hmms* were his way of trying to get his dad to be quiet. On the other hand, they could also be taken as a sign of agreement. Yuuki couldn't be sure. Ever since he was five years old, Jun had used this sound a lot. To avoid being hit by his father, or, more likely, to show his disobedience.

There was one occasion when Yuuki had seen through Jun's little game and completely lost it with the boy. Jun had stumbled when his father slapped him and he had grabbed a pair of scissors from the table, just for a moment. But he hadn't pointed them at Yuuki. He was still too much of a child to hate his father. Jun had held them so the tips of the blades were pointing at his own eyes, and begun to howl like a wild beast.

Yuuki finished his cold-water shower and left with his overnight bag of clothes.

He let out some heavy sighs on his way to the hospital. Jun had looked feverish to him, and he had wanted to put his hand on his forehead. But he couldn't even make that simple gesture of affection anymore.

He'd grown up longing for a family. A father and a mother and children. He'd imagined that this would bring constant laughter and happiness. He'd been in search of happiness when he'd decided to have children. Jun and Yuka were supposed to satisfy that craving he had in his heart. Yuuki had never even thought about his own children growing up and becoming parents themselves.

He wondered now whether he should have stayed single. Never fallen in love, never married, never had children. He should have just rotted away and died alone, despising and cursing his father.

He pressed his foot on the accelerator. He was on his way to the hospital, where his friend was in God knows what condition, and instead of being worried about him he found himself hoping that Anzai would save his own soul. Now Yuuki felt even more dejected.

# 11

The prefectural hospital had just been given a fresh coat of white paint and was dazzling in the midday sun.

Even though it was the Obon holiday, the parking lot was full, and Yuuki was forced to drive to the backup parking lot, which was quite far away.

He got out of the car and hurried as fast as he could to the hospital building. There was a large-screen TV set up in the ground-floor lobby showing footage from inside the Fujioka Municipal Sports Center. A woman was walking with a handkerchief pressed to her eyes, a police officer supporting her with an arm around her shoulder. It must have been shot right after she had identified the body of her loved one. Many of the people in the hospital lobby were expressionless as they watched the event unfold on the screen. Yuuki overheard an old lady sitting on the end of one of the sofas muttering, "I wish someone would weep for me like that."

Yuuki got Anzai's room number from reception and headed up by elevator to the fourth-floor surgical unit. Down toward the end of the corridor, on the right-hand side, he found Room 408. It appeared to be a single-occupancy room.

He knocked. After a short wait, the door opened a crack and the pale face of Sayuri Anzai peered out.

It was at that moment that he realized how serious it was. Yuuki had been worried, but he'd been caught up in the vortex of a huge, unforeseen disaster and hadn't had the capacity to think properly about other people's problems. And anyway, this was Anzai the invincible—probably even immortal. It was impossible to imagine this man affected by any kind of illness or injury.

Sayuri looked haggard. Anxiety, misery, fear—all were there in her face.

"Can I see him?" Yuuki asked. Sayuri nodded.

"Of course. But . . . Yuuki-san, I have to warn you. It's quite a shock."

Not really knowing what she meant, Yuuki walked hesitantly in and saw Anzai lying in the bed. His head was wrapped in white gauze and his arm was attached to a drip. Yuuki couldn't help himself.

"Anzai!"

He called out to his friend because his eyes were open. But Anzai didn't react.

It was just as Rintaro had said on the phone. Anzai was asleep with his eyes open.

Hold on . . . Was he really asleep? Those wide, twinkling eyes were the same as always. In fact, he even looked as though he were laughing at Yuuki, as if it were all one big practical joke. Any minute now he'd turn those eyes his way and say, *Hey there, Yuu!*

But his eyes didn't move. They seemed to be looking at something, but in reality they saw nothing. Yuuki took his friend's hand. It was warm. He squeezed it tightly, but Anzai didn't return the squeeze. Normally that big hand would be wrapped around Yuuki's shoulders and he'd be shaking him heartily.

The horror of it finally kicked in.

"Anzai . . . ? You . . ."

Sayuri opened up a folding chair and offered it to him.

"Mrs. Anzai. What hap—"

Yuuki stopped abruptly, not sure where to begin.

"It was a subarachnoid hemorrhage. They operated, but . . . They say he might have PVS."

Sayuri buried her face in her hands.

PVS? Yuuki's brain couldn't process what this meant right away.

"What . . . ?"

Sayuri shook her head.

"He blinks. But if you speak to him, he doesn't respond."

Yuuki couldn't find the right words. Sayuri fought off her tears and bravely set about making tea.

"Please don't worry about me. I have to get back soon."

"Do you really have to leave? Please stay and keep him company. He's lonely with no one to talk to him."

She forced a laugh.

It was more likely that Sayuri wanted someone to talk to. He'd seen it in her face—sitting by the bedside of her mute husband, she was wracked with despair.

Sayuri handed Yuuki a cup of tea, then sat down beside him. Her gaze turned to Anzai. Yuuki followed suit. His trademark goatee looked rather pitiful viewed from this angle.

"He was supposed to be going climbing with you, wasn't he?"

"He never set out?"

"Pardon?"

"I called your house that evening. We were supposed to take a train to the mountains, but I couldn't make it because of the plane crash. It looks like Anzai never got on that train, either."

"I suppose not. He collapsed in the street in Maebashi and an ambulance brought him here."

"Whereabouts in Maebashi?"

"Jotomachi or somewhere."

The entertainment district. He must have been out drinking. That was the most popular area for the Circulation Department to take their newsdealer clients. He'd probably been called to some last-minute dinner or something and he'd ended up missing the train, too.

"Was he drunk when he collapsed?"

"The doctor said there was no alcohol in his system."

"He hadn't been drinking at all?"

Yuuki found it very difficult to believe. No one loved drinking more than Anzai did. Whether it was a business dinner or just for pleasure, there was no way he'd be walking around Jotomachi sober. Or perhaps it had still been early, and he was on his way to one of his usual bars when it happened.

"About what time was it?"

"A little after two in the morning."

Yuuki's eyebrows shot up.

"Was he alone?"

"It looks like it. A passerby found him lying at the side of the road and called an ambulance."

Yuuki stared at Anzai's face.

A mystery. In the entertainment district at two in the morning, but not drinking. What could he possibly have been doing there all by himself?

"What does the doctor say?"

Sayuri's face clouded over.

"Worst-case scenario, he'll be like this forever."

Sayuri opened her handbag and took out a pocket diary. There was a piece of paper folded inside it, which she opened up. "PVS—Persistent Vegetative State" was written on it in masculine handwriting.

"They're going to try all kinds of treatment, but if he stays this way for more than three months that'll be the official diagnosis. I had the doctor write it down so I could learn the name. Not that I want to learn it . . ."

Normally very quiet and withdrawn, today Sayuri was unusually talkative. She was obviously suffering severe emotional shock. He thought about his next words carefully before speaking.

"There have been lots of cases of people regaining consciousness—a great many."

Sayuri's eyes flickered.

"Yes. I hope he's going to be one of them."

"Anzai's no ordinary man. I'm sure he's going to pull through this."

"Thank you."

He felt deeply sorry for her. There were financial considerations, too. How was General Affairs dealing with the situation?

"Has anyone from the company been to visit?"

"Yesterday his boss stopped by."

Yasuo Ito, head of Circulation. The muscles in Yuuki's neck stiffened.

"Did he say anything?"

"He said they would do everything they could. And that he should take his time and rest."

Take his time and rest? That was ironic. The company had a limit of six months' long-term sick leave. If Anzai were to end up in a persistent vegetative state, he would lose his job. His medical expenses would pile up. Yuuki suddenly felt very depressed.

"You'd better put in all the claims you can to the company. I'll back you up."

"Thank you. But Anzai's boss promised he'd do everything he could for us. I'm not sure about submitting claims . . ."

"It would be better to. The company won't do anything without them. And—"

Sayuri cut him off.

"I think it's terrible how hard they made him work!"

"I'm sorry . . . ?" Yuuki looked at her in surprise.

She hastily changed her tone to one more cheerful. "He was really looking forward to it."

"Er . . . to what?"

"Going climbing with you."

"Was he really?"

"After they operated on him, for just a brief moment he was conscious."

"He was?" Yuuki's eyes widened.

"Yes. And he spoke. He said, 'Tell him to go on ahead.'"

"Oh."

"That was a message for you, I think. My husband hadn't heard that you weren't able to go after all."

So Anzai had still intended to go. He'd missed the train but had planned to take the first one in the morning and catch up with Yuuki at the Tanigawa Climbing Information Center.

*"Tell him to go on ahead."*

Yuuki looked down at the bed. Anzai could well be scaling the Tsuitate rock face right at this moment, in his dreams. He wanted to curse him for being such a fanatic about it. His family—why hadn't he had a message for Sayuri and Rintaro? If he never woke up again, those would end up being his dying words.

"He told me the Tsuitate face is really terrifying."

"Terrifying?"

Yuuki was more than a little surprised. Anzai had actually called Tsuitate terrifying?

"Is that what he said?"

"Yes, he was afraid of it. My husband wasn't as tough as he looked. I don't know why he was going if he was that scared."

There was a faint sting in her words. So, she did feel it. Disappointment that he had spoken of his mountain-climbing plans instead of leaving his family with some final words to hold on to.

Yuuki's pager rang, as if to remind him to hurry up and get back. It was after 3:00 p.m. He slowly got to his feet. Sayuri shot him a wistful look. If she no longer had anyone to talk to, there'd be nothing but harsh reality left for her.

"Would you mind—" They had both started to speak at the same time.

"Go ahead," Yuuki offered, and Sayuri responded with a faint smile.

"Would you mind saying hello to Rintaro?"

Yuuki had been going to ask about him. He wanted to check on Rintaro before going back to the newspaper.

"Where is he now?"

"He went to the shop. He should be back any minute."

"Okay, then I'll just make a quick phone call from the lobby first."

"I hope I can count on you to keep in touch with Rintaro." She sounded as if she really meant it. "He's not a very talkative boy, but he really likes you, Yuuki-san. He was never all that close to his dad, though."

Yuuki was astonished. He'd visited the Anzai household several times and seen Anzai and Rintaro joking around together. He'd even been secretly envious. He was still pondering this new information as he went out into the corridor.

He took the elevator down to the ground floor and was heading over to the row of public phones when the glass entrance doors slid open and Rintaro walked in. He was thirteen, the same age as Jun, but about two sizes smaller. The plastic shopping bags hanging from each hand looked too bulky and heavy for his frame.

"Hi there!"

Rintaro responded by hurrying over to Yuuki. Right away Yuuki was looking into a pair of large round eyes, identical to the boy's father's.

"You're having a tough time," said Yuuki.

"Not really," replied the boy, turning red with embarrassment.

"I've just been to visit your father."

"I see."

"He'll wake up, I'm sure of it. Try not to worry too much."

Rintaro looked down at the floor. Yuuki put his hand on the boy's head and ruffled his hair with deliberate force.

"Be strong! You're a man. You have to look after your mother!"

Promising to visit again soon, Yuuki turned to leave. Right behind him he heard something heavy drop to the floor and, just as he turned back to look, two frail little arms were around his waist and Rintaro was hugging him as tightly as he could. Yuuki was taken completely by surprise, but he braced his legs so as not to lose his balance. The two plastic bags lay flat on the floor. A bowl of dried instant ramen had come rolling out. It was probably what Rintaro planned to eat at home by himself that night.

Yuuki's heart ached for the lonely boy.

He put his arms around Rintaro gently and pulled him closer.

**1**
**2**  It was almost daybreak and an enticing fragrance hung in the air. Yuuki crawled out of his tent to see the sturdy figure of Rintaro crouched down in the dry riverbed, grilling mochi rice cakes on a portable gas stove. He'd laid two paper plates on top of a large flat stone, and on these he'd put soy sauce mixed with sugar for dipping and some dried nori seaweed. Breakfast was apparently going to be grilled mochi wrapped in nori.

"Morning!"

Rintaro turned, looking a little surprised.

"Did I wake you?"

"I had to wake up just to stop you from eating everything," Yuuki replied with a laugh.

He looked up to see the morning sun just begin to hit the Ichinokurasawa ridgeline. A few stars were still visible in the sky. It was a magical sight.

"Wow! Beautiful!"

Rintaro also looked up.

"Yes, this is my favorite time of day, too."

Yuuki turned his head to the right and looked at the Tsuitate face. Its peak silhouetted in the morning mist, it stood there looking eerily like a stone pyramid.

"I really am afraid, you know."

"After you've eaten, it won't seem so bad."

Smiling amiably, Rintaro handed him a plate of wrapped mochi.

"Your father used to say he was afraid of it, too."

"Really?"

"Yes. Your mother told me."

"So Dad must have climbed it as a way to overcome his fear."

"No. He climbed up to step down."

"To step down?"

"It's a tricky one, isn't it? Your dad was always good at riddles."

They'd decided to set out at 6:00 a.m. Yuuki had been of two minds about it, but in the end he went ahead and broached the subject before they hit the trail.

"There's one thing I have to talk to you about before we get going."

Rintaro paused from clearing up the breakfast things and gave Yuuki his full attention.

"Do you remember back then when your dad was in the hospital and I visited for the first time?"

Rintaro blushed.

"I do. I remember it well. I remember clinging to you."

"Yes, that time."

Yuuki stretched out his back muscles.

"I have to apologize to you for something. I took advantage of you hugging me that day, and I've used you for something ever since."

Rintaro looked puzzled.

Yuuki needed to say that today's climb was going to be in memory of Kyoichiro Anzai. But before his attempt on Tsuitate, he wanted to confess everything that was on his mind. It was what he had been thinking about all the way here. He continued.

"That time at the hospital, it wasn't you I was hugging—it was Jun. I was so happy that you put your arms around me, but I really wished it was Jun who'd done it."

Rintaro's gaze didn't falter.

"About a year later, I took you and Jun to Mount Haruna. Do you remember? To tell the truth, my relationship with Jun was tense, to say the least, and things used to go very badly whenever the two of us spent any time alone together. I'd always wanted to take Jun to the mountains, but I couldn't work out how to do it. That's how I took advantage of you. Jun and I could be together if there were three of us. Fortunately, you and Jun had become friends. Of course, I was very fond of you, too. But—"

Yuuki hung his head.

"—your mother believed I was being a father to you, and thanked me for it. I guess you probably thought the same. You were thrilled when I invited you to go to the mountains with us. You looked at me the way you would look at a father. And it broke my heart to see it. Actually, it still pains me. And I really invited you for the sake of Jun and me."

Rintaro had loved him. That was the only real thing that Yuuki had been able to believe in back then. That was why he was always able to behave naturally around Rintaro. And he adored the boy. At times, he'd even wished that Rintaro was his son instead of Jun. Nevertheless, Yuuki had never given up on Jun. He'd wanted to start over from the beginning. To rebuild that father-son relationship.

A fresh breeze blew across the riverbed.

"I kind of understood," said Rintaro quietly. His eyes were as bright as usual. They weren't angry or disappointed.

"I had so much fun."

"Huh?"

"Back then, I used to look forward to Sundays so much."

His words lifted Yuuki's spirits.

"Yes, it was fun," he said, looking into the distance.

Every Sunday, Yuuki used to take Jun and Rintaro to the mountains. Climb a bit, stop to eat a packed lunch, then climb some more. It was always the same pattern, but it was true—it had been fun. Those were precious memories. Jun didn't really take it seriously, and never became much of a climber. On the other hand, Rintaro made steady progress, and it wasn't long before he was more skilled than Yuuki. Like father, like son. Yuuki truly believed that saying.

"Shall we make a start?" said Rintaro, getting to his feet.

"Can you forgive me?" Yuuki managed finally to get the words out.

Rintaro crouched back down and met his eyes. "You mustn't say things like that, Yuuki-san. You are kinder than anyone, and I should know it."

Yuuki felt a rush of emotion and struggled to hold back the tears. Rintaro abruptly spun on his heels and began to check the climbing equipment: rucksacks, rope, helmets, carabiners. Even from the back,

Yuuki could see that his earlobes had turned bright red. For a man as shy as Rintaro, this was a once-in-a-lifetime speech.

Yuuki looked up again at Tsuitate. Finally, he was going to confront it. "Yep. Let's go."

As Yuuki watched Rintaro sling his rucksack on his back, he recognized a change in the man's usually placid expression. This was a look he had seen numerous times in the past: Kyoichiro Anzai about to face off with a wall of rock.

They were about to set foot in Devil's Mountain territory. This time Yuuki really was going to take on the beast.

Rintaro set off walking; Yuuki followed. They were planning to pass through the main Ichinokurasawa valley, heading for Tail Ridge, the stepping-stone to Tsuitate.

They followed the gently sloping trail through the brush. Tsuitate was visible just to the right, ahead of them. It was a behemoth. Not even the soft morning sun could make that vertical wall any less fearsome.

They took stepping-stones across the stream, crossed back again, and detoured around the left of Hyonguri Waterfall. They skirted around a belt of shrubs, and from there the path began to climb. Rintaro advanced, sure-footed; neither too slow nor too fast, there was a fixed rhythm to his strides.

Approaching Tail Ridge, they followed the stream downhill a ways and crossed a snowy valley. The surface was rugged and uneven, and difficult to walk. The valley looked as if someone had scooped it out with a giant spoon, hence its nickname, Spoon Cut. It was dotted with rocks that had fallen or been swept down in an avalanche. There was no longer anywhere that could be called safe.

Yuuki's heart was beating fast. He knew they were now in the heart of Ichinokurasawa. He was supposed to walk this trail with Anzai seventeen years ago. Instead, he was walking it now with Anzai's son. If he raised his eyes, he could see the famous rock faces, all visible in a bunch. There was Takizawa Slab; Lower Takizawa, which rose perpendicular to the main valley; the inner wall of Eboshizawa. And finally, their destination—the Tsuitate face.

It took about forty minutes for them to reach the base of Tail Ridge. Rintaro turned around.

"Do you want to rest a minute?"

"No, I'm fine. Let's go."

Rintaro nodded and began to check the rock for holds. Last night there'd been a sudden shower, so the rock surface, polished smooth by many years of avalanches, was glistening with rainwater.

"Let's tie on."

It was reassuring to hear Rintaro's concern for him. It was obvious he could sense Yuuki's uneasiness. Normally they wouldn't tie on the rope at this point, but Yuuki was not at all confident about climbing this wet rock.

As he passed the rope through the carabiner he was surprised at how strong his sense of relief was. This was what it was all about, he thought. He was attached to Rintaro by a single piece of rope, and it was enough to give him the energy to climb.

"Here we go! Okay?"

"Okay!"

He set foot on Tail Ridge.

Rintaro mostly used his feet to climb. Yuuki had a more bent posture and relied heavily on his hands. He scrambled up as fast as he could below Rintaro. As they climbed, Tsuitate changed from a towering presence before his eyes to a heavy weight above his head. He'd never seen anything so intimidating.

*I don't know if I can do this.*

The voice that had answered him seemed far away in his memory.

*"There are plenty of guys like you who do it.*

*". . . set off climbing as fast as they can, utterly focused on what they're doing.*

*". . . the body gets overstimulated, reaches a level of extreme excitement. The fear makes them numb."*

Climber's high.

Something suddenly occurred to him.

That day, seventeen years ago, he had reached that *level of extreme excitement.*

He felt dog-tired. He'd spent far too long at the hospital, and by the time he'd run to his car and rushed back to the newsroom it was almost 4:00 p.m. He was greeted by the furious tones of the managing editor. He quickly got his head back into crash-coverage mode. The events at the hospital were already fading from his mind.

"You good-for-nothing!" Oimura roared. "What kind of leader vanishes like that without telling anyone where he's going?"

The reason the Firecracker had exploded was that, during Yuuki's absence, there had been a development in the story. The wires from Kyodo News were full of the breaking news. One of the survivors—the assistant cabin crew manager—had talked about the state of the aircraft just before the crash.

"At 6:25 there was a loud bang from somewhere above us, then my ears began to hurt.

"Inside the cabin everything went white. The vent hole under the cabin crew seats opened. A piece of the ceiling above the lavatories came loose. Right at the same time, the oxygen masks dropped down.

"The plane was rolling and oscillating quite badly. It seemed to have gone into a Dutch roll.

"In the end the plane descended at a very sharp angle. There were two or three separate strong impacts. All the surrounding seats and cushions, everything, was thrown around."

From her account, it was thought that the crash was probably caused by damage to the vertical tail or something toward the rear of the plane. This was the conclusion drawn in the Kyodo News wires.

Yuuki felt a surge of anger. It had been Japan Airlines management who had heard the testimony and passed on the information to the journalist. Just last night the prefectural police had set up a special headquarters to investigate criminal liability. The testimony of a witness would be vital to the course of their investigation. It goes without saying that, when building a case, the written account of an assistant cabin crew manager with specialized knowledge of the aircraft would be invaluable to the investigators. Despite this, Japan Airlines, who might very well end up being the defendants in the criminal case, had gotten in with someone connected to the survivor and managed to obtain her testimony first. What's more, they'd made it public. The testimony seemed believable, but could anyone be sure now that the information hadn't been doctored in some way to make it more favorable toward Japan Airlines?

If the purpose had been to answer the questions of the relatives and members of the public about conditions in the plane at the time of the crash, then they should have waited for the assistant cabin crew manager to make a full recovery, at which time she could have been interviewed by a delegation from the news media. It could have been left to the Ministry of Transport's Aircraft Accident Investigation Committee to listen to her testimony.

There were a lot of people at the *North Kanto Times* who thought that the next day's local news pages should center on this "vital testimony." The number of voices suggesting that it ought to be the newspaper's lead story began to grow, and Yuuki started to worry. He'd already decided that Sayama's eyewitness article was going to have the top spot, and he had no intention of moving it.

Just after five o'clock, Kasuya's potbelly made an appearance in the newsroom.

"Hey, what are we going to do with the testimony story?"

"Front page, second story."

In other words, he was treating it as the second headline story. He'd thought about banishing it to the second page of local news but he didn't want to rub people the wrong way. In the end, he was going to placate the chorus of voices calling for it to be lead with a compromise of second headline.

Kasuya looked doubtful.

"Going with the second spot, eh? I think it ought to be the top story."

"But—"

Yuuki emphasized the danger of the possible manipulation of the report by Japan Airlines. In his heart, he felt real indignation that the airline company had made their announcement at Haneda Airport. Japan Airlines Flight 123 had gone down in Gunma Prefecture. The assistant cabin crew manager was in a Gunma hospital, so her testimony had been obtained inside that hospital building. So why was the announcement made in Tokyo? Those ominous phrases "inherited accident" and "borrowed space" that they'd had to swallow so many times before were resurfacing.

Reluctantly accepting Yuuki's decision, the editor in chief left the floor and Yuuki set about reading all the wires and articles that had arrived in his absence. He was once again reminded that this was an unprecedented catastrophe. The number of hours he'd been away from his desk were in direct proportion to the size of the stack of papers.

121 bodies retrieved, 51 identified

Lamenting and clinging to the coffin

Was underlying cause tail strike seven years ago?

Aircraft had congested schedule—flew five times a day

Japan Airlines plans complete inspection of 49 jumbo jets in near future

Crash investigation: flight and voice recorders found. Analysis under way

JAL President, Takagi, informs Prime Minister Nakasone of his intention to resign

Prefectural police plan to question assistant cabin crew manager

U.S. President offers his condolences

Uenomura village office administrators paralyzed

Demand for travel insurance multiplies fivefold

Total compensation to reach fifty billion yen

Condition of four survivors improving

Just after seven in the evening there were angry exchanges in the newsroom. People were feeling exhausted and their patience was wearing thin. That was how Yuuki, who was deeply absorbed reading, managed to miss the oily voice behind him.

"Oi!"

He finally noticed that Nozawa, at the next desk, was calling him.

"What is it?"

Having finally gotten Yuuki's attention, Nozawa turned to look over his shoulder, and Yuuki did the same. Yuuki stiffened. The hooked nose and mustache of Ito, the head of Circulation—and Anzai's departmental chief—was right behind him.

"You have a minute?"

He had a strange way of speaking that sounded as if he had a mouthful of gum or something.

"Yes. What is it?" Yuuki asked cautiously.

"Yes, well . . . I was wondering what time the deadline was likely to be tonight."

"We're not extending tonight, so I assume we'll go to press at the usual time."

"Is that right? Well, that's fine, then. Because when the printing runs late and the paper doesn't reach the Circulation Department on time, we do get a lot of complaints from our newsdealers."

He spoke slimily, and for some reason he flashed Yuuki a meaningful smile.

Yuuki had never forgotten the first time Ito had spoken to him. It was shortly after he had started at the *North Kanto Times*, and the sound of the man's voice had chilled his heart. It was exactly like a voice he had heard many times as a child.

*"Hey, kid, I heard your mom's a pan-pan girl."*

Pan-pan girl. Street whore. It was something he'd heard way back when he was in primary school, some thirty years before. The person who had spoken his mother's secret out loud was a boy of high school age who used to hang around a nearby children's playground. The kid was in a different school catchment area from Yuuki, but they lived on either side of the boundary of neighboring districts. That must have been how he knew him. But he had no idea where the boy's home was, and he had no memory of them calling each other by name.

Yuuki never went back to that playground. In fact, he was afraid for a long time. Whenever he thought about running into that high school boy again, he'd be terrified of going out to play. He'd spotted him once at a distance and fled home as fast as his legs would carry him. He'd even had nightmares once or twice about being chased by him.

When he'd heard Ito speak at the office, he'd immediately recalled the boy's voice. And although fifteen years must have passed in the meantime, and it was normal for a voice to have changed a little, Yuuki was convinced that this was the same person. He looked up Ito's address on the list of personnel and, sure enough, his house was in the district next to the one where Yuuki had grown up. However, for some reason, he had no memory of what the high school boy had looked like. Only his voice had stuck with him. He must have been so afraid he hadn't dared look the boy in the face.

If that boy was indeed Ito, he must remember Yuuki, too. That fear had been living inside Yuuki ever since he started at the company. Back then, the boy had already been sixteen or seventeen and knew who Yuuki's mother was. So it wasn't too much of a stretch to assume that he also knew Yuuki's name.

Ito didn't give anything away in his behavior. It was a long time ago and he may well have forgotten about it. And anyway, it may not even have been him. Still, in a small gesture here, or a slight change of expression there, Yuuki would imagine he was listening again to that voice: "*I heard your mom's a pan-pan girl.*" He would flinch, and his skin would come up in goose pimples. The stink of the alcohol on his mother's breath and the smirking faces of the men would come back in vivid detail and he'd be overtaken by the urge to vomit.

He'd felt it all again this evening. Ito didn't seem to have any urgent business with him, yet he wasn't moving away from Yuuki's desk. It was as if he had some sort of evil agenda.

Yuuki reached for the next paper in the pile: *Ministry of Labor launches investigation into passengers' work-related death insurance.*

As soon as he began to read, Ito spoke again.

"Oh, yes, I just remembered . . ."

"Yes?"

Yuuki looked at him coolly.

"Today, you went to see Anzai, didn't you?"

"Yes, that's right."

"How was he?"

"How was he? Well, he was asleep."

"That's right. It's a bit of a problem."

Yuuki felt like yelling.

"And how about his wife?"

"What?"

"Anzai's wife? Was she there?"

"Yes, she was there."

"She say anything?"

Yuuki remembered what Sayuri had said to him: *I think it's terrible how hard they made him work!*

Anzai wasn't really interested in the newspaper company or the work. Or at least that's what Yuuki had always believed, so Sayuri's comment had been totally unexpected. Anzai had been overworked. Apparently Ito knew it, too.

In the past, Anzai had referred to Ito as his "lifesaver," but he had never explained why. He'd been a great admirer of the man. It was very difficult to fathom why. Just as the nickname the Black Box suggested, nobody really knew what kind of work the Circulation Department did. Everyone in the other divisions of the company seemed to find Ito, the department head, a unique and unidentifiable specimen.

Yuuki made a move to end the conversation.

"She was grateful to you—for telling her he should take his time getting better."

"Right. Anything else?" Yuuki jabbed his red pen at the article in front of him.

"She said a lot of things. How worried she was—things like that. You'd better send someone from General Affairs soon."

"Of course I will."

Yuuki turned back to his work. He'd decided to ignore anything else Ito might have to say. But then he felt the sharp gaze of someone else on him.

Oimura was watching him; or rather, glaring at him. On second thought, it wasn't Yuuki that he was glaring at. It was Ito. Or perhaps it was the apparently intimate conversation between Ito and Yuuki that had caught his attention.

But whatever the immediate reason, Yuuki could read that look. The staff of the Circulation Department were believed to be supporters of the *NKT*'s managing director. Oimura, the darling of the opposite faction, the supporters of the company chairman, was probably unhappy that Ito had even set foot in the Editorial Department. And he had most likely spoken ill of Anzai—Ito's junior—before for the same reason. It seemed to be a case of him tarring all the perceived "opposition" with the same brush.

Ito was returning Oimura's glare, and the two were practically baring their teeth.

Yuuki felt his brain go numb. He'd definitely reached the peak of fatigue.

"Here you are."

He heard the voice of someone from the copy team and the proofs of page two of the local news landed softly on his desk.

His eye went straight to a large advertisement on the lower half of the page.

"*We at Japan Airlines deeply regret the loss of so many precious lives in the crash of the JA8119 aircraft . . .*"

It was signed with the name of the Japan Airlines president. It was what was known as an apology ad. Right above it was a large article featuring a photograph of relatives of the deceased in tears after viewing the bodies of their loved ones. Yuuki leapt to his feet.

"Kaku-san!"

His blood seemed to flow backward in his veins. It was as if, after a huge fire, the arsonist had posted an apology on the same page as a report on the incident. There was no way he could accept the page in front of him. On top of that, there was the testimony of the assistant cabin crew manager to consider. It was all just too neat. And it wasn't only Japan Airlines. The *North Kanto Times* was equally guilty for placing the apology and the photos of the bereaved together on the same page.

Kamejima came running, his perfectly round face registering alarm.

"What is it? Is there a mistake?"

Yuuki pointed to the ad.

"Get rid of that."

"Why?"

"Just get rid of it. It's totally insensitive."

Kamejima stared at Yuuki, apparently not understanding.

"What's the matter? Are you okay?"

It was Kamejima's job to arrange the pages of the newspaper. Kamejima just didn't have the same level of enthusiasm for the content of the stories as Yuuki did.

"I don't have the authority to remove it. I'll have to consult with Advertising."

Yuuki thought of the Advertising Department, and general manager Kurasaka's furious face. He wasn't going to put up with that man's complaints this time. This was no hard-won advertisement. The advertising team hadn't put in hours of legwork on this one. The money the company would make from this ad was a windfall that had simply dropped on Kurasaka's desk.

"I'll take responsibility for it. Take it out."

"But—"

"Just do it!"

He hadn't meant to sound so angry. Kamejima screwed up his face. Everyone nearby was looking at Yuuki. He felt a surge of energy.

"How can we be so shameless as to put out a newspaper with this in it? This ad cost maybe two, three hundred thousand yen. If they want to appear to do the respectful thing, then tell them to buy flowers or something and take them to the crash site!"

Nobody said anything, which irritated Yuuki even more.

"Don't you have any feelings about it? This article above this ad!"

But then Yuuki's attention was caught by something else. He stopped blinking for a moment. Diagonally above the photo of the bereaved, in small font, and squeezed into a tiny box, was a familiar article.

*Report by Sayama on Mount Osutaka*

It was Sayama's feature piece, the one Yuuki had sent to Copy as the lead story. At some point, unbeknownst to Yuuki, it had been moved. And worse, to an inconspicuous corner of an inside page. The snakes. They'd done it again. His rage overflowed. He grabbed the proofs and marched over to Todoroki's desk.

Gold-Rimmed Specs was there. He was surrounded by five or six reporters from the JAL crash team, including Sayama and Hanazawa. His dark lenses were fixed on the faces of the reporters. No doubt he was making them listen to tales of his extensive reporting experience.

"Can you make space, please?" Yuuki said, brushing the junior reporters aside and slamming the proofs down on Todoroki's desk. "What the hell is this?"

Sayama started in surprise when he saw the treatment his article had been given.

Todoroki slowly removed his spectacles. He didn't even glance at the proofs. Instead, he fixed his raw gaze on Yuuki's face.

"What's the problem?"

"This article was supposed to be the lead story. Why is it on page two of local?"

"No idea."

"Don't play dumb!"

Todoroki got to his feet. "Who do you think you're talking to?"

"You! I've had enough of your pathetic games!"

They stared each other down, so close the tips of their noses were almost touching.

"I'll forgive you this time, if you go down on hands and knees and beg me."

"I know you're responsible for this shit! Put it back on the front page! Okay?"

"You need to speak to the managing editor."

Yuuki froze. Oimura was the one who had changed it?

"Why . . . ?"

Todoroki laughed scornfully.

"You know there's no way the managing editor is going to let a story about the Self-Defense Forces get top billing!"

He felt like he'd been slapped. He was right. The lead paragraph of Sayama's piece had a description of a Self-Defense Forces soldier.

Oimura became the new object of Yuuki's anger. There was nothing wrong with that article. He looked over at Oimura's desk, but he wasn't there.

"Where is he?"

"He said he was going to General Affairs."

Yuuki made to snatch up the proofs again, but Todoroki put the palm of his hand down to prevent him.

"Get off!"

"Hmm. I will if you get down and apologize."

All the reporters in the vicinity held their breath. Next to him, Sayama was staring at Yuuki's face. The gleam in Todoroki's eyes was as sharp as a knife blade.

"All these young kids have been watching. You'd better apologize properly."

Yuuki looked at him in disgust.

"There's no need."

"What did you say? You've been yelling at *me* when it was all *your* misunderstanding. Apologize!"

"You did the exact same thing yesterday. Shall I explain it in front of this group?"

Todoroki didn't reply. The look in his eyes was ferocious. Yuuki tugged once again at the proofs, but Todoroki refused to let go. There was a ripping sound, and Japan Airlines's apology ad tore in two.

"Don't for one second think this is over."

Ignoring Todoroki's threat, Yuuki made for the newsroom door. The young reporters all raced after him into the corridor.

"Yuuki-san," said Sayama, apparently acting as spokesman. "Of course, you can count on our support."

Yuuki ran down the stairs.

It was ten in the evening. He found it hard to believe that there would be anyone in General Affairs here at this time of night. Ground floor of the west annex. The General Affairs office.

Light was leaking out into the corridor. He pushed the door open to see Gunji, who'd joined the company at the same time as Yuuki. He was typing on a word processor. General Affairs were always recommending that the reporters use word processors, but no one would touch them. Who could write a proper article from the heart on one of those things? Yuuki felt the same way.

"This is a surprise. Don't see you here very often."

"Is our managing editor around here somewhere?"

Gunji gestured to the door at the far end of the office.

"The inner shrine."

He meant the office of the company chairman.

"The chairman's still here?"

"Don't speak too loudly. He'll hear you."

"Is he here?"

"Yes. He had some kind of meeting nearby and called in on his way home."

Yuuki headed for the chairman's office.

"Hey! Hey! What are you doing?" Gunji called after him. He sounded panicked.

"I've got urgent business," Yuuki replied.

He wasn't lying. The decision on the page layout couldn't be left until eleven or twelve o'clock. Because of the Printing Department's limited capacity, they always started work earlier with the pages that were ready, and printed bit by bit. The deadline for page two of local news was 10:30 p.m.

Yuuki stopped in front of the door. From behind him, he heard Gunji's voice.

"Are you one of us, then?"

"*One of us.*" He must be talking about the factions within the company. But there was no time for excuses or explanations. Without hesitation, he tapped his knuckles against the fine-grained wood of the imposing double doors.

# 14

It was the first time Yuuki had ever set foot in the chairman's office on the ground floor.

It used to be on the second floor, but Chairman Shirakawa had damaged his spinal cord in a traffic accident six months previously and been confined to a wheelchair. It had been necessary to relocate.

Right now the occupants of the office were Shirakawa in his wheelchair, his personal assistant, Manami Takagi, and Oimura, who was sitting on a large, curved sofa that looked big enough to seat ten.

"Well, sit down, then," said Oimura casually. Probably because the boss was present, he had the most congenial of expressions on his face. He had shown just the barest flicker of confusion the moment Yuuki entered the room. There was nothing whatsoever of the usual Firecracker about him.

"This is Yuuki," he said amiably. "You remember, I was just talking about him earlier?"

Shirakawa also looked cheerful.

"I know him already. The kid started here back when I was editor in chief."

"He's got the JAL crash desk right now."

"Well, you've really come up in the world, haven't you? I remember back in those early days when you were learning the ropes. You always were a serious pupil."

The awkward conversation continued. *Just talking about him earlier?* Was Oimura reporting in detail to the chairman everything that went on in the Editorial Department?

"Here you are." Manami placed a glass of iced coffee on the low table in front of Yuuki. She was stunningly beautiful. Up until three months ago she'd been employed by a housing corporation. It was rumored that Oimura had headhunted her on Shirakawa's behalf. Yuuki wondered what had happened to the last female assistant who used to push Shirakawa's wheelchair. Her name was Mina Kuroda or something . . .

It seemed the conversation between Shirakawa and Oimura was never going to run out of fresh topics.

Yuuki had to interrupt—he really was running out of time.

"Oimura-san, if you wouldn't mind . . ."

"What?"

Yuuki spread the proofs out on the table.

"Can you explain this? I asked for this to be the lead story but, somehow, it's mistakenly ended up here on the inside."

He was hoping that, in the presence of the chairman, Oimura might reveal his true intentions, but the managing editor kept his cool.

"It's not a mistake. They were my orders."

"Why?"

"It's obvious. There's no reason for a newspaper to do the Self-Defense Forces' PR work for them."

Yuuki leaned forward. "The article just happens to mention a soldier. It's got nothing to do with advertising."

"But that's what it ends up being. What do you think, sir?"

"What's that?"

Shirakawa was having his hair combed by Manami. This wasn't the place to be having this conversation. Yuuki leaned over to whisper in Oimura's ear.

"Could I speak to you outside?"

"Outside? The matter's been decided. There's no need for any more discussion."

"I don't believe so. I'd like you to reconsider."

Oimura turned to Shirakawa again.

"Sir, can you imagine the lead story of our paper being the heroic tale of some Self-Defense Forces soldier?"

"No, I can't."

Yuuki gasped. Asking the chairman's opinion? How had it reached this point already? It was unfair. Oimura had deliberately used the phrase "heroic tale." In any normal situation, there was nobody in the newspaper industry who would have taken that at face value. They'd assume Oimura was exaggerating or had some hidden agenda.

"Sir." Yuuki spoke quickly. "It's not a heroic tale. If you read it, you'll see."

Oimura rolled his eyes. But Shirakawa made no move to pick up the proofs. His hand was now in Manami's; he was enjoying a nail trim.

"Sir, please. If you would just read it."

In response, Shirakawa turned his head in Yuuki's direction.

"No, I don't think it'll work."

Yuuki stopped blinking. A final decision, made without any thought. But no, he wasn't going to give in that easily.

"But, sir, the reporter who wrote that article spent twelve hours climbing a mountain to do it."

"Yuuki!" Oimura rebuked him. "You're not thinking of defying the chairman, are you?"

"No, of course not. I'm just—"

"This is disgraceful. The chairman has given his opinion."

Shirakawa was observing their altercation with a slight smile on his face. Manami was now massaging his shoulders. *What a creep*, Yuuki thought.

He bowed deeply.

"Chairman Shirakawa, sir, please let it be the top story."

Shirakawa closed his eyes.

"You really have come up in the world, haven't you?"

The nuance of "come up in the world" was a shade different this time. Shirakawa was definitely on the point of losing his temper. Back when he'd been editor in chief, his nickname had been the H-Bomb.

Yuuki thought of Sayama's face. And his voice: *Yuuki-san. Of course, you can count on our support.* He made up his mind. Jumping to his feet, he picked up the proofs and took them over to where Shirakawa sat in his wheelchair. Oimura yelled something, but Yuuki ignored him and placed the sheet on Shirakawa's lap.

"Please, just read it. I'm begging you."

He bowed as deeply as he could.

There was a moment of silence as Manami stepped softly away from the wheelchair. Then Shirakawa's eyes snapped open.

"Desk chief—we don't want to hear your opinion!"

Yuuki stood up as straight as he could.

"Please read it," he repeated.

Shirakawa turned his bloodshot gaze on Yuuki.

"Are you trying to lose your job?"

Yuuki hung his head. But he hadn't lost his nerve, nor had he given up hope. He was trying not to punch the chairman. His heart was pumping wildly.

Could he be fired over something like this? Fine, let them fire him. If he gave in over this, he wouldn't keep the JAL command post anyway. Nobody would respect a leader who had killed his fellow reporter's story not once but twice.

He wasn't that attached to his life as a reporter. He'd done a miserable job, anyway. And it'd only get worse from now on.

And his family? It didn't matter anymore. It was all pretense anyway. His heart was in pieces. Could he tell his family that there was no way he could continue to live in constant fear of his son's moods? And when she heard he'd been fired, Yumiko would probably wash her hands of him. He'd be fine living all by himself. He'd felt this way for a long, long time. Much better alone—Yuuki clasped his forehead in his hands. He could no longer see clearly. He was tired.

And then, suddenly, in his mind, he was back in that dark place . . .

He was in the storage shed again. He could see his own tiny form. He was sitting, shaking, his arms hugging his knees.

Yuuki almost screamed. There was a throbbing in his ears.

He heard his mother's flirtatious voice . . . the men's wild laughter . . . a dog howling . . .

The loneliness that soaked into the marrow of his bones.

But then he saw other faces . . . Yumiko, Jun, Yuka.

It was enough that they were there. He needed them to be there. They didn't have to understand one another.

He didn't want to be alone. He never wanted to be that kid again, alone in the storage shed, hugging his knees . . .

His body swayed, but just as he was about to fall, he instead planted his feet firmly on the floor.

Through the thin membrane that was covering his field of vision, he saw the devilish face of Shirakawa. Yuuki reached down and, his hand shaking, picked up the proof of the article from the chairman's lap. First, he folded it, then twisted it, and finally he screwed it up into a little ball.

"I'm so sorry to have taken your time," he said, and with a casual nod of the head he left the room.

He walked through the dark corridors and climbed the stairs. The young reporters were gathered in the break area, apparently waiting for him to return. His eye met Sayama's.

It must have been written all over his face. Sayama turned and strode away. Immediately Hanazawa moved to block Yuuki's path.

"How did it go?"

"Hang in there."

That was all Yuuki could say. He set off back toward the newsroom. He heard a disapproving voice behind him.

"We expected more of you."

The newsroom was filled with pre-deadline commotion. Yuuki didn't head for his desk. He went straight for the blackboard.

*JAL desk chief: Yuuki*

He ran his palm through the chalk letters until they were obliterated.

Well into the night, it was as humid as ever.

Yuuki had left the office as soon as the morning edition had gone to press, but it was half past midnight by the time he arrived home. He was disappointed to see there were no lights on in the house.

Everyone was fast asleep. The warm, muggy air in the corridor was a cocktail of all the smells of the house, but the air in the living room was pleasantly cool. Yumiko must have only just gone to bed. He headed to the kitchen, where the dining table had been cleared. The pan on the gas stove had just a little curry stuck on the bottom. When he'd called in at home earlier, he'd told his wife he'd probably sleep over at the office, so there wasn't even a beer in the fridge, or snacks to nibble on.

Yuuki went back to the living room with a glass of barley tea, threw the proofs of the next day's paper on the table, and, without taking off his work shirt, sprawled out on the sofa. He turned on the TV. Right away the screen was filled with footage from Mount Osutaka. The news program was running late due to the earlier extended broadcast of the evening's professional baseball game. The female newsreader, in her somber suit and matching expression, was reading from a long script. There was nothing in it that Yuuki hadn't heard before.

As he stared absentmindedly at the screen, he began to regret coming home. He could hear the chairman's voice in his ears.

"Are you trying to lose your job?"

He'd given in to the intimidation. He'd failed, and now he felt ashamed. He'd failed to protect Sayama's article and betrayed his junior reporters. He let out a deep sigh and closed his eyes. He'd been clinging to hope when he'd set out for home—afraid of being alone, he'd wanted to see the faces of his family. But he couldn't.

Now that feeling of hope began to fade again.

A *failed family*. The phrase ran through his mind. A family was something he had tried to make for himself. His own dream garden. He'd tried to arrange these human beings in his miniature garden, but they hadn't grown together as planned.

He wasn't thinking this way just because he was alone at this late hour. Even if he'd returned to find the house bathed in warm light and Yumiko, Jun, and Yuka all sitting there ready to engage in lively conversation, nothing would have changed.

He suddenly had difficulty breathing. He realized he'd always been this way. Whenever he was at home, he couldn't wait to leave and get back to work. Despite the challenges that faced him there, he always felt more at ease, *at home*, in the workplace, because he could lose himself in the chaos.

He heard a hoarse voice. It was the TV. The newscaster had tears in her eyes. Just over her shoulder, an extremely shaky camera was showing a close-up of the bereaved families in tears in front of the Fujioka Municipal Sports Center.

Yuuki stared at the newscaster's face for a moment, then snatched up the remote and turned off the TV. He continued to stare at the dark screen. He imagined the staff at the TV station winding up the broadcast and cheerfully wishing one another good night. And the young newscaster staying frozen in her seat, turning down invitations to go for a drink or something to eat, crying her heart out alone in an empty studio.

"Crying's the relatives' job, not yours," he snapped.

He suddenly saw an image of Anzai lying in his hospital bed. Persistent vegetative state. In other words, a vegetable. He'd told Sayuri and Rintaro he was sure that Anzai would wake up, but it was merely to console them. He knew it was very rare for anyone to regain consciousness after being in that state.

"Oh, Daddy!"

Yuuki sat up quickly. In the doorway of the living room stood Yuka, in her pajamas. She was rubbing her sleepy eyes and looked painfully young. She was one of the tallest kids in the fourth year of primary school, but he'd heard that she wasn't considered quite tall enough yet for her sports club volleyball team and was a perennial benchwarmer.

"You okay? Just going to the toilet?"

His voice automatically took on that high tone it always did when he talked to his children.

"I wanted a drink of water . . . I was surprised to see you. When did you get home?"

"Just now."

"It's nice to see you. You must be working so hard."

She gave him a formal bow, just like they practiced in school. Yuuki felt tears pricking his eyes. He was a little slow to smile back.

"Yes, I'm back . . . No, I mean, thank you."

"Did the Tigers win?"

"Hmm, I'm not sure. No, hang on . . . Yes, I heard they lost today."

"Oh, what was the score?"

"No idea, sorry."

"Huh."

While he struggled to think of something else to say, Yuka's eyes were covertly watching to check out his mood. Ever since she'd been able to walk, Yuka had seen her father raise his hand to Jun. Her first-ever school report card had read, "She tends to observe the emotions of the stronger children, and adjust her behavior accordingly." It had given Yuuki a jolt to read it.

"Did Mayumi get a hit?"

"Sorry, love. I don't know."

"How about Bass?"

"I'm sorry. I don't know any of the details."

"That's right, you've been really busy with that plane crash."

"Yes, I have."

"Lots of people died, didn't they?" Yuka asked, wrinkling her brow in a very unchildlike way.

"Yes, very many. Five hundred and twenty."

"That's terrible."

"Right."

Yuuki put on the saddest face he could. He wanted to convey the true seriousness of the accident. To his daughter, at least.

"But there was a little girl who was saved, wasn't there?"

"Yes, there was. Daddy was so happy."

"Me, too."

"I see. You're a very kind girl."

"I'm not really," she answered, turning red.

Yuuki glanced up at the clock on the wall.

"It's really late, you know. Did you get something to drink?"

"Yes, I had some barley tea."

"Right, you'd better get back to bed now. You have to get up in the morning."

"Okay. Good night, Daddy."

"Night. Sweet dreams!"

Yuka waved a little hand to him as she climbed the stairs. Yuuki lay back down. The big smile he'd plastered on his face was beginning to make his face ache.

He'd noticed that Yuka hadn't taken a single step into the living room.

Yuuki stretched out both sides of his neck and loosened his tie. But he didn't take it off. He wasn't sure what to do. Should he go back to the office and sleep in the on-call room? That voice in the back of his mind was growling at him with growing ferocity even now. Already it was urging him up off the sofa.

It was the morning of August 15.

In the office of editor in chief Kasuya, Oimura and Todoroki had been joined by the chief copy editor, Kamejima, and other key figures from the management team. No one spoke to Yuuki when he walked in. Even the habitually cheerful Kamejima looked stern. Yuuki's authority as JAL crash desk chief was about to be revoked. Yuuki knew that the moment Todoroki opened his mouth to speak, that's what would happen, and he was prepared for it. He was even considering resigning the position before Todoroki got the chance to ask him to step down.

However, it turned out that the topic of the meeting was something completely different.

"Let's put our heads together and come up with some good ideas for today's layout."

Kasuya looked around the room. The editor in chief was desperate for some good ideas. Tomorrow morning's paper needed to include three major stories.

First, there were follow-up articles marking the fourth day since the Japan Airlines jumbo crash. Then there were the events to commemorate the critical fortieth anniversary of the end of the Second World War. And on top of that, Prime Minister Nakasone's visit to Yasukuni Shrine to honor the war dead.

The problem was the Yasukuni visit. How were they going to balance the space allocated to the Pride of Gunma, Prime Minister Nakasone? How were they going to portray his decision to visit? Good or bad? It was a headache for the paper of the PM's hometown. Since the day of the plane crash, Kishi's superior, chief political editor Moriya, had stayed in the background, but today he and Kishi at the political news desk were at the head of the table. It was Moriya who spoke.

"I think we should put Nakasone at the top right now," he said, deliberately jumping in to forestall the others' opinions.

Catching a whiff of the political section's maneuvering, Todoroki at once put on his chief local news editor's hat.

"You mean to take the JAL crash off the top page? It's only been three days since it happened."

"Let's make it the second story for today. Let's lead with YASU NAKASONE: THE LOCAL TIMBER DEALER'S BOY being the first postwar leader to pay a visit to Yasukuni Shrine. From the paper's point of view, this has to be the headline."

"No need to get so excited about it," said Todoroki bluntly.

"What do you mean, 'excited'?" replied Moriya.

The two colleagues glared at each other.

"It's nothing like the same thing as covering the prime minister's first visit back home, you know. We can't extol his virtues for visiting a shrine dedicated to war criminals. It's not only the opposition parties and religious groups who are going to kick up a fuss. What about China and Korea?"

"Why would they do that? They've no right to meddle in Japanese domestic affairs. What's wrong with a head of state offering prayers to his country's war dead?"

"What's happened to the separation of church and state? You can't deny that there's a suspicion of unconstitutionality when you suddenly change the rules of worship like that."

"I don't think you can lump all those issues together like that. This story compares favorably to the JAL crash."

"Five hundred and twenty people died in that!"

"And how many people died in the Maebashi City air raid?"

"Don't talk such shit!"

"Todoroki, aren't you the one that's getting excited?"

"What are you talking about?"

"The fact that you are rejoicing at the size of the accident. For all that you're going on about it being the world's largest air disaster, it's still just an inherited accident, after all. Don't forget that Japan Airlines isn't a Gunma Prefecture story."

Yuuki looked at Moriya.

*It's still just an inherited accident.* Yuuki knew someone had been bound to say it eventually, but he'd never imagined it would be tossed out like that in the middle of a turf war between the chief local and political news editors.

He looked away again. He'd recoiled at Moriya's words, but that was all. The JAL crash had been made light of. It had been trampled on. Yet he didn't feel any strong emotions welling up inside him.

Whatever happened, Yuuki believed that if the headline spot was conceded to Prime Minister Nakasone's visit, then the passion in the Editorial Department for the plane crash would quickly cool off. They were high on the sheer scale of the accident. Moriya had been spot-on when he'd said it. That described the mood in the newsroom perfectly. Getting excited about it wasn't so far off the mark, either.

Nobody in the Editorial Department had dared to think of the crash as an inherited accident. Quite the contrary—they'd used the fact that it was the world's largest to keep themselves enthusiastic and alert when they really should have been catching up on lost sleep.

Moriya and Todoroki's argument eventually died down. It had all been just for show. Unlike the big-name national newspapers, at the small, more simply structured papers such as the *North Kanto Times*, there was no deep-rooted antagonism between the political and local news sections. A born-and-bred local news reporter such as Yuuki was a rare thing—usually the people who made it to management had spent time in both sections.

At the *NKT*, most of the infighting was between the news-related and business-related departments. Then there were the two factions: the one that supported the chairman and the one that supported the managing director. But there was also another feud that was normally dormant but occasionally raised its ugly head. It related to the various managers' views of the famous rivalry between current and ex–prime ministers Nakasone and Fukuda. Sometimes, if someone was perceived as being a Fukuda or a Nakasone supporter, it would add extra fuel to the fire of an office dispute.

Kasuya had been fast-tracked to the position of editor in chief in part due to his skills in diplomacy, but also because he wasn't overtly political. However, the internal problems at the newspaper notwithstanding, the fight between the ex–prime minister and the current one, and the reality of the feud between both of the lower house representatives from Gunma Prefecture's Third District, still occasionally influenced the day-to-day makeup of the paper. To say nothing of the Liberal Democratic Party leadership election, which had been central to an earlier feud between the same Takeo Fukuda and another ex–prime minister, Kakuei Tanaka. Ever since Nakasone had betrayed Fukuda by suddenly switching allegiance to Tanaka in that election thirteen years ago, any reporter covering any aspect of the Fukuda-Nakasone rivalry had to tread ever so lightly, and be meticulous, cautious, and circumspect in their approach. Everyone present at the meeting knew that the current topic, the prime minister's visit to Yasukuni Shrine, could not be discussed without consideration of the Fukuda-Nakasone situation.

With a deep sigh, Kasuya issued a warning to all assembled.

"Moriya, if we lead with Nakasone's visit, how are we going to approach it? It's all about the content. As Todoroki has pointed out, we can't just extol his virtues. It's no puff piece."

"Of course we'll include comments from the opposition parties."

"Then we're just going to look as if we put the story up there as an excuse to take a swing at him. If our stance is the same as the *Asahi* and *Mainichi* newspapers, then that's how the Nakasone side is going to see it."

"True, but . . ." Moriya thought for a while, then continued. "The overall impression will be that Nakasone did something huge. If we're careful about the headline, I don't see any problem."

Kasuya folded his arms.

"If we do lead with it, how will the Fukuda side feel about it?"

"Well, of course, if we appear uncritical of Nakasone, they're bound to get their panties in a twist."

"Well, there's no hope of that . . ."

The *North Kanto Times* had a bitter taste left in its mouth after the Tanaka-Fukuda feud. Under the direction of Chairman Shirakawa (then editor in chief), they had avoided all criticism of Nakasone's actions and, as a result, their circulation figures had plummeted in Gunma's Third

Electoral District. And that wasn't the end of it. In the December general election of the same year, Fukuda had won the seat in a landslide, with an unprecedented 178,281 votes, destroying Nakasone. That figure was close to the total circulation of the *North Kanto Times* at the time. The top brass at the newspapers realized at that point what a terrible idea it would be to piss off Fukuda supporters.

Kasuya turned to the current managing editor.

"What do you think?"

"I think it should be fine to lead with it."

Oimura was lacking his usual self-assurance. He was a hater of the Self-Defense Forces, so it followed that he was anti-Nakasone. Chairman Shirakawa was pro-Nakasone, so he was caught in quite a dilemma. Kasuya had put the question to Oimura, sounding him out as a closet Fukuda supporter, but Oimura had neatly dodged the question. Kasuya sighed again.

"I guess we'll have to ask Iikura-san," he murmured, as if talking to himself.

A wave of tension ran through the room.

Until the year before last, managing director Iikura had also held the post of "editorial director." It was strongly suspected that he'd been released from that duty by Chairman Shirakawa under pressure from the local prefectural political and business community. There was no way of verifying this story, but the rumor that followed his being deposed was credible. Nowadays he was busy drumming up support within the company. He was reportedly consolidating his support base in Circulation and consequently stirring up trouble in that department. He had his eye on the chairman's position and it was rumored he was poised for an opportunity to attack. The rumor had gathered strength six months ago when Shirakawa had had his accident and been confined to a wheelchair. It had even reached the ears of Yuuki, who was usually completely out of touch with the internal machinations at the paper.

With the outward appearance of a true gentleman, managing director Iikura was frequently nicknamed the Clever Yakuza and was Takeo Fukuda's closest ally at the *North Kanto Times*.

Kasuya now turned to Moriya, with his Conciliator expression.

"Iikura-san had nothing to say about this upcoming Yasukuni Shrine visit?"

"Er, no. He never even called."

Despite being removed as editorial director, Iikura still liked to call the newsroom now and again to let them know "Fukuda's viewpoint" or "Fukuda's reaction." It was to unsettle them, a form of retaliation, or reverse intelligence gathering. The Editorial Department had tried to deal with this in several ways, but in the end their "Iikura inside information" was responsible for their clear coverage of the Fukuda side, and they weren't willing to give it up. The reporters assigned to Fukuda were able to get a far clearer insight into the politician's true opinions than they would have ever gotten from interviewing his private secretary.

"So why does he have nothing to say to us about this subject?"

"I think he's purposely waiting to see what we're going to do."

It was Oimura who had answered. He seemed to have perked up on hearing Iikura's name—his eyes showed signs the Firecracker was back.

"Purposely waiting?" Kasuya repeated. "Why?"

"He's going to find a way to use it against us somehow," continued Oimura. He was on a roll now. "If we lead with the story, he'll complain that we're buttering up Nakasone. If we put it as second lead, he'll say we're protecting him. Iikura is waiting for us to make a move. Without a doubt, that's the Clever Yakuza's MO."

Kasuya nodded gloomily. He was probably imagining how next month's executive meeting was going to go.

"Right, well, we'll do our best not to get dragged into his game. Oimura, what's your conclusion?"

"Well, we can't make it anything but the lead. As Moriya suggested, we print the opposition parties' criticisms, add a commentary piece."

"Commentary piece? Are we going to use Kyodo?"

"Kyodo's articles are too harsh. Better to get Aoki to write something lighter."

"No, I think commentaries are too dangerous. Everything in there is considered the opinion of the newspaper company. Best to go with something without a hint of subjectivity."

"Yes, I believe you're right, but—"

Oimura began to speak but broke off and looked pensive.

Everyone was silent. No one was really expecting him to come up with a solution. Not being able to read Iikura's thought processes was weakening their ability to decide on a course of action. Kasuya leaned back in his armchair and scanned the room.

"What do you think is the best plan of action?"

"Keep the JAL crash on the front page."

It was Kamejima who had spoken. Kasuya looked at him in surprise.

"Why do you think that?"

"If you look at our newsroom, you'd feel the same way. Everyone is completely absorbed by the disaster. If you tell them now that we're going to focus on Prime Minister Nakasone today, you'll never get them energized about it."

Kamejima's comment may have completely missed the substance of the discussion, but it was easy for Kasuya to go along with.

"That's a good point."

"Right? A newspaper is made up of living beings. We have to care about what we print."

Kasuya nodded and looked over in Yuuki's direction.

"What do you think?"

Yuuki returned the look in total silence. This is how he'd expected the conversation to go, but he hadn't prepared a response. Until yesterday, he wouldn't have hesitated to say, *Go with the crash.* But since then they'd killed one of his best reporters' articles, and last night he'd been forced to give in. The seeds of powerlessness had been planted in his heart, and they were steadily growing. His enthusiasm for the JAL crash had been seriously eroded. The frosty expressions of Oimura and Todoroki also made him afraid to come up with an opinion on the spot. He'd already lost the confidence of the JAL crash desk anyway. He was all too aware of that.

"What's wrong with you? I'm asking for your opinion."

Both Kasuya's expression and his voice betrayed his high expectations. Depending on Yuuki's response, he'd be able to go along with Kamejima's suggestion, or not. Yuuki realized that Kasuya was leaving the final decision up to him. He felt trapped. There was only one answer he could give.

"I don't care which one we go with."

Kasuya's disappointment was obvious. He sighed, not for the first time that morning, and, with no decision in sight, put an end to the meeting.

"We'll meet again this evening. Right now I'm going to see Iikura-san."

The newsroom was deserted. As they all left the editor in chief's office, Yuuki hurried to catch up with Kamejima. He intended to apologize for the previous evening, when he'd yelled at him to remove the Japan Airlines apology ad from the newspaper. He'd taken his anger and frustration out on Kamejima and, no matter what the provocation, he'd deviated from the normal protocol of keeping good working relations in the newsroom.

"Kaku-san!"

Kamejima turned, his moonlike face severe.

"What?"

"I'm sorry about yesterday," Yuuki said, bowing his head.

"It's fine."

"I'll make sure it doesn't happen again."

Kamejima snorted rudely.

"Look. I told you I don't care about that. I'm more bothered by what happened just now. What the hell was that?"

"Huh?"

"At the meeting. How can you say, 'I don't care which one we go with'? You're the one responsible for the crash coverage. It's been you from the start. Don't you even care anymore?"

Yuuki returned to his desk with a bad aftertaste in his mouth.

*"Don't you even care anymore?"*

He was envious of Kamejima for being able to say that. Actually, he found it surprising. How did he manage to be so properly sensitive to other people's feelings? Ever since he had started at the company, Kamejima

124

had worked exclusively in the copy section. He'd never had the chance to work out in the field like the reporters. He was always there in the newsroom, forever stuck in "today," creating the layout for the next day. That might be the reason—he never had a chance to meet up with real flesh-and-blood people outside the office, so he became good at assessing all the news that came into the office. It meant he was constantly sharpening his senses.

*"I don't care which one we go with—"*

His chest felt tight. He exhaled quickly and began to tidy up the papers on his desk. It wasn't yet eleven in the morning and already there was an impressive pile of wires from Kyodo related to the crash. His eye was drawn to a large photograph half buried under it. It was an interior shot of the Fujioka High School gymnasium, which was being used as a temporary morgue. The gym had been opened up to the press yesterday evening, but the negatives had been slow to arrive here at the head office, and the pictures hadn't made the morning edition.

The white coffins were neatly lined up with nameplates and bunches of flowers placed on top. Of the fifty-one bodies that had already been identified back at the municipal sports hall, forty-three were being kept here. As he examined the photo, Yuuki did a double take. He hadn't noticed it the night before, but on either side of the main door was a wreath. The photo was a blown-up, file-folder-sized photograph, so it was possible to read the name of the donors attached to the wreaths. The one on the right of the door read FORMER PRIME MINISTER TAKEO FUKUDA; on the left, PRIME MINISTER YASUHIRO NAKASONE.

It suddenly made sense—this was their constituency. Gunma's Third District was made up of Takasaki City and all the prefecture's western region. Uenomura in the Tano District, where the Japan Airlines plane had come down, as well as Fujioka City, where the deceased had been taken, were both part of that Third District.

It was an odd photo. He felt its strangeness all the more as he looked at it again. The wreaths hadn't been placed outside the gym; they were inside, leaning against the wall—deliberately in the view of the mass media, in the exact location where they had been given the go-ahead to take photographs. Again, that bile rose up in his throat.

"Good morning!"

Along with the cheerful voice came a hot cup of tea. But before he had time to say thank you, Chizuko Yorita was already on her way, a tray crammed full of tea and coffee in her hands. This must mean the newsroom was beginning to fill up.

Yuuki raised the cup to his lips. The tea washed away the nasty taste in his mouth, but he had no desire yet to start in on the pile of papers on his desk. Instead, he opened up the morning edition of the newspaper. Without even checking the page numbers, he was able to open it right at the sports pages. It was times like this when he felt as if he'd been in this job too long.

The Hanshin Tigers baseball team had lost again. This time it was 3–4 to the Yomiuri Giants. Mayumi had one hit from four times at bat.

"They might really win the championship."

He looked up at the sound of the voice. Kishi had just returned to his desk, carrying a large mug that he'd taken from Chizuko's tray.

"They lost. Yesterday, too."

"So, two losses after five wins in a row," said Kishi, pulling a face as if he were a Tigers fan. "Nothing to worry about."

"And from then on, they'll plummet right down the league. Isn't that their usual style?"

"You closet Giants fan!"

Kishi impersonated Oimura, then laughed. Gunma was one of the places that was being subjected to a blitz marketing campaign by the *Yomiuri Shimbun* newspaper. At the *North Kanto Times*, if you dared to mention you were a fan of the Giants, the baseball team owned by the *Yomiuri*, you'd be denounced as a traitor.

"But didn't you say your youngest . . . what's her name . . . Yuka, was a Hanshin Tigers fan?"

"She's an Akinobu Mayumi fan, though not because of his basehitting, I don't think."

"That's right. All the wives and daughters throughout Japan are Mayumi fans!"

Kishi laughed again. But then he put his mug down on his desk and lowered his voice.

"Tell me, how's it going with Yuka?"

"What do you mean?"

"Does she say you're yucky and all that kind of stuff?"

"Well, that came out of nowhere!" Yuuki said in shock.

"No, well . . ." Kishi frowned and clicked his tongue. "You know, you hear about it. I'm not sure if it's when they start getting their period, or what causes it, but when girls are in about the fifth or sixth grade at primary school they start to hate their fathers."

"Was Kaz like that?"

Yuuki had only met Kishi's daughter once, but he'd been shown an impressive number of photos of her.

"Yep. My younger, Fumiko, too."

"How old are they now?"

"First year of middle school and sixth year of primary. It's miserable—they treat me like some kind of germ. I get home from work and, as soon as I step foot in the door, it's like some magic disappearing act. Poof! They're gone."

Kishi spoke jokingly but, behind his laughter, the political editor looked depressed.

"I'm sure they'll grow out of it, won't they?" said Yuuki, partly out of concern, but also hoping for more information.

"I hear there's no guarantee. I couldn't bear it if they treated me like that forever. Seriously, I feel like crying sometimes."

Yuuki made a sympathetic noise.

"And I was so affectionate to them when they were growing up . . . You know, I wish I'd had boys. I've got to admit, I'm envious of you."

Yuuki desperately tried to think of another topic, but Kishi was too quick for him.

"Your Jun is the same age as Kaz, isn't he? He must have grown up."

"Yes, well, physically, maybe," said Yuuki, looking down at the floor.

"Well, you probably won't have any trouble with your Yuka, she's such a good girl."

"Oh, not really."

"No, she's a good girl. But that said, my Kaz and Fumi were just fine when they were still that age . . ."

As Kishi spoke, Yuuki noticed Oimura heading in their direction.

"Hey, Kishi!" Oimura said, plopping down on the corner of Kishi's desk. "I missed the chance to get your opinion back there. Just in case, let's hear it."

Yuuki swiveled his office chair around so that it seemed he was trying to stay out of the private conversation. In reality, he couldn't bear to look at the face of the ringleader in the killing of Sayama's article.

Kishi was expressing an opinion close to Nakasone's. It was natural that he would. Kishi had once been dispatched as a special correspondent accompanying Nakasone on one of his overseas trips. He even had a photograph of him posing with Nakasone on display in his living room. It had been taken on board the private government jet. It was obviously a photo op the government side offered to all the representatives of the press, so when Yuuki had seen the photo he'd been secretly scornful of a man who was so impressed by people in authority he would show off a photo like that with so much pride.

But now, following the discussion he'd just had with Kishi about his daughters, he'd changed his opinion of the man. The photo with Nakasone was above the TV, arranged in a row with photos of Kishi's daughters. It might not have been placed there for visitors to see. More likely he wanted his family to see it every day. That was what any man would want—to earn the respect of his wife and children—

"Well, we are getting a bit sick and tired of the whole JAL crash thing."

His attention was caught by Oimura's parting words to Kishi. *Sick and tired?* What an unpleasant phrase to use.

The Editorial Department staff began to arrive for the day. Soon the timer would be set for the evening deadline.

*"I don't care which one we go with."*

Yuuki couldn't settle down. He'd never approached an edition with such mixed feelings.

# 18

After lunch at the staff cafeteria, Yuuki returned to his desk and paged Sayama and Hanazawa. While he waited for their reply, he read over the crash-related articles in the morning's paper.

The top headline was 121 BODIES RECOVERED, 51 IDENTIFIED. The subhead was CAUSE WAS DAMAGE TO TAIL AREA. He flipped through the pages. Part one of the series that ought to have been the lead story, SITE OF A TRAGEDY: MOUNT OSUTAKA, looked a little sad, relegated to its inconspicuous position on the second local news page. His feelings of anger and self-reproach returned. He knew that, at this late stage, he was never going to get his feature series back on the front page. The whole idea was, so to speak, dead in the water.

Sayama called back first.

"You were trying to reach me?"

Sayama's tone was deliberately cold, stressing the distance between them. Yuuki kept it businesslike, too.

"Got anything for me?"

"The prefectural police have officially met with the assistant cabin crew manager now. I can give you about fifty lines on that."

"That was quick."

"Because Japan Airlines made the first move. The authorities were pretty mad about it."

"I can imagine. It amounts to obstruction of a police investigation."

"That's correct."

Sayama's use of formal language was making Yuuki very uncomfortable.

"Are you with the police now?"

"Yes. In the pressroom."

"Is Wajima with you?"

"No, he went out."

"If you see him, can you ask him to call me? He never answers his pager."

"Understood."

After he hung up, Yuuki sat and stared at the phone for a while.

It was obvious that Sayama had lost all enthusiasm. He wasn't even trying anymore. He'd poured his soul into that eyewitness piece and his bosses had trampled all over it.

The TV was showing the government-organized national memorial service for the victims of the Second World War. It was just as the ceremony was drawing to a close that Yuuki finally heard from Wajima.

"This is Wajima . . ." he began, in his usual faltering voice.

"What time can I expect your draft?"

"Eh?"

"Part two of the series. It doesn't matter that it's not quite what we'd hoped, we're still going ahead."

"Oh, okay, then Hanazawa'll write it."

For a moment Yuuki thought he'd misheard.

"What are you talking about? I told you to write it!"

There was silence on the other end.

"You're the deputy chief reporter at police headquarters, Wajima! Why would you ask Hanazawa, the number three, to write an article for you?"

"Well, I . . ."

Wajima searched for words, but Yuuki didn't need to hear his explanation. He could imagine what was going on. It was Hanazawa, along with Sayama, who'd been the first to climb Osutaka. Wajima, on the other hand, had attempted to climb it but had given up, exhausted. The result had been a switch in the balance of power between the number-two and number-three reporters.

"Wajima! You write it."

Again, there was no reply.

"I want it by five. Got it?"

Yuuki didn't wait for a response. He hung up. He wondered whether Wajima was thinking of leaving the paper. It wasn't just the work. When a reporter begins to be upstaged by the people below him, it's hard to survive.

He looked up. There was a throng of people in front of the TV set. He recognized scenes from Yasukuni Shrine. Prime Minister Nakasone, solemn in his morning suit, was climbing the steps to the inner sanctuary. Reaching the top, he paused and bowed deeply.

The editor in chief watched, a stern expression on his face. He still hadn't made the final call on whether to lead with Yasukuni Shrine or the JAL crash.

Yuuki's desk phone rang. It was Tamaki, the only reporter at the *North Kanto Times* with a degree in engineering. He'd been posted to the Fujioka branch office in place of Totsuka, and was under orders to follow the Ministry of Transport's Aircraft Accident Investigation Committee. That said, Tamaki wasn't a graduate in aeronautical engineering specifically. *NKT*'s hope wasn't to score a scoop; it was more to avoid being the only paper to miss out on everyone else's. However, Tamaki had some surprising news.

"I pretty much know the cause of the crash."

Yuuki couldn't respond right away. If this was true, it would be an incredible scoop. He pulled up his chair.

"Tell me."

"The pressure bulkhead was ruptured."

"What's that?"

"It's a hemispherical wall toward the back of the aircraft. It sustains the pressure in the passenger cabin."

"Could you explain a bit more?"

"When the aircraft flies at high altitude, the pressure in the cabin rises. In other words, compared to the outside air pressure, the pressure inside is higher. So the bulkhead has a substantial load pressing on it from the inside toward the outside."

Yuuki could picture Tamaki, with his earnest face and neat side-parting. He'd graduated from Gunma University and was in his third year at the paper, currently covering the Maebashi City mayor's office. That was really all Yuuki knew about him.

"Explain the complicated stuff later. For now, what's the upshot?"

"To put it simply, the wall broke under the load. I believe that, with the wall gone, the pressure of the air in the passenger cabin blew off the tail."

*Believe* . . . ? Yuuki lowered his voice.

"You didn't hear this from one of the investigation team?"

"Ah, no . . . I heard the investigators repeating the word 'bulkhead.'"

"So you got it through eavesdropping rather than a proper interview?"

"Well, yes."

"So they didn't actually say that the bulkhead broke?"

"No, they didn't go that far."

Yuuki's shoulders sagged. It was all no more than guesswork on the part of Tamaki. But there was also the possibility that he was spot-on.

"Tonight, sneak into the hotel where they're staying and try to collar one of the investigators," he ordered Tamaki.

"That's going to be a bit tricky. All the media have journalists camped out there. There's no way of getting past all the others."

"Just try anyway."

Yuuki hung up and turned to his neighbor.

"Kishi?"

"What?"

"Who do we have in the Ministry of Transport's press club?"

"No one. We used to have membership there at one time, but . . ."

"I see . . ."

If this was true, there was nothing for it but to get hold of one of the members of the investigation team. Would Tamaki be able to manage it alone?

Yuuki headed over to the regional news desk. A colleague by the name of Yamada sat there, his right hand absentmindedly in his trademark tousled hair.

"Hey, Yamada, what's Tamaki from the Maebashi office like? Is he a go-getter?"

"Tamaki? Let me think . . . It's kind of hard to get a sense of him. Not great, not terrible, either, I suppose."

Yuuki returned to his desk and looked at his phone. He knew there was only one person who would be able to answer his question properly—

Sayama. He'd know what kind of a reporter Tamaki was: his temperament, his abilities, how credible his information was.

As he was trying to decide whether to call Sayama, he heard someone calling him. It was that oily voice again. Yuuki mentally rolled his eyes and turned to face Ito, who had come right up behind him, as before.

"I need to speak to you."

"Of course. What is it?"

"Could I have about fifteen minutes of your time?" the Circulation chief asked, stroking his mustache. Yuuki frowned and looked up at the clock.

"Look, I promise you it'll take no more than fifteen minutes. It's about Anzai."

Yuuki turned pale.

"Has he taken a turn for the worse?"

"No, of course not," he said in his usual slimy way. "Nothing like that."

Ito nodded toward the door. Yuuki followed him out into the corridor. He had assumed that Ito intended to sit and talk in the break area, but the head of Circulation strode straight past the vending machines and started down the stairs. His self-confidence and egotistic manner bothered Yuuki. He was convinced once more that this man knew the truth about Yuuki's late mother.

Ito had prepared a space on the ground floor for them to talk. It was a little reception room where the Circulation Department met with their customers. Ito invited Yuuki to sit on the sofa. It was clear that he had some scheme in mind.

"We're really suffering at the moment. Anzai has left a big hole in our operations. Right now we've got three people running around trying to fill his shoes."

Yuuki decided to sit and wait. So far there didn't seem to be anything resembling a point in what Ito was saying. He deliberately studied his watch.

"You've had ten minutes already. If there's nothing you need, I'll be getting back to my desk."

Ito looked unperturbed.

"Dear me, you do seem to be in rather a hurry. I'll get straight to the point."

"We're run off our feet today."

Almost as if this was the trigger he'd been waiting for, Ito leaned forward and locked his fingers together.

"You mean with Prime Minister Nakasone's visit to Yasukuni Shrine?"

Yuuki watched Ito carefully. *The managing director's spy*—the phrase ran through his mind. Ito laughed, his eyes narrowing to slits as fine as thread.

"We're just a simple ramen shop stuck in the middle of two skyscrapers."

Gunma's Third Electoral District. It was the favorite phrase of the politician Keizo Obuchi. Stuck in the middle of the Fukuda-Nakasone rivalry, always forced to fight extra hard. Ito had just compared the *North Kanto Times* to Obuchi's position. He was laughing.

"How's it going to be covered in our paper?"

Yuuki wasn't at all surprised by the question. It was obvious that managing director Iikura had been dying to know what was happening in the newsroom vis-à-vis the Yasukuni Shrine visit and had sent Ito to find out. Ito had picked Yuuki to ask. In other words, he had been chosen as the Iikura faction's source of intelligence.

But why him? Because he hadn't been treated well. They saw him as an outsider in the Editorial Department. And he was also the man who had been about to set off for the mountains with Anzai, Ito's junior colleague.

Yes, he was sure that was it. Anzai must also have been a supporter of Iikura. Hadn't he looked up to Ito, calling him his "lifesaver"? He'd been Ito's right-hand man. Yuuki had caught their attention because of his friendship with Anzai. Without his even noticing it, he'd been labeled "managing director faction."

"Hey, what's the matter? No need to look so grim . . . So, are they going to make Yasukuni Shrine the lead story?"

Yuuki looked straight into Ito's narrow little eyes.

"What on earth do you have to gain by asking me that?"

But he already knew. His information would be passed on to the Fukuda side. Or, more to the point, passed on by a jumped-up little man acting under the supposed authority of Fukuda. Before the morning edition was printed, this sycophant would be explaining that "this kind of article is scheduled to appear." The most trivial, useless piece of information, but, as a journalist, Yuuki got it. There was always someone who could use information. Even the most trifling piece of C-grade or D-grade information could be used to smooth relationships and win friends. A tiny piece of information could buy a tiny amount of gratitude. If the process was repeated enough times, it grew into a sense of obligation, eventually blossoming into reliance and trust.

Yuuki stood up. Ito looked at him.

"Fair enough, but I heard you made a big scene yesterday."

"What are you . . . ?"

"In the chairman's office."

Suddenly everything was crystal clear. Ito continued.

"You understand? The chairman's a despicable man. We can't let a sexual pervert like that run our company!"

Yuuki was shocked into silence.

"As long as Shirakawa is in charge, there is no hope of you getting anywhere in this company. In fact, after yesterday, come autumn you'll probably be let go or, at best, transferred to the middle of nowhere."

Yuuki looked down at Ito.

"Better than selling my soul," he spat, and turned and headed for the door. The oily voice flowed along behind him.

"Hey, didn't you use to live in Nakashindenmachi?"

Yuuki stopped dead and turned his head slightly. Ito's eyes were wider now, like a cat that had just spotted its prey. But Yuuki couldn't return his gaze. He looked quickly away.

In that moment, he could see his mother's frail form, and the shifty-eyed men who used to slip out of their back door.

# 19

Four in the afternoon, and the newsroom was bustling.

Yuuki was at his desk, occupied with Kyodo News wires.

271 bodies recovered, 101 identified
Joint Japan-U.S. investigation gets under way
National public safety commission focuses on JAL's possible
    criminal liability

*"Hey, kid, I heard your mom's a pan-pan girl."*

Of course. The high school kid he'd met in that park way back—it was Ito after all.

He tried to keep calm.

Ito had gone too far. It was conceivable that Yuuki's secret was already out. The possibility of this happening had always been the thing that terrified Yuuki the most. But he realized that, if he were to discover that his secret was already out there, at least the worst part would be over. He was a forty-year-old man. How could whether his deceased mother had been a prostitute or not reasonably be seen as a blemish on his reputation?

Yuuki reached for the next wire. The red pen in his hand never stopped moving.

In the depths of his heart, there was a small wooden box.

Inside it, he had stuffed all the shame and disgrace that threatened to ruin his life. For many, many years he'd lived in fear, desperately concealing the box, squeezing the lid down as tightly as he could. But now that the lid had been opened, he found that all it contained was grief. In the chaos of postwar Japan, her husband having vanished into thin air, left alone with a hungry, crying baby, she'd been forced to depend on men. And then, in the end, she had lain there alone, at a funeral that no one had attended.

Yuuki kept on writing.

> Flight-path record reveals struggle
> Pilot's desperate attempt to control engine
> Thorough inspection of jumbo jets launched

"Yuuki-san?"

He looked up to see Yoshii from the copy section. There was a worried expression on his boyish face. He was in charge of today's front page.

"Could you make the decision as soon as possible? Which one is going to be the headline, JAL or Yasukuni Shrine?"

Yuuki craned his neck to check out the editor in chief's office. The door was shut. All the senior management were holed up in there for the rest of the morning's meeting.

"Looks like they're not ready yet."

"It'll be a real problem for us if they don't decide soon."

"For me, too. Looks like we're all going to have to wait a bit longer."

"But I don't understand why they're even considering Yasukuni. Why can't they just stick with the crash?"

Yoshii looked at Yuuki through narrowed eyes. He was a veteran copy editor in his mid-thirties but, with his slight build and childlike face, he looked much younger.

"If we stop leading with it after only three or four days, we'll be a laughingstock with all the other newspapers," Yoshii continued.

"Laughingstock?"

"Yes. I don't think we should even consider any other headline until the other papers do. No matter how others may see it, it's our local news story."

Yuuki began to feel a little guilty.

"Yuuki-san, could you go and talk to the bosses about it? You are the desk chief, after all."

"Only in name."

It was painful to have to admit this. And saying it out loud made it even worse. He was frustrated at himself, too, for not being able to be fired up by this topic of conversation. Or rather, he knew what he ought to have the guts to say, but the words just weren't there. Instead, he said something quite different.

"So you'll just have to prepare two alternative headlines, won't you?"

Yoshii returned to his desk, muttering under his breath. Yuuki let out a short sigh and glanced at the clock. It was almost five. Wajima still hadn't sent over his article for the crash feature series. As he turned back to his work, something on the next desk caught his eye. He'd seen a leg; a leg with no body attached. It was a photo from one of the newsmagazines—maybe *Friday* or *Focus*. Nozawa was sitting there, flicking through a magazine. It was the Mount Osutaka special edition. Every time Nozawa stopped at a page, Yuuki's eye was assaulted by a gruesome image of a different body part.

"That came out today?" Yuuki asked.

"I think we can use this," Nozawa replied, holding it out for Yuuki to see.

"Use it?"

Nozawa flicked his thumb and forefinger at one of the photos.

"This here, this is the JAL crash in a nutshell. Newspapers can't compete with this stuff."

"Why do you say that?"

"Ha!" Nozawa snorted scornfully. "Don't you get it? Ever since they heard that five hundred and twenty people were killed, everyone's wanted to see the bodies. The newspapers go on about how disastrous, how pitiful it is, they pile it on in platefuls, but they're no match for a single photo."

Yuuki wasn't sure how serious Nozawa was. It could have been his form of revenge for not having been named JAL crash desk chief.

"All those articles trying to make the readers cry—they're all the same," Nozawa continued. "Every day they write about the same thing—so and so, family member of the deceased. Who reads that stuff? No one wants to read the same shit over and over again."

"That's a naive thing to say," said Yuuki with a sigh.

"What do you mean?"

"Nozawa, have you ever written anything with the serious intention of making your readers cry?"

Nozawa began to say something but stopped.

"The mass media has the tendency to report people's deaths in the saddest way possible. Whether the public reads it or not, writing, assembling, distributing—that's what a newspaper's about. And if five hundred and twenty people have died, then we are going to write five hundred and twenty pieces that make the readers cry. That's our job."

Yuuki's heart felt as bleak as he sounded.

"I'm sure there are people out there who cry about complete strangers. I suppose it's a matter of personal taste whether you prefer to look at a photo or read some sentimental piece. We can't get caught up in worrying about that kind of thing," said Yuuki.

There was a pause.

"You're being philosophical about this. Definitely out of character for you."

"Nozawa?"

"What?"

"I can hand in my notice anytime. If you want the JAL desk chief job, just let management know."

Nozawa folded his arms and looked Yuuki in the eyes.

"I heard you had a falling-out with the chairman."

"News travels fast."

"Anyway, I've got no interest in taking over."

"This kind of accident happens only once in a lifetime."

"It's too big. There's nothing interesting about it. It's fine—go ahead and cover it. Your way. To the bitter end, Don Quixote."

And with that, Nozawa turned his back on Yuuki.

Don Quixote? If Yuuki hadn't been the one sitting in this seat right now, he'd have laughed out loud at the name. Nozawa had nailed it.

He gathered together all the articles relating to the cause of the crash.

Ministry of Transport investigators rule out R5 door as cause

Defect in tail connector may have created resonance

Possible damage to tail linkage

Vertical tail came off at the root

Extreme pressure on the root; turbulence theories

Horizontal stabilizer also damaged?

U.S. Federal Aviation Administration: large aircraft suffer from fast deterioration

Mystery of 30-minute "figure eight" flight path

Full effort into wreckage investigation

It took Yuuki a while to get through all these. The term "bulkhead" was nowhere to be found. He began to think he'd been misled by Tamaki.

Next, he turned his attention to the articles dealing with the bereaved families.

Slow progress in identification of victims

Air crash dead return home

He thought about how these two would seem to cancel each other out if they appeared together on the same page. If he was picking a headline story, he'd probably go with the former. It had a stronger impact. If he had to choose a second story only, AIR CRASH DEAD RETURN HOME would make a good sentimental piece.

He finally looked up from his work. Kishi had just been to see what the situation was in the editor in chief's office.

"Have they decided?"

"Looks like they're leaning toward Nakasone. But they're still fighting over the content."

"Did Kasuya meet with managing director Iikura?"

"No. Seems he's not at work today."

"Vanished into thin air, huh?"

"Apparently. Seems he's not at home, either."

"He's like *Jaws* or *Alien*. Scarier when you can't see him."

"You seem pretty laid-back," said Kishi with a broad smile. "So you have the crash stuff sorted out?"

"The Kyodo News part," Yuuki replied. "How about you?"

He took AIR CRASH DEAD RETURN HOME from the pile, convinced now that he was picking the second story.

"We're waiting to get the lead piece from Aoki in Tokyo. He must be having a tough time with it. He's not as talented at writing as he is at talking."

Yuuki laughed.

"By the way, Yuuki . . . Is it really okay with you?"

"Is what okay?"

"Putting the crash into the second slot."

Kishi's expression was dead serious.

"It's not my decision."

"So it seems."

Just as they broke eye contact, Nozawa's sharp voice pierced the air.

"Hey, they can't just come in here like that!"

By the entrance to the newsroom stood a woman in her early thirties with a forced smile on her face. She held the hand of a little boy. They appeared to be mother and son. Nozawa got to his feet and marched over to them.

"Outsiders aren't allowed in here. You'll have to leave."

"I'm sorry," said the mother, bowing nervously. "I wondered if you had any spare newspapers."

"You'd better try downstairs."

The mother had a slight accent that wasn't familiar to Yuuki. She was very plainly dressed, but from a distance it looked as if she'd had a heavy hand with her eye makeup. Her little boy was about five or six, and he must have thought his mother was being bullied because he was glaring daggers at Nozawa.

The boy turned his gaze on Yuuki. Yuuki tried to smile back at him, but all the muscles in his face suddenly froze.

"It's down the stairs on the right-hand side. There's a newspaper vending machine. You can put coins in."

"Thank you so much. That's very kind of you," she replied, bowing to Nozawa. The boy took his eyes off Yuuki.

Yuuki felt a frisson of fear. He knew that look. There'd been a time when he'd had the same look himself. *I'm going to look after my mom.* That painful day when he'd sworn that oath. The day he'd understood that his father was never going to return.

A wave of something rushed over him, and he snatched all the copies of the *North Kanto Times* up off his desk—today's, yesterday's, the day before yesterday's . . . a total of thirteen days' worth of papers—and stuffed them into a large envelope. His eye fell on the headline he'd been preparing: AIR CRASH DEAD RETURN HOME.

He ran wildly down the stairs and caught up with the mother and son at the bottom.

"Here," he said, holding out the envelope. The mother, who had been on the point of opening her purse to use the vending machine, turned in surprise.

It was as Yuuki had thought. What had looked at a distance like heavy eye makeup was in fact the dark circles of someone who had been constantly weeping. Yuuki looked down at the floor.

"Here are the papers from the last thirteen days. You're welcome to take them."

A huge teardrop rolled from the woman's eye.

"Thank you . . . so much . . ."

She opened her purse with a trembling hand. As she did so, it was spattered by several more teardrops.

"You don't need to pay for them. Here."

Yuuki handed her the envelope. Through the glass doors of the lobby, he could see a black hearse parked outside. The woman bowed her thanks several times and left. The little boy had scowled at him the entire time.

Yuuki went back upstairs, but he couldn't bring himself to go into the newsroom.

*"Crying's the relatives' job, not yours."* It didn't matter how many times he told himself that. He turned and went back downstairs, taking the steps slowly, one by one, and then he noticed the big *North Kanto Times* signboard. That was why she'd told the driver to stop.

What part of the country was that accent from? Every prefecture in Japan had its own local newspaper. There'd certainly be one in whatever area she was from. But the accident had happened here in Gunma. She must have figured that this newspaper would have more details about the crash than the others. That was why she'd asked the driver to stop at the office of the *North Kanto Times*. The plane crash that had robbed her of her husband— she believed she would get the most informative stories here.

Yuuki looked down and used his tie to dry his eyes. Then he bounded back upstairs.

This time, he returned to the newsroom. Kishi and Nozawa watched him in silence. Ignoring them completely, he went over to his desk, opened the drawer, and pulled out a photograph. Then he headed over to the editor in chief's office and pushed open the door.

Editor in chief Kasuya, managing editor Oimura, senior political editor Moriya, chief copy editor Kamejima—they all turned to look at him.

"Let's lead with the JAL crash."

The room remained hushed for a few moments. Kasuya finally broke the silence.

"No, we're going with Nakasone—"

Yuuki didn't let him finish.

"That's just to keep the Clever Yakuza quiet, right?" he said, placing the photo in the center of the table. It was the photo of the makeshift morgue with the two wreaths. And the two names.

"I'll print it in this size. This way, Fukuda and Nakasone will both stand out."

He seemed to have taken everyone by surprise. Yuuki looked at every face in turn.

"The crash has to remain our top story. Five hundred and twenty people lost their lives, and it happened here in Gunma."

Of course, it was the man seated at the lowest spot at the foot of the table who was the first to nod in agreement—Kamejima.

Six in the evening.

The layout for the next day's paper was finally done. The top story was the continued coverage of the Japan Airlines crash. There was a much shorter article about Prime Minister Nakasone's visit to Yasukuni Shrine, over to the left-hand side of the front page. It had been less of a decision and more of a settlement. Thanks to one single photo, the balance between the Fukuda and Nakasone factions had been preserved. Yuuki's ingenious plan had delighted Kasuya; and Oimura and Todoroki, unable to roll out any of their usual objections, had mournfully acquiesced.

"The crash is top again today!" Kamejima called out. A fair number of people in the newsroom applauded. Most of the Editorial Department was absorbed by the accident. It was gratifying that the big story about their "hometown" prime minister visiting Yasukuni was no longer headlining. It felt as if the *North Kanto Times* had shown some guts, developed a backbone.

When Yuuki had left editor in chief Kasuya's office, Chizuko Yorita had been waiting at his desk to get his dinner order.

"Yuuki-san, what are you having today?"

"Hmm . . . I think I'll have cold Chinese noodles from Raku-raku Tei."

"Cold noodles?"

Chizuko glanced over her order sheet. She was obviously checking to see if there was anyone else having the same thing.

"Am I the only one?"

"Yes. Everyone else is too chilled from the air conditioner."

If there were too many different orders, it would delay the delivery.

"What's the most popular?"

"Um . . . today the top order is *gomoku* fried rice. There are eight others who've ordered it."

"That'll be fine."

Yuuki sat down and began to look over the latest wires. He'd only been in Kasuya's office for twenty minutes but during that time the world's biggest single-aircraft airline disaster had not taken a break. News articles were being churned out in massive numbers. Time for the red pen again . . .

> Exhaustive search for remaining bodies
> Uenomura residents prepare to assist
> NTT communications sets up 340 temporary phones for relatives
> Two reporters in critical condition from fatigue, dehydration
> Ministry of Transport orders all four airline companies to inspect
> tail assembly
> U.S. investigation team arrives at Mount Osutaka

He could still feel the burning behind his eyelids.

Hugging the bundle of newspapers to her chest, the woman had pulled her little boy along by the hand and climbed back into the hearse. It would be a long time before Yuuki would be able to forget the image of that mother. As she'd accompanied the remains of her husband's body back to her hometown, she'd stopped off at the *North Kanto Times* to buy some copies of a local newspaper. Because the accident had happened on their turf, she'd been convinced that they would have the best coverage. Naturally, they must have . . .

*Naturally* . . .

She'd taught him something. Detailed, informative articles. Beyond any doubt, that was why local newspapers existed.

He felt a tap on his shoulder and turned to see the back of Kamejima's head as he hurried away, a spring in his step. Yuuki chuckled, then remembered something. He looked up at the clock—half past six.

His mood, which had been somewhat softened, now became tense again. The feature article series—he still hadn't received the manuscript from Wajima. He'd told him to have it done by five. He'd paged him several times, but there'd been no response. Maybe Wajima wasn't going to write it. But if he didn't, he'd be fired.

He got back to his reading.

Gunma police question assistant cabin crew manager

Nodai Niko baseball nine pledge to win second round for teammate

3:30 p.m.: rain forces halt of recovery operation

Third regional coast guard HQ delivers Sagami Bay tailpiece to Gunma police

He skim-read all the articles, then turned to the man on his right.

"Kishi?"

"Huh?"

Kishi's pen kept moving, but he was listening. Aoki's commentary piece on the Yasukuni visit was already covered in red ink. Yuuki spoke more sharply to distract him from his work.

"Is there any space in international news?"

"Why?"

Now he had Kishi's full attention. He picked up several of the articles.

"These articles are about the U.S. investigation team and Boeing. Could you fit them in?"

"Shouldn't they be on the front page?"

"I want to make the front all about the bereaved families. If you've got space, I'd like to use it."

"Just a sec."

Kishi glanced over the papers on his desk. He was normally in charge of the front page but, ever since the crash, Kishi had been handling both the national and international political pages.

"Hmm. I think I could fit in two or three, if they're short."

"Please. And this one? It's about the Ministry of Transport. Can you put it on the national page?"

"Huh?"

Kishi looked amazed.

"Why do you want to scatter them all over the place? Put them all together on the local news pages."

"Unless we increase the number of pages, I can't fit everything in," said Yuuki, sorting through his papers. "Every day I have to discard at least a third of what I have."

Kishi gave a wry smile.

"Yuuki, you can't use everything. We have enough articles here to open a shop. We can only fit so many columns on a page."

"I'm not trying to use everything. Just as many as I can."

"But the other pages have their own agenda."

Kishi sounded as if he were complaining, so Yuuki threw him a stern glance.

"I'm just saying you'd better give it your best," Kishi continued.

"What the hell?"

"The *Asahi* and the *Yomiuri* are putting out huge, flamboyant spreads. And here we are, putting odds and ends here and there."

"Really? I thought we were holding our own pretty well."

He didn't really know the truth of the situation. Every paper was scrambling for information, and it was impossible to grasp who was ahead in terms of volume of information, or how substantial the content of that information was. The scale of the accident was just too big. Three whole days after the plane came down, the continuing, very real problem was how to deal with the enormous wave of information that poured from Mount Osutaka like a tsunami. The *North Kanto Times*'s staff had no time to analyze the pages of the other publications, to sort through the mixture of the brilliant and the mediocre and scrutinize it piece by piece.

However, the one thing that Yuuki did know was that they were not winning the fight. The national newspapers had any number of reporters permanently stationed at their local branch offices. In a local turf war, the regional papers could capitalize on their geographical advantage by using human wave tactics to overwhelm them. However, when it came to the journalism related to the JAL crash, there was no guarantee that the *North Kanto Times* would be able to dominate by numbers. If you added the number of journalists from Kyodo News Service to those from the *North Kanto Times*, the total was impressive, but this massive, unprecedented accident had set off less of a local battle and more of a full-scale war. The national newspapers had gone all out and sent in troops not only from Tokyo but from all other prefectures throughout Japan. And it wasn't only personnel they'd sent. They'd provided backup in the form of helicopters, communications equipment—everything the modern reporter needed. It may have made it look like war, but it was obvious that, if it turned out to be a long, attritional struggle, the *North Kanto Times*, with its lack of resources, equipment, and personnel, was eventually going to be defeated.

"We're not going to give up without a fight," said Yuuki, jumping to his feet and dumping a pile of papers on Kishi's desk. He called out across the room in the direction of the regional news desk.

"Yamada?"

Yamada raised his head to respond, his untidy hair shaking with the movement.

"Yes?"

"Could you get this onto your regional news pages?"

Yamada came running over.

"What do you need?"

"A story from Uenomura. Can you put it in the northwest section?"

When Yamada saw the running title of the story that Yuuki gave him, he became agitated.

"But, Yuuki-san, this is an article to do with the JAL crash."

"It doesn't matter. It's about how the village office and the local fire department are playing an active role in things."

Yamada scratched his disheveled scalp. The regional section was divided into five different areas and was a compilation of neighborhood events and soft stories such as A RARE FLOWER HAS BEEN DISCOVERED.

"I'm so sorry. The northwest region is already finished."

"Has it gone to press?"

"No. It hasn't gone down yet."

"Then you can redo it."

"Come on, Yuuki!" Kishi pitched in. "If you're going to make him change it, you'd better at least run it by the bosses."

"Yeah, yeah. I'll talk to them tomorrow," he said dismissively.

Yuuki checked the clock once more. Picking up the phone, he dialed Wajima's pager number again, then got to his feet.

"If Wajima calls back, come and get me," he said to Kishi, and walked over to the copy team's island. He handed a pile of papers to Yoshii, who was in charge of the front page.

"You did it, Yuuki-san. This was the way to go."

Yoshii was in an excellent mood, thanks to the JAL crash retaining the headline position. He had the proofs of the page spread out on his desk. He'd drawn the rough layout with a pencil and written some possible headlines at the top. Scraps of paper with ideas scribbled on were scattered about: "ID-ing the dead rough going"; "Sorrow of the silent homecoming"; "The flight path of the crash—toward an explanation"; "Body recovery continues night and day"; "Relentless rain on Mount Osutaka."

"Have you decided on the headline?" Yuuki asked.

Yoshii tapped his forehead with a ruler.

"Give me fifteen minutes. I can't quite find the right phrase."

"No hurry," said Yuuki affably. But then he leaned in to whisper in Yoshii's ear.

"I can't say anything for sure, but there might be a late scoop coming in."

"About . . . ?"

Yuuki could see Tamaki's face and the word "bulkhead."

"The cause of the crash."

Yoshii went pale.

"In that case, the whole page will have to be redone."

"It's a long shot. It's probably not going to happen, but just keep it in mind."

"Got it."

"And don't tell a soul."

"Understood."

On his way back to his desk, Yuuki's eyes met those of Inaoka, who was in charge of the *North Kanto Times*'s letters-to-the-editor page, titled Heartfelt. He'd been writing for the arts and culture pages for many years and was due to retire next year. Inaoka called him over.

"Wow, Yuuki. You've got a tough job there."

"Not really."

"We're getting heaps of letters about the crash."

Yuuki was reeled in by Inaoka's words: How about using readers' contributions as part of his feature series?

"What kind of letter's the most common?"

"There are all sorts."

Inaoka flipped through a pile of letters and postcards.

"First, you've got the people who were impressed that four people survived. Next, the ones who talk about the importance of improving air safety. And then the words of encouragement to the police and fire rescue teams. But the biggest group are the ones sending condolences to the families. Mostly from our regular readers."

Regular contributors to the column writing condolence letters to the bereaved relatives? Yuuki felt gloomy just thinking about it. He didn't mean that there was anything wrong with the contributors. These people were the newspaper's most fervent and reliable supporters, but there was also a malicious element among them. This particular group was the kind who only put pen to paper to express their outrage about something or other—in other words, they were the ones who were out to cause trouble. They were always on the lookout for a good topic to moan about. They borrowed freely from others' opinions and writing styles and categorized every event under the heading of "Love" or "Justice." The Japan Airlines crash was perfect fodder for them. The death of five hundred and twenty people and the misery of thousands more bereaved relatives and friends. They were bound to seize the opportunity to demonstrate their boundless goodwill by strenuously wielding their pens.

No. He had seen that woman's tears with his own eyes and vowed to write detailed, informative articles. These readers who want to be seen as "good people"—perhaps they were not so different from Yuuki himself.

"Inaoka-san?" Yuuki asked, putting both his hands on the desk. "Could you put together a special feature on the JAL crash using letters from only nonregular contributors?"

"No regular contributors? Yes, I suppose . . . I might just have enough."

"Are there any contributors who have written in for the first time ever?"

"Yes, of course. Mostly housewives and high school kids. I got one from a junior high school girl, too."

"Could you put those together, please?"

"Hmm . . . not one single regular contributor?" Inaoka smiled at Yuuki a little helplessly. "You see, they'll kick up such a fuss later—it'll be, *You put together a special feature and didn't include me!*"

He'd heard this before. Some of these contributors even had a contest going to see who could get the most letters published. To every writer whose letter was chosen, the *North Kanto Times* would send a pen with the newspaper's logo. The pens were a status symbol conferring rank. There were many who adorned their breast pockets with a whole line of these pens when they had one of their get-togethers to boast about their achievements . . .

"Just ignore them, then."

Yuuki had meant to say this in a normal tone of voice, but for a split second Inaoka looked terrified. He must have sensed the arrogance about the local news section in Yuuki's attitude. Yuuki had heard that, back in the day, Inaoka had campaigned to expand the paper's arts and culture section but had been completely shut down by his local news colleagues.

*Arts and culture isn't real reporting. Try eyeballing a dead body once in a while!*

"Got it. Got it. I'll focus on the new names," Inaoka said, rearranging his facial expression. "Today's column has already gone to press, but I'll put something together for tomorrow."

"Thank you. I appreciate it."

Yuuki made a point of bowing extra respectfully.

His eye fell on an unopened envelope. The address was written in the unsophisticated, looping handwriting of a young girl. She'd addressed it "To Mr. Heartfelt."

What were her thoughts? What had she written?

He pictured it as a love letter to the *North Kanto Times*, and it was as if Yuuki had been wafted back to his desk on a gentle breeze.

The evening food delivery was arriving at the newsroom. Yuuki, on his way back from the men's room, was intercepted by a member of the copy team named Jinbo. Today Jinbo was in charge of the second local news page. He'd been running, and the proofs he held in his hand were fluttering.

"Yuuki-san, please get it to me quickly."

He was talking about part two of the feature series. On the right side of the page there was a blank space reserved for Wajima's article. The two walked back together to the newsroom.

"I think it'll be here. Just wait a bit."

"What? The draft? You mean you don't even have it yet?"

Jinbo followed Yuuki right to his desk. His face was flushed.

"But it's already ten past seven."

"What's the deadline today?"

"We'll have to send it down at eight thirty at the latest."

"Eight thirty? Why so early?"

"It's going to be crazy after that. They're still in there discussing the special news page, so we've got to get the rest of them sorted out early."

"I see. I'll get on to it."

"Seriously, please hurry. The layout team will get mad at me."

Yuuki saw that Jinbo was genuinely worried. He was around twenty-five or -six years old. Until last year, he'd been a reporter at the branch office in Tatebayashi City. At this company, to be assigned to the copy team while still very young meant that you were either considered by management to have shown you were an excellent all-around reporter and you'd been favored, or you'd been sent out from headquarters to work in the field but been sent back again, branded a failed reporter.

Jinbo fell into the latter category. Yuuki hadn't heard the reason, but he knew that several people in management had expressed sentiments along the lines of, "We won't be sending him on any more assignments until hell freezes over."

This would be his last try. Praying that this time he'd respond, Yuuki paged Wajima. Failed reporter . . . Jinbo's flushed face began to merge in Yuuki's head with Wajima's listless one.

Yuuki practically inhaled his fried rice. Both the rice and the accompanying sauce had gone completely cold.

He suddenly wondered—had Rintaro eaten this evening? He cleared up his bowl and chopsticks and made a call to Anzai's home number. He let it ring awhile, but no one answered. Yuuki felt relieved. The boy was probably at the hospital. At least he wasn't home alone.

His phone rang the moment he hung up. He guessed it would be Wajima, or, if not, Tamaki with an update on the bulkhead situation.

"This is Yuuki," he said.

"Hello. Tamaki here."

"What's up? Did you get confirmation?"

"No, that's what I'm calling about. The investigation team members have all gone back to Tokyo."

"Gone back?"

"Yes. Because it started raining this afternoon."

"So . . ."

Someone was going to have to chase them up in Tokyo. That was Yuuki's first thought, but he rejected it. The *North Kanto Times* had no staff at the Ministry of Transport, so all the national papers would be suspicious if they suddenly tried to make a move up there. Yuuki took a quiet breath.

"Will they be back tomorrow?"

"Yes, they're coming. They're going to carry out a joint investigation with the Americans."

"Then we'll have to go on the attack tomorrow evening."

"I suppose so. Well, I'll give it a try."

Tamaki had never been on the police beat, so he had no experience of working the night shift. His replies didn't inspire the greatest confidence, but next the conversation turned to the cause of the crash and his words became much more fluid.

"I'm pretty sure now that it was the bulkhead. They say the exact same aircraft had a tail-strike accident seven years ago at Osaka Airport, right? It looks like they didn't fix it properly afterward. At that time, it wasn't only the fuselage but the bulkhead, too, that was damaged and had to be repaired. I reckon the repairs were inadequate. It's likely that metal fatigue set in, the bulkhead was unable to withstand the high pressure from the interior of the plane and was blown off. And with that kind of force, almost certainly the tail would have been demolished in an instant."

Yuuki listened in silence. *Pretty sure; I reckon; it's likely that; almost certainly*—this man spoke in vague, elusive terms. Not a single straight yes or no. He recalled Yamada's evaluation of Tamaki. *"Not great, not terrible, either, I suppose."* Yuuki was now starting to have pretty strong doubts of his own.

"I read about the tail-strike incident in the Kyodo press. I remember it was written that the underside of the fuselage had to be repaired. But the article never mentioned the bulkhead."

"That was probably because the journalist who wrote that piece didn't know about the bulkhead. If he didn't ask any specific questions about it, then neither JAL nor the Ministry of Transport would have been able to tell him anything."

He had a point, Yuuki thought. It wasn't as if he had blind faith in the Kyodo News reporters. Every media company was the same—they had sharp, incisive reporters as well as ones who were completely unfocused. Still, to say the reporter didn't know about the bulkhead—again, that was pure conjecture on the part of Tamaki. If it was fine to fill in the gaps in knowledge with guesswork, then there would be nothing for investigative reporters to do. They wouldn't be needed in the first place. Yuuki knew immediately that he'd better send someone as backup for Tamaki.

He put down the phone and stood up.

"Yoshii!"

Yoshii's boyish face appeared over the copy team's island of desks. Yuuki made an X sign with his arms, indicating that the scoop was off, and

Yoshii raised his ruler to confirm he'd gotten the message. Beyond Yoshii, at a desk by the wall, Todoroki looked puzzled. Clearly, he'd caught the exchange but without understanding it. Yuuki sat back down and folded his arms.

Backup for Tamaki? There wasn't any question who it should be. He had to send Sayama. When it came to digging up a story, he was the absolute best the *North Kanto Times* had. Tomorrow he would have Sayama and Tamaki latch on to the investigation team, have them throw out the topic of the bulkhead and see if they could get a bite.

He felt surprisingly little excitement. The *North Kanto Times* was on the brink of landing a worldwide scoop. But Tamaki's information was built on a very brittle foundation of truth. Yuuki's biggest concern was not the scoop itself but rather how Sayama would react to being asked to help.

Someone shouted over from the copy team's island.

"Yuuki-san! Has it still not arrived?"

Jinbo was holding up the proofs of the second local news page, that flushed expression back on his face. Yuuki checked the clock. A quarter to eight. They'd reached the deadline. Giving up on paging Wajima, Yuuki called the prefectural police press club directly.

Sayama picked up.

"Yuuki here. Is Wajima there?"

"He's out."

"Where's he gone?"

"He didn't tell me, but I think he might be writing his article over at the parliamentary press club."

"Are you sure he's really writing it?"

There was no reply. Someone at the other end was making an announcement. A man's name and address were repeated two times. Someone from police public relations must have been giving a press conference. It sounded as if one more body had been identified.

Yuuki asked again.

"Is Wajima writing that article?"

"I think so . . ."

It sounded as if Sayama was tiptoeing around, or avoiding, something. As if he was talking not to Yuuki but to someone completely different . . .

Wajima was right there next to Sayama. Yuuki was sure of it. He cupped his hand over the mouthpiece.

"If he doesn't write it, he's finished."

. . .

"Sayama! What's going on?"

Through the earpiece, he could make out Sayama's rough breathing.

"You can only focus on the scene when you're there, *at* the scene. We don't need people who aren't there on the ground, such as yourself, telling us what's what."

Sayama was going to take it upon himself to convince Wajima. That was how Yuuki interpreted this.

"Okay, then. Tell him I need it by ten past eight. A fax will be fine."

"If I find him, I'll let him know."

"Make sure you do."

Yuuki replaced the receiver. He'd decided to leave the other matter till later. If he'd brought it up now, Sayama wouldn't have had time to get on Wajima's case.

But what if he hadn't even started writing it yet? It'd be too late. Yuuki began to riffle through the articles on his desk. He picked out several that were about the right length to fit in the empty frame on page two. A sigh escaped him, but he didn't really have any particular feelings about Wajima, to whom he had barely ever spoken.

This time, Yuuki turned to his left, to his grudge-bearing neighbor.

"Hey, Nozawa?"

"What?" Nozawa replied languidly. He was leaning back in his chair, reading the sports section of a national paper.

"You know Wajima? Is he really bad?"

Nozawa screwed up his face in disgust.

"He's completely useless, that one. Hanazawa may be younger, but he's way better."

"Because Hanazawa made it up to the crash site?"

"That's not even the half of it. Wajima's a complete wet blanket."

Yuuki couldn't see Nozawa's face behind his sports article as he doled out the abuse. He lowered his voice.

"Does he have any special talents?"

"He's got a teacher's license."

"Really?"

"He's one of my team. Don't worry about him."

"I'm not worried."

On that note, Yuuki put an end to the conversation. On his other side, Kishi, who'd been trying to listen in to the conversation, showed no reaction.

Yuuki looked over at the fax machine in the corner. Eight o'clock came and went . . . three minutes past . . . five minutes . . . ten minutes.

He waited until a quarter past before getting to his feet. Beside him, Kishi let out a deep breath. But then the light on the fax machine began to flash.

"Wow, he made it just in time," said Kishi, unable to hide his excitement. As Yuuki had guessed, he, too, had been totally caught up in the drama.

Nozawa still had his nose firmly in the sports section, but Yuuki could tell he was only pretending to read. From the angle of his body, he might have been watching the fax machine the whole time.

The machine spat out its paper. Jinbo came running over, a huge smile on his red face.

The handwriting was Wajima's. Yuuki picked up the first few pages that came through and took them back to his desk.

The article was about the retrieval of the bodies. It was a mediocre piece of work. But because he'd done it, there was still a shred of hope for Wajima's existence as a reporter.

Yuuki must have been utterly absorbed by the article, because he seemed to be the last person at his island to react to the voice behind him.

"I'm sorry I'm late."

It was Hanazawa standing there, looking like a university student in his casual T-shirt. His gleaming eyes and the awkward, prickly vibe he was giving off hadn't changed since he'd returned from Mount Osutaka.

Yuuki spun his chair around. Hanazawa was holding a sheaf of papers.

"What's the article?"

"It's for the series, of course."

"I'll use it tomorrow. Leave it with me," said Yuuki, businesslike, spinning his chair back around.

"Tomorrow?" Hanazawa's voice was near-hysterical. "Why aren't you using it today?"

Yuuki turned his chair around again to look at Hanazawa.

"Today we're using Wajima's piece. I'm just looking over it now."

Hanazawa narrowed his eyes and said something under his breath. It sounded a lot like, "That idiot."

Yuuki started to get angry.

"If you've got something to say, just say it!"

"Wajima never even made it up that mountain!"

"He climbed it yesterday."

Hanazawa laughed scornfully.

"That doesn't count! It had to be the first day."

*The first day.* That turn of phrase bugged Yuuki. Some reporters, including Hanazawa, had made it up Mount Osutaka on the day after the crash. That was what Hanazawa called the first day. It was as if this had given him special rights and he was going to insist on them.

Yuuki lowered his voice.

"It doesn't matter if it was the first day, the second day, or whenever—he still climbed the mountain."

"It's not the same thing! It was only a true accident scene that first day. After the police and the Self-Defense Forces arrived, by that second day so many of the bodies had been cleared up. Yuuki-san, you can't possibly understand. You just sat around in this cool, comfortable room. You never climbed that blazing-hot mountain."

"Hanazawa!" shouted Nozawa, but Yuuki motioned him to be quiet. Technically, Nozawa was Hanazawa's boss, but this was Yuuki's fight.

Hanazawa was looking defiantly at Yuuki. His attitude was one of total insolence. It was remarkable how a timid-looking twenty-six-year-old reporter with only three years' experience could have undergone such a transformation, merely by climbing a mountain and visiting the site of an accident.

"Hand it over."

"Huh?"

"If it's good enough, I'll put it in today."

"Yuuki-san!"

This shriek was from Jinbo. Wajima's article was still only halfway proofread. Yuuki's next words were for him.

"I'll read it right now."

With that, he grabbed Hanazawa's copy and turned back to his desk. Without picking up his red pen, he began to read. Three pages . . . five pages . . . seven pages. His hand stopped turning the pages. His eye stopped reading. He was transfixed by one particular word.

He reached over, grabbed Wajima's article by the corner, and handed it to Jinbo.

"I'll check over the rest of it at the galley stage. Can you set it first?"

"That's not fair!" yelled Hanazawa. "You'd already decided what you'd go with. You're a cheat!"

Yuuki snatched up the copy in one hand and then grabbed the neck of Hanazawa's T-shirt with the other.

"Come with me."

Hanazawa panicked.

"Wh-where are you taking me?"

"I'm borrowing him," Yuuki announced to Nozawa, and he dragged Hanazawa toward the door and down the corridor to the break area, where he sat him down on the farthest sofa.

"What the hell's your problem?" said Hanazawa, readjusting his T-shirt.

Yuuki, who'd made sure he'd seated himself at a distance from the other man, leaned toward him.

"Wajima's your senior, right?"

"What the . . . ? I never expected to hear that kind of thing out of the mouth of Yuuki, the police beat specialist. Is there such a thing as juniors and seniors in the reporting world? It's a matter of being the best at getting a story, period."

Pretty arrogant for a reporter who'd spent a mere three years on the police beat, Yuuki thought.

"Okay, I've got a question for you. What kind of story do you think you've got here?"

"What do you mean?"

"You climbed a mountain. That's it. There's no proper story here. Do you plan to keep bragging forever that you were the one who climbed Mount Osutaka?"

"Bragging? Are you kidding? God, that sums you guys up, doesn't it? You're still living off the Okubo/Red Army thing."

Yuuki felt a sharp ache in his temples.

"When did I ever talk to you about Okubo or the Red Army?"

Hanazawa looked away.

"They're always talking about it—Nozawa and the rest. How, at the end, you all went up to that lodge on Mount Asama? You were all just observers, right? Slurping your instant noodles?"

"That's true."

"What I saw was nothing like that. That was a real honest-to-God accident scene."

"So that's why."

"Why what?"

"Why you wrote an article like this."

"Like what?"

Yuuki flicked through Hanazawa's article. There it was, on page seven. He pointed to a word—"entrails." Then he looked Hanazawa straight in the eye.

"Put yourself in the readers' place—how do you think they're going to feel when they read about the corpses' entrails? What they looked like, what state they were in."

Hanazawa didn't flinch.

"Yeah. I gave that a lot of thought. Their relatives won't be reading this. Nearly everyone on that plane was from another prefecture."

"What if they did read it?"

"They won't. Anyway, I'm sure they're too busy to read newspapers right now."

"Okay, and what about the regular readers, then?" Yuuki demanded, his hand curling into a fist. "Here at the office we check over the news late at night, but remember, most people read the paper in the morning, over breakfast."

"That's too bad. I was just writing what really happened."

"You—"

"Okay, that's enough. First of all, you don't have any right to lecture me. Second of all, that article that Sayama and I risked our lives to send—you bumped it down to the second page. And now that great plan you told us about has been sidelined into something completely insignificant. Do you have some sort of grudge against us or something?"

"No."

"So, then, please tell me why it's ended up like that."

"You'll get it when you've been at this company another ten years."

"Another ten years? Are you fucking kidding me? I can see what you're doing. You're jealous. Because only Sayama and I were able to climb that mountain. That's what it comes down to. I've had incredible, terrible experiences. It doesn't matter how much you all go on acting so self-important—that just won't do anymore. Five hundred and twenty people—five hundred and twenty!"

Hanazawa seemed unable to stop himself. That peculiar gleam was in his eyes again.

"Wajima's account is fake. What I described—that's the true accident scene. The corpses, the entrails, shouldn't we write about everything? Isn't it a newspaper's mission to make sure this never happens again? If we don't paint a true picture of the full fucking misery, then what's the point? If you say you won't publish my article, I'll take it somewhere else. I can't do this anymore. It was horrendous. There were corpses everywhere. Literally as far as the eye could see. There was not one decent, normal thing about it. Scattered all over—"

His voice was cut off by Yuuki's hands around his throat. Yuuki pushed until Hanazawa's head touched the wall behind him. Even then the man was still trying to speak.

"Just remember this," Yuuki said through clenched teeth. "Those five hundred and twenty people didn't lose their lives for you to get off on it."

Hanazawa stared back at Yuuki with bloodshot eyes. Then, suddenly, those eyes began to pour tears; big, fat tears that wouldn't stop coming. Yuuki shuddered. It was just like that mother—the one who had brought her young son to the office with her to buy copies of the newspaper. She had cried just the same way.

He let go of Hanazawa's throat. The young reporter continued to sob. It was as if he had no idea why he was crying. As if there was nothing else he could do but hang his head and weep. Something inside had connected, and something else had begun to dissolve.

Yuuki stayed where he was on the sofa.

*"It was only a true accident scene that first day."* That was the reality of it. And Hanazawa had seen it—the true accident scene of the crash of a Japan Airlines jumbo jet that had caused the deaths of five hundred and twenty people.

## 2 2

Midnight had passed. It was now August 16.

There were very few people left in the newsroom; it was even quiet enough to be able to hear the TV.

The *North Kanto Times* had put together their fourth morning edition since the crash. Any moment now the rotary press was about to roar into action.

Yuuki was going through the remaining wires on his desk. He picked up Kamejima's cheery tones as he arrived back from the printing room.

"The JAL crash has made the top story four days in a row. It's a new record."

"Care for a quick one?" said Kishi, miming sipping from a sake cup.

"Yeah, let's go," Yuuki replied, without hesitating. He'd been weighing whether to go home or not, and now Kishi's suggestion had tipped the scales in favor of the latter.

He'd done a respectable job with his pages. The thought put him in good spirits. Until last night, he'd been overwhelmed, trying to find his bearings. He'd been swallowed up by this huge accident that had come out of nowhere, and he'd been out of his depth. He'd begun to feel how insignificant he was and had lost sight of why he was even in the business of making newspapers.

Today had been different. Ever since he'd met that mother and child, things had changed inside him. Here and there throughout the paper were signs of Yuuki's hand, his opinion. He wasn't vain enough to think that he had managed to tame the story of the accident completely, but he'd gotten just a fingertip on the reins. He was feeling a modest amount of self-confidence and a definite sense of accomplishment.

"Yuuki, you ready to leave now?"

"Sure."

The two men descended the semi-lit staircase.

"By the way, what happened to Hanazawa?" Kishi asked.

"He went to the on-call room. I think he's been asleep there."

"Did he talk to you about it?"

"Yes. Well, bits and pieces."

"Is he going to be all right?"

"I think so."

"I heard he hasn't eaten anything for two days."

"Seems not."

"So the crash site was that bad . . ."

"I guess so."

As Yuuki carefully made his way in the dark, he thought about Hanazawa. Mount Osutaka was the first time in his life that he'd ever seen a dead body. He'd finally confessed as much to Yuuki in the on-call room, once he'd calmed down. He'd spoken haltingly, his face expressionless, about how he'd never had any previous encounters with death. His parents and grandparents were all in good health. He'd been three years on the police beat and had seen his fair share of accident and crime scenes, but for some reason he'd never crossed paths with any dead bodies. He'd always wanted to see one, he admitted. What kind of a police reporter didn't? He'd felt that, without having seen one, he was a poor role model for younger reporters. They say you should be careful what you wish for. Mount Osutaka had fulfilled his wishes in a way he had never imagined . . .

Outside, the heat wrapped itself around Yuuki's face.

"Ugh! Even at this time of night!" said Kishi.

The two men automatically crossed the Annaka prefectural route and headed toward a little *yakiniku* barbecued-beef restaurant on the opposite corner. Sojahanten was run by a South Korean couple who had lived in Japan all their lives. If you were going drinking in this neighborhood at this time of night, this was the first place you'd think of.

"Yuuki-san, you're quite the samurai, I hear," said the master, his eyes crinkling when he saw them come in. He must have overheard that Yuuki had been made the JAL crash desk chief. He seemed impressed that Yuuki had found the time, in the midst of everything, to come out for a drink.

Yuuki didn't respond to the remark. Over to his right, he'd just spotted Todoroki sitting in the Japanese-style tatami room. He was sitting on a *zabuton* floor cushion across from Nozawa, sharing a beer.

This irritated Yuuki immensely. Just yesterday, he and the chief local news editor had had a very public altercation in the middle of the newsroom. Kishi must have heard it and, without letting on, he had brought Yuuki here. Typical Kishi—he was attempting to bring about a reconciliation.

"Let's sit down."

Kishi was all innocence as he led Yuuki to the tatami room.

"What kind of shit are you pulling here?" said Yuuki through gritted teeth. He felt like leaving right there and then. But that would be the coward's way out.

Todoroki looked just as surprised to see Yuuki, but Nozawa appeared to be in on the plan. Kishi had probably asked him to bring the section chief here. He was clearly an accomplice, but Yuuki knew Nozawa too well. He was sure he had no intention of encouraging him to shake hands with Todoroki. Nozawa was much more likely to hope that their relationship would sour even further, fueled by a generous dose of alcohol.

"A bottle?" the master called out from behind the counter.

"Make it a mug," Yuuki replied. He had no intention of staying any longer than necessary.

The atmosphere in the room was just as Nozawa must have hoped. Wordlessly, Yuuki plopped down on the *zabuton* diagonally opposite, or as far away as he could get from, Todoroki.

In the past, this group would often drink together after work. Back when Todoroki was deputy lead reporter at the police press club, Yuuki, Kishi, and Nozawa had all still been rookie reporters. They were yelled at daily by Todoroki and his boss, the then–lead police beat reporter, Oimura.

The master brought Kishi and Yuuki mugs of beer.

"Do you want any barbecue?"

"Yes, please," said Kishi.

Todoroki looked at Kishi.

"This was a very good idea of yours."

"Sorry?"

Kishi smiled politely. He had no idea what Todoroki was talking about, but Todoroki looked back at him with a serious expression.

"With *zabuton*, at least he's already down on his knees ready to apologize."

Yuuki looked up sharply. Todoroki was looking away from him, his face rather flushed, but he couldn't be drunk. He and Nozawa had been here since about ten—in other words, they'd already been drinking for a couple of hours—but Todoroki had always been able to hold his liquor.

Yuuki had had no intention of saying anything, but now that Todoroki had insisted on dragging up the whole thing again, he decided to stand his ground.

"I've nothing to apologize for," he said brusquely.

Todoroki removed his gold-rimmed spectacles.

"Oh, yes, you have. Your abusive language yesterday."

"Okay, everyone, cheers!" said Kishi, trying to be upbeat as he raised his mug of beer. But Todoroki ignored him.

"Yuuki, what was it you said to me? Do you remember?"

"More or less."

The two glared at each other across the table. Oblivious, the master arrived and began arranging marinated meat on the hot griddle.

"There's no more or less about it," said Todoroki from behind the cloud of smoke rising from the griddle. He sounded perfectly calm. "Managing editor Oimura dropped your Mount Osutaka article from the front page. You thought I'd done it and you laid into me. You insulted me and used offensive language in front of a group of junior reporters. That's pretty much an accurate summary of what happened, wouldn't you say?"

Yuuki's gaze dropped to the meat browning on the grill.

"So why aren't you apologizing? You're the guilty party."

"Hey, Yuuki?" Kishi interrupted. "It's true—you did jump to conclusions there."

"Shut up!"

Todoroki scowled at Kishi, then turned his attention straight back to Yuuki.

"'I've had enough of your pathetic games.' That's what you said yesterday. What did you mean by that?"

Yuuki raised his mug to his lips.

"Exactly what I said." He took a sip. "The day before, you dropped Sayama's eyewitness article. You were jealous because of the world's biggest airline disaster. It made you feel inferior."

"Why would I feel inferior?" asked Todoroki, as Nozawa poured him another mug of beer. How he must be enjoying this . . .

"Because Okubo/Red Army is everything to you."

"Of course it is."

"But the JAL crash is so big, it eclipses them completely."

Both men took a large gulp of beer. Todoroki was the first to put down his mug.

"So you're saying that's the reason I killed Sayama's article?"

"You didn't tell me that the rotary press was broken."

"I already told you, that was your misunderstanding."

"What exactly did I misunderstand?"

"Even if I'd told you about the broken printer earlier, how would that have changed things? At that time, Sayama and Hanazawa were still up the mountain. Our paper doesn't have any wireless phones. You wouldn't have had any way of telling them that we couldn't extend the deadline."

"True. I wouldn't." Yuuki drained his beer. "But you're not being logical."

"I'm sorry?"

"Let's think about it—say I'd been told that evening that the printer was broken. I could have begged Kyodo News to let me borrow their wireless system for a few seconds. I could have gotten them to contact their reporters up on Osutaka to give a message to Sayama and Hanazawa—*No extended deadline today*. If I could just have let Sayama know that, then he could have calculated how fast he could get down the mountain. He could have gotten me his report before midnight, and the next morning Sayama and

Hanazawa's names would have been in print on the front page of the *North Kanto Times.*"

"You think things would have gone that smoothly, do you? Kyodo might have refused to let you use their wireless. And, even if they'd agreed, there's no guarantee that the Kyodo reporters would have met up with Sayama and Hanazawa on Mount Osutaka. And then, say they had, hurrying down a mountain like that in the black of night? You had no way of knowing whether they'd make it by midnight. It'd have taken nothing short of a miracle for that article to have made it into the next day's edition."

"You've given yourself away."

Yuuki had meant to say it in his head, but somehow he had spoken the words aloud.

"What's that? What do you mean, given myself away?"

Yuuki had no intention of backing down.

"Nothing you just said made any sense. It's the same way you were thinking that night. You thought, if you didn't tell me about the broken printer, you'd be able to make up some kind of excuse later."

"That's enough!"

"You're right that it would have taken a miracle to get Sayama's article in the paper. But there was still a chance that miracle might have happened. And you—"

"I said, that's enough!"

"You started the fight. You'd better see it through to the end."

"Don't you dare yell at me, you—"

"You nipped that miracle in the bud. Because of all your Okubo/Red Army shit, you killed Sayama's article!"

"Yuuki!"

Todoroki slammed his fist down on the table and, in response, Yuuki squared his shoulders.

"Why did you get in their way? Was it so you weren't outdone by a couple of young reporters? Was it because for you all—I s'pose I mean for us—the Okubo/Red Army was a crushing defeat?"

Todoroki's eyes widened to twice their usual size. Kishi's, too. Nozawa turned around to stare. Then Todoroki tried to speak.

"We . . . we lost? Lost to who?"

Everyone knew Yuuki had crossed a line. No one had ever before dared to put "Okubo/Red Army" and "lost" together in the same sentence.

"Tell us, Yuuki. Who did we lose to?" Kishi looked as if he'd just seen a ghost.

"Isn't it obvious? All the national newspapers—the *Asahi, Mainichi, Yomiuri,* and even the *Sankei.*"

"But we beat them, didn't we . . . ?"

"That's just how you prefer to remember it."

"But we won! We destroyed them!"

Nozawa had joined the conversation. There was a blue vein visible at his temples.

"We may have, a few times. But we were beaten many times over."

"Surely it was the other way around?" said Kishi. "I guess we were beaten a few times, but still—"

"Have you really forgotten?"

Yuuki glanced back and forth between Kishi and Nozawa. He'd long assumed that the word "lost" was simply taboo. But he'd been mistaken. Both of these men genuinely believed that they'd "won."

"You two are talking about the early days of the Okubo case. I'll admit, back at the beginning, we were running circles around the rest. But as the case grew bigger, and the head offices of all those other papers started sending their reporters, everything was turned upside down. They were all writing amazing stories. But the Okubo case still went better than the Red Army one. In that one, we were totally extinguished. The National Police Agency in Tokyo released one story after another, and we were helpless. We were completely outplayed. North Kanto lost to Tokyo."

Total silence enveloped the room.

It was just as Hanazawa had said during his rant earlier that evening. In the final stages of the Red Army siege, the *North Kanto Times's* police beat reporters had been in high spirits as they'd entered the lodge on Mount Asama. But they'd ended up being forced to stay far away from the action— distant observers. The only thing they'd gotten out of the experience was an appreciation for the taste of cup noodles, the previous year's new culinary sensation. Hanazawa had seen through the whole thing.

Nozawa was the first to speak.

"It's true that there was nothing we could do at the lodge, but that case was Nagano Prefecture's. Of course we were outdone. Our hands were tied. But the executions at the hideouts on Mount Haruna and Myogi, we were the winners there."

"Kyodo News was. We did nothing. We just wandered aimlessly around the mountains. We didn't write any of the informative articles. It was hard on our bodies. We thought we were going to die of cold and exhaustion. That's how we deluded ourselves that we were fighting the Tokyo guys on equal terms—"

Yuuki quickly averted his eyes as a shower of beer came flying his way. Todoroki's expression was demonic. He parted his tightly pressed lips and the beer shower was followed by a torrent of abuse.

"It's all true, every word," Yuuki replied, calmly wiping his face with the sleeve of his shirt.

"I can't believe I'm hearing this! Anyone who despises the *NKT* so much ought to just leave. Get the hell out of our company!"

"Haven't they already?"

"What?"

"Takahashi-san, Nozaki-san, Tadara-san—they all left right after the Red Army case. They were all poached by the *Yomiuri* or the *Sankei*. They left the *NKT* because they knew we'd been completely outdone. They despaired at people like you, who kept on insisting, 'We won, we won.'"

Yuuki was seething.

"And we really need to take a thorough look at why it was we lost. We need to teach the young up-and-coming reporters how to avoid losing again in the future. Instead of droning on and on for over ten years about how great we were, we could have put that time and energy into having proper meetings where we made a swift decision to start using wireless phones or something useful. Do you understand? Even now, the *North Kanto Times* has failed to move on in any way from the Okubo/Red Army era. Mark my words, we'll lose again this time on the JAL crash."

With a loud clatter, the empty beer bottles on the table in front of Todoroki toppled over into one another. Yuuki readied himself for the punch he knew was coming. But Todoroki didn't move. His body stayed there swaying, his eyes glinting as they bored into Yuuki's. Or rather, didn't connect with Yuuki's. Yuuki saw that the editor's pupils were unfocused.

Was he drunk? Surely not. Todoroki, drunk on this amount of beer? He must be getting weaker . . .

Yuuki had lost his enthusiasm for the fight. He looked away and drained his beer.

The meat on the hot plate had turned to charcoal. Kishi sat quietly, his arms folded. Even Nozawa looked meek. Yuuki moved on to spirits, ordering *shochu*, but it didn't matter how much he drank, he still felt clearheaded.

After a while, Todoroki got up and staggered over to sit by Yuuki. Without making eye contact, he poured a generous slug of *shochu* into Yuuki's glass. Half of it spilled onto the table.

"You know Tadara—the one who went to the *Yomiuri*? . . . Did you ever hear what became of him?"

Yuuki shook his head.

"He died. He was forced to tour the country nonstop. In the end, he was up in Hachinohe in the north and his body just couldn't take it anymore."

Todoroki paused to take a sip of *shochu*.

"They asked me, too—to leave *NKT*."

This was news to Yuuki.

"Who?"

Todoroki glanced over at Kishi and Nozawa. They were huddled together, deep in their own private conversation.

"Don't tell this to anyone."

"I won't."

For a brief moment Todoroki looked unusually pleased with himself.

"The *Asahi*."

"Why didn't you go?"

"I couldn't. Shirakawa had just made me take one of his damn dogs."

Todoroki spat out the words, and immediately laughed self-deprecatingly. Yuuki chuckled, too. Everyone at the company had heard the story of "The Emperor's Puppies." Chairman Shirakawa had been editor in chief at the time, and when his pet dog had a litter of five puppies, he had distributed them among his staff; to Kasuya, Oimura, Todoroki, as well as to the chief political editor at the time—Moriya. And also to the man who was to become general manager in Advertising, Kurasaka. Brilliant and capable reporters had been leaving the company one after the other. It must have caused Shirakawa quite a headache. Behind the gift of the puppies was the unspoken message, *You're my right-hand man.*

"It was so emotionally manipulative. Puppies are so cute. Even after the boss had a go at you at work, you'd go home and there'd be a little piece of him fawning all over you. It was a living creature . . . You couldn't just throw it away. Of course, they're all dead now, but for five to ten years the boss succeeded in managing his personnel perfectly through the medium of dogs!"

"It wasn't completely perfect. Didn't the managing director tempt Kurasaka-san away from the Editorial Department and set him up in Advertising?"

"That's not what happened. Kurasaka was kicked out."

"Kicked out?"

"He got too close to Fukuda. There was a rumor for a while that Kurasaka's older brother was going to run for the prefectural assembly and he was working behind the scenes to win Fukuda's support. That really incurred the imperial wrath."

Yuuki nodded sympathetically. It was a very predictable story, but it had really piqued his interest. After a few moments of silence, Todoroki continued.

"I feel as if we're living on dreams and illusions. I never wanted to do this kind of work."

Yuuki gave him a puzzled look, but he'd recognized it right away. Todoroki wanted to talk some more about the *Asahi* job.

"The whole country, the whole world, everything becomes bigger at a newspaper like that. All their reporters are doing exactly the same thing. Relentlessly investigating, listening to people's stories, that's it. Getting a story from a big name makes it big news. But that doesn't mean they've done a big job. It's exactly the same effort that it takes to get a story from a small name. What reporters do, everyone . . ."

Todoroki was starting to go around in circles. He was slurring his words, too. His eyes had a strange look about them.

Yuuki had just made his mind up to go back to the office and get some sleep when Todoroki suddenly grabbed his tie and pulled on it with surprising force.

"Are you listening to me?"

Todoroki's face was as pale as death.

"Remember this! The minute local newspaper reporters admit they've lost, it's all over. Doesn't matter how badly they were beaten, they never ever admit to it. Got it?"

With this final, honest confession, Todoroki slumped drunkenly onto the tatami floor. Yuuki looked down at his unconscious face. He recalled something his mother had taught him.

*Never trust a man who needs to get drunk before he can speak his mind. Those people are not living an authentic life.*

Long ago, Todoroki used to say something similar.

*If you drink, just laugh. If you get drunk, just sing. Tomorrow we can talk . . .*

Suddenly Yuuki realized he was drunk. It wasn't long ago—it was a mere ten years or so. He looked around the restaurant. Behind the counter, the master reminded him of an Egyptian mummy as he sat there dozing.

Back then, even the master was still young. His wife was still full of life and used to help out in the restaurant at night. They had an extremely attractive daughter by the name of Chan Hi. Kishi had been madly in love with her. It had been a matter of life and death for him. Nozawa had jumped up onto the counter and done impersonations of the singer Linda Yamamoto. The master's wife had yelled at him in Korean, but he used to seize any moment she wasn't looking, and did it over and over. Todoroki had jeered at him. Oimura had clapped. From time to time, Kasuya had turned up and thrown lots of money around. They'd all sung the "NKT song" together—a song that had originally been the fight song at some university. Arms around each other's shoulders, they'd belted it out at the top of their lungs.

Everyone laughed back then. Yuuki thought about how he used to laugh. He'd been happy. He felt as if he'd gained fathers and brothers and a home all in one go. This place had everything. It was the full package. It was filled with smiling faces and lively conversation . . .

Todoroki began to snore. Kishi and Nozawa were apparently still deep in conversation.

Yuuki got to his feet. *When did all of that disappear?*

He stumbled out into the street. Mixed in with the ringing in his ears, he could hear that song . . .

"*. . . we won't stop writing, we won't give up, until the day we die.*"

# 23

Yuuki was staring up at the ceiling, which was yellow-stained from years of cigarette smoke. Or perhaps not . . . it could have been his vision that was tinted.

He realized that he was lying on one of the newsroom sofas. He recalled collapsing on it the previous night—well, the sky had already started to lighten, so he must have been drinking until around four . . . or was it closer to five?

He'd been dreaming. About Anzai. He'd gone to visit him at the hospital, but the bed had been empty. There was graffiti on the wall: LIAR! In the dream, Yuuki had decided that the message was directed at him, because he'd broken their promise to climb Tsuitate. Anzai was missing from his bed because he'd set out by himself to Mount Tanigawa.

"Are you ready to get up?"

Chizuko Yorita's smiling face swam into focus above him. Her long hair hung down, almost brushing Yuuki's nose.

"Um . . . Yes. What time is it?"

"It's already ten. Do you want something to drink?"

"No, thanks."

"Some water?"

"No, I'm fine."

Yuuki waited for Chizuko to move away before sitting up. He noticed that there was a light cotton blanket over him. He had no memory of dropping by the night-shift room last night, so it must have been Chizuko who had put it there.

He turned to look across the room. Todoroki's desk was unoccupied. Not surprising. It was still early. In fact, the only people here right now in this great, sprawling room were Chizuko and himself, and staff from the cleaning company.

"How's Nodai doing?" Yuuki asked. The TV was on, but it was too far away for him to make out the score.

"They've got a huge lead," Chizuko replied cheerfully. She twirled her duster like a cheerleader's pom-pom.

The first game of the day in the Koshien baseball tournament was the second-round match for Nodai Niko High School: the local team whose player had lost his father on Flight 123.

"What about Hanazawa?"

Chizuko paused from wiping down the desktop.

"It looks like he's gone home. He wasn't in the on-call room."

"I see. Thanks."

As Yuuki pondered this, another question occurred to him.

"Yorita?"

"Yes?"

"Is it true you're being transferred in the autumn? You're going to one of the branch offices?"

"Oh, you heard?"

Chizuko suddenly looked radiant.

"Yes. The Maebashi office, isn't it?"

"Right. I'm so excited!"

"How old are you?"

"What . . . !"

"You might as well get used to it. They're going to be asking you the same thing over and over. After all, you are going to be the first-ever female reporter at the *North Kanto Times*."

"I'm not the first. There's Hirata-san in the arts and culture section."

"That's not reporting. More like hostessing," said Yuuki dismissively. "If you're going to be a reporter, then do it properly. They're only going to pamper you in the beginning. They'll get tired of it after a while."

The charming smile disappeared.

"Ri-right."

Yuuki got up from the sofa. He knew he reeked of sweat. The cold air from the air conditioner hadn't reached his part of the room yet.

"Yuuki-san?" Chizuko gave a quick bow. "Please tell me everything you can about the work."

"Sorry. I've got nothing."

Chizuko didn't even flinch. By now she was used to reporters being blunt. She followed Yuuki over to his desk.

"It'd be great if they put me on the police beat to start with, don't you think?"

"I suppose."

"But . . . er . . ."

Yuuki had begun to sort through the wires on his desk, but he stopped and turned to face her.

"But what?"

"Oh, never mind. It's nothing."

"Just tell me."

"Erm . . . it's just temporary, but I heard I get a week's training at the prefectural police press club."

"So?"

"What kind of person is the lead reporter there—Sayama-san?"

She was blushing. Sayama was approaching his mid-thirties, but still single.

"Surely you know Sayama?"

But Chizuko waved her hand to indicate that she didn't.

"The police reporters, they hardly ever come up here."

Yuuki looked into the distance. Sayama's remark from the previous day was playing in his head.

*"You can only focus on the scene when you're there,* at the scene. We don't need people who aren't there on the ground . . . telling us what's what."

If Yuuki had been in Sayama's place, he'd most likely have given up on Wajima. There was no point in dangling a rope for someone who had no intention of trying to climb up. People who truly wanted to ascend would do so somehow, even without a rope.

Chizuko was still waiting for an answer.

"Sayama is—"

Of all the adjectives that came to mind, Yuuki surprised even himself with the one he picked.

"—good-hearted."

Chizuko didn't look particularly pleased. This was the first time she'd ever heard Yuuki use terms other than "a good reporter" or "a bad reporter" to describe his junior colleagues.

"Excuse me, Yuuki-san?"

Yuuki turned to see the tanned face of Miyata from the Advertising Department just walking into the newsroom. Or Miyata from Anzai's hiking club, as Yuuki preferred to think of him.

"Er . . ."

It was Chizuko who spoke. Yuuki turned and gave her a hard stare. Miyata had obviously come up to speak to him, and here she was, still stuck to his side.

"Twenty-seven," she said abruptly. Her expression was deadly serious. "I'm twenty-seven years old. I'm not going to waste this opportunity. I don't care what happens—I'm going to work as hard as I can. Please give me advice. Please."

*"I've got nothing."* The same phrase rose up as far as his throat, but he swallowed it back down. He watched as Chizuko walked away, her back straight and proud.

Miyata now replaced Chizuko at his side. He had a worried look on his face.

"What's up?"

"Nothing much," he said, pulling up a chair. "I was out doing my rounds this morning and decided to drop in at the hospital to see Anzai."

Yuuki had guessed the conversation would be about Anzai, and he prepared himself for bad news. But that wasn't it. Miyata had something quite different to tell Yuuki.

It turned out that Miyata had run into another visitor at the hospital— an old climbing acquaintance of Anzai's by the name of Suetsugu. According to Suetsugu, Anzai's previous climbing partner had lost his life on the Tsuitate rock face, and since then Anzai had disappeared from his role at center stage of the climbing community.

"Did you know about that, Yuuki-san?"

"No . . ."

"But you and he were planning to climb Tsuitate."

"Right."

"Why the same mountain where he lost his partner . . . ?"

That was the burning question. Yuuki folded his arms in the hope of calming his racing heart.

"*I climb up to step down.*"

"Has this Suetsugu gone home?"

"I think he went to the library."

"Which library?"

"He asked me for directions to the prefectural one. Are you going to try to meet him? I think you'll probably make it—it was only about thirty minutes ago."

Yuuki stood up.

"What does he look like?"

"You'll recognize him right away. He's wearing really tiny shoes."

"Eh?"

"About the size of a primary school kid's."

Yuuki could guess the reason. He looked at Miyata, who nodded.

"Yeah, I'm pretty sure he must have lost all his toes to frostbite."

## 2 4

It was about a fifteen-minute drive from the *North Kanto Times* headquarters to the prefectural library. Yuuki drove carefully; he still had the sense that he was looking at everything through yellow lenses. In addition, he'd had a sharp pain around his temples ever since waking up.

He spotted Suetsugu even before getting out of his car. As he was parking, he saw a solidly built man entering the library. He couldn't actually see his shoes, but the man had a peculiar, jerky gait.

Yuuki hurried in through the main entrance and looked around. The man had just entered the building.

"Suetsugu-san?"

The man turned, and Yuuki took in a wide, friendly face, deeply suntanned. He looked to be in his mid-forties—just around the same age as Anzai.

Yuuki approached and offered his business card. He quickly explained who he was, dropping the names of Anzai and Miyata.

"I'm sorry, I don't have a business card."

Suetsugu laughed quite innocently, but with a touch of what sounded like pride.

Even if there were several varieties of rock climber, Yuuki would still have placed Suetsugu in the same "easygoing and openhearted" category as Anzai. His shoes were very small. They looked to be made-to-order, and from their appearance and Suetsugu's overall balance, it was fairly safe to assume that he didn't have any toes left at all.

Yuuki invited him to go to the café on the third floor, and Suetsugu agreed, but he wanted to look in on the first floor on the way. Apparently there was a memorial collection dedicated to Anzai's previous climbing companion somewhere in the local history section. Seeing as he had come all the way to Gunma Prefecture, he thought he would take a look at it.

"Actually, I had a copy, too, but it was lost in a fire about six months back," said Suetsugu. Even while describing such terrible misfortune, he didn't stop smiling.

They inquired at the desk, and a few minutes later the librarian brought them a thick A4-sized book entitled *Birds*. It was rather old and looked nothing like a regular book. There was no binding; the right edge was tied up with glossy green-colored string.

Suetsugu took an extremely long time to climb the stairs up to the third floor, so Yuuki had heard most of the story before they even arrived at the café. The accident had happened about thirteen years earlier. Anzai and his partner had tackled Tsuitate's Cloud Ridge by route number 1. Just before the overhang at its crux, Anzai, who was climbing in the lead, slipped and set off a rockfall. He yelled out, "Rock!" to alert his partner below, a man by the name of Mitsugu Endo, but Endo was unlucky. A large piece of rock hit him right in the forehead. Death was almost instantaneous. He was never able to say goodbye to his loved ones and died there and then in Anzai's arms.

Yuuki realized he had a vague memory of that climbing accident. He had just started at the *North Kanto Times* and, although he hadn't been directly involved in covering the story, he remembered reading a fairly detailed article on the death of a young climber. But he had never imagined that the man's climbing partner had been Anzai.

Yuuki bought two iced coffee tickets from the machine in the café.

"You know, I couldn't believe it when I heard the news. Endo was a superstar in the rock-climbing world. He was also tougher than anyone. Just the year before, he'd climbed Chomolungma. Or—"

"I know. Mount Everest."

"Yep, Endo became a Mount Everest summiter. In conditions well below freezing, and about a third of normal oxygen levels. What do you think he did the moment he reached the peak?"

"Er, no, I can't guess."

"According to the Sherpa who climbed with him, he didn't plant a flag or even take a commemorative photo."

"So, what did he do?"

"He looked at the sky."

"At the sky?"

"On a clear day in midwinter at the summit of Mount Everest, they say you can see a flock of cranes."

Suetsugu looked pensive.

"Endo was looking for those cranes. But because he didn't climb in the severest part of the winter, he never saw them. He was standing on the highest point of this earth and wanted to see the birds flying even higher above him. He wanted to climb even higher—like the birds. Maybe that was what he was thinking."

*Birds.* The title of the book suddenly made sense. Suetsugu went on.

"Anzai loved climbing just as much as Endo did. If it weren't for the accident, I'm sure he'd have been a summiter, too, within a couple of years."

Yuuki pondered Suetsugu's words. Anzai had been a hard-core rock climber after all . . .

"It really was just a very unfortunate accident. No mountain is ever completely safe but, from Anzai and Endo's point of view, Tsuitate was just for warming up. I suppose that's what makes it all the more dangerous. It robbed Endo of his life, and Anzai of the joy of mountain climbing."

Suetsugu picked up *Birds* and looked at the cover. He seemed to be struggling with his emotions.

"This string, it came from the rope that tied them together that day."

Yuuki's eyes were wide with amazement.

"Anzai unwound that rope and made this binding himself. Even now, my chest hurts thinking about how he must have felt as he was making it. He vowed never to bind himself to anyone and climb again. That was the decision he made that day."

Yuuki shivered. He hesitated awhile, deciding whether to put his thoughts into words. Eventually, he swallowed and leaned across the table.

"Actually—"

"Yes?"

"Anzai invited me. To climb Tsuitate with him."

"Did he, now?"

Suetsugu stared at Yuuki.

"So you're into climbing?"

"I'm a total amateur. I've just been playing around at ski resorts, really."

Suetsugu sat there for a while, lost in thought. Yuuki waited awhile, but it didn't seem as if he were going to speak. He leaned even farther across the table.

"May I ask you a question?"

"Yes, of course."

"*I climb up to step down.* Do you know what it means?"

Suetsugu shook his head.

"Is it a proverb or some kind of saying in the climbing community, perhaps?"

"I've never heard it before. Who said it? Anzai?"

"Yes."

Suetsugu thought awhile longer but finally just sighed. He seemed to have given up.

"It's been thirteen years since that accident. Perhaps, after all that pain and anguish, that was where Anzai was at mentally. I'm truly sorry, but I don't know what it means."

"I see."

Suetsugu had a reservation on the bullet train to get back to Hamamatsu, so Yuuki hurried to get in one last question.

"Is there really such a thing as 'climber's high'?"

"Yes, there is. It's quite a terrifying phenomenon."

"Terrifying?"

Yuuki was confused.

"It's where your mind gets taken over by excitement or stimulation, and you become immune to any sense of fear, right?"

"Yes, that's it."

"So you stop feeling afraid, right? So then, why is it that you say it's terrifying?"

"It's terrifying when it leaves you. If the feeling of climber's high starts to wear off, it's horrific. All that fear that you've stashed away has built up inside your mind, and it comes bursting out. If it wears off and you're half-way up a rock face, you just freeze. You can't take another step."

But now it was Yuuki who froze.

"*It's when the body gets overstimulated, reaches a level of extreme excitement. The fear makes them numb.*

"*. . . They climb in a mad frenzy and, before they know it, they're at the peak of Tsuitate. An incredible feat.*"

He wondered why Anzai hadn't told him the full story of climber's high. It must have been so as not to panic him, with his limited experience.

Yuuki was utterly flummoxed. In one short conversation, he had learned so much new information about Anzai that he found he couldn't picture his friend clearly anymore.

But there was still one thing he needed to know. What had driven Anzai to tackle Tsuitate one more time?

And why had he picked Yuuki as his climbing partner?

Yuuki gave Suetsugu a lift back to Maebashi Station, then drove straight to the prefectural hospital. He'd been thinking of visiting Anzai ever since dreaming about him that morning.

It had been a lively journey to the train station. Suetsugu had been glad to be saved the taxi fare. In Yuuki's car, he had regained his original, easygoing personality. He told funny stories about the early days of Anzai's relationship with Sayuri, his future wife, and how he had ended up working at the *North Kanto Times*. But he didn't talk about himself; not a word about which climbing club he belonged to, or what mountains he'd climbed. And there was no hint at whatever fateful climb had ended with him forever wearing those tiny shoes. Only when he got out of the car at the station did he suddenly turn serious.

"If Anzai wakes up, please call me."

Yuuki wondered if Suetsugu was the man who had taught Anzai and Endo to climb.

It was almost midday when Yuuki knocked on the door of Anzai's room.

"Come in!"

Sayuri sounded surprisingly perky. Wondering if there was some improvement in the situation, Yuuki entered the room. The first person he noticed was Rintaro, sitting at some distance from the bed on a folding chair. He was fiddling with a yellow rubber ball. To Yuuki's "Hey," he gave the typical half-hearted greeting of an adolescent boy. The reddening of his cheeks suggested that he was remembering with embarrassment how, two days previously, he had hugged Yuuki in the hospital lobby.

"I'm sorry you had to come all this way when you're busy," said Sayuri.

Yuuki recoiled ever so slightly at how cheerful Sayuri looked. But it wasn't just how cheery. Perhaps he was imagining it, but she almost looked more beautiful.

Yuuki walked over to the bed.

Anzai's eyes were still open, their brightness still as surprising as before. He didn't even look pale. Yuuki had the urge to call his name but, knowing the disappointment he'd feel when there was no reply, he held back.

PVS. The acronym didn't mean much to him. But "vegetative state" was a term that could not fail to hit home.

"Yuuki-san, please sit. I'll make some tea. Or would you prefer something cold? We have barley tea and orange juice."

"Please don't trouble yourself. I'm sorry, I can't stay for long."

"Oh, that's a pity. Please stay awhile. Anzai'll be disappointed if you leave so soon. Won't you, darling?"

Her tone was flirtatious, and she caressed her husband's cheek as she spoke.

Yuuki was puzzled. Sayuri's behavior was a huge contrast to two days ago, when she had barely been able to force a smile. Now she was bustling around the hospital room, full of life. He had to ask.

"Did you get some good news about his condition?"

"Ah, no. We still don't know anything."

Her expression clouded slightly, but that was all. She reached into the fridge and pulled out a jug of barley tea, poured Yuuki a glass, and handed it to him with a big smile.

She'd made her peace with this. That must be it. But it had only been forty-eight hours . . .

Sayuri kept glancing over at Anzai. She even smiled at him. Suetsugu had explained it in rather old-fashioned-sounding terms: "The two of them were a match made in heaven. You know, they eloped together." Yuuki had known that the couple were very close, but Sayuri's behavior today made him uncomfortable. He felt as if he were intruding on their personal space.

He checked on Rintaro. The boy looked bored.

Thirteen years old. Sayuri's long-awaited child. Born three months after Endo's death. He'd heard all this from Suetsugu.

He searched around for a topic of conversation.

"Did Nodai Niko win?"

"Yes. Nine to one."

"Wow. That's a really good score."

"Yeah, it was a total slugfest."

Rintaro seemed to be into the conversation. Yuuki looked at the rubber ball the boy was holding.

"Do you like baseball?"

"No, not really."

"You wanna go and throw a ball around for a while?"

"Huh?"

Rintaro looked around the hospital room. Yuuki laughed.

"Outside! I mean outside. There's a bit of grass we could play on."

"Oh . . . okay," he said nervously.

Yuuki got to his feet. Sayuri had her back to him, wiping Anzai's hands with a wet towel.

"Sayuri-san, do you mind if I borrow Rintaro for a while?"

"Thank you. That'd be very kind."

Sayuri looked jubilant as she bowed her head. Yuuki was perplexed again to see how delighted she seemed to be, to be clearing the room of people. He forced himself to rethink. This might be the only chance he'd have to visit for a while. And today he'd have to head back to the office right after playing catch with Rintaro. He was going to have to put his thoughts from the car journey into action right now.

"Sayuri-san, do you happen to have Anzai's diary?"

"Yes. He was carrying it when he collapsed."

"Would you mind if I borrowed it for a couple of days?"

"Not at all. Why?"

For a moment a concerned look crossed her face. Yuuki chose his words very carefully.

"It's about when he collapsed. There's something I don't understand about it. Two o'clock in the morning and he hadn't been drinking. If it's all right with you, I'd like to look into it a bit more."

"I see . . . Thank you."

He'd managed it without much persuasion. Sayuri went straight to the locker and retrieved the notebook.

Yuuki did mean to investigate Anzai's movements on the night in question, whether for work or for personal reasons. What was he doing in the entertainment district stone-cold sober? And why did he collapse the very night before he was due to climb Tsuitate with Yuuki?

All the anecdotes he'd heard from Suetsugu were running through his mind. He was determined to solve the mystery of Anzai's behavior and how it was connected to those stories.

"Here it is."

Sayuri passed him a small black leather-bound diary.

"Thank you."

Yuuki slipped the book into his trouser pocket. Rintaro was waiting for him just beyond the door, looking very apprehensive.

"Right, let's do this!"

"Okay."

They took the elevator down to the ground floor and went out the side entrance. What Yuuki had imagined to be a large area of grass turned out to be a courtyard covered in weeds.

"Okay, let's have it," said Yuuki brightly, stepping backward to adjust the space between them. Rintaro threw the rubber ball toward him. He didn't seem to be particularly good at sports. His throwing style was a bit awkward.

As they tossed the ball back and forth, Yuuki remembered all the times he'd played catch like this with Jun.

"Okay, I'm going to throw you a curveball."

"What?"

"Try to catch it."

Yuuki wrapped his fingers tightly around the ball and threw it sidearm. Right as it was about to reach Rintaro, the ball curved sharply to the left and shot on past, Rintaro having set himself to catch it directly in front of his chest.

Rintaro didn't even move. Then, after a beat, he turned his head to see where the ball had gone. When he turned back to Yuuki there was a flushed smile on his face.

"Wow!"

"Good, right?" said Yuuki, beaming proudly.

Rintaro ran to fetch the ball and made a long throw to send it back.

"This time I'm going to throw a drop ball."

"A drop?"

"Nowadays they call it a forkball."

He clowned around a bit, making a show of wrapping his fingers around the ball like before, and then released it overarm and slow. Rintaro waited with both hands in front of his chest, but this time the ball dropped suddenly and hit him right between the legs.

"Ow!"

Rintaro doubled over, both hands clutching his nether regions. It was only a rubber ball—it shouldn't have hurt that much. But then Yuuki realized: Rintaro was bright red in the face . . . with laughter.

Yuuki had no idea how much longer the two of them kept on playing. The pager on his belt kept on buzzing; perhaps Rintaro pretended not to hear it. Five more minutes, then another five. Yuuki found room in his heart to give Rintaro this small gift of his time. And, as he played, it came to him.

He was JAL crash desk chief and he was going to keep on taking this responsibility seriously. He would pour all his energy into publishing detailed, informative articles. In other words, he was going to try to win. He was never going to repeat the mistakes of the Okubo/Red Army era. That said, he was also ready to admit defeat if he had to, and let the next generation take over from him.

He let rip another drop ball. He could see Jun's sullen face in the back of his mind; a total contrast to the joyful sight of Rintaro rushing around after the ball. For a moment, Rintaro had made him feel like a proper father.

As they climbed from Tail Ridge to Anseilen Terrace, they were directly under the Tsuitate face.

Yuuki followed the figure of Rintaro in the lead, step by step, across the bedrock. The base of Tsuitate's rock wall was practically grazing his left shoulder, its top reaching way up into the heavens. It was an overwhelming feeling.

Rintaro paused and looked up, evidently scoping out their route. He had to strain his neck, bending his body as far back as it would go, and looked as if at any moment he might topple backward. But the only way was to look straight up.

"A little farther," he said, picking up his pace.

Just as he'd predicted, not five minutes later they passed through a small thicket of bushes, and suddenly their field of vision opened right up, and they were on Anseilen Terrace, the kickoff point for their attempt on Cloud Ridge route number 1.

Now it was time to prepare for the serious part of their climb.

Two nine-millimeter ropes, carabiners, pitons, aiders, slings, climbing gloves . . .

"Shall we set out in about fifteen minutes?" said Rintaro casually.

"Sure."

But Yuuki wasn't quite sure. He was already short of breath from the less challenging climb they'd just done. That, and he still wasn't quite mentally prepared for the formidable Tsuitate. He put on his climbing gloves, then pulled them off again. He took a deep breath and took in his surroundings.

"Anseilen Terrace—the perfect name for this place."

Anseilen—the German word for tying climbers together with a rope—this was the place to do it. To unite your whole self with your partner. To put your trust in him. And then climb.

"But that's right," continued Yuuki with a laugh. "Anseilen was supposed to be your name. Anzai Rentaro in the Japanese order—or Anzai Ren for short. But your mother put a stop to that one, otherwise right now Anseilen would be standing here now on Anseilen.

"Yuuki-san, where did you hear that?"

"What?"

Yuuki was surprised to see confusion on Rintaro's face.

"Don't tell me you never heard that story?"

"No, no, I've heard it. Just not the part where my mother put a stop to it."

"She was opposed to the name, wasn't she? Your father told me."

"The story I heard from Mom was different," said Rintaro, looking grim. "Dad announced that he wanted to call me Rentaro, and my mother agreed."

"Really? Is that true?"

Rintaro nodded and continued.

"Dad went to the city office to record the birth, but when he came home two hours later there was a different name on the birth certificate. It was my dad who changed it to Rintaro. That's what Mom told me."

Yuuki was dumbfounded.

"I don't get it. How can that be?"

"I guess my father spent those two hours thinking it over," said Rintaro sadly. "And he decided that he wouldn't be taking his son to the mountains, that he would never teach his son how to climb."

"Oh."

Yuuki suddenly understood. Mitsugu Endo—the man whose death Anzai had caused. Three months after that terrible accident, Anzai had a son. He must have struggled with the decision of whether to keep on climbing or to stop. Rintaro's name was testament to his final decision.

Very quietly, Rintaro began to speak.

"I think my father must have been in a lot of pain. I don't think he had any idea how to behave around me. Probably the only way Dad would have known how to show affection would be by teaching me how to climb."

It seemed he couldn't make up his mind what to call Anzai—Father or Dad.

"I suffered, too. My father was so awkward around me that I remember always being anxious. I never understood his pain, but I could see that it was hard for him to handle."

"Anzai really loved you," said Yuuki.

He'd spoken spontaneously, and Rintaro humbly nodded his appreciation.

"I believe he did. But he never found a way of showing it. And then he passed away without ever being able to. I was completely lost after that. I ended up not being close to my mother, either."

Yuuki thought back to that time. He recalled that day at the hospital when Sayuri had seemed so cheerful.

The husband and wife had been a match made in heaven. But Anzai's job in the Circulation Department of the *North Kanto Times* involved going to parties and receptions at night. On weekdays, he would drink; Sundays, he would lead the hiking club on trips to the mountains. Their loving relationship had already turned into something to reminisce about, relegated to memories in old photo albums. The man she had eloped with was shut away somewhere in her heart. After the accident, the sadness could be let out.

With Anzai sleeping, she had a second chance, an opportunity to revisit the early honeymoon period of their marriage. Along with despair came a new kind of warmth. For the first time in a long while, Sayuri had her husband by her side all day every day. Anzai wasn't dead, just asleep, and now Yuuki realized that Sayuri had been free to love him to distraction.

"Back then, you were the only person I could rely on, Yuuki-san. Every time we had a date to meet up, I could barely wait to see you."

There wasn't a hint of sadness or bitterness in Rintaro's words. Just nostalgia.

"Today I'm going to rely on you," said Yuuki, looking up at the awe-inspiring face of Tsuitate.

The first phase: the overhang that seemed to cover them completely.

It jutted out like the eaves of some giant's castle in the sky; the feature was known in the climbing world as a "roof." This would be the first obstacle they would need to overcome on Cloud Ridge route number 1. Once they'd surmounted this hurdle, they'd continue up the vertical wall. This was the very same route that Mitsugu Endo had taken when he was killed by a falling rock.

Yuuki gulped loudly.

"You'll be fine as soon as you can feel the rock with your hands."

Yuuki nodded wordlessly and reached up. The rock was cold to the touch. The texture of something mineral, inorganic. Something about it felt different from the rock faces he had scaled at the ski resorts. The feel of atmospheric pressure on a three-hundred-meter vertical wall, perhaps? Or was it just nerves at his first-ever encounter with this formidable rock face?

No, it wasn't just fear. The solid rock beneath his palm gave off some sort of energy. As he stood there, his hand on the rock, a strange thing happened. His mind became calmer, and then clearer.

"Let's do it!"

The words came out, unforced.

"All right. Let's go."

Rintaro looked amicably at his climbing buddy.

There was a gust of wind. Yuuki took his hand off the rock face and looked up one more time at Tsuitate. His fear was now turning to something more like anticipation. Those were the same emotions he had felt back then, on the fifth day of the Japan Airlines crash story.

August 17, 1985. That was the day that a local newspaper in Gunma boldly competed for the world's biggest scoop.

As he gripped the steering wheel, Yuuki could still feel the squishiness of the rubber ball. Slipping into a parking space, he glanced at the dashboard clock—ten past two—and his pager began to buzz again.

He bounded up the stairs and into the newsroom. He arrived at his desk to a very shocked look from Kishi.

"Hey, were you caught in a shower or something?"

Yuuki's shirt was soaked through.

"I was playing catch."

"In the midday sun?"

Looking at Kishi's stunned expression, Yuuki realized that he hadn't even noticed how hot it was. He had started out playing as a way of making Rintaro feel better, but he'd ended up so focused on the game that perhaps it had been as much for himself as for the boy.

"Anyway, what's all the paging about?"

"That," Kishi replied, gesturing to Yuuki's desk.

He hadn't spotted it right away because of the mountain of papers that dominated the work surface, but stuck underneath a paperweight were about ten sheets of paper from a company memo pad. The memo on top had Tamaki's name on it.

*Urgent. Please call.*
*The accident investigation. Pressure bulkhead. Ruptured.*

The words lit up like neon signs in his head.

Yuuki dialed Tamaki's pager number, immediately followed by Sa-yama's. He put down the phone and began to look through the rest of the memos. The sight of one name made him freeze. He glanced at the next desk. Kishi was working on some draft copy, his red pen occasionally moving across the paper.

"Kishi?"

"Yeah?"

The face that turned to Yuuki was without expression.

"Sorry that you had to take my calls."

"Just don't go out again. They're lining up to get in touch with the JAL crash desk."

Kishi's expression and tone were perfectly normal. But he couldn't quite hide that there was something wrong.

Yuuki guessed it was the fallout from the previous night's events. Yuuki had dared to voice the view that during the Okubo/Red Army era the *North Kanto Times* had been totally outperformed by Japan's national newspapers. Those words had been intended to pierce the armor that protected Todoroki's reminiscences, but the intensity of Kishi and Nozawa's reaction had surprised Yuuki. Their memories of their days as reporters had been sullied, and many of these memories were ones they shared with Yuuki. It was going to be hard for Yuuki to clear the air and convince his two colleagues that he hadn't meant to insult them.

His phone began to ring.

"This is Sayama. Did you call me?"

"Yes, I did."

He'd been sure that Tamaki would call back first, so, to start with, he stumbled over his words.

"Are you . . . you're at the police press club right now?"

"That's right."

Sayama's tone was just as cold as yesterday.

"I need to talk to you. Can you get back here?"

"They're still announcing the identified remains."

"Is there no one else who can cover for you?"

"There's only Moriwaki."

*Only.* Well, it was too bad. Moriwaki was a rookie reporter who had just started to go on assignments this last month.

"Moriwaki'll be fine for that. Get him to take over, and get out of there."

"Is it something you can't tell me over the phone?"

"Right. Not over the phone."

He said it with as much force as he could.

"Try to get here in twenty minutes. I've got a meeting at three-thirty."

". . . Okay."

While Yuuki had been talking to Sayama, a large heap of new Kyodo News wires had been deposited on his desk. One headline caught his eye.

BODY RECOVERY FINALLY AT 60%

Yuuki divided the wires roughly into piles. He looked back over the memos as he paged Tamaki one more time. His neck stiffened when he got to a particular piece of paper. That one name was enough to cause his body to react involuntarily: Ayako Mochizuki.

The note said she'd like him to call back. There was a phone number with a Takasaki City area code. She'd called at one o'clock that afternoon. There was nothing to say what it was about.

Yuuki guessed it must be something to do with Ryota Mochizuki. A feeling of apprehension came over him. A car accident. He had never been able to shake the belief that it had been suicide. And Yuuki had pushed him toward it. He couldn't deny that fact.

He was sure that Mochizuki's mother was called Kuniko, so the next possibility was the woman Yuuki had run into at the cemetery the other day, the young woman of around twenty who might well have been Ryota Mochizuki's cousin. The one who had glared at Yuuki. She was probably Ayako. The incident felt like something that had happened a long time ago, but the monthly observance of Mochizuki's death had been only four days earlier. That same evening, Flight 123 had come down. All sense of time seemed to have become completely skewed since then.

But what could she possibly want?

Yuuki craned his neck to look over toward the editorial administrative section. He'd recognized the handwriting on that particular memo as belonging to Chizuko Yorita. Even if she didn't know what the call was about, she might be able to tell him something about the tone of the caller's voice.

But there was no sign of Chizuko, and the surface of her desk was immaculate.

"Kishi, where's Yorita?"

"What? Oh, yes, Chi-chan's at the Maebashi branch office this afternoon."

Yuuki had seen her this morning when he'd woken up on the sofa. He'd appreciated her cheerful smile.

"I thought she was transferring at the beginning of September."

"Kudo-san came and insisted to managing editor Oimura, said he needed her to transfer early. Tamaki and others have been assigned to the JAL crash, so when she's not too busy she's been helping out at Maebashi."

Yuuki nodded. Kudo, the Maebashi branch chief, was something of a panicker. He was about to turn fifty, but still, anytime the workload got a little too much, he'd lose it completely and come crying to headquarters.

It'd be too awkward to chase her down with a call to the branch chief.

Yuuki sat for a while, tracing the other number with his thumb before finally calling.

He got the answering machine. The message on the tape wasn't the prerecorded one, but Ayako's own. It was a clear, strong voice, without warmth.

He gave the paper's name and his own in a monotone, promised to call back again, and hung up. He was afraid that she might call again at an awkward moment, so he'd decided it was better to say he'd call her.

The breeze from the air conditioner felt stronger than usual, probably because his shirt was still damp with sweat. Or maybe because Chizuko Yorita wasn't there. She always brought a cover for her knees and would turn the air conditioner to a higher temperature as soon as she arrived at the newsroom.

Yuuki held the front of his collar closed with his left hand while he checked through the rest of the memos. Over half of them were from Tamaki. He began to regret having played catch with Rintaro for so long.

He'd been so late back to the office that he and Tamaki had completely missed each other. There was still no reply on his pager, but Uenomura was pretty remote. It was the kind of place you would normally assume had poor reception.

Yuuki thought about it. If Tamaki had called him four or five times in quick succession, it must mean that he had succeeded in making contact with a member of the investigation team and must already have managed to get evidence supporting his bulkhead theory.

This didn't necessarily mean Yuuki's confidence in Tamaki as a reporter had increased. For now, all Yuuki could do was wait for him to call back. In the meantime, he decided to deal with the rest of the memos.

There was nothing urgent. Miyata, the hiking club member from Advertising, had left a message asking if Yuuki had managed to meet Suetsugu, the rock climber who knew Anzai.

Yuuki couldn't forget his conversation with Suetsugu. Kyoichiro Anzai's climbing partner had died on Tsuitate. Anzai had blamed himself for the accident and retired from the climbing community.

Yuuki felt something nagging at him. He lifted himself out of his chair and pulled Anzai's diary out of his pocket. On the black leather cover, "1985" was embossed in gold lettering. He opened it to find every single page covered in black ink. Every day was filled with fine writing, detailing Anzai's schedule.

He checked August 12. First thing in the morning, Anzai had taken some client or other golfing. A memory from that day suddenly came rushing back—the red T-shirt with the sweat stain in the shape of a baby's bib. Even his mustache had been glistening with sweat. That day had been a scorcher. Anzai hadn't mentioned that he'd had to play a round of golf out at the prefectural course that morning before he'd turned up at the staff cafeteria. But it wasn't only golf. That same afternoon, up until evening, he'd visited five different newsdealers. And on the same day, the twelfth, there was something written in very tiny lettering in the margin. Yuuki concentrated on trying to read it. It looked like "LH."

Yuuki blinked hard several times to try to get his eyes to focus. LH? Or, possibly, the first letter was a C . . . ?

He turned the page. August 13. The only page on which Anzai had used blue ink instead of black. "New attempt on Tsuitate." The lettering was bold and clear and circled several times over.

He remembered something Sayuri had said.

*"He was really looking forward to it . . . Going climbing with you."*

Yuuki shook off the sentimental feelings and moved backward through the diary. Most of Anzai's schedule involved variations on entertaining newsdealers and other shopkeepers. Yuuki couldn't help grumbling out loud when he saw what the average working day consisted of for an employee of the Circulation Department. Drinking alcohol, playing mah-jongg, singing karaoke; rounds of golf, hot-spring resorts, fishing trips. Riverside barbecues, bowling competitions—they were all there in his schedule. On every page, he spotted the name of some famous—or infamous—bar or club. The same "LH" turned up regularly. It appeared first on June 7, and then with more frequency, until, by August, it was scribbled in about every other day. It must have been a bar or some other place he used to entertain clients. However, unlike any of the other places, the annotation "LH" was always written in the margin, outside the allotted space for each date. Yuuki guessed it was some sort of special code.

But his interest in LH soon faded when he discovered several totally unexpected entries in the diary for August: "Okuma," "Isozaki," and "Oribe." These three names were known to anyone connected to the *North Kanto Times*. These men were three of the most prominent business owners in Gunma Prefecture, and also external members of the paper's board of directors, holding consulting and supervisory roles at the company. Judging by Anzai's notes, Yuuki could guess that, along with the head of Circulation, Ito, they'd made the rounds of several high-end hostess clubs.

It was a huge discovery. There had long been a rumor that managing director Iikura's faction was meeting night after night to lay the groundwork for overthrowing Chairman Shirakawa. They were aiming for a majority at the next board meeting. Here was Iikura's oily-voiced right-hand man, Ito, along with Anzai, the man who idolized Ito and saw him as some kind of great benefactor. Their job had been to butter up and win over the external directors, one by one. And here it was recorded—dates, places, names. The scene brought to vivid life by notes on a page.

However, rather than feeling disgust at this revelation, Yuuki thought he might have caught a glimpse of what had led to Anzai suffering a sub-arachnoid hemorrhage. His schedule had been packed, particularly the past three or so months. Every day, every night, he'd been charged with entertaining clients and conducting behind-the-scenes negotiations. However fond of drinking he might have been, staying out into the early hours for someone else's benefit, flattering and wooing them, must have been a huge burden on Anzai. He'd had one day off a month. Sayuri had let slip the words *"I think it's terrible how hard they made him work!"* And now, suddenly, Yuuki saw how right she was. But at the same time he realized that Anzai had used that precious day of rest for his trips into the mountains with the hiking club.

He thought back again to Anzai's behavior that day in the office cafeteria. According to his diary, he had been out the previous night schmoozing somebody, then spent the whole of the following morning playing golf in the blazing heat. Despite all that, he hadn't seemed tired in the least. He'd never breathed a word about his work or the behind-the-scenes maneuvering. His eyes had had their usual twinkle, and he'd chatted happily about the next day's climb. About taking the 7:36 evening train out of Gunma-Soja station. After promising to meet at the station, they'd gone their separate ways. But somehow or other, Anzai hadn't gone to the station at all. Instead, he'd collapsed at 2:00 a.m. on the streets of Jotomachi, with its wall-to-wall bars.

LH snuck back into his head. If it was a bar, then he could assume that was where Anzai'd been. But if that was the case, something jarred. If he'd been planning to go drinking that evening, then how could he possibly have managed to meet Yuuki at 7:30 at Gunma-Soja Station? Perhaps he was just going to drop by the bar early and then go on to catch the train. Or perhaps Anzai never had any intention of climbing Tsuitate? No, it was more likely that he'd always intended to climb but, when suddenly faced with the reality of it, he'd lost his nerve. And so, after parting from Yuuki at the cafeteria, he'd headed off to LH instead. Maybe he'd planned to apologize to Yuuki later by inventing a story about suddenly having to work.

More than ten years after he lost his climbing partner on Tsuitate, Anzai had started up a hiking club at the newspaper. Yuuki didn't get the thinking behind that decision. Perhaps it was Anzai's fondness for the mountains that had propelled him to do it. But if, as Suetsugu had said, he hadn't been able to get over the death of his friend, surely leading these casual hikes, to a hard-core climber such as himself, must have been like some kind of self-imposed prison sentence? Atonement, bordering on masochism. But then the addition of Yuuki to the club had shaken up Anzai's routine. Badgered by Yuuki to go rock climbing, Anzai had ended up taking him to Mount Haruna's ski resort. Perhaps that had led to a change in his mental state.

*"Hey, Yuu. Let's take a shot at Tsuitate!"*

It had been Anzai who'd suggested it, but now that Yuuki finally knew the whole story, he couldn't stop thinking about the storms of conflict that must have raged inside his colleague's heart.

Yuuki turned to look at the door behind him. The core of the layout team—known as the three o'clock shift—were just arriving for work. The newsroom was getting noisy once more.

When Nozawa's sour face made its appearance again at the desk to his left, Yuuki caught a look of relief on Kishi's face. Apparently even Kishi was uncomfortable being alone with Yuuki now.

Nozawa didn't bother making eye contact with Yuuki. He just dropped his shoulder bag on the floor and called across to Kishi.

"I stopped by the city office on the way to work and saw Yorita in the reporters' room."

"Yes, she's been transferred early."

"Is she going to be all right? I've never seen her look so terrified. She can't even write a simple ten-line report."

"Everyone's like that when they start out."

"But anyone can write something that simple on their first day."

"Well, maybe you could."

*Stop pretending you and Chizuko are the best of friends!* The sense of isolation that had swept over him dragged up these bitter thoughts.

Nozawa turned to Yuuki.

"I heard that Anzai from Circulation's in the hospital."

Yuuki grunted in response. Four days. That was about the usual delay in news reaching one department from another.

"Anzai? Is that true?"

Kishi was genuinely taken aback. Strong as an ox—that was Anzai's image in the company.

"Someone from the city firefighting office passed it on to Kudo, the Maebashi branch chief. Seems he had a subarachnoid hemorrhage and was taken to the prefectural hospital."

"A hemorrhage!"

"Yeah, seems he was running and suddenly collapsed."

Anzai was running? Yuuki looked at Nozawa.

"Is that information reliable?"

"Someone saw him, apparently."

"Hey, never mind that—what's his condition?" said Kishi, addressing Yuuki as well as Nozawa.

"It's death from overworking."

This was what Yuuki had been thinking ever since reading Anzai's diary. Now he'd put it into words.

Kishi's face froze.

"What are you talking about? Don't mess with us, Yuuki. He's still alive, isn't he?"

"Of course I'm joking," said Yuuki crossly, and got up to meet Sayama, who had just entered the newsroom.

Sayama had quite an expression on his face. It was different from his usual aggressive look. The tension and shadow that had shrouded him ever since he came back from Mount Osutaka had also vanished. He had the face of a fully fledged police beat reporter.

As soon as Yuuki recognized that look, it finally registered with him— the *North Kanto Times* had the potential to be a contender. They were going to beat all the big names in global media to the biggest scoop.

Yuuki had Sayama wait for him in the break area while he gave some directions to the copy team.

When he returned, Sayama was sitting in the corner of the sofa, a paper cup of cola in his hand. It felt as if he was sending Yuuki a message that he wasn't even ready to let his senior colleague pay for his cheap hundred-yen drink. Yuuki sat down, leaving about the space of a person between them.

"Did Hanazawa come in today?"

"He's climbing Osutaka."

"Again?"

"He climbs it every day. It's become his routine. At any rate, I think he'll get a great article out of it."

Yuuki hadn't known any of this.

"What's going on with Wajima?"

"What did you want to talk to me about?"

"Is he at the press club?"

"Writing an article about the personal belongings of the deceased. Hurry up and tell me what this is about. I'm worried about leaving Mori-waki in charge."

Yuuki nodded. He sat up a little, looked around to check that no one was listening, then leaned back in.

"It's about Tamaki from the Maebashi branch."

"What's he done?"

"What's he like as a reporter?"

Sayama didn't reply. He took a sip from his paper cup. It was clear from the look on his face that he had no intention of selling out the reporters at the accident site to the desk chief. Or, if Yuuki took the cynical view, that Sayama had nothing particularly praiseworthy to say about Tamaki as a reporter.

"Anyway," Yuuki continued, "he's got hold of a story."

"What kind of story?"

"The cause of the crash."

Sayama's eyebrows shot up.

"Have you heard of a thing called a pressure bulkhead?"

"It's the dome-shaped piece at the rear of the fuselage. It maintains the pressure at a constant level inside the aircraft."

"You're pretty knowledgeable."

"I'm just the same as the prefectural police. We're all starting by learning what makes a plane able to fly."

"Well, that bulkhead couldn't withstand the pressure and it ruptured, blowing off the tail. At least, that's what Tamaki tells me."

"Where did he get this from?"

"One of the members of the crash investigation team."

He saw Sayama's pupils dilate.

"The problem is, he only overheard the conversation. And only the word 'bulkhead.' He didn't actually hear that it had ruptured, or that it had blown the tail off. That part was all his own theory."

Sayama thought for a moment before replying.

"Tamaki studied engineering at university, didn't he?"

"Yes, but it wasn't aeronautical engineering."

Yuuki stole a glance at Sayama, who was clearly giving this some serious thought.

"It might be fake information."

"I don't think so."

"All right, then. The story is true. Or at least we have to believe it is. Take a leap of faith."

Yuuki felt relieved.

"I want you to gather the evidence. Get up to the accident site and try to talk to the investigation team."

"You're asking *me*?" Sayama looked at Yuuki for the first time. "Why don't you get Tamaki to do it? It's his story."

Sayama was showing his immaturity. His voice oozed with bitterness. Yuuki sat up a little straighter.

"Do you honestly think Tamaki's up to the job?"

Sayama was silent.

"Just think how big a story this is. I need a reliable person on it."

Still no answer.

"Do it! You're the *NKT*'s top police reporter."

Sayama inclined his head ever so slightly. He wanted to be part of this international scoop. Any investigative reporter worth their salt would.

Yuuki clapped his hands.

"Good. Get going right away. Try to get there while it's still light. And check out the investigation team's lodgings."

"Where's Tamaki right now?"

"I'm trying to locate him. You start with the village office. I'll let you know as soon as I find him."

"Who should I go after?"

Sayama's look became sharper.

"Make a proper story out of this. Go for the top—the head of the investigation team."

"Kanae Fujinami?"

"That's the one. It doesn't matter how late it is. Corner him in the toilet or the bathhouse changing room and get it out of him."

They exchanged a look. If anyone had been watching, they'd probably have thought the two men were glaring at each other.

Sayama swallowed hard.

"Got it. I'll do it. On one condition—it stays as Tamaki's story. I'm fine being behind the scenes on this one. I'm serious about that."

It felt as if it had been a long time since Yuuki had heard such invigorating words.

"Of course. Ha! If Tamaki gets the Chairman's Award, he'll be over the moon."

Sayama grinned, but only for a moment. He became serious again right away.

"Right. I'm off," he said, getting to his feet.

"I'm counting on you."

The job had brought the two of them closer again. But it was precisely because this was something beyond their usual job.

Yuuki set off back to the newsroom. He could feel his heartbeat pulsing faster than usual. He was going to publish a world scoop in the *North Kanto Times*. He was on a real mission, but this was only the first step.

He met Kishi at the door. There'd been a call from Tamaki. Yuuki looked down the corridor, but Sayama had already gone. He hurried back to his desk. If only the call had come in three minutes earlier they could have made all the arrangements on the spot. The receiver was still off the hook. He grabbed it.

"Yuuki here."

"Finally got hold of you."

Tamaki sounded in good spirits.

"I heard you'd been trying to reach me. Have there been any developments?"

"Yes. It's definitely the bulkhead. I was about to start writing my—"

"Wait!" Yuuki cut him off. "Where are you calling from?"

"What?"

"The location of the phone."

"It's the public phone in the anglers' lodge."

"Speak as quietly as possible, okay?" Yuuki's tone sounded threatening.

"O-okay."

"So tell me. How do you know it's the bulkhead?" Yuuki had his hand around the mouthpiece as he spoke.

"Well, it turns out that Harasawa from the investigation team is a good friend of my seminar professor back at university, and it seems my professor asked him what caused the accident. And apparently Harasawa told him it was most likely the bulkhead."

*It seems. Apparently. Most likely.*

Hearsay was just one level above eavesdropping. He'd just accepted this story and begun writing an article?

"So you're working on a draft?"

"A draft?"

Yuuki took a deep breath. Surely Tamaki understood why he had to get working on a draft right away? If it was late at night, and you waited until all the supporting evidence was gathered before you started your article, you'd never make the deadline. So instead you sent a draft of the article to headquarters and rushed around afterward to get the rest of the facts.

"All right, then, get the piece written ASAP. A fax'll be fine. Make sure you give me a call before you send it."

"Okay."

Tamaki sounded buoyant once more. Yuuki also felt the information had gained some credibility now that there was another source involved.

"And one more thing . . ."

Yuuki put it into simple terms.

"Even if you're sure of the truth of your story, it's still hearsay right now. It needs proper researching. Do you understand?"

"Yes, of course. I'll be sure to do that."

"Sayama from the police beat is on his way."

"Don't worry, I can do it myself."

Yuuki ignored him.

"Meet Sayama at the village office. Tell him every single piece of information you have."

The telephone receiver picked up what sounded like a small shriek.

"Why? I can do this!" Tamaki said, sounding reproachful. "Sayama-san doesn't know the first thing about airplanes. Even if he manages to talk to an investigator, he won't be able to follow any of the technical explanations."

So he'd been planning to discuss the cause of the crash directly with someone from the accident investigation team. It was difficult to explain to Tamaki, who had no experience of being on the night watch. Things could be resolved in a matter of seconds. There was one question to put to the accident investigator: *Was the rupture of the pressure bulkhead the cause of the crash?* But there wasn't a government employee in the whole country who would give a straight answer to that question. What was needed was a reporter with the skill to seize exactly the right moment to coax a yes or a no out of someone. Sayama was just such a man—responsible for covering accidents all over the prefecture, he interviewed policemen 365 days a year.

"That's Sayama's job."

Tamaki sounded despondent.

". . . I understand. I'll take Sayama with me."

"No. Let him do it by himself. You'll be my support. I want you to report every detail of Sayama's movements."

*People don't divulge their secrets when there's more than one person present.*
Suddenly Tamaki flared up.

"I'm really not happy about this. I was the one who overheard them talking—it was my story. And now you're handing it over to Sayama!"

Yuuki wanted to tell him what Sayama had said earlier. Yuuki hadn't realized how much Tamaki was willing to fight for his story. Perhaps, if Tamaki got to experience the police beat for a while, they might make a hard-hitting reporter of him yet.

"Each man to his own. Let Sayama do it."

"But—"

"Are you listening?"

". . . Yes."

"Sayama will be there just before five. Whether this story lives or dies depends on your support. I'm counting on you."

He had ended up having to resort to flattery in order to win Tamaki over.

Kishi and Nozawa had already started walking toward managing editor Oimura's office. The August 17 meeting to decide the layout of the next day's paper was just about to get under way. This might be the front page that put the *North Kanto Times* into the history books.

Yuuki strode after his two colleagues. *God! It's freezing in here*, he thought, but just for an instant. He put it down to the fact that he was trembling with excitement, and thought no more about it.

The meeting had begun with idle chitchat.

Editor in chief Kasuya was in a buoyant mood. This morning's paper, which had delicately managed to maintain the balance between Fukuda and Nakasone, had been well received by all parties.

"Even Iikura-san found the time to give me a call. The managing director had nothing but praise for the front page, even though I'm sure he'd been rubbing his hands in glee, waiting for his opportunity to attack."

Oimura looked dubious.

"I can't help finding it suspicious that he just happened to call at a time like that. The Clever Yakuza's up to something for sure . . . Yep, he definitely has something up his sleeve," he continued. "Kasuya-san, you really should be careful."

"Yes, I know, I know. But the managing director always likes to give his opinion about the layout of the paper."

"You're naive. That guy has no interest whatsoever in the contents of the paper. The only thing he's interested in is appearances."

Yuuki was on edge the whole time the others were talking. At this very moment, his trouser pocket contained proof of the managing director's faction's toxic handiwork. Probably someone of Kasuya's status in the company was aware to some extent of what was going on and, as Yuuki had no allegiance to either faction, he didn't feel obliged to reveal his hand. However, he did feel that Oimura's cautiousness was a lot more appropriate than Kasuya's optimism.

Kasuya turned his attention to Yuuki.

"Good job yesterday. The idea to use that photo, well, it was inspired."

Yuuki gave a vague nod. His attention was on Todoroki, who had just entered the room. He looked exactly the same as always. Glancing at Yuuki from behind his dark lenses, he sat down next to Oimura and folded his arms. The previous night, he had drunk himself into oblivion at Sojahanten. Yuuki wondered how much of their conversation Todoroki remembered.

"So, about today's layout . . ."

Finally, Kasuya had started on the work at hand. His smiling face was still turned in Yuuki's direction.

"First of all, the JAL crash. How are we dealing with that?"

"I thought we'd lead with Nodai Niko's second-round win at the Koshien. Emphasize the tragedy of the team member's father."

Immediately Oimura, sitting across from Yuuki, frowned. Surely he wasn't going to object?

"What other crash-related stories do you have?" asked Kasuya.

Yuuki consulted his notes.

"The press conference interview with the survivors. The joint U.S.-Japan investigation. The storage of the remains. Meetings with the bereaved families. Continuation of the series on the second page. They've started to return possessions to the families now, so coverage of how that's going."

"I see."

Yuuki made no mention of his possible scoop. It'd be madness to talk about it now. Not everyone in the Editorial Department was his ally. There'd even been a couple of cases in the past where information was leaked to a rival paper.

"I think it's about time to take the JAL crash off the front page."

Naturally, it was Oimura who said this. Something must have irritated him, because there was already a hint in his eyes of the Firecracker being lit.

"For now, today, let's lead with the crash. Koshien and the bereaved families in one story. But I don't want every page crammed with crash articles. I think, unless we have a really strong story, tomorrow we should drop it from the headlines. There are plenty of reporters covering other big stories around the prefecture."

Oimura glanced at Yuuki before continuing.

"You know, this morning's edition just wasn't right. All the national and international news pages were jammed full of crash articles. And not only that—how did the crash end up spilling over onto even the regional news pages? Explain yourself, Yuuki."

His opponent had made the first move. But now he knew why Oimura was so irritated. He was telling him not to saturate every page with articles about the JAL crash. To gather together a wider assortment of news stories in less depth. To be fair, this was good practical advice for putting together a newspaper.

But Yuuki wasn't about to give in. Or rather, this was the one point he was absolutely not willing to back down on. He was not going to change a thing about his current editing policy. The *North Kanto Times*'s coverage of the crash, which had started out all at sea, was now being very well received. And it was the words of that one bereaved widow that had given him the impetus to get it to that point. He wasn't going to chicken out that easily, just because Oimura was attempting to intimidate him with his trademark scowl.

"We're the local paper. We can't fall behind the other press when it comes to information on this crash. I used all the space I possibly could. And that's what I plan to keep on doing from now on."

"Such arrogance." Oimura locked on to Yuuki. "You can't just do whatever you feel like. Who do you think you are? Make no mistake about it, being JAL crash desk chief means you have authority only over the crash coverage. You're not desk chief for the entire NKT. We have a whole variety of articles that need to be published on a variety of pages. You can't just start dropping them at will!"

Yuuki lost his temper.

"I'm not leaving out any important news; only the page-filler stuff."

"What a narrow-minded perspective! There are people who want to read those 'filler' stories. If there isn't any variety in the news we offer, the whole format of the paper will collapse."

"But—"

"I don't think it's a problem. For once, we should stop worrying about the format."

It was copy chief Kamejima who had jumped in.

"What do you mean by that?"

Oimura had lowered his voice a good octave. He may have held the higher position in the company, but Kamejima was his senior both in age and in years of service.

"I mean that we should try to include all that we possibly can about the crash. We need to do everything we can not to lose out to the national papers or the *Jomo*. Once the crash disappears from their pages, I want us to have the conscientiousness and the sheer guts to keep leading with it for another week."

Kamejima wasn't jumping in just to help Yuuki out—it was clear that he passionately believed what he said.

"I know that our status is a bit vague. We're a Gunma local newspaper, but we tried widening our base into Ibaraki and Saitama Prefectures. That was the big thing three years ago, wasn't it? But that was a total failure. We tried putting out an evening edition with not much substance to it, and it fizzled out after six months. This time, let's really go for it. We will never again have the opportunity, in any of our lifetimes, to write about anything on this scale. All the copy team are completely on board. If we keep at it like this, we can outdo the other newspaper companies, and it might not be too outrageous to hope to be in the running for the Newspaper Association Prize."

Oimura was silent. The Firecracker had failed to ignite properly.

"Well, Kamejima certainly makes an interesting point there," said Kasuya vaguely.

The general feeling in the room seemed to be that Kamejima had won the battle but, just because of that, it would be very dangerous to offer any words of support. There was the danger of setting off a much more violent explosion. That was definitely the way Yuuki was thinking about it, in any case.

Today, besides the regular articles, was the day Yuuki had planned the JAL crash special feature on the Heartfelt readers' page. But he knew it was a difficult topic to pitch. As chief culprit in the angering of Oimura, he knew that if he mentioned it now, it would throw the whole meeting into an uproar. If he didn't broach it sensitively, there was a chance the entire approach of detailed, informative coverage would be nixed.

Todoroki was acting strangely, too. He was just sitting there with his arms folded, downcast, staring at the floor. He hadn't spoken a word and seemed completely indifferent, but if Yuuki and Oimura were to clash a second time Yuuki knew that Todoroki would end up on Oimura's side.

Kishi and Nozawa were silent as well. Who knew what side they would take? All in all, the odds were firmly against him.

Yuuki switched modes. He had another idea to bring up besides the issue of in-depth coverage.

"Right, is that everything?"

Just as Kasuya made a move to end the meeting, Yuuki jumped in.

"One more thing."

"What is it?"

*Just don't say anything rash.* He could read the message in the Conciliator's eyes. He nodded imperceptibly and continued.

"I'd like to distribute the *North Kanto Times* to the bereaved families while they wait for news of their relatives."

"While they're waiting? You mean up in Fujioka City?"

"Yes. At the East Municipal Middle School gym and the other centers. There are around two or three thousand bereaved family members waiting for the autopsy reports. How about giving them copies of our newspaper?"

"Are they going to pay for it?"

"Certainly not. It would be free of charge."

"How many copies?"

"Say a thousand? No, actually, I think five hundred should be enough."

"That's easy for you to say."

"I'm told that the families are all packed in there like sardines, with no proper access to information. I think they'd be delighted to have a newspaper to read. They'll get the most detailed and informative stories here. That's what all the bereaved relatives believe."

He spoke fervently, but Kasuya wasn't quite convinced.

"Well, I'm sure that's true, but . . ."

"We ought to do it."

This unexpected support came from none other than Todoroki. And his voice was swiftly followed by Kamejima's.

"It's a great idea. Let's do it. The families will certainly appreciate it.

Not to mention it's a great way to broaden the appeal of the paper beyond the prefecture."

Oimura was quiet, but there wasn't any sign that he was going to object. That seemed to be the decider for Kasuya.

"So, if we go ahead with this, when should we start?"

"The earlier the better. How about tomorrow?" said Kamejima.

Kasuya was taken aback, but Yuuki was ready to back Kamejima's suggestion.

"The JAL crash and the articles about it are essentially temporary. If we delay getting this off the ground, the number of family members up at the center will dwindle, and there'll be no point in distributing the papers at all."

"I understand your point, but the Editorial Department can't decide this alone. Delivery is going to be a problem. We need the cooperation of Circulation. Oh, and Accounting. If we start distributing copies for free, you can guarantee they'll all start complaining."

After grumbling a while longer, Kasuya called an end to the meeting.

Yuuki made a point of trying to catch Todoroki's eye as he got up to leave, and nodded his thanks. But Todoroki left without acknowledging him in any way. Perhaps he hadn't noticed. But one thing was clear to Yuuki: he owed Todoroki one.

"Huh? Is there something else?"

Seating himself back behind his desk, Kasuya noticed that Yuuki hadn't moved from the sofa. They were the only two people left in the editor in chief's office.

Yuuki got up and approached the desk. Within the department, there was no one who would be able to give as much information about a "night on the town" as Kasuya. Another name for the Conciliator might be the Considerate One. His gentle manners had once made the young reporter very popular at the city's hostess bars. Now older and rounder, he still made what he referred to as his thrice-weekly "patrol" of his favorite bars in the entertainment district.

"Sir, there's something I need to ask you."

"What? I hope it's not something that's going to cause trouble."

"I think it might be the name of a bar or something. Have you ever heard of a place with the initials LH?"

"LH?"

Kasuya stared into space for a moment, but it didn't take long for him to come up with an answer.

"It has to be Lonely Hearts. That's the only LH that comes to mind. Yes, it's a little bar around the back of the Joden Plaza."

So, one of the places Anzai took clients after all.

"Don't recommend going there, though. Not that place," Kasuya added.

"Why's that?"

"Mina Kuroda works there."

Yuuki couldn't immediately put a face to the name.

"You don't know her? The woman who used to push the boss's wheelchair until about three months ago."

Oh, yes. The young woman who used to be Chairman Shirakawa's PA before Manami Takagi joined the company.

"She left because she said that the chairman used to touch her inappropriately. No one working for the chairman is welcome at that bar now."

Yuuki snorted. If you put it another way, anyone working for managing director Iikura was probably welcomed with open arms . . . But now it was all beginning to make sense. Anzai had been visiting Lonely Hearts to make contact with Mina Kuroda. She was probably a cog in the scheme to oust Chairman Shirakawa. She could expose him. He'd touched her inappropriately. This was bound to be part of the managing director's plan to oust him.

"Is that all you need? I've got to call on Circulation. Ever since we've had the deadline almost permanently extended for the JAL crash, that Ito keeps bugging me about the delays in delivery. And when I break it to him that we're going to need to deliver free copies to the relatives of the crash victims, I can't imagine how unpleasant he's going to get."

There was a stabbing pain in Yuuki's gut at the sound of Ito's name.

"I'll go and talk to Circulation."

Kasuya's face was a mixture of astonishment and delight.

"You'll do it?"

"Well, I was the one to suggest it. I'll sort it out."

"That would be a great help. Then I'll deal with Accounting," said Kasuya, adjusting his tie.

Yuuki left the editor in chief's office. The newsroom was alive. He returned to his desk and sorted through the latest stack of wires and drafts.

His heart felt heavy. He thought of Anzai's twinkling eyes, which held not one ounce of malice. And his other persona—advance guard for managing director Iikura's army, on reconnaissance missions around the entertainment district.

It was impossible to survive at a company without becoming embroiled in its shadier side. The thought caused Yuuki to experience a whole medley of emotions. He decided to give them full rein for now.

It was around five o'clock when Yuuki headed down to the ground-floor Circulation office.

He stopped by at General Affairs on the way and got ahold of his colleague Gunji. Yuuki was after information about the relationship between Chairman Shirakawa and his former assistant Mina Kuroda. He really wanted to know what she'd suffered at his hands. They had talked in a tiny room tucked away in a far corner of the floor, but Gunji was a great advocate of neutrality in the workplace and refused to give anything away.

"I don't know anything. Truthfully. The chairman locks his office door from the inside, so no one knows what goes on in there."

Yuuki felt this told him a lot of what he wanted to know. Chairman Shirakawa and Mina Kuroda had been alone together in a locked room . . .

The door to the Circulation Department was wide open.

As Yuuki walked in, a head bobbed up at the desk in the far corner. It was Ito. Apart from him, there wasn't another soul in the office. The room was cramped and dark, and it lived up perfectly to its nickname the Black Box. It housed the Circulation Department exclusively; the shipping department had its own, much larger room elsewhere.

"Well, well . . ."

Ito took his time getting up. He gestured toward a sofa, one that looked jarringly plush in these surroundings. Ito was the first to speak.

"Wow. Excellent front page this morning. They tell me it was your idea. Good job, good job. Pretty slick of you to keep the balance between Fukuda and Nakasone with a single photo. Managing director Iikura was full of admiration. 'Really scored one there,' he said."

That irritating voice had lost not one drop of its oiliness. Yuuki expected excess saliva to start dripping from the edges of the Circulation chief's mouth at any moment.

"So what brings you all the way down here today? Have you been thinking over what we talked about yesterday?"

"What was it we talked about again?" Yuuki responded coldly.

"You remember. How we need to get rid of our pervert of a chairman."

*In other words, about becoming a member of the managing director faction.*

"Wouldn't you consider taking over from Anzai for a while? And I'm sure there must be other people up in the Editorial Department who you could bring along with you? After all, it's not like you and I don't go way back."

Yuuki decided to postpone discussion of the Editorial Department's business for now.

"Ito-san, I'm going to tell you right now, your threats don't work on me."

"What? There's no need to be like that. Surely you don't think you're the only one who's had it tough?"

He wasn't sure what Ito meant, but he certainly wasn't prepared to get on to the topic of his mother.

"Seems Anzai was worked pretty hard."

"Now, that is just slanderous. Nobody made him do anything. He was just the most genuinely hardworking employee I had."

"All those secret meetings with the external board members were a result of your direct orders, I'm sure."

Ito looked unperturbed. There were traces of amusement around his eyes and mouth.

"Is that what his wife told you?"

So this was what Ito had been trying to get out of Yuuki in that uncomfortable conversation two days ago. He was concerned that Anzai had passed on the truth to Yuuki, via Sayuri, about all his underhanded political maneuvering.

"Not at all. I read it in Anzai's diary."

The smile vanished from Ito's face.

"Really? Do you think it's appropriate for you to mishandle his personal property?"

"I have his wife's permission."

"I see . . . And? Are you intending to show that diary to the bosses?"

It was clear Ito was worried. Yuuki was tempted to tell him that he'd already shown it to them.

"I'm asking you about Anzai. He used to call you his lifesaver. I heard it was you who headhunted him from the newsdealer's where he was working and brought him to work at the newspaper."

Yuuki had heard this from Suetsugu during their chat at the library. For a while after the accident on Tsuitate, Anzai had been kind of "out of it," to use the older man's words. As is apparently quite common in the climbing community, Anzai didn't have a regular full-time job back then but scraped by doing part-time work. Lived in a tiny rabbit-hutch apartment with Sayuri. Sayuri had run away from home and moved in with Anzai, and the couple did not marry until she became pregnant with Rintaro. This love of Anzai's life was the daughter of a traditional Japanese sweet maker and had fallen in love with him when he used to visit their shop to buy *daifuku*, sweet bean-filled rice cakes. Or that might have just been Sayuri's version of the story, Yuuki supposed . . .

But without a doubt, it was thanks to Sayuri that Anzai got back on his feet after Endo's death.

*"It was a shock. I just happened to be looking out of the window at the time."*

Anzai had told Suetsugu the following story. Sayuri had been in the last month of pregnancy and had fallen in the street on her way home to their tiny apartment. Anzai had watched from the window as she got shakily to her feet, all the while gently stroking her belly as if to protect and comfort the child inside. There was blood pouring from the palms of her hands and from her knees.

*"Sayuri didn't even notice she was injured. Even when the blood started dripping all over the place."*

The incident had shocked Anzai out of his depression and made him realize that he needed to step up and provide for his wife and the baby that was due so soon.

Shortly after that, he responded to an ad for a live-in employee at a newsdealer's called Yoshikawa. He started out delivering newspapers, graduated to door-to-door fee collecting, and kept on moving up until he'd made enough to rent a bigger apartment for him and his new family. It was his superhuman work ethic at that time that had caught the eye of Ito at the *North Kanto Times,* and he brought Anzai in to work for him. The not-so-young couple with their brand-new baby were absolutely thrilled that Anzai had been given the opportunity to work for one of the top companies in the prefecture. It was absolutely true that Anzai had looked up to Ito as his lifesaver and benefactor.

Ito had made maximum use of Anzai's feelings of indebtedness. In fact, Ito had probably lured Anzai to the company in the first place for the express purpose of having him eventually do his dirty work. For his part, Anzai was in no position to refuse any job that he felt uncomfortable doing. It was his benefactor who was asking, so he must have just gritted his teeth and gotten on with it. He was hardly able to complain, having no academic qualifications, and having been recruited mid-career. If he were to refuse an order, he'd be out of the company. That was the fear he'd been living with.

"Congratulations on making such good use of Anzai."

The smile returned to Ito's face.

"He was an employee. They're there to be used."

"You sent Anzai after Mina Kuroda. To get evidence to bring the chairman down."

"What a shocking thing to come out with! Such conjecture! Anzai was a hard worker. I was the most shocked of anyone when I heard what had happened to him."

Fixing Ito with a stare, Yuuki spoke.

"Beginning tomorrow morning, I need five hundred extra copies of the paper delivered to Fujioka City."

"What? I haven't heard anything about this."

Yuuki explained the Editorial Department's plan. It was obvious Ito was disgusted by it.

"That's going to be a problem. Say we deliver to all three of the families' standby locations, that's one hundred and seventy copies per location. Each of the newsdealers employs the minimum staff to cover their deliveries. They can't manage that many more."

"They don't have to deliver every single copy separately. All they need to do is drop off a pile at each standby location. Anyone who wants to read it can just pick up a copy themselves."

"You editorial people have no idea. That's why you come up with nonsense like that. In rural areas and up in the mountains there aren't any exclusive *NKT* newsdealers. We're forced to share with our rivals. The shops all handle *Asahi* and *Mainichi*, too, so we can't be asking them to do special deliveries just for us."

*Such a spineless snake,* Yuuki thought. But he had another suggestion ready.

"How about if our delivery van just drops them off directly at the standby centers?"

"That'd be completely out of their way. After Fujioka, that van has to go to Manba in the Tano District, to Nakasato, and then all the way up to Uenomura. It'll be late getting to those newsdealers."

"It'd take them no more than five or ten minutes, surely?" Yuuki hadn't expected this last comment to infuriate Ito so much.

"For God's sake! Those five or ten minutes are critical to the newsdealers! They're up every morning at one or two a.m. with all their staff, stuffing those papers into plastic bags. They have to take all the flyers and ads and fold them up inside every single copy, one by one. After that's finished, they have to divide them up by destination. There's a whole elaborate plan of attack they have to go through every single day. It's like a battle. Ten minutes' delay and the newsdealers lose it completely. They're on the phone complaining to us every minute that passes."

His usual careful enunciation had vanished.

"If we're not careful, our readers get their delivery late. And a newspaper that's delivered after breakfast time has no right to call itself a *news*paper."

So the Circulation Department also took great pride in their work. It was the first time Yuuki had thought about that. But still, this was the head of the Circulation Department—as well as a manipulative puppet master and political operator. In the course of this short conversation, Ito had shown him two different faces, and Yuuki's dislike and distrust of the man had grown considerably.

"So you're telling me that you refuse to accept five hundred extra copies?"

"Now, that's not what I said. The whole JAL thing is finally calming down. If the newsroom can get a move on with the proofs, get that printing press turning quickly . . . then perhaps we can squeeze out an extra five or ten minutes to stop at the standby locations."

"So you'll do it?"

"Yes, as long as you get yourselves properly organized."

Having extracted this promise from him, Yuuki responded to Ito's last barb.

"Sometimes we can't get the proofs together early."

"Because you're having so much fun putting them together, I suppose," sneered Ito.

"Having fun? What the hell does that mean?"

"That's what it looks like to us. There are always crowds of people standing around with serious frowns on their faces, pretending to consider it all so deeply, but when all's said and done, you're just having fun doing jigsaw puzzles with the news. It's all about the thrill you get as the deadline approaches. Isn't that what's really going on?"

Yuuki's eyebrows shot up.

"Accident and crime articles are often last-minute. It's vital to get the very latest information in there."

"That's not what the readers expect. It's all just masturbation on the part of the Editorial Department. Just put yourself in our shoes for once. All the trouble you cause with your self-indulgent games, all the messing around, it has repercussions on all the other departments, you know."

"What's the point of a Circulation Department that can't even deal with customers' complaints?"

Ito's narrow eyes slowly widened.

"What did—?"

But Yuuki couldn't help himself.

"Night after night, you burn through company money, entertaining shopkeepers and newsdealers. I'm just asking, what's the point of all that?"

"I told you already. To get the newsdealers to give us equal footing with the other newspaper companies. What would happen if they decided they didn't want to sell *NKT* anymore? Are you assholes going to go up to the mountains and go house-to-house delivering papers? If the newspaper home-delivery system breaks down, it's all over for us. All we can do is take them out, wine and dine them, and make them happy to deliver our papers."

"That's a very convenient argument. How many copies of other newspapers do they really sell up in the mountain regions? It's got to be an insignificant number. The *NKT* is the newsdealers' bread and butter. So it's a give-and-take relationship. We scratch their back, they'll scratch ours. How much money do you waste on all those pointless indulgences?"

Ito banged his fist on the table. The two men glowered at each other.

Ito's desk phone and Yuuki's pager rang at the same time. Yuuki got up, and Ito followed suit. The Circulation chief narrowed his eyes again.

"I really wouldn't act so smug if I were you. A newspaper isn't all that big a thing in the long run. Why don't you try putting out an edition with two or three blank pages in the middle? We can sell it for you, no problem."

They turned away from each other. Yuuki started toward the door, then spun around. He called over to Ito, who had already put the receiver to his ear.

"There's one thing I forgot to tell you—we're going to have to push back the deadline. We in the Editorial Department appreciate your understanding."

It was almost six o'clock, and a cigarette fog hung over the newsroom.

Yuuki's phone rang the moment he reached his desk. It was Sayama. He'd arrived in Uenomura and met up with Tamaki. Before going to the village office he'd taken a few moments to check out the inn where the accident investigation team was staying. He'd discovered that the side entrance was kept unlocked.

For now, Yuuki occupied himself with the wires on his desk.

Huge victory for Nodai Niko High; tell bereaved teammate "We did it for you"

Tears during school song; bereaved family watches from standby center

Survivor testimony: panic in the passenger cabin

"Unfasten your seat belt!" father yelled right before impact

Inquest confirms there were originally more survivors

Struggle continues to ID deceased, now at 181

Fuselage cut open to remove remains

Solemn funeral service for thirty-six dead

Ashes transported home

"Yuuki?"

He was interrupted by the voice of Inaoka from Heartfelt, the readers' letters page. The older man was pressing his hands together in a gesture of apology.

"I'm so sorry that I haven't been able to get the special feature on the JAL crash together today."

"Why is that?"

"I'm afraid I have four or five letters left over from the anniversary of the end of the war. Today's the last day I can really use them. The content is rather interesting and I don't want to have to discard them."

Yuuki was secretly relieved. Oimura was already on the point of explosion, and he had neglected to run his idea for Heartfelt past the higher-ups. He thought it was probably best to give Oimura a day or two to cool off. It wouldn't have been appropriate for him to order Inaoka, as a colleague far senior to him, to postpone publication, so he'd been in a quandary. If Inaoka were to put together the JAL crash special feature today, as they'd planned, he'd have had to prepare for the barrage of criticism and invective that would come raining down from a furious Oimura. Anyway, for Inaoka to change the plan was the best possible outcome all around.

"When do you think you'll be able to put it together?"

"Well, tomorrow is the legal advice special, and I can't really take space away from that, so how about the day after that?"

"That'll be fine. Thank you."

Yuuki bowed, but then, as he spun his chair back around to face his desk, he felt a little dizzy. Yes, he'd caught a cold or something—ever since he'd been back in the newsroom, his forehead had felt a little fever-ish. Lack of sleep, his fury at Ito, the anticipation of having a huge scoop right there at his fingertips—any of these could be the cause of it. He'd refused to acknowledge it, but just now he'd started to get chills running up and down his back.

He got up, crossed the newsroom, and switched the output from the air conditioner down from five to three. Then he stopped off at the editorial admin island, where there was a vacant desk that was used as a kind of medicine cabinet. He opened the drawer, found some medicine for colds, and swallowed it without water. On his way back to his own workstation his legs seemed a bit wobbly, but he wondered if it was just because he had finally acknowledged that he might have a cold. For now it was better to persevere until the deadline. He got back to the wires.

Japan-U.S. joint investigation team arrives at the crash site
Tailpiece fell in the sea off Shimoda, tide calculations confirm
Piece of passenger cabin roof drifts ashore
Engine #4 found

He knew that, somewhere in the back of his mind, he had doubts about Tamaki's story. Although he was concentrating deeply on reading the articles, he didn't miss the sound of the fax machine kicking into gear. He glanced up to see Kishi getting to his feet.

"It's probably for me," Yuuki said, forcing himself not to sound too excited. He leapt up and nimbly made it to the fax machine before Kishi. As he'd expected, the cover sheet read "Tamaki, Maebashi." Tamaki had forgotten to call before sending the fax. The intro began to come through.

*On the 17th, following investigations into the crash of the Japan Airlines jumbo jet that left 520 people dead, the Ministry of Transportation's Aircraft Accident Investigation Committee announced the most likely cause of the crash to be "rupturing of the pressure bulkhead, situated at the rear of the aircraft." The same aircraft suffered what is known as a tail-strike accident at Osaka Airport seven years ago, and it is believed that inadequate repair work done at that time on the damaged bulkhead contributed to the accident. Because of this, investigators—*

A shiver ran down Yuuki's spine, but this time it had nothing to do with having a cold. The fax continued to churn out paper. Yuuki stood close to the machine to shield its contents from prying eyes, grabbing each page as soon as it came out. He turned each page over and piled them upside down.

There were twenty-three pages in total. A hundred and fifteen lines of print. A real epic work. Yuuki took them back to his desk and, with a red pen in one hand, created a kind of wall with his arms and shoulders and began to read.

It was a long-winded draft. Clearly a lot of effort had been put into it. It was a mixture of fact and conjecture and lacked coherence in places. It required major surgery.

First Yuuki slashed anything that was superfluous. Then he excised all the risky passages. Then he nipped and tucked, connecting the sections neatly together until they formed a coherent article. He read it over once more and removed some more of the surplus. A good story didn't need any excess flab. The bare bones were all that should remain.

He put down his red pen and looked at the clock: 8:15 p.m. He'd spent an hour fixing the article. He put the proofs into a neat pile. Thirteen pages, sixty-three lines—about half of what he'd started with.

He slipped the proofs into his desk drawer and picked up the phone. He dialed the extension for Yoshii in the copy team and watched him reach for his phone. He kept his voice low.

"Yuuki here."

Yoshii's childlike face glanced over.

"The thing we talked about yesterday, it's happening tonight."

Even from across the room, Yuuki could see Yoshii's expression freeze. There was a beat before he replied.

"How many lines?"

"Only about sixty. Can you prepare another mock-up, separate from the Nodai Niko High School one?"

"Got it. When will you have it ready?"

"Can you have the layout ready by tenish?"

"Easily."

"Speak to you later."

As soon as Yoshii replaced the receiver, Yuuki dialed Tamaki's pager. Fifteen minutes later, Tamaki called back.

"This is Tamaki. Did you page me?"

His voice was loud and upbeat. Yuuki kept his own voice low.

"I read your article."

"It was a little too long, wasn't it?"

"Don't worry about that. I want to know how things are going at your end."

"Sayama-san is on standby on the hill at the back."

"Hill at the back?"

"There's a small hill covered in bamboo right behind the inn. You can see right into the building from it."

Yuuki gave a small nod.

"And the accident investigators?"

"They ate dinner a while ago, they've already been to the bathhouse. Now they seem to be chatting in the lounge."

"And the other media?"

"Same as always. They're all loitering around the inn."

"How about your position? How far away are you from the inn?"

"I'm at a public phone a little way down the road. It's about a fifteen-minute round-trip."

"I see. Right, I won't call you again unless there's a major development. I'll expect a call from you."

"About what time?"

"Call me when Sayama gets into the inn."

"Understood. Um, one more thing . . . Sayama-san wanted me to ask you something."

"What?"

"When's tonight's deadline?"

For a moment Yuuki didn't know what to say.

But of course—Sayama had set off to Uenomura without asking about the deadline. There was still some lingering fallout from the incident with Sayama's eyewitness account. Perhaps Yuuki had subconsciously avoided the topic with Sayama.

He looked up at the clock again. It was 9:45 p.m. But it wasn't the hands of the clock that Yuuki was studying. He was staring at the space between the figures 12 and 2.

He made up his mind in seconds.

"One a.m.," he whispered into the mouthpiece. "And depending on the situation at your end, I can wait until half past."

"Half past one? Can you even do that?"

"Give Sayama the message."

"Okay. I will."

Yuuki hung up.

He could sense the strained atmosphere on either side of him. Both Kishi and Nozawa were clearly dying to know what was going on. Their silence spoke volumes.

Yuuki pulled the pile of Kyodo wires toward him. His heart was beating faster than usual, and his breathing was agitated. But it wasn't the cold he'd caught that was causing this; it was the contents of his desk drawer.

It was ten to ten by the time he'd finished reading all the wires. Ten more minutes . . . Yuuki waited.

"Ten o'clock!" People in the newsroom began to get up from their seats. A special late-shift team had been put together in order to cover the JAL crash, but about one-third of the staff of the newsroom were leaving at ten, as usual. The remaining shift was known as the "last call." They wouldn't leave the building until the final proofs were ready.

Yuuki carefully slid open his desk drawer and retrieved Tamaki's manuscript.

"Kishi? Do we have an *NKT* staff directory?"

Kishi was half standing, stuffing papers into his bag. He stared at Yuuki for a few moments, then picked up a booklet from his desk.

"Here."

"Thanks."

Yuuki found the page he was looking for and propped it open with a paperweight. He pulled Tamaki's manuscript closer and added at the end of the intro: "Akihiko Tamaki, Tatsuya Sayama." It was the first full-name credit in the history of the *North Kanto Times*.

Yuuki looked over at Kishi.

"Do you have any plans tonight?"

"No. Nothing in particular."

"Could you keep me company on the last call?"

Yuuki handed him Tamaki's manuscript. Kishi took it and began to read. His expression changed. He gave Yuuki a sharp look, then laughed. Yuuki glanced at Nozawa, who quickly pretended to be absorbed by the proofs of the entertainment pages.

"Nozawa!"

No reply.

"Take a look at this for me. And when you've finished, pass it to Yoshii."

Without waiting for a response, Yuuki got up. Even as he set off across the newsroom, he still wasn't sure where he was heading. To see editor in chief Kasuya? Or managing editor Oimura? Local news section chief Todoroki? Which one of the three should he talk to?

This time yesterday, he wouldn't have hesitated to go straight to Kasuya's office. He would have deliberately insulted both Oimura and Todoroki by going over their heads. He felt no sense of duty toward Oimura. And Todoroki had been responsible for killing Sayama's eyewitness article. Still . . .

Yuuki headed for the row of desks by the wall. Todoroki was at his.

"Chief?"

The dark lenses looked up. Yuuki put both hands on the desk and leaned in close.

"I've got a scoop."

"On what?"

As Todoroki glared at him, Yuuki silently pleaded that the local news chief wouldn't kill it this time.

"The cause of the crash."

Behind the lenses, Todoroki's eyes widened.

"Is it a sure thing?"

"Pretty much. I'm just waiting for corroboration."

Todoroki turned to look at the wall clock.

"Will it be late?"

"Probably."

"What do you plan to do?"

"I want the deadline extended an hour to one a.m. And if we don't make that, then another half an hour. That's what I told them up at the crash site."

He'd worded it so that Todoroki was free to make the call. His boss folded his arms.

"One thirty—so you're going to have two proofs ready."

Yuuki nodded. The first galley proofs would be made with the Nodai Niko High School story as the lead, and they would go to press. The pages would be collated and loaded into the delivery vans. This had to be done, otherwise there would be substantial delays in the deliveries to remote locations. This was all going to happen right after midnight. But the moment he heard from Sayama, the printing press would be halted. The front-page galley proof would be replaced by a new one headed CAUSE OF CRASH RUPTURED BULKHEAD, and the rest of the copies would be printed. It all depended on what time Sayama called, but it was probable that only about thirty percent of the prefecture would receive the second edition with the scoop headline. If the call came really close to half past one, then only Maebashi City would get the second edition. If they were lucky, maybe some of Takasaki, too.

That was the problem.

"But if the second edition doesn't make it to Fujioka or Tano, then there isn't really much point in the scoop," Yuuki pointed out.

"That's true. But if the delivery van going to Fujioka and Tano is the last to leave—if the copies come off the press at two a.m. and they use the Kan-Etsu Expressway—they can be up in Uenomura in two hours. The papers would be with the newsdealers by four."

"I think it'd be worth doing."

"Circulation will be furious."

The plan was exactly what Yuuki was hoping for. His expression communicated as much to Todoroki.

There was a moment of silence.

"Okay, then. Deadline's one thirty," said Todoroki briskly. "Just one thing: the first edition goes to print at twelve fifteen. The scoop goes out to Maebashi, Fujioka, and Tano only."

Yuuki had no objection.

"And you're going to need to detain the Fujioka and Tano van."

"I'll use the old-fashioned method."

"You mean . . . ?"

"Yep."

"It's a whole new era now."

"I can't think of any other way of doing it."

Yuuki turned and left. He'd gone only a few paces before Todoroki's voice stopped him.

"Yuuki!"

He turned only his head.

"Have you spoken to Kasuya and Oimura about this?"

"No."

The eyes shifted slightly behind their lenses. Yuuki knew that now he'd paid back the debt from earlier in the day.

Time to banish idle thoughts and focus everything he had on getting that scoop.

It was 11:30 p.m.

The newsroom was eerily quiet. Everyone was sitting, waiting for a single telephone call to come in, with Yuuki right there at the center of it all.

The date was about to change. Lots of nervous eyes turned to watch the wall clock and, just at that moment, Yuuki's desk phone rang.

The tense voice came over the phone.

"Tamaki here."

"Did he get into the inn?"

"Yes. He managed to slip in through the side door."

"The investigators?"

"Still in a meeting."

"Got it. Go back to the hill. Watch them for another fifteen minutes, then call me again."

"Okay."

The public phone was fifteen minutes' round-trip from the inn, so the next call would come at half past midnight. Of course, if Sayama came rushing out of the inn before that time, there would be no need for Tamaki to check in.

"Sayama's inside the inn," Yuuki told Kishi. In the total silence of the newsroom, his words carried all the way to the copy team's island. It caused a small commotion, and Kamejima pumped his fist in the air.

The door opened and Yoshii came running in. He'd been down to the Production Department on the first floor. His cheeks were bright red from the exertion, which made his face look even more boyish than usual. He was clutching the rolled-up proofs of the front page.

They spread the mock-up of the second edition out on the desk. Usually they'd run off ten copies; today, there were only three—one for Yuuki, one for Kasuya in the editor in chief's office, and one for Yoshii. All three copies had "not to be removed" stamped in the top right-hand corner. Kishi and Nozawa leaned in to read.

RUPTURED BULKHEAD PROBABLE CAUSE OF CRASH

The size of the headline was unprecedented, a full-on assault to the eyes.

Yuuki read carefully through the article below, checking each sentence. He felt a clammy sweat break out on his forehead.

"This is going to be amazing," Kishi muttered to himself.

Tomorrow morning, this front page was going to be revealed in its full glory. Every newspaper throughout Japan would publish their own version of the story. It would be distributed to news agencies all over the world, translated into hundreds of different languages; people of all nationalities would read an article by the *North Kanto Times* . . .

Kishi beckoned Yoshii over.

"It's good."

"Okay."

Yoshii rolled the proof back up awkwardly, and set off again, running out the door.

There was a rumble from below. The press had begun to print the Nodai Niko High version.

The phone rang. Yuuki glanced up at the clock. It was exactly twelve thirty.

"Tamaki here."

"How's it going?"

"I caught a glimpse of Sayama."

"Where?"

"In the toilet. The one near the lounge."

"The rest of them?"

"They're still talking."

"Got it. You—"

He was cut off by a loud crash. He recognized it as the sound of the newsroom door being flung open.

Ito marched into the room, accompanied by several of the Circulation Department's junior employees.

"Someone tell me what is going on up here."

Teeth bared, Ito stood and surveyed the room. He hadn't spotted Yuuki yet, as he had his back turned.

"Printing's delayed by fifteen minutes yet again! Yet again!"

Yuuki frowned. He'd screwed up. When he'd met Ito earlier that evening, he'd relayed the news that the deadline would once again be delayed. This had put Ito on his guard. He must have stayed back late in order to keep an eye on the Editorial Department.

"And the keys? Where are the keys to the van?"

Yuuki held his breath. They were in his pocket. The keys to van number 5—the vehicle heading for Fujioka and the Tano District.

Oimura and Todoroki came running out of Kasuya's office, followed by the editor in chief himself, who was looking rather worried.

"Get out!" Predictably, it was Oimura who barked the order. The Firecracker was definitely lit. "The newsroom is off-limits. You Circulation schmoozers can't just wander in here at will!"

"Who are you to talk to me like that? I don't take shit from the chairman's little Chihuahua!"

"You're one to talk! Iikura's pet puppy!"

"You're nothing but a bunch of thieving animals. Give back the keys! We know you've got them. It's not the first time you've pulled a childish stunt like this."

There was loud jeering from close to the newsroom door. Any moment, people were going to come to blows.

"Yuuki. Go downstairs!" called Kishi. "We'll move the crash desk to the first-floor production area."

It was a good plan. Yuuki nodded and got up from his desk. He was still holding the telephone receiver. He put it to his ear and found he was still connected.

"Tamaki, from now on, call me on extension 3301."

He replaced the receiver and turned around, only to be caught in the seething Ito's direct line of sight.

"Yuuki!"

His oily voice reverberated through the office.

"It's you, isn't it, you little fucker? Give me the keys!"

Ignoring Ito completely, Yuuki began to walk toward the door, Kishi and Nozawa on either side of him. But the opposition also made their move. Two of the junior employees from Circulation moved to block their exit.

"Get out of the way!" Yuuki barked, and instead of slowing his pace, he walked straight at them, maintaining eye contact. The two men faltered.

"Stop him!"

This time it was Ito's command. The young Circulation staff desperately tried to cut Yuuki off, but Kishi and Nozawa advanced on them, like young sumo wrestlers protecting their *yokozuna*. The junior members of the copy team also joined their ranks.

The two sides came together. But the Editorial Department had the superior number. Somehow, a space was opened up, through which Yuuki saw he could pass. He dodged to one side and slipped through the doorway. It was right then that he heard it.

"Son of a whore!"

Yuuki stopped dead. He turned back to see a vulgar grin on Ito's face, and suddenly his head felt fizzing hot. All he could see were his own tiny, shivering kneecaps as he cowered in that storage shed. He ran at Ito, fists raised. In an instant, a couple of people had grabbed him by the shoulders, others by the chest and waist. Kishi was among them.

"Yuuki, save it for later."

"Let go of me!"

He struggled to get free, but the arms were wrapped too strongly around him. The entire Editorial Department swarmed in a single mass out into the corridor, Yuuki being swept along in the center of the throng. It felt as if his feet were barely touching the floor. The staff of the Circulation Department chased after them down the stairs. The employees of the first-floor Production Department, clearly intrigued by the uproar, came running out into the corridor.

"Stop the Circulation guys!"

In response, the junior Production staff positioned themselves just inside the doorway. As Yuuki and the rest of the Editorial Department poured through the door, they threw all their strength against it and shut it tight.

"Don't let them in!"

"Lock it!"

Yuuki shook himself loose from the grips on him and sank into the nearest chair. He was out of breath. His throat was dry. His face felt like it was on fire and he was sweating bullets.

From the other side of the door, he could hear the voices raging.

He slowly leaned back in his chair and looked around the Production Department. There was quite a crowd of young staff there from the Editorial and Production Departments. *Just you try and break in here.* That was the expression on everyone's face. He was safe here. Everyone was his ally.

Nevertheless, he felt truly alone.

"Yuuki?"

Kishi was beckoning to him from in front of the worktable. Yoshii was at his side. It seemed the second version of the front page was ready.

As Yuuki moved to join them he looked up at the clock. It was 12:55 a.m. There was only just over half an hour left. As he walked he noticed something strange about his trousers . . . Surely he hadn't dropped the keys? Panicked, he stuck his hand in his pocket. His fingers came into contact with something cold and metallic. But at the same time his brain registered the texture of leather. All of a sudden, Anzai's voice was there inside his head.

*"I climb up to step down."*

He saw a flicker of light. If only he could just have some peace, some time to think, he was sure he could solve the riddle that Anzai had left him.

**3 3**

Extension 3301 was silent. The phone in question sat on a desk close to the middle of the office. Yuuki sat waiting, his arms and legs crossed. A crowd of roughly twenty people was gathered around him. The room felt stuffy and overheated.

1:15 a.m. . . . . Yuuki stood up. Fifteen minutes to the deadline. He couldn't sit still any longer. His chest was on fire and it was all he could do to stop himself from exploding.

What was Sayama doing? How many times had he screamed this inside his head?

Yuuki approached the wall that held the air conditioner, but never took his eyes off the clock. 1:16 . . . 1:17 . . .

Todoroki was sitting on a metal chair. He'd taken off his glasses and his exposed eyes were glued to his wristwatch.

Kasuya and Oimura were nowhere to be seen. They were probably still outside in the corridor, facing off with Ito and the rest of the Circulation Department. The distant sound of angry voices could be faintly heard.

Yuuki tore his gaze away from the clock and looked at Todoroki.

"What's going to happen to the five hundred copies for the families in the standby facilities?"

Todoroki looked up.

"They can drop them off on the way back. We don't need to use the delivery system. It'll be good enough."

Todoroki turned his attention back to his wristwatch, and Yuuki turned his to the wall clock.

1:19 . . . 1:20 . . .

*Maybe we'll have to wait until tomorrow. Try again. Go for it then instead.*
1:22 . . . 1:23 . . .

His prayers weren't working. But he knew that the moment he gave up, fortune would fall in his lap. When he was working cases out in the field, this was always what happened. He allowed himself a momentary, rueful half smile.

The telephone rang.

Yuuki turned his head, and suddenly the eyes of all the people crowded around extension 3301 were on him. Nobody moved. Then Yuuki was on his feet and running. He snatched the receiver off its hook.

"Sayama here."

His voice was calm and low.

"I got to speak to Fujinami."

"And?"

"If he were a police officer, it'd be a yes."

Yuuki groaned. Sayama had asked the lead investigator, Kanae Fujinami, about the bulkhead, and got a probable yes from him. But Fujinami had refused to confirm absolutely that the cause of the crash was the rupture of the bulkhead. Intimation, facial expression, manner; Sayama had only been able to draw his conclusion from these signs. And what Sayama was saying was that it *seemed* to be a positive response. If Sayama had gotten the same response from one of the police officers he normally dealt with, officers famous for their perfect poker faces, he could safely have read this as a conclusive yes. That was what Sayama was telling him.

However, Sayama's problem was that this was someone he had never interviewed before. A man with the unique post of accident investigation specialist. Sayama had no existing data, no baseline reaction, to which he could compare this man's responses. In other words, no matter how close to a definitive yes this might appear to be, Sayama was not able to fully confirm.

Yuuki sank down into his chair and repositioned the receiver against his ear. It was already slick with his own sweat.

"So you're saying you can't be one hundred percent sure."

"Right."

"How about the others?"

"The *Mainichi* seems to be up to something."

"I see."

The other press bodies were moving on the story. Normally, telling this to the editor was a favorite ploy of a reporter desperate to get his own scoop into print. And normally, the editor would take it with a grain of salt. But right now there was no trace of raw ambition, no restless impatience. Sayama's words were to be taken at face value; the *Mainichi* newspaper could very well be sniffing around the bulkhead story, too.

1:26 . . . 1:27 . . .

You could have heard a pin drop in the room.

Could they run the story? Yuuki ran over all the possibilities in his head.

On one hand, the story was probably accurate. And a chance like this would never come around again. They had to print it. If it turned out that the cause of the crash was not a ruptured bulkhead, it could, at the very best, be said that the investigators were presently looking into the possibility that it was. To write the piece as conjecture would probably be acceptable. And the cause was very likely to be confirmed afterward. The language used in the headline, and in the article itself, would have to be diluted to "probable" and not "definitive." But that was okay. It was doable.

And yet, having made its decision, his mind was now beginning to backpedal.

Five hundred and twenty dead. The biggest single aircraft disaster in history. This article would be read all over the world. Was it acceptable to make this kind of decision to publish a major news story about such a momentous event this flippantly? The reporters, the desk chief, the editorial staff were all about to put the information into print without definitive proof. Was that really okay? What if it took investigators more than a year, or even three years, to come up with a proven cause? If the *North Kanto Times* published an incorrect theory now, the consequences of the false alarm they triggered could continue to affect the investigation indefinitely.

So what should he do?

He was afraid. It was extremely unlikely that they were wrong. Were they about to let this chance slip from their grasp? It wasn't only Sayama and Tamaki but the man in command of the JAL crash desk—Yuuki himself—whose names would go down in *North Kanto Times* history along with this scoop.

He looked at the clock. The minute hand was pointing directly downward. The deadline had arrived.

Do it!

Yuuki leapt to his feet and, as he did, something clattered to the floor. It was a set of keys. The keys to the number 5 van, the one that headed up to Fujioka City and the Tano District. They'd fallen out of his pocket.

Suddenly, he panicked. His knees began to shake.

*Stop the press!* The words were right there in his throat. Or rather, they'd made their way up from his throat and were already on his tongue. But they wouldn't make their way out of his mouth.

"Yuuki! We're going for it, right?" Kishi shouted.

Then everyone was yelling at once.

"Let's do it!"

"We've got this. A worldwide scoop!"

But Yuuki didn't move. The tip of his shoe rested against the keys to the van.

Van number 5 would be going to Fujioka and Tano. The victims' relatives would get a copy. This morning's edition would be read by many of the bereaved families waiting for news of their loved ones.

Yuuki looked up at the ceiling.

*"Thank you . . . so much . . ."*

He saw that mother again, holding the hand of her young son. Bereaved family members. It wasn't the world who needed to know the truth, it was the victims' families. People who had lost a close family member needed to know as soon as possible what had caused their loved one to be stolen from them. Why had their father, their mother, their child, been forced to perish there on Mount Osutaka?

A clear-cut, definitive cause.

He looked down at the floor. It felt as if he were looking into hell. He bent down, picked up the dropped keys, and headed toward the door.

"Hey, where are you going? Yuuki, wait!"

Shaking off Kishi's hand, he pushed his way through the crowd. Todoroki called out his name. He didn't react. He marched straight over to the door, unlocked it, and passed through into the corridor.

Everyone's eyes were on him, particularly Ito's bloodshot ones. Yuuki silently handed him the keys to van number 5.

"Sorry for all the trouble. I'll be sending you a written apology tomorrow."

*We can't see the mountains today.*
*No clouds in the sky, yet we can't see them.*
*No rain falling, yet we can't see them.*
*Why, why, Grandma?*
*Why can't we see the mountains?*
*Well, my child,*
*The mountains are grieving.*
*Why, why, Grandma?*
*Why are the mountains grieving?*
*Well, my child,*
*Since long, long ago*
*They've grieved for the dead*
*Because since long, long ago*
*The mountains have been there.*

Yuuki sat straight up in bed. *Where am I? Ah, yes, the on-call room.*

The phone on the bedside table began to ring. Automatically, Yuuki reached behind him to pick it up.

"This is Sayama."

*Sayama, lead police beat reporter,* he thought, and then everything came rushing back.

"Ah. Great job last night. What time is it?"

"Just before six."

Yuuki had instructed him to go back to the inn first thing in the morning and try to make contact with the investigation team again. But if it wasn't even six yet, it was too early.

"Has something happened?"

"The *Mainichi* published it."

"Published what?"

"The pressure bulkhead. That it was the cause of the crash."

Yuuki tried to blink the sleep out of his eyes.

"Hello?"

Yuuki said nothing.

"Hello? Yuu-san?"

Again, nothing.

"Look, I think you made the right decision, Yuu-san. It wasn't the kind of story to gamble on. That's how I feel, anyway."

Without a word, Yuuki replaced the receiver. He got out of bed, pulled on his trousers, and buttoned his shirt on his way out of the on-call room. He descended one flight of stairs and entered the newsroom. Young Moriwaki was on the night watch. He scrambled to his feet and bowed to Yuuki as he walked in. First year on the police beat, his face was puffy from lack of sleep.

"Has the *Mainichi* come?"

"Oh, sorry. I'll go and get it now."

Moriwaki left a breeze in his wake as he rushed out of the newsroom. At this time in the morning there was hardly anyone in the building, so Yuuki heard every step as Moriwaki ran down the stairs and back up again. The nimble footsteps approached the door, then it was flung open and Moriwaki rushed in, a stack of newspapers in his arms.

"Here you are," he said, handing Yuuki the *Mainichi*. Yuuki took it and spread it out on his desk. There was no need to leaf through. It was the top story.

BULKHEAD RUPTURE PROBABLE CAUSE

Strangely enough, it was almost the exact same headline that the *North Kanto Times* had planned for their second edition. The content of the article was also very similar. The reasoning was that the rear pressure bulkhead had ruptured, causing the air in the passenger cabin to shoot outward and the tail to disintegrate in midair. Seven years earlier, the bulkhead had been damaged in a tail-strike accident at Osaka Airport, and it had been gradually deteriorating ever since.

*Shit!*

The hand holding the newspaper shook a little. Without really knowing what he was doing, he grabbed the centerfold of the open paper and held it high above his head. The next moment it was flapping through the air like a giant moth. From his desk across the room, Moriwaki watched wide-eyed.

Yuuki slumped back in his seat and didn't move. Everything seemed to have gone dark. He waited for the phone calls. Or, more specifically, for the jeers and angry voices. Who would be the first? Editor in chief Kasuya? Managing editor Oimura? Or would it be the local news chief, Todoroki?

Thirty minutes passed . . . An hour . . . Seven o'clock came, but still no one had called.

Respectful silence? Compassion? Or, as it was still an inherited accident after all, perhaps they just didn't care that much. Maybe no one had ever really believed in the possibility of a scoop in the first place.

Yuuki walked out of the newsroom and kept going. He reached the parking lot, got into his car, and set off in the direction of Takasaki City. Should he go home? He wasn't sure. He just wanted to put some distance between himself and the *North Kanto Times*'s headquarters.

He was consumed with regrets. He was the one who had made the decision to kill the bulkhead story, because the families had trusted him to print an accurate account and he had been too tempted by the chance of a scoop.

But still he regretted it. And having come so close, the disappointment was all the more bitter. He felt utterly dejected.

He could hear Sayama's voice in his ear. He'd called him "*Yuu-san.*" "*I think you made the right decision, Yuu-san.*"

And Yuuki had put the phone down without answering him. He'd been so obsessed with his own misery that he hadn't bothered to respond to Sayama's words.

*Thank you.* That's what he should have said. If he could just have said that simple phrase, he would have been able to feel proud of himself again. The same opportunity would never offer itself again. *Life is just a series of moments.*

Yuuki gripped the steering wheel with both hands. He pumped the accelerator twice, then three, four times. The speedometer needle shot up.

Jun was home alone. He was in the living room, watching TV in his pajamas.

"Where's your mom?"

"Weeding," he replied, without looking up.

"Yuka?"

"Weeding."

They must be at the local park. Everyone in the neighborhood took turns to help with its upkeep.

Yuuki sank down on the couch. He stared for a while at Jun's back and his broadening shoulders. He could see Jun getting annoyed with him, as usual. First his foot started tapping, then his shoulders began to twitch. *Don't sit behind me. Go away.* That was what he was saying to his father. But today it wasn't so obvious.

"Jun?"

No reply.

"Hey, Jun!"

"Yeah?"

The boy didn't turn his head, but the twitching of his shoulders became more pronounced.

"Is there anything you'd like to do?"

Utter silence.

"In the future, I mean. Is there anything you really want to do?"

"No."

"Nothing at all?"

"Nope."

"I was the same, you know, when I was your age."

"Huh."

"I just dreamed of eating a huge meal, you know—just that sort of thing."

"Huh."

He had a hunch that, at some point, Jun was going to explode. Perhaps he'd suddenly grab his father, or even swing a metal bat at him . . .

And if it came to that, he would just let himself be hit. He should let himself bleed the equivalent amount of pain and distress he'd caused Jun in the past.

"I think I'll take a nap."

Yuuki was mostly talking to himself. He got up, and at once Jun's twitching slowed. Yuuki cut through the living room and into the corridor. He climbed the stairs.

He always escaped this way. Always telling himself he'd do something about it next time. How, next time, he'd try to have a deeper conversation. That they were father and son living under the same roof and there'd be plenty of time.

Yuuki paused at the landing. Was it true? Was there still plenty of time for Jun and him? *Life is just a series of moments.*

Yuuki went back downstairs. Back down the corridor and into the living room. Jun looked around when he heard his father's footsteps. He probably thought it was Yumiko, come to tell him off for still being in his pajamas. The expression on his face was cheerfully mischievous, as if he were about to stick out his tongue. That innocent thirteen-year-old face reminded Yuuki of the bashful Rintaro.

But Jun had already turned back to the TV. He was obviously trying to cover up his mistake.

Yuuki's heart welled up.

"Jun, do you want to come climbing with me sometime?"

Tsuitate stretched up like a sword piercing the serene sky.

"Okay, here goes!"

Rintaro, climbing in the lead, seemed to float his way up the rock face, the only sound the rattling of the carabiners suspended from his harness. They were at the huge rock wall with its series of overhangs. Cloud Ridge route number 1's first pitch was about twenty-five meters. The first hurdle—that first roof—wasn't directly above their heads, but it required them to take a route that leaned toward the left. The first, more gently inclining pitch could be free-climbed without using any equipment.

Yuuki was standing on Anseilen Terrace, looking upward as he cautiously let out the rope connected to Rintaro. The ace of the local mountaineering club—Yuuki was fascinated to watch the young man's perfect climbing style. It made him feel good. There was no trace of hesitation or stress in the rhythmic way he moved his hands and feet. As his tall frame moved steadily upward, it was as if gravity didn't exist.

About midway through the pitch, Yuuki heard Rintaro's cheerful voice.

"Yuuki-san! If I fall, make sure you catch me, okay?"

He felt the tension release in both shoulders. He knew this kind of banter was an example of Rintaro's consideration for other people. Yuuki was alone on the terrace and feeling a little nervous and tense.

"Okay! You can count on me!" Yuuki shouted back, as loudly as he could.

The speed at which Rintaro was ascending was even faster than it looked. If he didn't pay enough attention, the rope that Yuuki was letting out, or belaying, instead of remaining at just the right level of slack, would become too taut. Even so, Rintaro kept climbing comfortably and soon reached the spot that marked the end of the first pitch—nicknamed the Two-Person Terrace. It was a space in which two adults could just about stand side by side.

Tying the rope to bolts that had been left behind in the rock, he quickly made sure he was secure on the terrace, then looked down at Yuuki.

"All right, you can start now. Begin by letting your body relax and stretch into it."

"Got it. I'll take it easy."

Contrary to his words, Yuuki's knees were wobbly and he was trembling with fear. But he obstinately grabbed hold of the rock.

It was pleasantly silent.

It was the same feeling he got when he woke up at the crack of dawn. The cold-water tap . . . the handle of the fridge . . . the knob on the gas cooker . . . the cool feel of things that had been left untouched overnight— he felt all these in the rock. He looked up. The first overhang dominated the view above him—a huge protruding roof. He hurriedly pushed the thought from his mind. His first goal was to reach the Two-Person Terrace, where Rintaro was waiting for him. Without rushing, without getting flustered, with a steady rhythm. It was what Kyoichiro Anzai had taught him, long ago.

Suddenly he was assaulted by a wave of nostalgia.

"Hey, Yuu. Let's take a shot at Tsuitate!"

He had never forgotten the sound of that booming voice. Nor Anzai's beaming smile whenever he spoke.

"There's a fine if you back out."

"Tsuitate's no big deal when you have middle-aged superpowers!"

It had never occurred to him that Anzai might be forcing his smiles. But in that moment, Yuuki believed he'd been laughing from the bottom of his heart.

And yet back then, as an employee of the North Kanto Times, Anzai had been in deep distress. He believed he owed a debt of gratitude to the chief of the Circulation Department, and had been talked into being the foot soldier and general gofer for the managing director's faction. He'd been entertaining the external board members night after night, supporting the maneuvering and plotting of the breakup of the chairman's faction. And in the end, he was ordered to arrange the reveal of the sex scandal by constantly turning up at the bar where the chairman's former personal assistant worked.

Even that night, right before he was supposed to climb Tsuitate with Yuuki, he was at that bar. Then, sometime after leaving the premises, in the dead of night, he'd collapsed in the street in the middle of the entertainment district.

Lonely Hearts. A short while afterward, Yuuki had paid a visit to that bar. Chairman Shirakawa's ex-secretary, Mina Kuroda, had the kind of delicate features that suggested she might have some foreign blood. It turned out to be true that she'd been subjected to constant sexual harassment from the chairman and had ended up leaving the company because of it. And it was also true that Anzai had paid her many visits to find out the details of this harassment. Mina commented on how sullen he always was, never cracking a single joke. So Anzai had taken the job very seriously. When Yuuki asked about that particular night, Mina had lots to say. The owner had asked her to work at another branch that night. It was one in the morning by the time she turned up at Lonely Hearts. When she walked in, Anzai was sitting at the bar. As soon as he saw her, he got to his feet and approached her, saying, "I need to talk to you. This will be the last time." Mina had flinched. She'd just had a quarrel with one of her best customers and was in a bad mood. She told the bar owner that she was going back to the other branch, and she walked out of Lonely Hearts. When she saw Anzai follow her, on reflex she broke into a run. Apparently, he was yelling so loudly for her to stop that she got frightened and dodged into a backstreet to give him the slip.

Anzai had collapsed at around 2:00 a.m. Shortly before that, someone had seen him running. So he must have been looking for Mina in the streets of the entertainment district when it happened.

Anzai must have decided to try to sort everything out the night before he was due to climb Tsuitate. *This will be the last time.*

He was planning never to ask her again about the sexual harassment.

He hated making her feel bad. That was probably what he wanted to tell Mina.

But it was all just guesswork. Anzai, in his hospital bed, hadn't been able to answer any questions. His eyes had nothing to say. Those big, twinkling eyes had stared at the ceiling without seeing a thing. They shone brightly in the rays of summer sun that entered through the hospital curtains; they glowed in the autumn sunset. Yuuki had watched how Anzai's eyes reflected all the seasons.

"Just one more. You've got it."

Rintaro's voice was right above him. All the past seventeen years seemed to be contained in that voice.

It had been around the time that the pale winter light had begun to shine into Anzai's eyes that Rintaro had started to spend time at Yuuki's house. Yuuki would bring him over on his days off, or for dinner. Yumiko was always glad to have him. Yuka was also very quick to take to him. His presence made everything peaceful. Somehow, Rintaro possessed that mysterious power. At first Jun was uncomfortable in the presence of this boy the same age as him, but he, too, gradually warmed to him. Eventually he would invite Rintaro into his room to hang out together. Yuuki was optimistic. He had almost given up on repairing his relationship with Jun, but now that Rintaro had been brought into the family he felt there might still be hope for them.

In the early summer of the following year, Yuuki invited Jun and Rintaro to go hiking with him in the mountains. After that, they went all the time. The two boys finished middle school, entered high school, then Jun went on to university. Rintaro took a job in a local factory, but even after their lives diverged they would still all three meet up once or twice a year to go to the mountains.

"The rock right there's a little fragile. Better to take the right side."

"Got it."

Yuuki was almost at the Two-Person Terrace. He increased his pace ever so slightly. He'd started out a little awkwardly, but now he felt as if he'd gotten a feel for the rock. As he sped up, his fear seemed to leave him and he felt the same way he always had when he climbed at the Mount Haruna ski resort. Anzai used to take him, then later Yuuki would take Jun and Rintaro. It was a climbing course filled with memories for him.

"Great job."

When he arrived at the terrace he was greeted by Rintaro's grinning face.

"It was nothing. I'm fine."

"You seemed to really find your rhythm in the second half there. At first you were clinging a little bit to the rock."

"Yep."

"How are you feeling?"

"Fine. Like I can do this," Yuuki replied, wiping his brow with a towel.

He hadn't noticed how much he'd sweated. He turned his face toward the gentle breeze that blew up from the valley. The slab beneath his feet shone white in the morning sun. Beyond that was the main Ichi-nokurasawa Valley. The winding mountain stream that they had just been walking along was already distant scenery. He loved this feeling. They'd completed only the first pitch of their climb, but already they were in a different world.

Rintaro was staring at a plume of smoke rising from somewhere down in the foothills. The lower part rose straight upward until it was picked up and scattered by the mountain breeze.

From the tinge of sorrow in his expression, Yuuki guessed he was remembering his father's funeral. It was a ceremony that Yuuki would never forget as long as he lived. The funeral hall was packed with scruffy-looking "rock jock" types, among them a man with a familiar jerky walking style. It was Suetsugu, the man he'd met seventeen years earlier at the prefectural library. During the funeral procession, an unexpected thing had happened. The men had lifted the coffin up onto their shoulders. Suetsugu had called out in a loud voice, "Higher, lift him higher! Raise Anzai up to the proper height." The men had stretched their arms as high into the air as they could possibly reach. The coffin had seemed to merge into the distant peaks that marked the prefectural border.

"This is where your father wanted to climb."

A tear rolled from his eye, and Rintaro smiled in response.

"Weren't you the one who wanted to climb? I can read it in your face—you must have wanted to climb this with Jun."

Yuuki was too surprised to respond right away.

Rintaro had always been with them. Not once had Yuuki and Jun been to the mountains by themselves. *Next week, shall we go, just the two of us?* How many times had he practiced those words in his head? But he'd always been so scared of rejection that he'd never actually said them out loud. *I'll just see how we get along for now. Maybe next time. After the three of us have been one more time . . .*

And somehow, he'd missed the chance. Seven years ago, Jun had moved to Tokyo to work for an office equipment maker and the climbing trips had stopped. Today's climb was in memory of Anzai. The occasion had inspired Yuuki to call Jun's apartment, but he'd only gotten the answering machine. Typical. They'd never really connected. Now that Jun was financially independent, Yuuki couldn't find a way to finally repair their relationship. He could only pray and hope that, one day, when Jun married and became a father himself, he would not repeat his own father's mistakes.

"Yuuki-san?"

Rintaro suddenly looked very uncomfortable.

"What's the matter?"

"It's nothing. Well . . . I've got something I really need to tell you."

"What is it?"

"Something I heard from Jun a long time ago."

"From Jun? How long ago?"

"Around the time we started high school," Rintaro replied, looking at Yuuki. "He told me he was so happy the first time his dad asked him to go climbing with him."

Yuuki was lost for words.

"He was so happy? Is that what Jun said?"

"I'm sorry that I never told you."

"It's no problem, but . . ."

It was that day. The day that the *North Kanto Times* had their JAL crash scoop stolen by the *Mainichi*. That morning.

"I was afraid to tell you," Rintaro continued quietly. "I was afraid that, if I did, you wouldn't take me climbing anymore. You all treated me as if I was one of your own, but I was still terrified. As long as you and Jun didn't get along, I knew I was safe. That was the way I thought back then."

Yuuki thought over all the ways he'd used Rintaro. He regretted it intensely. But Rintaro would forgive him. Yuuki had good reason to believe that. He'd grown up into such a broad-minded, openhearted man.

He knew that Anzai would have wanted to go climbing with Rintaro.

"*I climb up to step down*"—he believed he understood the true meaning of those words . . .

"Okay, then, let's try this," said Yuuki with a smile. "From now on, you're climbing with your dad and I'm climbing with Jun. This way we're even."

Rintaro gave him a huge grin. His pleasant laugh was carried on the wind and spread throughout the mountains.

"You know what's interesting? Everyone who comes to the mountains is suddenly able to speak frankly and honestly."

"Right. Why is that? It must be the air, or the scenery."

"That's not it."

Rintaro's smile shrank a little as he spoke.

"I think it's because it might be the last conversation they ever have in this life. They don't even realize, but that's what they're thinking subconsciously."

Yuuki nodded gravely.

"Well, I've got it all out now," he said. "There's nothing left, so shall we get going?"

"Well, I still have something left to say."

"What?"

"I'll tell you when we reach the top," said Rintaro, blushing. He gave a shy little laugh.

"So, in other words, I might never hear what you have to say."

The dark rock loomed over them. The first overhang. That giant roof that jutted out at least three meters. Time to make a start on the second pitch. The smile faded from Yuuki's face.

"It'll be fine. We'll definitely be continuing this chat at the top."

Rintaro spoke with unusual force. Then, with his right hand, he reached up toward the overhang.

Yuuki slept for about two hours, then went out again.

Before going back to the office, he drove to Maebashi City Hall and popped into the press club on the third floor. He wanted to get hold of Kudo, the famously panic-prone Maebashi branch chief and the man who had been tipped off by the fire department about the circumstances of Anzai's collapse. Or at least that was what Nozawa had claimed.

Chizuko Yorita was alone in the press club room, sitting at the desk by the window, writing. The other branch reporters must have been busy covering the JAL crash.

"Is the branch chief around?"

Chizuko looked up at the sound of Yuuki's voice. Her face was flushed.

"No, he's not."

Her tone was unexpectedly harsh.

"Where's he gone?"

"Dunno," she said, her tone unchanged.

She turned her attention back to the NKT-branded writing paper on her desk, but her pen didn't move. She was having trouble writing—another thing Nozawa had mentioned.

Kudo was probably at the *keirin* cycle track, gambling. And yet he'd gone crying to headquarters that he needed Chizuko to fill in. That the crash had taken most of his junior staff and there was no one to do the work.

Yuuki decided to wait and see if Kudo came back. If he didn't, he'd go on back to headquarters. He sat on the sofa and looked at all the different newspapers arranged on the coffee table. The *Mainichi* was on the top. The headline leapt out at him: BULKHEAD RUPTURE PROBABLE CAUSE.

He suddenly felt very thirsty.

"Yorita? Could you pour me a coffee?"

There was no reply.

"Yorita?"

Again, silence.

Her face was hidden by her long hair.

Yuuki got up and headed to the little kitchen off in the corner.

"I'll make it."

Chizuko spoke sharply as she hurried across the room. Her face was bright red, her forehead crumpled into a frown.

"It's fine. Write your article."

"I'll make the coffee."

"It's not going to taste good if you do it with a face like that."

Chizuko glared at him, tears in her eyes.

"Stop treating me like we're back at headquarters. It seems I'm only here to serve tea and coffee anyway. None of the women reporters from the other companies are forced to do this, you know."

He reached out and knocked the mug out of her hand. It fell to the floor and smashed.

Chizuko froze.

"I'm not asking you to make me a coffee because you're a woman. I'm asking you because you're a rookie reporter and therefore junior to me!"

Yuuki stormed out of the room.

Even after getting into his car, he still felt agitated. Even though he'd just spoken the words that everyone used to say to him back when he was a junior reporter, there really had been no need for him to get so angry.

The word "bulkhead" was still burned on his retina. Lingering regret . . . He hadn't been able to move on yet.

He'd go to the office and see what everyone's reaction was.

No one at the time had spoken up to object to Yuuki's decision.

And yet, a mere four hours later, the *Mainichi* had appeared with its magnificent scoop adorning its front page.

Chizuko's face had been as red as a monkey's—

He clicked his tongue several times, then turned the steering wheel in the direction of the highway.

The staff at the *North Kanto Times* took two weekends off a month. However, today was the third Saturday of the month, so the front doors of headquarters were wide open.

Yuuki trudged up the stairs to the Editorial Department with a heavy heart. The familiar shabby old door to the newsroom felt like an impenetrable wall today. It was going to require some nerve for him to pass through it.

It was just turning two in the afternoon, but there was a sluggish atmosphere in the room. To be fair, it was probably the aftereffects of the phantom scoop. An intense high followed by an acute low.

Everyone Yuuki passed on his way to his desk nodded at him without making eye contact. The only person at Yuuki's island of desks was Nozawa. He was leaning all his weight back on his chair, ostentatiously absorbed in a copy of the *Mainichi*. At least, that was how it seemed to Yuuki in his current frame of mind, although Nozawa didn't appear to have picked up the newspaper just because he saw Yuuki coming.

"Sorry for all the trouble last night," said Yuuki curtly as he took his seat.

"Hmm."

Nozawa didn't even bother to look out from behind his newspaper.

Yuuki looked around the newsroom defiantly. Around half of the editorial staff were already there, but the wall-side row of seats belonging to the managerial staff was empty.

"Where are the top brass?"

"They're all in the editor in chief's office," replied Nozawa, as if he wasn't that interested. "The managing director and Ito from Circulation came storming in a while ago."

Yuuki nodded. They'd disrupted the newspaper delivery in order to get a deadline extension. It was pretty obvious that Ito had gone running to his boss, Iikura, to get him to inflict the maximum punishment on the Editorial Department. No doubt Kasuya and the others were having to grovel.

There were two piles of Kyodo News wires on Yuuki's desk. Thinking he'd better get his written apology out of the way first, he pushed them to one side for now, opened his desk drawer, and took out some writing paper. Depending on the attitude of the bosses, he thought he'd better be prepared to write an informal letter of resignation, too.

"Yuuki-kun?"

He looked up to see Kamejima's moonlike face, minus its usual smile.

"Good work last night."

"I should be saying that to you."

"At least you created something of a fantasy for us all. Sorry for the copywriter's cliché, but last night felt a bit like A *Midsummer Night's Dream*."

Kamejima, at least, didn't seem to harbor any ill will toward him. His words seemed more like ones of sympathy for Yuuki's situation. For some reason, though, Yuuki found this really irritating. Perhaps it was because someone who had never been involved in fieldwork could never understand the true misery felt by a failed reporter.

Yuuki couldn't help it—his tone turned harsh.

"Is there something you wanted?"

"Well, now that we know it was the pressure bulkhead, what do you want to do with the article we prepared yesterday?"

"We don't have enough supporting evidence to publish it." Yuuki's tone was final.

Kamejima's eyes grew wide. "What? Haven't you heard?"

"Heard what?"

"Look. Here . . ."

Kamejima scrabbled through the pile of Kyodo wires until he found the one with the headline he was looking for.

INVESTIGATION INTO JAL'S CRIMINAL LIABILITY

Yuuki's heart skipped a beat. An investigation into criminal liability? What . . . ?

He began to read the article.

*Following the crash of a Japan Airlines jumbo jet, law enforcement authorities, including the National Police Agency, the Gunma Prefectural Police's special investigation unit, and the Metropolitan Police Department, will announce by the 17th their intention to investigate Japan Airlines on a possible charge of professional negligence resulting in injury or death. Law enforcement is attaching the greatest importance to the statement by the Ministry of Transport's Aircraft Accident Investigation Committee that the cause of the accident was damage to the fuselage due to rupture of the pressure bulkhead, resulting in the gushing of pressurized air from the passenger cabin, damaging the vertical tail—*

Yuuki was speechless. The accident investigation team had now officially revealed the pressure bulkhead to be the cause. In other words, the Ministry of Transport had confirmed the *Mainichi* newspaper's article. But that wasn't all. All the different branches of law enforcement appeared to be completely on board with the investigating team's findings, and were making their move as one.

Yuuki began to sweat as he considered once again the magnitude of the scoop that he'd let slip through his fingers. He turned to Kamejima.

"We'll follow with the same headline."

He bravely emphasized the word "follow." It was time to stop feeling sorry for himself, let go of any regrets, and get on with his job.

Kamejima nodded in agreement and started to walk to his desk, but he suddenly stopped and turned back.

"Oh, yes. I meant to tell you—this morning *Jomo* dropped the crash from its front page. We should really keep going with it—keep on pushing it with quantity and quality of information. It doesn't matter whether we have a couple of scoop stories or not. What matters is that we have overall victory.'"

Yuuki waited for Kamejima to get out of sight, then brought his fists down hard on his thighs. But it wasn't Kamejima he was angry with; he was wondering why senior management hadn't summoned him.

Early that morning he'd left the office and gone home to sleep. And while he'd been away, not only had the cause of the crash been confirmed, there had been significant corroborating announcements made by the law enforcement agencies. Despite these developments, not one member of the management team had thought to page Yuuki. No, come to think of it, it went back even further. They hadn't even called him when they'd discovered that the *North Kanto Times* had been scooped by another paper.

This time, he understood. They thought the coverage of the crash was other people's business. The management of the *North Kanto Times* really believed that they could count on interviews and articles from Kyodo News. A jumbo jet had come down in a local newspaper's home territory. Five hundred and twenty lives had been lost. And still the whole thing was being treated like an inherited accident. As if someone else had just rented their space.

Yuuki stared pointedly across the room at editor in chief Kasuya's office door. They weren't in there discussing how best to cover an aviation disaster of unprecedented proportions. No, they were putting valuable time and care into discussing some petty internal squabble.

He no longer felt like writing a letter of apology. He put the paper back in the drawer and turned his attention instead to the wires and articles on his desk, scanning for possible headlines.

> 90% of bodies retrieved, 276 identified
> Identification gargantuan task; dental records and fingerprints
>     crucial
> Angry families break through police barriers to search the crash site
> "My love to the children"—letter written to family just before the
>     impact
> "Live life to the full" scribbled on company stationery

Yuuki frowned at the office door again. As he did, his vision slowly began to distort.

He was just the same as them. Content to sit behind a desk, constantly fretting over petty internal squabbles. He had an urge to do something big. Something that would tear at his heart.

He picked up the phone and dialed the *North Kanto Times*'s direct line at the prefectural police press club. Sayama picked up right away.

"Yuuki here."

"What is it?"

The icy tone was back. Yuuki had expected it, so he wasn't fazed. He went ahead with his idea.

"Is Hanazawa climbing Osutaka again today?"

"Yes, he is."

"Tomorrow, I'm going with him. If he gets in touch with you, please let him know."

Sayama didn't respond.

"Did you get that?"

"Yes."

"What kind of restrictions are in place on the mountain?"

"As long as you have a company armband, you're allowed to enter the crash zone."

"What time does he usually climb?"

"He sets out from the village office around five or six every morning."

"Where can I meet up with him?"

"Like I say, it'll have to be the Uenomura village office. They sleep in the first-floor lobby."

"Today I'm going to cover the bulkhead thing."

There was a short pause.

"Is that why you want to go up the mountain?"

There were barbs in his words.

"What do you mean by that?"

"Nothing. It's just not something you need to leave your desk for. We've got enough on the crash site."

"I just want to see it one time. All I have in my head is Kyodo News journalists' point of view."

He slammed the receiver down.

A crime scene should be covered by a crime scene specialist. He understood what Sayama was telling him. He knew that already, but he couldn't understand the reasons behind Sayama being so openly hostile to the idea. He'd completely shut Yuuki out. That had to be it.

Hearing a sound, he looked up.

The editor in chief's door was open, and managing director Iikura and Ito were just coming out. His eyes met Ito's and locked on to them as the Circulation chief approached. Yuuki got to his feet.

"You've changed a lot."

It was Iikura who spoke. He had the smooth skin of a man much younger than his sixty years. He also had the sharpest eyes of anyone at the company, but right now those eyes were glittering with amusement.

"How could the man who pulled off the feat of balancing the coverage of Fukuda and Nakasone with a single photo pull such a foolish stunt as you did last night? Do you possess two separate brains?"

Yuuki had heard around the office that Iikura enjoyed toying with people by throwing impossible questions at them.

"I'm sorry for the trouble I caused last night," said Yuuki, neglecting to bow.

"That's not the face of someone who's truly contrite. Do you also have two tongues?"

Yuuki didn't respond.

"Or is it that you had two—or even three—fathers, and somehow failed to learn any manners from any of them?"

Yuuki threw Ito a look of total contempt. He'd discussed Yuuki's past with Iikura.

"Well, anyway, none of that's worth worrying about," Iikura continued, taking a half step toward Yuuki and patting his upper arm. "Don't try to overreach yourself. Stick to the level of work that suits you. Use Kyodo articles wherever possible. We're paying them enough money."

Yuuki felt more discouraged than angry. If this man were to overthrow Chairman Shirakawa to run the *North Kanto Times*, nothing would change at all.

"Sir, have you been to visit Anzai in the hospital?" he called out to Iikura's retreating back.

Iikura turned his head.

"Anzai . . . ? Oh, that guy. No, not yet."

"Please pay him a visit. It's because of you that he collapsed."

"Hey!" snapped Ito.

Iikura signaled him to be quiet.

The gaze he turned on Yuuki was one of breathtaking ferocity.

"Words are fearsome weapons. The spoken word is surprisingly powerful. It has a stronger tendency to stick in the mind than the printed word."

Having allowed Yuuki a glimpse of his true nature, the Clever Yakuza strolled calmly out of the newsroom.

Kasuya was languishing on the sofa, a flannel over his forehead.

"I give up. Iikura is like a snake. And he's persistent. He got me to put it in writing."

"Put what in writing?" Yuuki asked, confused.

"Well, I'd have to tell you sooner or later anyway. I had to promise that for the next month the deadline would be midnight, and no later."

Yuuki was horrified.

"You didn't agree to that?"

"I had to. Even had to write it down."

"Midnight? Even if there's a major incident?"

"Even if there's a major incident."

"But we've still got the JAL crash to cover."

"The JAL crash is finished. There's nothing we can do."

They both sighed. Neither Oimura nor Todoroki said a word. They simply sat there, grim-faced. If their opposition had been the Circulation chief alone, they might have had a chance of success, but now that he had the backing of the managing director, it was a hopeless cause.

"So, what shall we put in today?" Kasuya asked Yuuki, without much enthusiasm.

Yuuki checked his notes. Since Sayama had poured cold water on his idea of climbing Mount Osutaka, his mind had been unable to focus properly on his job.

"The front page needs to follow up on the bulkhead thing. And then there's Koshien. Nodai Niko is playing in the third round, so let's put them on the front page, whether they win or lose. For the local pages, I thought I'd go with a feature on the letters written by some of the crash victims."

"What's that?"

"It seems they've discovered several letters and notes that passengers wrote to their families just before the plane went down. I haven't had the chance to read any of them but, even if it's just a few scribbled words, I believe it's newsworthy."

"Okay. Go with that," said Kasuya, sounding a little offhand.

"And I have all kinds of connected articles to put in on the other pages."

Yuuki prepared himself to hear Oimura's objections, but the managing editor wasn't even looking in his direction. What kind of sorcery had Iikura managed to work on him?

"But it really is a pity," said Kasuya, stretching.

Yuuki stared at him, willing him to shut up, but the editor in chief continued.

"That thing last night, if we'd pulled it off, we'd all be celebrating now. Even Iikura wouldn't have been able to complain."

When an ex-reporter starts thinking about things from that perspective, it's over. What was worse, Kasuya was editor in chief. No matter how much Yuuki might have objected, if Kasuya had wanted to print it, he could have.

"So, are we done?"

Kasuya looked from Oimura to Todoroki and then, lastly, to Yuuki.

"Don't give your letter of apology to General Affairs. I'll take care of it, so any rough bit of old paper's fine."

Yuuki bowed his head in silence and got up to leave. Just as he was heading for the door, Oimura spoke up.

"Kasuya-san, don't you think you're being too soft?"

Yuuki stopped and looked over his shoulder at Oimura. He seemed perfectly calm.

"I think making Yuuki desk chief was a mistake."

"Oimura!"

Kasuya's intention had been to get Oimura to lay off Yuuki, but it had the opposite effect. Oimura just turned the volume up.

"This incident just made it clear to me. He's a total coward. Every time he has to make a big decision, he just runs away. That sums up his capability for the job right there."

Now Yuuki turned his whole body to face Oimura.

"I'm not going to defend my ability, but when did I ever lose my nerve? Go ahead, give me a specific example."

"Who are you to talk to me like that?"

The fuse had been lit and the Firecracker was starting to burn.

"Ever since you were a rookie reporter. Whenever you were ordered to write something, it was all, *Oh, dear, I haven't got enough evidence. I need another day to research it.* How many scoops have you missed out on with all that nonsense?"

"Really? And how many stories have you written without proper research and ended up printing a bunch of misinformation?"

"You insolent shit. I don't have to hear this from you."

Kasuya raised his voice.

"Drop it, both of you!"

Todoroki was also on his feet, ready to pull the two men apart in case they came to blows. Oimura just bellowed all the more.

"Thanks to you, we've all been shamed. Sneered at by Iikura, criticized by Ito. All because of your cowardice. You weak-willed, spineless—"

Yuuki exploded.

"So why didn't you just speak up last night? Tell them to run it? What's a managing editor there for? To quibble over trivialities and get paid for doing nothing?"

"You stupid little—!"

The blood had drained from Oimura's face. Kasuya and Todoroki grabbed him by the shoulder and arm to hold him back.

"You've gone too far, Yuuki," Todoroki warned him.

But Yuuki continued to stare Oimura down.

"You're only making this much fuss because it's Iikura. If you're going to kick up a stink, then why didn't you do it when we lost the scoop? You're a former police beat reporter. Do you have no pride?"

Having said what he wanted to say, Yuuki turned and walked away.

The argument must have been overheard. Every single face in the newsroom was turned in his direction. Yuuki came stomping through the center aisle back to his desk. Kishi was standing there, transfixed. It looked as if he had only just arrived at work. His bag was still over his shoulder.

"Hey, what's going on?"

"Nothing."

"Ah, the *Mainichi* thing."

"If that was all, it'd be okay."

Yuuki dropped into his chair with a thud. His chest and stomach felt as if they were about to explode.

"Hey, Yuuki—"

"Wait."

He'd just spotted Oimura. Instead of returning to his desk by the wall, the managing editor had marched straight out of the newsroom. Possibly on his way to the office of the chairman to discuss Yuuki's reassignment. Fine. Go ahead. He'd even supply his own letter of resignation if necessary.

Kishi approached a little timidly.

"Sorry about the timing, but there's something I need you to hear."

"Tell me later."

Yuuki tried to cut Kishi off, but he blurted it out . . .

Did he say *punched*?

Yuuki looked up at Kishi for the first time and lowered his voice.

"Hanazawa punched someone? Who?"

Kishi leaned in very close to whisper in Yuuki's ear.

"Kurasaka."

Yuuki felt a sharp pain in his stomach. Kurasaka from the Advertising Department. That prick who'd lectured him when he'd cut the ad for the shopping mall opening the day after the crash.

"Why did he punch him?"

"No idea. What I do know is that it happened up at the crash site."

Yuuki couldn't believe what he was hearing.

"You mean Kurasaka from Advertising was climbing Mount Osutaka?"

"Looks like it."

"But why? Oh, my God, he wasn't sightseeing, was he?"

"Dunno."

"So where did you hear this?"

"They're all talking about it in the Photography Department. Seems that one of the guys from there—his name's Tono, I think—was climbing with Hanazawa today, and he saw the whole thing."

"Did you ask Tono directly?"

"He's in the darkroom right now."

Yuuki let out a ragged breath and in the same moment noticed that his fists were clenched. He was sure they'd been that way since he'd been in the editor in chief's office. He unclenched them to see that his nails had left red marks on the palms of his hands. He clenched them again, hard, until it hurt.

It was true there were plenty of people he wanted to punch. Every day it was a race against time to create fresh news. There were always disagreements and fighting.

But a newspaper company had the same structure as any other company. It didn't matter what the provocation might have been, a junior employee couldn't punch a senior colleague and get away with it. He'd lose his job. What was worse, Hanazawa had made a very poor choice in punching Kurasaka, of all people.

Kurasaka had worked on the political desk until last year. He'd been lured to the Advertising Department by the promise of being made manager. Yuuki didn't like to jump to conclusions, but something Todoroki had let slip when he was drinking suggested that Kurasaka had been ostracized by Chairman Shirakawa and thrown out of the Editorial Department. Yuuki recalled how, right after Okubo/Red Army, when reporters were leaving left and right, Shirakawa was trying to persuade his employees to stay by giving them puppies from his own dog's litter. Kurasaka was one of the recipients of a puppy, and yet he was still kicked out of the department. To this day, he still bore a grudge toward Shirakawa and the Editorial Department that was under his control. Yuuki had caught a glimpse of Kurasaka's twisted psychology when, on the day after the JAL crash, Yuuki had discarded one of the paper's ads. He'd been in the wrong, but Kurasaka had hurled all kinds of abuse at him, as if he were getting revenge on the whole department that had spurned him.

*"You guys have no idea how hard we work. You all have it so easy . . ."*

*You don't have to earn a single yen for the company. We're the ones who earn your living for you."*

He could see that bright red square face. That was the man Hanazawa had punched.

Yuuki grabbed the phone and dialed Hanazawa's pager. He waited five minutes but there was no call back. Next, he called the prefectural police press club, but nobody answered. He called back repeatedly until a young woman finally picked up. It was a reporter from another newspaper.

"There's nobody here from the *North Kanto Times*," she said, sounding a little annoyed.

He paged Sayama, and Hanazawa one more time. Still no answer. He reached for the list of extension numbers. He found the number for the Advertising Department and dialed.

"Hello. This is Advertising."

"I'd like to speak to Miyata."

"And who's calling please?"

"Accounts."

It took a while but eventually Miyata came to the phone. Yuuki could picture the confusion on his tanned, bespectacled face when he answered, believing it to be the Accounts Department, then discovering it was Yuuki.

"What's going on?"

"I want to ask you something in confidence."

As a fellow member of the hiking club, Yuuki felt he could talk to Miyata.

"It's about Kurasaka-san."

"He's taken the day off."

"I know. I heard he went to Mount Osutaka."

"Er . . . no . . ."

Miyata faltered.

"Have you been told not to say anything?"

"Um . . . not to anyone in the Editorial Department."

"Well, I already know. Keep your voice down. Tell me why Kurasaka-san went to Mount Osutaka."

"I'm sorry, he never said why . . . But it was probably to get some material."

"What do you mean, '*material*'?"

"Put simply, it's stuff to talk about, conversation material. We always try to stock up on good topics of conversation for when we visit our advertisers."

The blood rushed to Yuuki's head. Kurasaka was trying to use a visit to the JAL crash site as a gimmick to attract advertisers.

"At our morning meetings, we're all supposed to share our ideas for attracting new advertisers. We have to come up with a new one every day, so it's quite a challenge."

Miyata didn't sound concerned. Apparently this was normal to him. Without any reporting experience, he wouldn't have associated the manufactured pictures he'd seen on the television with corpses and the stench of death.

But Kurasaka should have. He'd spent a long time in the political section, but as a rookie he'd also spent time at accident and crime scenes. He'd even been a member of the support crew during the Okubo and Red Army cases.

This same Kurasaka was now using the JAL crash as a business opportunity. And Hanazawa had been so enraged by this that he'd punched him. That must have been what happened, but still it was hard to see how. Kurasaka was an intelligent man. It was very unlikely that he would have told a reporter that he was climbing the mountain to gather material for conversation.

"Does Kurasaka know Hanazawa? He's one of our reporters."

"Yes, the boss requested him specially. They're from the same town, apparently—Yoshiokamachi."

Yuuki could guess some of the story. Hanazawa, Kurasaka, and the young employee from Photography, Tono, had climbed Mount Osutaka together. But what had happened after that? Why had Hanazawa lost it . . . ?

"This phone call never happened, okay?"

After hanging up, Yuuki reached over to Kishi's desk.

"I'm just going to drop by the Photography Department. If Sayama or Hanazawa calls back, please forward the call."

"No problem."

Yuuki got up slowly. His legs felt stiff. He walked calmly as far as the door, but as soon as he reached the corridor, he broke into a jog and finally bounded up the stairs.

What had happened on Mount Osutaka? Yuuki couldn't forget the sight of Hanazawa two days earlier, his self-control completely gone, sobbing his heart out.

The door to the Photography Department was closed.

Press photographers tended to be a bad-tempered bunch, so there were lots of young reporters who were afraid to enter this room.

Yuuki had to hop over a pile of muddy hiking boots in order to get in. Four or five photographers were sitting in a group, smoking.

"Is Tono here?" Yuuki asked the assistant manager, Suzumoto.

"He's in the darkroom. He should be out . . . Ah, there he is."

Yuuki spotted Tono's sweat-stained T-shirt across the room. He ran up and tapped him on the shoulder, and led him back into the darkroom he'd just come from.

"Can we turn on the light?"

"No problem."

Yuuki turned on the fluorescent light and sat down on a nearby stool. The smell of developing solution assaulted his nose.

"Please tell me what happened today between Kurasaka and Hanazawa."

Clearly perplexed, Tono scratched his scalp, with its neat crew cut.

"Suzumoto-san told me I had to keep it to myself."

"And I'm going to tell you the same thing. If this story gets out, it'll mean the sack for Hanazawa. The other guy is Kurasaka. You know what that means, don't you?"

Tono bowed his acknowledgment. He was in his fourth year at the company, and was all too familiar with Kurasaka's character from their run-ins at the Editorial Department.

"Tono?"

Yuuki raised his voice to compete with the loud whirring from the ventilation fan on the old-fashioned air conditioner.

"I'm going to go and make sure that Kurasaka never breathes a word of this."

Tono studied Yuuki's face for several moments.

"I understand. Okay, I'll tell you what happened."

He sat on the stool directly in front of Yuuki and leaned toward him.

"The three of us climbed Osutaka this morning. They'd worked hard on getting that trail put in, and it was in pretty good shape, so it only took us about two hours to get to the crash site. When we got there, we split up to do our own thing. After a while Kurasaka came up to me and asked me to take some photos with his camera.

"With his own camera?"

"Right. It was one of those cheap instant cameras you can set the date and time on. Well, I couldn't refuse. He gave me directions: 'Take this, get that'—you know—so I just took the photos as he instructed. And then, in the middle of it all, he told me to take a photo of him."

Yuuki felt sick. Surely not—

"So I did as he said. I took a picture of him standing in front of the main wing, which had JAL written on it."

A *commemorative photo.*

"Tono!"

In response to Yuuki's exasperated groan, Tono shifted closer, as if to signal that he had reached the main part of the story.

"The thing is, that kind of stuff wasn't all that unusual up there. There were idiots from other companies doing the same thing. There were even members of our team posing for photo after photo and making peace signs in front of the wreckage."

"Is that true?"

"Yes, I'm afraid it's the honest truth."

It was very difficult to believe that anyone would take commemorative photos at a scene where five hundred and twenty people had just lost their lives. Yuuki did his utmost to stay calm.

"So, that wasn't the reason that Hanazawa punched Kurasaka?"

"No, well, not directly. Hanazawa was standing a little way off, watching Kurasaka. After I'd taken about five pictures, he came over. 'Don't you think that's enough?' he asked him, perfectly calmly. Because all around us there were police and Self-Defense Forces guys practically performing a bucket relay of body parts. Hanazawa had become very nervous about Kurasaka's behavior, particularly as he was wearing an NKT armband. Anyhow, at this point Kurasaka listened to Hanazawa and stopped posing for pictures."

"So then what happened?"

"He caught him."

Tono's expression hardened.

"Caught him doing what?"

"I saw it, too—Kurasaka picked up a bit of broken fuselage or a scrap of insulating material or something and tried to slip it in his pocket."

Yuuki was speechless. Kurasaka had tried to take home a souvenir. Or perhaps it was intended to be a small gift for one of their advertisers . . .

"And what then?" said Yuuki, his voice turning hoarse.

"Hanazawa threw himself at Kurasaka and kicked the hand that was holding the piece of fuselage. He made him empty everything out of his pockets on the spot. He grabbed him by the collar and pulled him behind a tree. Then he began to lay into him. Punched him over and over. In the face, in the stomach . . ."

Yuuki's eyes nearly popped out of his skull.

"And then?"

"Well, I stopped him. But I was a bit late—Kurasaka's face was pretty messed up, he'd even lost a few teeth. There was so much blood . . ."

Yuuki closed his eyes.

"What did Hanazawa do after that?"

"He went back down the mountain by himself. A little while later, I helped Kurasaka down, too. I drove back to Maebashi and dropped him off at a hospital. Then I came here."

"Did Kurasaka say anything to you in the car?"

"Not a word. He had a towel pressed over his mouth. He put the passenger seat back and stared ahead the whole time."

Yuuki got up.

"Which hospital?"

"Mori General. They're open on Saturday evenings. And they have a dental surgery, too."

"What time did you drop him off?"

"Um . . . about an hour ago."

"Was it busy?"

"The parking lot was full."

"Then he should still be there."

"I suppose."

There was a knock on the door.

"Just a minute!"

Yuuki spoke quickly to Tono as he moved to open the door.

"What about the film from Kurasaka's camera?"

"I've got it."

"Did he ask you to develop it?"

"No. Not after all that."

"Even if he asks you, don't develop it."

"Of course not," said Tono angrily. "Even I wanted to punch him. If my wife wasn't pregnant, I might have done it."

Yuuki nodded.

"What'll happen to Hanazawa?" asked Tono, looking worried.

Yuuki didn't answer. He left the darkroom and headed down the stairs. He left the building by the back door and hurried to his car.

He hadn't been able to offer Tono any consoling words. It was going to be tough to protect Hanazawa. Or rather, this thing couldn't be resolved by dealing with Hanazawa alone. He was sure that Kurasaka was a puppet of the managing director's faction. Which meant that Iikura was bound to get involved once more. The editorial management would be beset by accusations that they were raising violent reporters, and the managing director's faction would be rounding up their troops to make sure this reached the ears of the external board members.

If this happened, Hanazawa would be beyond help—not just because the managing director faction was making such a fuss but because the Editorial Department would have no choice but to let him go in order to calm the situation down.

Yuuki bit his lip and hit the accelerator. Now that he knew the reason Hanazawa had resorted to violence, he felt a lot more concern and sympathy for the man. He felt exactly the same way Tono did. If he'd been there on Mount Osutaka with them, he'd have punched Kurasaka, too.

At any rate, the most important thing was to get hold of Kurasaka as soon as possible and persuade him not to talk. Most likely in vain. But it didn't matter. He had no intention of slowing down.

## 4 0 .

Despite it being five o'clock on a Saturday afternoon, there was quite a crowd of patients in the ground-floor lobby of Mori General Hospital. They had probably been enticed by the gorgeous, brand-new building, Yuuki guessed.

On the sofas in front of the Oral Surgery Department he counted at least twenty people waiting. He began to walk up and down the rows, looking for a ruddy, square face, but Kurasaka wasn't there. Would he have gone home? Or gone back to work? But he'd taken the day off to climb Mount Osutaka, so that wasn't likely. And anyway, at five o'clock on a Saturday, the Advertising Department would be deserted.

Yuuki approached the reception desk. After confirming that Kurasaka's name wasn't on the list of patients, he headed for the door. But then he heard a voice behind him.

"Hey there. It's been a while."

He turned to see an elegant man in a suit. It was Shimagawa from the prefectural police department. If you hadn't known he was a policeman, you'd never have guessed. He had the look of a well-dressed salaryman. Two or three years Yuuki's senior, he was a detective born and bred. Yuuki had heard that he was currently head of the Forensics Division.

"Yes, I'm sorry I haven't been in touch."

In fact, it was the first time they'd met in five years, when Yuuki had been taken off the police beat. Yet Yuuki had the feeling they'd met much more recently. He realized it was because he'd seen the detective in footage from Mount Osutaka, issuing commands to the Azami riot police squad.

"How's it going at the accident scene?"

"Haven't you been reading the news?"

"No need to be sarcastic," replied Yuuki with a smile.

"We're identifying the victims through dental records and finger-prints."

"I see."

Yuuki glanced over Shimagawa's shoulder at the sign on the door of the Oral Surgery Department.

"I'm sure the police must have an incredible amount on their plate right now."

"You, too, I'm guessing."

"Right. Actually, we're all feeling a bit helpless."

"Now, that word's taboo."

"What?"

"We're all locals: you at the *North Kanto Times*; us, too." His features remained completely unruffled. "How does an airplane fly? That's about our starting point."

Yuuki was startled. He remembered that Sayama had said almost the exact same thing to him. Was that one of Shimagawa's lines? In the near future, the prefectural police were planning to start up a separate division for dealing with emergencies. With his extremely precise and calm intellect, Shimagawa was very popular with his junior officers, and was reportedly at the top of the list of candidates to head up that new project.

"Well, it looks as though it's going to be a long case. It's ours, and we have to deal with it. There's no escaping the fact that a jumbo jet crashed in Gunma Prefecture."

Yuuki felt as if someone had stabbed him in the forehead. The police were utterly dedicated to the task.

He hadn't realized it in the beginning. He'd started out believing that this crash was too much for the prefectural police to handle. He'd even dared to underestimate the members of the police force by assuming they felt the same way. Earlier that same day he had read the Kyodo News report about the criminal investigation and had paid attention only to the words "National Police Agency."

And yet, this man was determined. He was going to investigate the matter of criminal liability in this massive air disaster. Or, to think of it in another way, how had he, Kazumasa Yuuki of the *North Kanto Times*, approached this major disaster?

"Well, I have to get going," said Shimagawa, turning to leave. "Maybe we'll meet in about another three years."

In another three years . . . A jumbo jet had gone down with the loss of five hundred and twenty lives. Would that be how long it took to prosecute this case?

Yuuki spent some time staring into space. It occurred to him that, whenever they got to that point, it would be the very moment they would need Hanazawa of the *North Kanto Times*. Someone who had witnessed the immediate horror of the accident scene. Someone who had felt it keenly and shed tears for the victims. Someone who had been so haunted by the image that he had felt compelled to climb that mountain over and over, day in, day out. Hanazawa was the only one. Over the next thousand days, as the police investigators assembled the case for the prosecution, Hanazawa should be the one to follow and report on their work.

Yuuki couldn't stay still for another moment. He hurried out of Mori General Hospital and got back into his car.

He was lost. Kurasaka lived in Rokkumachi, a residential area of Maebashi City. He'd been to the address once before, a long time ago, to drop off some documents. He remembered it being two doors down from a big house with its own traditional Japanese-style storehouse. With that memory, he'd come looking for the house, but the area had undergone some kind of large-scale rezoning and the streets looked completely different. Yuuki drove at a snail's pace around the whole neighborhood about three times, hoping to spot that distinctive storehouse, but to no avail.

His pager began to buzz. It was already 6:30 in the evening. For sure, the copy team would be starting to complain that they hadn't received any articles on the crash yet. He knew it'd be quicker to call somebody at the newspaper and get them to look up Kurasaka's address for him. He'd been keeping an eye out for a public phone booth for a while now.

He finally found one on the edge of a children's playground. It wasn't a phone booth per se, but it had a small shelter over it to keep the rain off. He stopped the car and ran toward it, fumbling in his pocket for change.

He called his own extension, and Kishi answered.

"Copy's freaking out."

"I'll be back as soon as I can. For now, could you find Kurasaka's home address and telephone number for me?"

After getting the information from Kishi, Yuuki asked if there'd been any response to his earlier pages. Apparently Sayama had called back to say he was in the pressroom at the prefectural police station, but there'd been no contact from Hanazawa.

Yuuki guessed that the two men were together. As he walked back toward his car, he checked the note he had written. The third block of Rokkumachi. He was sure that it was just a little way to the south of where he was. Should he walk? Or go by car and perhaps stop to ask the way? Feeling lost, he looked around. He stopped when he saw a white mask, the kind that people wore over their nose and mouth when they had a cold.

About fifteen meters away, the man wearing the white mask was crouching down near the entrance to the children's playground. The mask was large and covered the whole lower part of his face.

It was Kurasaka. Yuuki instinctively moved closer to his own car and watched him covertly. First of all, he was wondering why he was crouching down like that.

It soon became clear. Kurasaka had a dog with him—a very old dog.

*Wow,* Yuuki thought. *It's still alive.*

The same dog that he'd gotten as a gift from Shirakawa . . . That was right after Okubo/Red Army, so it must be about thirteen years old now. Or even a little bit older—he wasn't sure exactly when the puppies had been born. When he thought about it, the dog must be positively geriatric.

About the size of a Shiba Inu, the dog looked as if about half its fur had been torn out, the way it was molting in great patches. It appeared to be defecating right now—or at least it was trying to, but its legs were too unsteady.

Kurasaka reached out and supported the dog's torso with one hand, while with the other he patted its back in encouragement. He was looking into the dog's face with a kind and gentle gaze.

Yuuki quietly opened his car door and slipped into the driver's seat. He adjusted the rearview mirror so that he could see Kurasaka. Now he was picking up the dog's droppings with a small shovel and putting them into a plastic bag. Then he stood up and began to walk. The dog followed. Kurasaka's steps were almost painfully slow—keeping pace with the elderly Shiba Inu.

Yuuki started the car and drove away. He turned at the first corner and merged onto the main road. He was filled with a mixture of pity and disgust.

Kurasaka had just wanted to play at being a reporter. He needed to get ads into the newspaper, so he'd climbed Mount Osutaka in search of material he could use in conversation. He'd wanted to show the advertisers that he wasn't just an adman; he was also a serious reporter. He wanted to be able to tell them that he'd visited the site of the world's biggest plane crash and show them photos and fragments of the fuselage to prove it. He wanted them to be impressed. That was the only reason he had climbed Osutaka. But on some level, any ex-reporter forced to leave the News Department would be prone to a tendency to show off. Maybe it was nostalgia.

So, while pretending to be a reporter, he'd ended up being punched by a real one. Yuuki knew that Kurasaka's pride wouldn't let him tell anyone. Right about now he'd be thinking up a plausible reason for his missing teeth.

Yuuki took a deep breath. Perhaps Mount Osutaka refused to allow anybody with dishonest motives to climb it.

He looked into his own heart.

The traffic light turned red. It stayed red a long time. In his mind, he began thinking through his plan of attack for the newspaper. However unpleasant or uncomfortable it got in the newsroom, he was going to have to stick it out as JAL crash desk chief.

## 42

It was half past seven when Yuuki got back to his desk. It was snowed under with papers, and a mini-avalanche seemed to have occurred, flowing onto Kishi's territory. Before leaving, he had turned in only the two front-page stories: CRIMINAL LIABILITY INVESTIGATION and PRESSURE BULKHEAD.

He pulled his chair up, cracked his knuckles, and rotated his wrists a few times before attacking the first job of sorting them by topic. Next, he started work on the story that would head the local news pages—FAREWELL MESSAGES. As he read, his eyes and throat began to burn.

A businessman, knowing that he was about to die, had written a good-bye letter to his family. He'd scribbled the names of his wife and children, and then . . .

But Yuuki found he couldn't read it. It was too blurred.

Yuuki rested his face in his hands and tried as hard as he could to focus on the letters on the page. But it was impossible. The images that entered his eye were passing through the thalamus, but the meaning was failing to register in his brain.

"Daddy is really sorry. Goodbye . . . Please take good care of the kids. I'm grateful that I got to live such a happy life."

He turned to the next letter.

"Look after the kids."

And then another one.

"Live life to the full." "Grow up to be wise and good."

Yuuki realized he could give these letter writers a voice.

Determined, he got to his feet. He cupped his hands around his mouth to amplify his voice and shouted across to the copy team.

"Kaku-san! We're changing the top story!"

He could see the expression on Kamejima's round face change.

"What the—?"

"Drop that third story about the new mountain trail. We're printing the farewell letters."

Kamejima came rushing over.

"What are you talking about? They'll be fine on the local news pages."

Yuuki held out the article for him to see. Kamejima looked dubious but began to read. A couple of moments later, he abruptly turned his back to Yuuki.

Yuuki had Kamejima make a huge number of copies of the article and distribute them to all the members of the Editorial Department. There wasn't a dry eye in the room. There were even some who had to excuse themselves to go to the men's room to cry.

Yuuki set about choosing the other stories related to the crash.

Nodai Niko loses to South Ube

. . . Ah, *they lost*, he sighed to himself.

Ministry of Transport orders reconstruction of plane
Collision with mountain ridge, one engine fell off
Bulkhead and other items added to inspection list
No inspection ordered for SR-type 747 aircraft
JAL administration put profit above safety
Pilots' working hours excessive
Loss of pressurization robs ability to think
Voice and flight recorders to be made public; Upper House committee passes resolution

Yuuki took a break and checked the clock. It was almost nine. Kishi and Nozawa had already gone home, and Yuuki was alone at the island of desks. He reached both arms high into the air and stretched, turning his head from side to side at the same time.

He went back to editing, but it was as if he could feel it through his skin—something had changed in the atmosphere of the newsroom. The excitement had faded and been replaced by a sense of calm, of composure. The bustle and the noise were still there, but the fervor, the seething frenzy under the surface, was gone. The dry, prickly feeling that until yesterday had hung in the air had been somehow dampened down. One way to put it would be that it was a "before the JAL crash" atmosphere.

They were over the peak. The phrase rattled around in Yuuki's brain.

Tomorrow's edition, for August 18, which was put together today, the seventeenth, was almost done. The crash had happened the night of the twelfth. He counted on his fingers . . . today they were making their sixth "JAL crash page." Tomorrow it would be a week, one business cycle. Perhaps this was causing each person to stop and think.

Last night, the paper's failure to run with the bulkhead story had damaged morale, and everyone's enthusiasm for crash-related news had cooled a little. The revelation of the cause of the crash was a huge scoop to the mass media. Having let that slip through their fingers, they were not likely to get their hands on a scoop of that magnitude for a good while. If they did, it would probably be about the police's legal action. The search of the Japan Airlines premises. Arrest of the responsible parties. Or the decision to send them to trial. They could be the first to pry out the details and get one over on the other papers. But this wasn't going to be tomorrow's article— or even the day after tomorrow's. Just as Detective Shimagawa had made clear, they were going to have to wait another three years for those stories.

It had been like living in a dream—the world's biggest air disaster.

The newsroom had been hypnotized by it all, and chaos had ensued. They'd spent the whole of that first night without sleep, waiting to hear the location of the crash site. They'd rejoiced when they heard there were survivors. They had been worked up into a state of fevered anticipation over the bulkhead theory, then plunged into despair when they couldn't run it. And now, tonight, the whole newsroom had shed tears over the victims' final letters to their loved ones, bringing a kind of calm to the turmoil. Yuuki had felt a sense of peace returning to him, too.

He was still going to make sure he wrote detailed, informative articles. His mind was clear and unwavering. Now that JAL crash fever was cooling down, Yuuki had no idea how much longer the post of JAL crash desk chief would exist. There was very little chance that, after their altercation that morning, Oimura would quietly back off. But right until the moment he was relieved of his command, he was not going to deviate from his plan. He was convinced this was his duty.

It turned ten o'clock. Yuuki had finished all his editing and picked up the phone. He paged Hanazawa again, and then the man who had come up with the bulkhead story, Tamaki. Neither called back.

Next, he tried the police press club room. Right away, as if he'd been expecting the call, Sayama picked up.

"I've got two requests for you. First, please let Hanazawa know he's got nothing to worry about."

"About what?" Sayama asked, feigning ignorance.

"I know he's right there with you. Tell him he doesn't need to worry about what happened on the mountain."

". . . Okay."

"Second, another message for Hanazawa. Tell him that, although I said I was going to climb Mount Osutaka tomorrow, I'm not going to after all."

"Really? So when are you going to come?"

"I don't know."

There was a pause as Sayama considered this answer.

"So, you're not postponing, you're canceling. Is that what you're saying?"

"That's right. I think your eyes should be enough."

Confident that he'd expressed his feelings clearly, Yuuki got ready to hang up, but Sayama hastily stopped him.

"Just a minute, please. I'm putting Hanazawa on the line."

The line was quiet for a few moments, long enough for Yuuki to hear that the police were announcing the names of the most recently identified victims. Ever since the crash, no one in the press club had had a moment of sleep.

"This is Hanazawa."

He sounded depressed.

"Like I just told Sayama, you have nothing to worry about."

"Thank you so much."

"Are you planning to climb again tomorrow?"

"Yes, I'm taking Wajima with me."

Wajima. Yuuki felt relieved at the mention of the timid reporter's name.

Yuuki replaced the receiver, but then something occurred to him. He grabbed it again, checking the phone list of branch offices as he dialed.

"Hello. *North Kanto Times*, Maebashi branch."

"This is Yuuki. Could you pour me a coffee?"

"You idiot!" replied Chizuko, laughing. It felt like the first time he had ever heard her natural speaking voice.

"Why don't you get Sayama to show you how he writes articles?"

She called him an idiot one more time and hung up.

It was half past eleven. The proofs of the front page were ready.

*"I'm grateful that I got to live such a happy life."*

There was a hushed silence in the newsroom.

*Could he have written a goodbye letter like this one?*

Yuuki's thoughts turned to Anzai, lying in his hospital bed. He'd never had the chance to say goodbye to his family before falling asleep. After his operation, he had had a brief moment of consciousness, but all he had said was, "Tell him to go on ahead." A message for Yuuki to go ahead and climb Tsuitate—or at least that was what Anzai seemed to be saying.

*"Live life to the full."*

*"Grow up to be wise and good."*

Yuuki pictured Rintaro's young face.

Of course, Anzai hadn't known he was about to die. But Yuuki still wished he had left his son some kind of farewell message. Even just a few words. If he'd managed to do that, how much more reassured Rintaro would have felt.

A voice echoed from the sky above.

"Yuuki-saaaan! Can you hear me?"

"Yes! I can hear you perfectly!"

"I've reached the belay station. You need to unhook your carabiner and start to climb."

Yuuki was looking directly upward from Two-Person Terrace. Viewed from here, the first overhang was intimidating. Rintaro had just successfully traversed it. Now it was his turn.

He grasped the rope as tightly as he could. The other end had disappeared over the top of the overhang. But he wasn't afraid, because he knew Rintaro was there.

"I'm going for it!"

"Stay calm."

Using the rope as his guide, Yuuki began to climb toward the left edge, where the overhang began to jut out. There was a slight rift close to the center. He knew that was the weak point. Edging sideways like a crab, he moved cautiously up until he'd reached the underside of the roof. He looked up, uneasy. Nothing but unyielding, dark rock stretched out above him. There must be some way out from under this roof. He was now at the toughest part of Cloud Ridge route number 1. Climbers would call it the crux of the whole climb. It required equipment that looked like a mini-rope-ladder, known as an aider or a stirrup. He needed to hook this aider onto pitons that had been hammered into the rock and left as a climbing aid. This called not only for good technique and balance but also Yuuki was aware that if he didn't climb quickly and efficiently, the drain on his stamina and his time would have a significant effect on the rest of the climb. It wasn't even beyond the realm of possibility that, if he messed up too badly, he would end up having to make camp there overnight, hanging from the ledge.

This was all from stories he'd heard from Rintaro. In preparation for their attempt on Tsuitate, they'd spent hours at the ski resorts practicing with the aider, but today was the first time Yuuki had ever used one to climb an overhang.

"I've reached the underside!"

"Right, you need to be fast and focused."

Yuuki did exactly what Rintaro advised. He attached his aider to the first piton and stepped on it. He felt himself suspended from the roof, buffeted by the wind. The breeze that had felt so pleasant on his cheek had turned into something devilish. He moved up the rope steps, stretched out an arm, and hooked the aider onto the next piton. Again, he climbed the rope ladder to the top. He repeated the same steps over and over, climbing at a steady pace. It was like clambering across the monkey bars in a children's playground. There were moments when his back was completely parallel to the ground way, way below, and it was hard to keep his balance. He knew that Rintaro, up in the lead, would be using all his concentration to work the rope to support Yuuki's climb. The route was meandering and, if Yuuki wasn't careful, there was a danger the rope could stop moving smoothly.

His assault on the overhang continued for about an hour, but then he found himself at an impasse. The next piton in the rock was too far away for him to reach. He would need to place his foot on the very highest rung in order to reach it with his hand. But if he placed his foot there, he'd be very likely to lose his balance. He couldn't summon the courage he needed to take that step.

His chest felt tight and he was as short of breath as if he had just finished a hundred-meter sprint. With the incline at more than ninety degrees, he was losing power fast. He was beginning to experience what Rintaro had explained to him before they'd set out. His feet weren't on the ground, and therefore they were unable to support his weight. He was forced to rely on his arms for the most part, and they were getting weaker. The tips of his fingers clinging to the aider were going numb.

He jumped at a loud clang from the rock face below. Something had fallen out of his pocket. He twisted his neck to look and watched a carabiner bouncing merrily away down the rock wall at a speed it had never previously experienced. A chill ran down his spine. He turned his head back. Right in front of him was the thick edge of the overhang. There was no other way to cross it than to place his foot on the top rung of his aider, yet he couldn't bring himself to do it.

Fifty-seven. He suddenly became very aware of his own age.

He called up to his climbing buddy.

"Hey! Please be ready. I might fall!"

"Don't worry. If you slip, I'll pull you up."

Rintaro sounded cheery. Pull him up? Yuuki was sure that would be impossible. But then he heard Rintaro's voice again.

"Yuuki-san? You need to be brave and step on that upper rung."

Yuuki was struck with admiration. There was no way that Rintaro could see him, but he was able to read the situation completely, including what was troubling him. This was enough to invigorate him. If Anzai had been alive, how proud would he be right now?

*"I climb up to step down."*

Anzai had wanted to go climbing with his son, that much was certain. But he'd never been able to free himself from the painful place he'd been in since the death of his climbing buddy. Still, he had been determined to climb Tsuitate with Rintaro someday. For that reason, he'd made the decision to "step down" from the NKT. He'd gone to Lonely Hearts that night to change his life, to shed that other version of himself that he'd become. To prepare himself for his fresh assault on Tsuitate.

Yuuki was going to be Anzai's witness. Anzai had finally achieved a level of financial stability, but he was still connected to his life as an employee of the *North Kanto Times*. He'd been ready to sever his connection with the company, and that was why he was going to climb Tsuitate with Yuuki. He'd been planning to return to the life of a rock climber. *Please see the person I'm going to become. Be my witness.* That was what Anzai had been saying to Yuuki.

*"Tell him to go on ahead."*

Anzai wanted more than anything to come here to Tsuitate.

"Yuuki-san?"

Rintaro was calling him. It was as if Yuuki could see his face. He was worried, but acting as if he weren't.

Yuuki smiled. This time, it was Jun's face he could see. That day, seventeen years ago, when he'd turned around, mistaking his dad for Yumiko. That awkward smile. The first time his dad had suggested they go to the mountains together. He'd been really happy—

It felt as if the stiffness in his limbs had melted away; his airways opened up and he breathed in new air. There was no other way. If he didn't step on the upper rung he wouldn't be able to cross the overhang.

He recalled the decision he had made seventeen years ago. On the seventh day of the Japan Airlines crash story. The last decision he ever made as JAL crash desk chief. The toughest and most awful decision he'd ever made. The result of which . . .

Yuuki shut his eyes. He moved his right leg and stepped on the upper rung of the aider. His body began to tremble. To hell with it! He brought up his left leg, too.

He snapped open his eyes, stretched his body as far as he could, and reached out for the piton. Five centimeters more . . .

Yuuki was going to conquer Tsuitate.

It was August 18. Yuuki was in the office at 11:00 a.m. There was a reason for being there earlier than usual. The night before, he had called the deputy chief of the company's Book Publishing Division, a man by the name of Kaizuka, at home, to sound him out about the possibility of putting together a volume about the crash of Flight 123. He'd expected to be refused point-blank, but to his surprise Kaizuka had been enthusiastic about the idea. They were meeting this morning to talk about the specifics.

The idea of documenting the crash in book form had been rolling around in Yuuki's head ever since they'd crossed the peak that marked the end of the first phase of the crash.

Or, another way of looking at it might be that they were through the preliminaries and had finally reached the main part of the case. It was going to take a long while to finish identifying five hundred and twenty victims. Then there were the personal belongings to sort through; the opening of the mountain for the families of the dead to pay their respects; the removal of all the plane debris; not to mention the joint memorial service that was planned, and the ongoing crash investigation. None of this was going to die down anytime soon.

Be that as it may, whenever an accident or a crime is drawn out over a long period, it inevitably becomes difficult to maintain morale. Already it wasn't only Yuuki who was beginning to feel this strain—he'd been seeing the symptoms of it throughout the newsroom. Even if the news when it first breaks is earth-shattering, it will by its very nature lose its freshness over time, eventually becoming completely stale.

Yuuki knew this from experience. Reporters and their editors tended to get themselves into a rut researching and writing about one particular case. They would find themselves waiting for the next story. Sometimes, without even realizing it, they were anxious for the next big case that would surpass the one they were working on.

Yuuki wanted to make an exception. He wanted the coverage of the crash of Flight 123 to keep going, to keep its freshness. That was one of his reasons for wanting to publish the book. He wanted to plant the seed of an idea that even the most fleeting moments at a newspaper could be captured forever in a book, and he wanted to slow the fading of memories within the company.

Another reason for publishing the book was his sense of obligation as JAL crash desk chief to reward the efforts of his staff. He intended to send as many of the young reporters as possible up to the crash site. By this point, one week after the disaster, he'd managed to send more than fifty people up Mount Osutaka but, because of the sheer numbers, most of the articles they'd produced had never made it into print. They languished in Yuuki's desk drawer. Now that the moment had passed, many of them could never be used. Yuuki planned to read over these rejected manuscripts, edit them as needed, and then compile them into a book. This way the JAL crash news team would all have their names recorded for posterity. As long as they expressed the wish to write, Wajima could tell the story of his deep regret at having failed to climb Osutaka, and Tamaki his anger at the failure of the JAL desk chief to run his bulkhead scoop.

Yuuki pondered this as he climbed the stairs of the paper's headquarters. He stopped at the first floor and took the connecting corridor to the west annex. He was momentarily blinded by the sunshine pouring through the corridor skylights. Today was going to be another scorcher.

He opened the door to the Book Publishing Division. Considering it was Sunday morning, a fair number of faces turned to look at him, Kaizuka's among them.

"You look very busy."

"Ah, a lot of our self-publishing customers are only available to meet with us on the weekend."

Yuuki had a bad feeling about this. Kaizuka seemed completely different from how he had been on the phone—as if Yuuki's presence was an unwelcome interruption.

"So, let's talk in here," said Kaizuka, ushering Yuuki into the department chief's office.

Yuuki quietly acquiesced, but inwardly he was cursing Kaizuka. If he'd already brought the topic up with his boss, the Book Publishing Division chief Moro, that meant the idea was going nowhere. He'd deliberately approached Kaizuka first because he knew the man was an ex-reporter.

Moro glanced at Yuuki and Kaizuka and waved a vague hand in the direction of the sofa. With exaggerated regret, he closed the book he was holding, took off his reading glasses, and placed them back in their case. Running his fingers through the longish hair that fell below his ears, he got up from his desk. He was definitely the smug, know-it-all type.

"What kind of book are you thinking of publishing?"

"Something like a document of the Japan Airlines crash."

"Something *like* a document?"

Moro spoke scornfully. He sat down opposite Yuuki and crossed his arms and legs exaggeratedly. His body language let Yuuki know he was waiting for a better explanation.

Yuuki wasn't going to let any of this get to him.

"I've come to find out whether the *NKT* would be able to publish a book of this kind."

"But what kind of a book are you talking about?"

"The kind of book that sums up the JAL crash in *North Kanto Times* style. Made up of memoranda and photos from our reporters. A record of the accident."

"A record? If that's what you want, why don't you make a scrapbook out of old newspaper articles?"

"Because I want to leave a proper record, an official one. Because the world's biggest plane crash happened here in our prefecture."

"How many copies do you plan to print?"

"Well, I haven't . . ."

Yuuki didn't know how to reply. He hadn't yet turned his thoughts to the practical side of things.

Moro's know-it-all expression evolved into a triumphant one.

"Who are you planning to sell this book to?"

This was a question Yuuki had expected. Most of the publications put out by the *North Kanto Times* were privately printed, self-funded books. For example, if a former school principal wanted to put out his memoirs, he'd first research how many pupils he had taught over the years. If an instructor of ikebana or the tea ceremony wanted to publish her book, she'd work out how many students she had, and they'd print that number.

This was the system that Moro himself had put in place. In his younger days, he'd made a bit of extra pocket money writing the "autobiography" of a politician to hand out during an election, as well as the success story of an enigmatic entrepreneur. He wasn't a particularly skilled ghostwriter, but his reputation had somehow spread and these days more than a dozen requests "for Moro-san to write my book" were received every year.

Yuuki decided to go all out.

"I'm hoping to sell it in the regular bookstores to the general public. I believe they would be happy to stock it."

"I'm sure that, if I were to ask them, they'd agree to put it in their local publications section, but I don't think it'll sell. Not something of that sort."

"On the contrary, I think there'd be a lot of interest."

"But I heard there were hardly any passengers on board from Gunma."

*Hardly any?*

Yuuki was startled. Well, no. He'd been aware of it from the moment he'd walked into the room. There was something missing from both Moro's desk and the table in front of him. There wasn't a copy of today's *North Kanto Times* anywhere in the room. He looked Moro straight in the eyes.

"There was one passenger on board from Gunma Prefecture."

Moro was completely taken aback. He looked away.

"So, it's hopeless. Out of the question."

He'd had no idea.

Suddenly there was a movement at Yuuki's side, as the clearly uncomfortable Kaizuka leaned forward.

"How about the people who like to read photo magazines?"

"What are you talking—" Moro said in a low, measured tone. His eyes were filled with contempt; it was clear he enjoyed intimidating his direct subordinate. Kaizuka shrank back a little, but he'd apparently decided that, having worked for a while in the Editorial Department, he ought to back Yuuki up. He spoke rapidly.

"If you print it on cheaper paper, mostly in black-and-white, then the cost and the number of days spent producing it can be kept to a minimum. We can pay for the project by taking preorders from the police, members of the Self-Defense Forces, and the fire department. And if it's in the form of a magazine the bookshops'll sell quite a few, I imagine."

"Are you a complete idiot? It'll be in direct competition with *Jomo's Illustrated Gunma*. They got money from the prefecture to print that; we'll be funding the whole thing ourselves. If it doesn't sell, we'll lose money."

"But the prefecture funded that book because it's about the prefecture's activities; it's completely different from something like the crash. In our case, from what I understand from Yuuki, we'll be digging much deeper into the subject. And its style will be newspaper journalism. It'll set us apart from what the *Jomo* book is doing."

"That's already been done by *Friday* and *Focus* magazines. Do you really think that readers who've already seen those shocking photos are going to want to look at some well-mannered, illustrated book put out by a newspaper company?"

"That may be true, but—"

*Never mind. Don't worry about it.*

The words got as far as Yuuki's throat.

Moro turned his irritation on Yuuki.

"It's the same with regular books, too. The *Asahi* or the *Yomiuri* can produce them at lightning speed. We can never hope to compete with them in terms of content or production."

"I can say with all certainty that no other company has spent anything like as much time as our reporters have at that crash site on Mount Osutaka."

Yuuki had answered on reflex, but Moro turned a deaf ear and spoke even more vehemently.

"You are so sure of yourself, aren't you? So conceited. A local newspaper has to do things the local way. In other words, economically. You editorial staff get all carried away about an accident. I think you need to tell your bosses it's time to calm down."

"I haven't spoken to my bosses about this yet," Yuuki said, getting to his feet. Moro's loathsome voice followed him out of the room.

"It's ridiculous. Knowing we're already in the red, the Editorial Department wants to put out a book to brag about what they do."

So that was what he was really thinking. Yuuki didn't bother to stop and respond.

This time, no one in the outer office met his eye. En masse, as if they had an urgent deadline, they sat with their red pens, poring over privately funded manuscripts and what looked like thick piles of galley proofs.

He supposed it was better not to make a profit out of the JAL crash. Telling himself this, he stomped off along the corridor, his footsteps echoing loudly.

Yuuki ate lunch alone in the basement cafeteria, then headed back up to the Editorial Department. The newsroom was still sparsely populated. Yoshii at the copy section island called out a "Good morning!" with a vague bob of the head. He looked half asleep. Yuuki recalled his tense expression on the night they'd chased the bulkhead scoop; it already felt like the distant past.

There were three mountains of documents on his desk. It had become a familiar sight. The central mountain was the highest, consisting of thick article drafts, all contenders for today's top news. The remains of the Nodai Niko High School baseball player's father had been identified in the pre-dawn hours. Early that morning Yuuki had gotten a call at home from Sayama, who was working at the prefectural police headquarters. He was heading out to try to get some background.

Yuuki took his seat and picked up the phone. He dialed the extension of Kaizuka in the Book Publishing Division, and he answered right away.

"This is Yuuki. Sorry about all the trouble I caused you back there."

"Don't worry about it. I'm sorry I couldn't be of more help. You might try getting your managing editor, Oimura-san, to give him a push. Way back, it was Oimura who introduced Moro to his wife."

As Yuuki thanked him and hung up, a coffee cup appeared next to the phone. He looked up to see Chizuko Yorita smiling at him.

"Sorry I lost it with you the other day."

"Looks like you're feeling much better. You working here today?"

"I'm to go back there at three."

"Where do you prefer?"

"I'm not sure yet."

"You'll pick it up. You'll be writing front-page articles in no time."

"I hope so."

Chizuko's hair swung as she moved on to the administrative affairs island. She didn't seem to be in the best spirits yet, Yuuki reflected as he watched her leave. He turned his attention back to his own desk and once more picked up the phone. This time he dialed the extension of the Advertising Department. He wasn't going to give his name, just in case, but luckily it was fellow hiking club member Miyata who answered.

"It's Yuuki. And, again, can we keep this between us? Any news of Kurasaka?"

"He took today off, too. At the last minute."

"Did he give a reason?" Yuuki asked, feeling a little worried. Would he say he was taking the day off because he'd been beaten up by Hanazawa on Mount Osutaka? He hoped that wasn't the rumor going around the company.

"It seems he slipped on his way down Mount Osutaka and took quite a painful fall. I guess he just wasn't used to climbing."

"Right, I see."

Yuuki heaved a sigh of relief. He was about to hang up when he suddenly thought of something.

"Miyata? Have you been to see Anzai recently?"

"Yes. I went last night."

"How was he?"

Miyata's voice took on a sad note.

"No change. Anzai-san was just lying on the bed . . . His eyes are wide open. He looks completely awake. But the doctor says that he's going to have to diagnose persistent vegetative state. That's what his wife told me."

"How does she seem?"

"Actually . . . oddly cheerful . . . Though I think she must be putting up a front."

"I suppose so."

"And their son, I feel really sorry for him. He was sitting in the corner of the room looking very depressed. At this time of year he should be out enjoying the school holidays, but . . ."

These distressing words weighed on Yuuki's heart. He thought of Rintaro's crooked smile and high-pitched laughter when they'd played catch in the hospital courtyard. Of course—his voice hadn't even broken yet. After hanging up, Yuuki couldn't shake the gloomy feeling left by this insignificant realization.

Oimura and Todoroki were at their desks. Yuuki checked the clock on the wall above their heads. Half past one. Still thirty minutes to go before the meeting to decide today's JAL crash coverage.

Yuuki paged Tamaki and skimmed a couple of pages from the central mountain of papers.

> One week since the nightmare accident; search continues under
>     the blazing sun
> Analysis of voice recorder; interim report due this week
> More goodbye messages discovered
> Executive vice president of JAL offers 1.5 million yen condolence
>     money to bereaved families
> Seventh-day memorial service; flowers and incense at the crash
>     site
> Ministry of Transport Aircraft Accident Investigation Committee
>     finishes reconstruction of bulkhead
> Haneda and Narita airports to inspect all bulkheads
> Same class aircraft as crashed JAL plane suffers engine trouble in
>     Hong Kong
> The tail-strike accident in Osaka; repairs were carried out by
>     Boeing

A sound nearby broke his concentration. Kishi had just arrived.

He looked like he was dying to say something.

"What are you smirking about?" Yuuki asked.

"I turned forty yesterday."

"And I turned forty last month," Yuuki snorted. "It wasn't all that happy or amusing."

"There was a truce—a birthday truce."

Kishi looked even more pleased with himself.

Yuuki suddenly understood what he meant. Kishi's two daughters, who usually treated him like "some kind of germ," had been kind to him last night.

"Kaz and Fumi?"

"It was the first time in ages. The whole family celebrated together. In fact, I thought I was going to cry."

"Do you think this means an end to hostilities?"

"I'm not sure about that. I'll have to see what happens when I go home tonight. But I have to say, I think there may be signs of a permanent cease-fire. What do you think?"

Yuuki nodded a little too enthusiastically, then reapplied himself to his work in order to banish Jun's face from his mind. The telephone rang.

"Tamaki here. Did you page me?"

His voice sounded relatively calm. Yuuki spun his chair around so that he had his back to Kishi.

"I'm sorry for what happened, Tamaki. We couldn't get your story into print."

No reply.

"I'd like you to stick with the investigation team. I hear they've rebuilt the bulkhead up at the crash site."

There was a long pause before Yuuki heard Tamaki's strained voice in his ear.

"Yuuki-san, I won't bring this up again, I promise, but can I ask you one thing?"

"Sure."

For a while there was silence on the other end of the line.

"Go ahead. It's okay."

"If it hadn't been you on the crash desk, Yuuki-san, would my article have gone to press?"

Yuuki considered the question.

"Yes. It probably would."

"I understand. Sorry for asking."

"If anyone's going to apologize, it should be me. Just don't forget, you have a long future ahead of you."

Empty words. No matter how long Tamaki did this job, he would never again encounter an accident of this magnitude. Yuuki already understood this, and a young reporter like Tamaki wouldn't need much imagination to understand, too. But this was all he could say. Still, as recently as one week ago Yuuki himself had never imagined that anything bigger than Okubo/Red Army would ever again take place in Gunma Prefecture.

Over by the wall, Oimura and Todoroki stood up and headed off to editor in chief Kasuya's office. It was exactly two o'clock.

Yuuki picked up the notepad on which he'd scribbled his ideas for articles and headlines, and followed. His phone call with Tamaki had felt almost like a purification ritual. Now he was prepared to face the management who wanted to move away from the JAL crash coverage on to something new. Yuuki was ready to motivate them to continue to fill the pages with detailed, informative articles. He was one hundred percent convinced that this was the single most important task left for the JAL crash desk chief.

"So, Yuuki, what's on the menu today?" Kasuya asked.

Yuuki checked his notes.

"The body of the sole victim from Gunma Prefecture was ID'd, so I want to have that as the front-page headline. Related articles on the first and second local news pages to make a full spread."

Kasuya and Todoroki nodded. Yuuki looked at Oimura. He was looking over some documents that he'd brought in with him, and there was no sign of any reaction. Yesterday, they'd almost come to blows, so Yuuki wondered if that was influencing his behavior.

Kasuya turned to Oimura a little anxiously.

"What do you think?"

"I've no objection to that. Just . . ."

Oimura threw a quick glance in Yuuki's direction, then slipped one of the documents he'd brought onto the table.

"These four need to go on the front page."

Yuuki picked it up. There were four tentative headlines in list form.

FUJIMIMURA MAYORAL ELECTION TO BE ANNOUNCHED TOMORROW

AKAGIMURA ASSEMBLY VOTE TO BE ANNOUNCED TOMORROW

CURTAIN UP ON KUTSATSU MUSIC ACADEMY

FINALS OF GUNMA PREFECTURAL YOUTH BASEBALL TOURNAMENT

"Of course, we'll have to include head shots of both of the Fujimimura mayoral candidates, photos from the opening concert at the music academy, and, for the baseball, obviously we need a shot of the winning team's celebrations. Got it?"

Oimura's tone was condescending. He was leaving no room for negotiation.

"Well, the elections for sure—"

Yuuki pointed to the other items on the list.

"But the music academy can go on the second page of local and the youth baseball will be fine on the sports page."

"Impossible," Oimura replied in his most serious voice. "The Kusatsu Music Academy is sponsored by the Agency for Cultural Affairs and Gunma Prefecture. You wouldn't understand these things, but it was a star-studded lineup. The master cellist Pierre Fournier, the BBC Symphony Orchestra's first French horn player Alan Civil, and the conductor David Shallon were all invited to participate. A prefectural newspaper is obligated to lead with a story like that."

"But that kind of story really doesn't mesh with ones about the JAL crash. It's just too cheery. And the youth baseball tournament definitely shouldn't be on the front page."

Oimura pulled out another piece of paper and handed it to Yuuki. It was a photocopy of a preview announcement from the Kusatsu Music Academy that had appeared in the arts and culture section a few days earlier. In celebration of the three hundredth anniversary of the birth of Bach, there was going to be a fortnight of events with the theme "Bach and Sons." In the mornings there would be a series of master classes, and in the afternoons lessons open to the general public, as well as concerts and a whole array of different events.

"Can you imagine how much work went into arranging something on this scale? Schedule planning, negotiating with the overseas musicians, arranging accommodation, rehearsals, PR. It took them a whole year. All with the goal of creating today's opening event. The sweat and tears of a lot of citizens of this prefecture went into this. Don't force them to sacrifice all that. Flight 123 went down. Five hundred and twenty people died. But that and this are completely separate things. This music festival is unique; it's attracted interest from overseas. Don't you think it has as much news value as the Japan Airlines crash?"

It was difficult to know how to respond. Yuuki had to admit that Oimura had made some very good points. And Yuuki knew that, just as he had prayed on that first day, if the jumbo jet had crashed on the Nagano Prefecture side of the border, even he would have had the attitude that it was someone else's accident. He would probably be relaxing on the sofa at this very moment, watching the coverage on TV.

"I completely understand about Kusatsu Academy. But I have to say that I find the idea of featuring a photo on the front page of the winners of the youth baseball tournament tossing their coach in the air way too insensitive. Especially as the dead man from Gunma was the father of one of the Koshien players."

The Firecracker shot back immediately, "You could also see it in the exact opposite way. The boy's father loved baseball. Perhaps the boy would be happy to see the photo. It'd be a nod to his father's memory. That's the way we have to think. The point is, there are many ways to see the same thing."

"But—"

"It's Chairman Shirakawa who ordered us to put the baseball on the front page," Oimura snapped, apparently losing patience with Yuuki. "NKT owes its circulation numbers to printing as many people's names as possible in relation to sports and accidents. Long ago, it didn't matter how small the event, we always printed the results and the names of the participants. If kids' names appear in a newspaper, then the parents buy it. That's how we built up our readership. That's the legacy built by our chairman. Circulation was at a mere fifty thousand copies when he started out at NKT. Don't trample all over that."

Yuuki was doing the calculations. Four articles and two photos. It wouldn't take up too much space. He wouldn't have to give up the top spot. Or, to look at it another way, by agreeing to publish those four articles, he would be completely free to use the rest of the front page however he liked. He could be as lavish with the crash piece as he wanted. In the end, it wasn't that bad a deal. He nodded his acceptance.

Kasuya looked relieved. It seemed the Conciliator would not be required on this occasion.

"Well, that's decided, then. To tell the truth, I agree with Oimura, too. The crash coverage is all well and good, and it still deserves our focus, but we should return to some extent to regular *North Kanto Times* coverage. The JAL crash won't last forever, and we should think about our future. We need to leave something for future generations to work on. So, are we done?"

Yuuki hesitated for a moment, then raised his hand slightly.

"Sir, I'd like to say something."

"What?"

"Today I called in on the Book Publishing Division."

He'd agreed to Oimura's demands, and the meeting had ended peacefully. Now would be his only chance to bring up the topic of the book.

"The Book Publishing Division? What were you doing there?"

"I went to sound them out about the possibility of putting out a book on the JAL crash."

Oimura wasn't the only one to pull a face. Kasuya also looked openly concerned. Yuuki knew why. The company had never published a book about the Okubo/Red Army cases. Yuuki had a hazy recollection that Kasuya and Oimura had negotiated with the publishing arm. Moro, who was already heading up the division back then, must have turned them down. So the cases that had been their personal gold medals, Okubo and the Red Army, never got put into book form. Putting together a book about the JAL crash, a case that had suddenly come out of nowhere, was not going to do anything to save their honor. Put another way, it had no emotional appeal for them. Just from looking at their faces he could read their warped way of thinking.

"You really like to blow your own trumpet, don't you, Yuuki?" said Oimura snidely.

Yuuki didn't respond. He snuck a glance at Todoroki. He had no expression. Or at least it seemed that way.

Ever since he and Todoroki had almost come to blows over whether he'd killed Sayama and Hanazawa's eyewitness story, it was as if Todoroki no longer had to express his dislike of Yuuki so strongly. Yuuki suspected that Todoroki, ever since he'd destroyed the young reporters' opportunity for recognition, had been feeling pangs of guilt. Or perhaps at last he'd been moved by the sheer scale of the accident and decided it was finally time to let go of the Okubo/Red Army era.

"So, what did old Moro have to say?" asked Kasuya, without any genuine interest.

"Well, he—"

But Yuuki was interrupted by a light knock at the door and the entrance of Chizuko Yorita. She came over to Yuuki and, after handing him a message, bent down to whisper in his ear.

"This person is here to meet you."

Yuuki wondered why she didn't say the visitor's name. Puzzled, he checked the name on the note.

Ayako Mochizuki—it felt like a slap on the cheek. Cousin of the late Ryota Mochizuki. He suddenly remembered. She'd called the office the day before yesterday. He'd called back the number with the Takasaki City area code, but she hadn't been home. He'd left a message on the answering machine that he'd call back again, but it had slipped his mind.

That was right around the time that the possible bulkhead scoop had suddenly surfaced. He'd been completely distracted.

"What's up?"

Kasuya was watching him curiously.

"Oh, nothing."

He had no desire to say this name aloud in present company.

"Do you have a visitor?"

Kasuya looked at both Yuuki and Chizuko expectantly.

"It's an acquaintance."

The lie popped out. Yuuki turned to Chizuko.

"Please show her to the visitors' reception area. I'll see her as soon as the meeting's finished."

"Yes."

"Actually . . ."

Chizuko stopped and turned back.

"On second thought, please show her to the basement cafeteria. And get her something to drink."

Chizuko nodded, a knowing expression on her face, and left the room.

"So, can we go on?"

Yuuki nodded, and Kasuya got straight back on topic.

"So what did Moro say?"

"He questioned whether anyone was likely to buy a book like that and then completely shot me down."

Kasuya and Oimura nodded, as if they would have expected no other outcome. The look on their faces was a peculiar mixture of hate for Moro and relief that Yuuki had been rejected. Todoroki let out a long, silent exhalation. So he'd felt the same way as the other two after all.

Yuuki took a deep breath.

"I strongly believe that NKT should leave a proper record. A plane crashed here in Gunma, a prefecture without any flight paths. I admit that it does have some aspects of an inherited accident, but it remains true that the world's biggest air disaster happened right here in our prefecture. It'd be shameful for a newspaper company to just let this opportunity slip by. Simply for the sake of a local newspaper's pride, we should print a few copies, if only that. We have to do it."

There was very little reaction from the three managers. Kasuya and Oimura in particular looked as if Yuuki's whole speech had washed right over them.

To be honest, Yuuki was distracted, too. Ryota Mochizuki's death had been, to all intents and purposes, a suicide. There was no call to get sentimental. For the past five years his mind had been working hard to convince him of this. But now the appearance of Ayako Mochizuki threatened to upset the balance between his mind and heart. He was gripped by a sense of unease.

It was about twenty minutes later that he eventually made it down to the basement.

He sped up involuntarily. His were the only footsteps echoing in the deserted corridor. He got to the cafeteria and saw a young woman in a white T-shirt sitting by the wall with the high windows.

They recognized each other right away. They'd met only six days earlier, at the Takasaki City crematorium. As before, she was glaring at Yuuki as he approached. Or at least that was how it seemed to him.

There was nobody else in the cafeteria. Even the dishwashing area was silent. The staff must be on their break.

Ayako stood up as Yuuki approached, and bowed very properly. Backlit by the window, her T-shirt and brownish hair were surrounded by a halo of pale light.

Yuuki sat down opposite, and Ayako introduced herself briefly. As he'd suspected, she was Ryota Mochizuki's cousin; the only daughter of Ryota's father's younger brother. She was twenty years old, a second-year student at Gunma Prefectural University. Her face was still that of a child, but Yuuki could see both strength and intelligence in her eyes. Once he knew for sure who she was, he felt very unsettled. He found her expression impossible to read.

"First of all, I owe you an apology. I promised to call you back, but I didn't."

"I expect you were very busy," she replied, with the hint of a smile. There was no sarcasm or criticism in her tone but there was something else there, as if she had put a lot of thought into how to respond.

"Every day I read the articles about the Japan Airlines crash. I'm taking media studies and the history of journalism at university."

Yuuki squinted at Ayako.

"And so what is it you wanted to meet with me about?"

Ayako held Yuuki's gaze.

"I've been given a far more valuable experience than anything I could learn at university."

There was nothing to do but wait for her next words.

"These past two days I've been waiting for your phone call. But it never came."

"I'm sorry about that."

"I know. You were busy."

"Yes."

"People's lives. There are big lives and little lives, aren't there?"

Yuuki swallowed. His mind went around in circles. But Ayako's words brought an ache that began to spread inside him.

"Heavy lives and lightweight lives; important lives, and lives that are . . . not. Those people who died in the JAL crash—their lives were extremely important to everyone in the mass media. I've learned that recently."

Yuuki couldn't think how to respond.

"I lost my father eight years ago in a traffic accident. Thanks to a scholarship, I was able to graduate from high school, and now I get a grant to attend university. I wasn't lonely. Ryo-chan's mom and dad have been really kind to me. And Ryo-chan was just like an older brother."

The ice in Ayako's cold coffee had completely melted. Yuuki noticed now that she hadn't even taken the straw out of its paper wrapper.

"My father was a plasterer. He was a really gentle man. I can't tell you how much I wish he hadn't died. He didn't do anything wrong. He was crossing the road on a pedestrian crossing, but he was hit by a speeding motorbike."

She put both hands to her chest and took some deep breaths, as if trying to stop the tears from coming.

"He was in critical condition. There was a small article in the newspaper. After I started at university, I looked it up in the library. It was what you call a 'below-the-fold' piece, wasn't it? Right at the bottom of the local news page, twelve lines of print."

She paused. Yuuki didn't say anything.

"He died three days later. But no one wrote about his death. If you die more than twenty-four hours after an accident, the police don't count it as a traffic death. And so my father's death was never included in the official statistics."

Ayako looked searchingly into Yuuki's eyes.

"Newspaper journalists forget, don't they? My father wasn't anybody famous. It didn't matter to anyone if he departed from this world. His life was little, lightweight and unimportant. That's why, once they'd taken him to the hospital in serious condition, the reporter forgot all about him."

Ayako pulled out a handkerchief and dabbed her eyes. She breathed in deeply, then let it out again with force. When she'd regained control, she raised her reddened eyes and nose to look again at Yuuki.

"And Ryo-chan. You forgot him, too, didn't you? Right away. When I came up to the Editorial Department, everyone was there laughing and joking away. Once the article had been printed, that was it. Over. He worked with you all, at the same company, in the same newsroom, but none of you ever thinks about Ryo-chan anymore."

"That's not true."

It wasn't self-justification. It was for Ayako's sake that he said it.

"Everybody remembers him."

"Liar."

"I'm not saying that we all remember him all the time. But we do remember. It's true."

His chest contracted. He recalled the phrase used by Sayama: "desertion in the line of duty." Thanks to the dishonor that had been brought to Mochizuki's name, Yuuki had survived at the newspaper.

Ayako clenched her jaw.

"You're the one who caused Ryo-chan's death, aren't you?"

"Yes, I did," said Yuuki, looking Ayako straight in the eyes.

"So—" Ayako managed to look challengingly at Yuuki through her tears. "I want you to make sure that you never forget him."

Yuuki nodded.

"I want you always to think of Ryo-chan's name."

Yuuki bowed his head, more deeply this time. He felt as if his heart was being squeezed to its limit.

"I always remember him. Every fifteenth of the month since it happened."

Ayako's voice seemed to catch on her shaking lips.

"Is it wrong to love a cousin so much?"

For a while, neither spoke. After what felt like minutes had passed, Ayako got up.

"When I called you the other day, it was because my aunt had asked me to. She wanted me to tell you not to come and pay your respects anymore."

Yuuki also stood up.

"I understand. Please let her know that I won't go again."

"And one more thing—"

Ayako reached into a plastic bag and pulled out two pages of A4 writing paper, folded in half, and handed them to Yuuki.

"This is what I think about little lives. I want you to run it on the Heartfelt page. I wrote in before, but it must have been rejected."

"I see. I promise we'll publish this one."

"Thank you."

Once again, Ayako made a proper bow, then made her way out of the cafeteria. Yuuki listened to her footsteps fading away gradually until they could no longer be heard. Suddenly he was overcome with exhaustion. He sank back into his chair. His body seemed to be made of lead.

Twenty years old. A young woman half Yuuki's age who already understood so clearly the true nature of the media.

The weight of a life.

The media might pretend that every life was of equal importance, but they selected people, graded them, decided whether their lives were—as Ayako put it—"heavy" or "lightweight," then imposed that set of values on society.

The death of a famous person. And the death of someone who wasn't.

A tragic death. And one that wasn't.

The face of an old woman came into his head—the woman he'd seen that day at the prefectural hospital on his way to visit Anzai. He remembered how she'd been watching the news on the big-screen TV in the lobby, and they'd been showing footage from the Fujioka Municipal Sports Center. It was when they'd showed a young woman, a handkerchief pressed to her eyes, being supported by a police officer. The elderly woman sitting on the end of the couch had muttered something.

*"I wish someone would weep for me like that."*

She'd envied those people—the ones who had died in the plane crash—because she had no one who would grieve for her when she was gone. The old woman understood.

All those faceless people in that hospital waiting room.

Yuuki managed to summon up an image of Ryota Mochizuki's face.

A little life . . . A lightweight life . . .

No! A life was never little or lightweight. But—

Yuuki deliberately cut himself off mid-thought. He checked his watch. It was already beyond half past three. He forced himself to his feet and stretched out his back.

No matter what happened, he was not going to run away from the Japan Airlines plane crash.

He left the cafeteria and, as he made his way back along the corridor, unfolded Ayako Mochizuki's letter and began to read. Its contents brought his feet to a stop. He could feel the blood draining from his cheeks.

The letter was almost word for word exactly what Ayako had just said to him back there in the cafeteria. But then there were the last four lines, which shook him to the core.

*To all those who didn't cry at the deaths of my father and my cousin: I won't cry for you either. Not even for you who lost your lives in the world's greatest, most heartbreaking accident—I have no tears.*

"Maebashi, ninety-six degrees!"

It had turned five o'clock, but the temperature in the newsroom was still rising. Yuuki was at his desk, correcting drafts.

Voice recorder: captain was calm
Bulkhead was badly warped
Number of identified victims reaches 342

From behind him, he heard Sayama's and Hanazawa's voices.

"Yuuki-san?"

He didn't turn around.

"Yuuki-san, can we have a word?"

He ignored them, so they walked around and peered at his face.

"Hey, Yuuki-san?"

"What?"

He looked at them so sternly that they both gulped.

"Ah, we just wanted to thank you for yesterday."

"It's fine."

"I'm sorry for all the trouble I caused you. Thank you so much for dealing with the . . . er, situation."

"I said it's fine!"

The two reporters looked at each other and stepped quickly away.

Yuuki massaged his temples with his thumbs. His skull hurt from the ringing in his ears. It was his mother's voice, singing.

*Little things don't scare me, big things can't be fixed*
*Little things don't scare me, big things can't be fixed*
*Little things don't scare me*
*Little things don't scare me*

His least favorite lullaby ever.

Yuuki put his hand in his pocket. He could feel a scrap of paper in there.

At first he'd thought it must have been revenge on him. And that would have been fine. If that had been the case, he could have just crumpled the paper up and thrown it away.

But it wasn't.

Ayako Mochizuki had completely exposed herself. Her name, her address, her age, even that she was a second-year student at Gunma Prefectural University—all that information was included in her submission.

She hadn't released an arrow under cover of darkness. There was no pseudonym. She was prepared to take full responsibility. She wanted her letter to be published and would deal with any reactions and repercussions it invoked.

A twenty-year-old girl.

He couldn't throw this letter away. He'd reached that conclusion more than an hour ago, but he still couldn't . . .

He got out of his seat.

He could think of many reasons not to print it, but if he peeled them away one by one, like the skin of an onion, there at the core was self-preservation.

He grabbed the telephone. He checked her number, and dialed.

After five rings, she picked up.

"Hello. This is Mochizuki."

"This is Yuuki from the *North Kanto Times*. Thank you for coming in today."

"Oh . . . right. What do you want?" she said in a firm voice.

"That letter. Do you really want us to print it?"

"Are you going to?"

"Yes."

"Thank you. Please do."

Yuuki moved his mouth closer to the receiver.

"Aren't you afraid?"

He heard a sound that might have been a slight chuckle.

"Aren't you the one who's afraid, Yuuki-san?"

"Yes, I am."

This time it was Yuuki who chuckled.

He replaced the receiver, stood up, rearranged his features, and headed over to the central island of desks. Inaoka, the man in charge of Heartfelt, saw him coming and raised a hand.

"The JAL crash special feature is all nicely put together." Yuuki produced the piece of paper from his pocket. He unfolded it and placed it in the middle of Inaoka's desk for him to read.

"If you've got something similar in content, could you replace it with this one?"

"Hmm. A twenty-year-old female university student. Yuuki, you dark horse!"

But that was the end of any joking around. Inaoka's eyes grew wide when he got to the end of the letter. He turned them on Yuuki.

"Wha— Are you . . . This?"

"Yes, this."

Inaoka physically recoiled for a moment, then recovered and looked defiant.

"Come on. You're kidding, right? Are you trying to get my retirement brought forward a year?"

"I promise I won't make trouble for you, Inaoka-san. Just include it. Please?"

"It's awful! Why do you want to publish such a horrible letter? It's disrespectful to the victims of the crash and their bereaved family members."

"It's the opinion of a respectable, upstanding citizen. Common wisdom dictates that the media shouldn't stifle opinion."

"But—"

Noticing the commotion, people from the copy island and beyond had started to gather around. Ayako Mochizuki's letter was being passed among them.

"Whoa!" came the rather loud reaction from Kamejima. "Yuuki, ignoring how unpleasant this letter is, in a way it really hits the nail on the head. But our paper isn't some little private newsletter! It's going to be read by all sorts of people."

A number of voices were raised in opposition.

"This is suicide! If we publish this, tomorrow morning there'll be a shitstorm of protest calls!"

"Mochizuki . . . ? She's not related to Ryota Mochizuki, by any chance?"

Everyone turned to look at Yuuki.

"She's his cousin."

An eruption of sighs and jeers.

"So what?" Yuuki looked around defiantly.

Kishi leaned in to whisper in his ear. "Yuuki, I don't know what's happened here, but stop. This is too much."

"If you don't know what's happened here, then keep out of it."

Yuuki met Nozawa's eye. Normally, each would have broken eye contact with the other immediately, but now they held each other's gaze.

"Yuuki!"

The familiar angry tones of Oimura came from somewhere behind him. The managing editor was holding the letter.

"Have you lost your mind? The families of the dead read this newspaper! Wasn't it your idea to deliver copies for free to the families waiting in Fujioka? More than a thousand grieving relatives are going to read this anonymous defamatory smear! Have you forgotten that?"

"Defamatory smear?"

"It's libelous! The families won't stay silent. They'll come complaining to the newspaper. What are we going to do if that happens? What are you going to do when the NKT ends up the subject of someone else's media coverage?"

"The relatives aren't going to complain."

"Hey, we're not going to escape scot-free just because the letter was written by a private citizen. If we publish it, we'll be held responsible."

"Well, obviously."

"Are you fucking kidding me?" yelled Oimura, grabbing him by the collar. "Are you trying to destroy the *NKT*? Do you think it's fun to offend the victims' grieving families?"

Yuuki grabbed Oimura's collar in turn and pulled it as tight as he could.

"What makes you so sure that the victims' families are going to react that way? Don't you think that people who have lost their own flesh and blood will understand how that young woman feels?"

You could have heard a pin drop in the newsroom.

"I'm printing the letter. Got it?"

Yuuki's face was right up in Oimura's. It looked as if the Firecracker had already finished exploding. There were even signs of fear running through the muscles of his pallid face.

Several people rushed over and separated Yuuki and Oimura.

"The last four lines are the problem," began Inaoka, looking at Yuuki, then Oimura. "If we could cut those lines, it'd be fine. It'd be more of a general observation."

"No cuts!"

Inaoka looked panicked.

"Cutting isn't uncommon. We always have to edit the letters because of special restrictions. There isn't a letter we print that hasn't somehow been altered."

"I don't want you to alter anything except perhaps the name. Publish it just with initials."

"But—"

"Is a letter that's been edited a true letter? Call yourself an ex-reporter?"

Lost for words, Inaoka just stared into space.

"Yuuki-san?"

Sayama now stood in front of Yuuki.

"I know how much you're still affected by the Mochizuki case. But you don't need to feel obliged. He killed himself. It's not your fault."

Yuuki closed his eyes.

"Don't say it."

But Sayama wasn't put off that easily. His tone of voice was now the same as when he talked about his own father's suicide.

"I can never forgive anyone who makes another feel responsible for their death. It's unforgivable to put it on the living and cause them to suffer after you're gone. That's the most cowardly way to die."

"I told you not to say it!"

Yuuki opened his eyes again and scanned the room.

"All I want is to make a newspaper. A real newspaper, not just pages of newsprint. We've all gotten so busy that we're missing the signs. The *North Kanto Times* is on its last legs. We've all become the playthings of the executives, and the rot has set in. If we fail to print this letter, you all will spend the rest of your whole working lives just churning out more pages of newsprint."

The newsroom was filled with the sound of breathing, nothing else.

"Let's publish the letter in its entirety," Yuuki continued. "An hour from now, anyone who doesn't want to be involved had better go out and get themselves a cup of coffee."

There was no time to scream.

He lost any sense of a foothold, and his body suddenly plummeted. What was surely only a moment felt like eternity. The rope made a zipping sound and then went taut. His body jerked violently to a stop.

*First overhang, Tsuitate rock face.* Yuuki found himself dangling in midair under the giant roof.

He heard a worried voice calling down from above.

"Are you okay?"

He couldn't see Rintaro, up there above the eaves of the roof, keeping Yuuki's rope secure.

"Are you hurt?"

Yuuki couldn't reply right away. The shock of falling had completely robbed him of his ability to think. All he could see was the ground, far below him. He realized that he was hanging upside down.

"Yuuki-san, stay calm. Please tell me what your situation is right now."

Now he recalled what he'd been doing just before he'd fallen. He'd almost cleared the first overhang, mounted the final rung of his aider, reached up as far as he could with his right hand to hook another aider to one of the many pitons covering the rock wall. He was going to make it. But just as that thought had crossed his mind, his leg had begun to wobble. His knee unlocked, and his foot had slipped off the aider's rung.

But he hadn't fallen more than about a meter. Rintaro had stopped his fall. And yet, even in his relief, Yuuki was still in a desperate state.

"Yuuki-san! Can you hear me?"

Yuuki called out into the void.

"Yes, I hear you."

"Do you have any injuries?"

"I'm all right . . . I think."

"Are you completely suspended? Did you get separated from the aider?"

"No . . ."

He realized he wasn't totally in midair. His right leg was tangled in the lowest rung of his aider, and bent to an angle of approximately forty-five degrees. That was what was holding him in his upside-down position.

"My leg's caught in the aider. I'm hanging upside down."

"Got it. Right, let's try to pull you up a bit and get you upright again. Grip the rope with both hands. Brace your leg so that it doesn't get separated from the aider."

"Okay."

"Here we go."

The rope began to move with impressive force. His upper body was pulled steadily upright. He felt all the blood that had pooled in his head begin to flow back down.

"How is it? Are you back up again?"

"Yes."

"Grab hold of the aider and steady yourself."

"Got it."

"Now rest for a moment. Take some deep breaths and try to get as calm as possible."

"Okay, I'll try."

His words sounded weak to his own ears.

He looked up. This giant dark rock was blocking his way. It seemed to be looking down on him, sneering. His mouth was completely dry. His hands and legs were trembling. His stamina and willpower were all completely used up. But worse than anything, terror had entered the core of his being and was eating away at his mind.

*I can't do it. I can't climb this thing.*

Just as he was about to lose his nerve completely, Rintaro called down to him again.

"Are you ready to go for it?"

Yuuki didn't reply.

"One of the aiders is still usable, right?"

Rintaro was talking about the one he'd had in his hand right before he'd fallen. One end of it had been attached to his waist to prevent it from falling.

"It's fine."

"Great. So, let's go."

Silence.

"Yuuki-san, let's go. While you're still feeling it."

It wasn't only his words—Yuuki could feel Rintaro's message of encouragement through the tension of the rope. *If you wait too long, then you really won't be able to climb anymore.*

But he just couldn't get that fire started in his mind. The urge to climb simply wasn't there anymore. It felt shameful, but he had to admit it.

"I'm sorry. I don't think there's any way I'm going to get over this roof."

"No, you're fine. You can do it."

"It's impossible. The piton is too far away. I can't reach it."

"No way. It can't be."

Rintaro was so matter-of-fact, it made Yuuki a little angry.

"I tried it just now and it was hopeless. I stood on the very top rung of my aider but I still couldn't get there. Even the closest piton is out of my reach."

"You should be able to reach it, because . . ." Rintaro's voice suddenly grew more forceful. "Because it was Jun who placed that piton there."

What?

Yuuki looked up, and it finally registered—all the metal pitons hammered into the rock—most of them were ancient and covered with rust. But one of them, the one closest to him now, still had a faint silvery sheen.

"I'm sorry I kept it from you until now. The thing is, last month we climbed together."

Yuuki's mouth was hanging open. *Together . . . ? Jun and Rintaro . . . ?*

"We came to check out the route. I'm sorry to be rude, but because it was going to be your first-ever real climb."

Rintaro's voice became more cheerful.

"Jun was saying, 'My dad's not so young anymore. He's not going to be able to get over this roof.' And so he added one more piton."

Perhaps because Yuuki couldn't see Rintaro's face, the words carried an impressive strength of their own.

*Jun left it here for me.*

That fire was lit.

He curled his fingers into a fist and pulled with all his strength. This was one of those moments when you truly understand that human beings are almost entirely ruled by their emotions.

He raised his head and began to ascend the aider. Step by step, carefully, so as to keep the shaking to a minimum, he climbed up to the very top rung. The silver-colored piton seemed much closer this time.

He reached over his head with the other aider. Reprimanding his leg for shaking in fear, he stretched out his knee and arm as far as they would go. Every muscle in his body groaned. He thought his arm was going to be pulled out of its socket. Five more centimeters . . . three . . . he knew he could reach it. It was because he believed he could that he was able to hold this extreme pose for ten, twenty seconds.

The tip of the aider touched the piton. He wasn't sure whether it was sweat or tears that got in his way, but he missed seeing that crucial moment.

*Click.*

That beautiful metallic sound reached his ears. It seemed to echo through the mountain.

Perhaps he hadn't wanted to interrupt this father-son dialogue, but Rintaro stayed quiet, wordlessly working the rope as Yuuki climbed, and doubtlessly offering a silent prayer of thanks. Yuuki thought about how this rope connected him to Jun, now far away in Tokyo. And also to the Jun of that other day, seventeen years before.

**50**

Yuuki left the office just before ten in the evening.

He drove out of the parking lot with Ayako Mochizuki's hoarse voice still haunting him.

*"People's lives. There are big lives and little lives, aren't there?*

*"Heavy lives and lightweight lives; important lives, and lives that are . . . not. Those people who died in the JAL crash—their lives were extremely important to everyone in the mass media."*

He'd been so moved by these words that he'd vowed to ensure by any means possible that her letter would be printed on the readers' letters page.

The final four lines were burned into his retina.

*To all those who didn't cry at the deaths of my father and my cousin: I won't cry for you either. Not even for you who lost your lives in the world's greatest, most heartbreaking accident—I have no tears.*

He gripped the steering wheel with all his might.

He had to publish that letter. He couldn't back out of it. As he thought about the possible reaction from the victims' families, his stomach seemed to have detached itself from the rest of his insides and was rolling around. Would the newspaper be inundated with calls? They would be reading the *North Kanto Times* up in Fujioka City as they waited for their loved ones' remains to be identified. Yuuki supposed that, if there was so much as one single protest from a family member, he would be forced to leave the paper.

He was almost home. This would be the first time since the crash that he had arrived home before Yumiko had gone to bed. Today Inaoka, as the man in charge of Heartfelt, had taken over the job of seeing the next day's edition go to press. His attitude had been one of chivalry mixed with a kind of desperate abandonment.

"Yuuki, this page is my job. I'll be responsible for the final layout. You go home."

Yuuki took him up on his offer. He was longing to see Yumiko's face. It was very possible that he was going to lose his job, and he felt that he needed to talk this over with his wife tonight.

Of course, Inaoka had stayed in the newsroom. But not a single other person had left, either, despite Yuuki's offer for them to distance themselves from the publication of the letter. Even Oimura had stayed at his desk, making a whole slew of phone calls. He was probably doing everything in his power to make sure that, whether there were complaints from the bereaved families or not, Yuuki would be fired from the paper. By the time Yuuki parked in front of his house, he was convinced this would be the outcome.

Ever since his days on the police beat, he'd always taken his own key and let himself in when he came home. Tonight, as soon as he stepped through the door into the humid *genkan* entranceway, he could hear laughter coming from the living room. Yumiko and Yuka . . . and he could also hear Jun.

Everyone was still up. He hurried down the short corridor, feeling a mixture of happiness and confusion.

"Wow, you're early!" said Yumiko, with a look of surprise.

Yuka was kneeling on the floor in front of the TV, her legs splayed out to the sides.

"Hi, Daddy!" she called out to him in a cheerful voice. Cross-legged next to her sat Jun. Their eyes met for a split second, but the moment his dad stepped into the room he abruptly turned his back and fixed his gaze on the TV screen. There was an exciting-looking dinosaur film on. Yuuki guessed it was the kind of thing they showed during the summer holidays.

Yuuki sat down at the dining table and took off his tie. The sofa was a little too close to Jun for comfort. He was afraid that if he sat there it might provoke Jun to jump up and break the family circle.

Smiling, Yumiko came over.

"Do you want something to eat?"

"No, thanks. I already had something."

"So, did something good happen today?"

"Huh?"

Yuuki saw that Yumiko was laughing.

"Does it look as if it did?"

"Actually, it does. You look happy about something."

*Happy . . . ?*

Instinctively, Yuuki rubbed his cheek.

"Shall I run a bath for you? We all just took showers today," said Yumiko, picking up Yuuki's tie. She sounded a little reluctant. She wasn't overtly worried about saving water, but perhaps it was in the back of her mind.

"Yes, please," Yuuki replied.

Instead of going into the bathroom, Yumiko headed to the kitchen. She got out two bottles of beer from the storage space under the kitchen floor and put them in the fridge. Yuuki turned his attention to the two children in front of the TV.

"Yuka, how was the Yomiuri Giants versus Taiyo Whales game?"

"Oh, I don't know. After *Touch* I watched *Sailor Moon*."

Yuuki already knew this would be her answer. She was only interested in Hanshin Tigers games.

Back in the newsroom, they'd been showing an NHK special broadcast: "What Happened to the Tail?—Analysis of the Japan Airlines Plane Crash." The word "analysis" gave the feeling that time had lapsed since the crash. The eye of the storm had already passed.

Yuuki rolled his neck and shoulders uncomfortably. Next in line was Jun. He tried to think of something to say to him, but he couldn't find any words.

There was something he needed to talk about, though.

"Hey."

He was addressing Yumiko, who'd just come back from the bathroom.

"What?"

"Sit down a minute. I've got something to tell you."

He told her the short version of what had happened to Anzai. She was utterly amazed.

"I've never heard of that before. I mean, asleep with your eyes open. So he's a vegetable?"

But she was a reporter's wife. She remembered she needed to avoid discriminatory and offensive terms. She quickly rephrased it.

"Sorry. I mean, is he in a vegetative state?"

"Yes. They call it a persistent vegetative state, or PVS."

"Is it possible to regain consciousness?"

"In exceptional cases."

Yumiko let out a deep sigh and slumped back into her chair.

"His poor wife," she murmured under her breath.

"The Anzais have a son, Rintaro."

"I know. He's about the same age as Jun."

"I'd like to invite him over to the house sometime. His mom's busy at the hospital. It'd be nice to have him over for dinner or—"

Yumiko cut him off.

"Sounds good. Bring him over anytime. I'll try to help out as much as possible."

Yuka was watching them. Jun's head was turned just far enough to hear what his parents were saying.

"I hope you two will help out, too," Yuuki managed to say as casually as he could.

Yuka's eyes lit up.

"Hey, Daddy. What's he like?"

"He's a really good kid. A little quiet, maybe."

"Is he good-looking?"

"Hmm . . . I'm not sure about that. I know he has a really kind face, though."

"Okay."

"Hey, Jun?" He caught his son just as he turned back to the TV.

"That boy's dad is a really good mountain climber. He taught me how to climb, too. Let's take Rintaro with us mountain climbing sometime."

He watched for Jun's response, but instead he got an earful of Yuka's shrill voice.

"That's not fair! I want to come, too!"

"Of course you can come. But I know you've got volleyball on the weekends."

"Ahh! What a pain. I think I'm going to give up volleyball."

"Which mountains?" asked Jun flatly. His gaze landed somewhere around Yuuki's torso.

"Mount Haruna or Myogi. Actually, there are loads of places. It's great. The air's really clear. It's exhilarating, going up to a high place."

Yuuki gestured excitedly as he spoke. Jun was looking off into space. But he didn't look lost—more as if he was letting his imagination run free.

"What do you think? Should we go?"

". . . I'll think about it."

Having given this vaguest of promises, Jun turned back again to the TV. Yuka got hold of her brother's shirt and began shaking him. "Jun, it's not fair. It's not fair." She was clearly annoying him, yet Yuuki could still see the trace of a smile on his face.

Yuuki lay in the bath and thought things over. He felt a mixture of guilt and, to a lesser degree, contentment. He'd used Rintaro to pique Jun's interest. Of course, Rintaro would be thrilled. The experience was sure to be good for him. But Yuuki knew that making these kinds of excuses for Jun's behavior didn't make it any better.

He scooped up a handful of steaming-hot water and splashed it over his face.

It had been a long day. Everything he'd done and felt drifted through his mind.

Ayako Mochizuki . . . "*Heavy lives and lightweight lives . . . Important lives, and lives that are . . . not.*"

There was no point in thinking about it anymore. He'd made his decision: Ayako's letter was going to appear in tomorrow's paper.

Something Yumiko had said to him popped into his head.

"*So, did something good happen today?*"

He wondered why she'd asked him that. She'd said he looked happy. Surely not. He'd been tense and worried at the thought that he might be leaving his job.

When he got out of the bath, Yumiko was alone in the living room.

Yuuki was both relieved and a little disappointed to see that the TV screen was dark.

"They've gone to bed?"

"Just now."

"It's not really cold yet, but never mind," said Yumiko, pouring two glasses of beer.

Yuuki sat on the sofa and picked the copy of the *North Kanto Times* up from the coffee table. Turning it over, he checked the TV schedule on the back page. Only a few days ago it had been full of the words "JAL crash." Now the program titles were again peppered with exclamation points and question marks; proof that the usual variety and comedy programs had regained their prominence.

"Can you turn on Channel Four?"

"Something on the crash?"

"Yeah. After the sports news it looks like they're doing a documentary."

Yumiko switched on the TV and came to sit by Yuuki.

"I'll just have the one," she said, picking up a glass.

Yuuki was finding it difficult to broach the subject of what had happened at work. He wanted to quit. He thought that, if only Yumiko could read his mind, then he wouldn't need to find the words.

"Sweetheart?" said Yumiko, without taking her eyes off the screen. He peered at her profile and saw a hint of something determined.

"You shouldn't get too upset about it."

"About what?"

"This thing with Jun. He doesn't hate you, you know."

Yuuki froze.

"How can I explain it? I guess he's just tactless, awkward. He doesn't know how to mend fences. He's very much like you, really."

Yuuki didn't answer. Yumiko turned to look at him.

"He'll get over it. He just needs to grow up a bit first. I'm sure he understands. You used to hit him because you didn't know how to communicate with him. Don't be too impatient. Take it slowly."

Silence.

"Are you listening?"

"I have to put my trust in you," said Yuuki. "Be their sunshine. If you're there for them, Jun and Yuka will be okay."

"Sunshine? Yuck!" Yumiko burst out laughing. "Being a bit overdramatic, aren't you? That's why Jun can't get close to you, you know."

There was a kind of understanding that came from being a married couple. As well as things that, despite being married, they would never understand. Right on the boundary between these two states, Yuuki felt a little sad.

He could hear his mother singing a lullaby. He'd wanted her to be his sunshine. That had been his strongest desire in his youth.

Yumiko soon went off to bed, and Yuuki was left alone in the living room.

The sports news was over and he still didn't know the result of the Giants versus Whales game. Nor could he concentrate on the crash documentary. He just sat and stared into space.

The plants on the windowsill that had faded in the sun; the white wall clock he'd bought for one of their wedding anniversaries—what number was it again? The patchwork quilt Yumiko had made back when she was really into that kind of thing; the woodblock-printed calendar Yuka had won as a first prize—so it must have been three years ago; the black skid mark on the floor left by the tire of one of Jun's toy cars; the wooden carved figure and the vase with the artificial flowers, both of which seemed to have been dumped haphazardly; the *noren* cloth hanging that they'd bought on a family trip to a hot spring. Nothing expensive, but everything precious to him, each piece representing a family memory.

If he was kicked out of the company, had no job, he'd probably have to sell this house. A reporter was useless for anything else. There was not much work for writers out here in the provinces. It would be pretty much impossible to make enough to support a family of four. He'd have to move to Tokyo. But he didn't have any connections or know of any job openings in the capital. Even if he set out with the hope of new beginnings, would there be anyplace willing to give an unskilled forty-year-old a chance?

He'd lose his family, move to a tiny apartment in a small town somewhere. But Yumiko could still be the sunshine for his children.

He laughed at himself, at his childish way of thinking. He was forty, after all.

Yuuki cursed the years that had accumulated while he'd been idling his life away. He cursed that innocent woman, Ayako Mochizuki, who'd turned up unexpectedly right at the crossroads of his life.

## 51

*You mustn't chase the stars*
*You mustn't chase the moon*
*Chase the beasts, in the forest*
*It's dark, it's dark, deep in the forest*
*The stars are asleep, deep in the forest*
*The moon is asleep, deep in the forest*
*You are asleep, deep in the forest*
*You mustn't chase the stars*
*You mustn't chase the moon.*

Yuuki greeted the sunrise from the sofa.

It was morning, and he hadn't slept at all. He'd sat up all night waiting for the morning delivery. Now the hands on the clock showed a little after five. There was a noise coming from outside—an engine running and stopping, then running again. The newspaper deliveryman was making his way up the street on his moped.

At ten past five, Yuuki slowly got up from the sofa and walked to the front door. He stuck his feet in a pair of sandals and went out to get the stack of newspapers from the mailbox. Back in the living room, he pulled out a chair and sat at the dining table. He broke his usual habit and opened the *North Kanto Times* before the others.

READERS' LETTERS: HEARTFELT

It was titled "Japan Airlines Crash Edition."

He scanned the letters. Ayako Mochizuki's was there, right at the end. Just as he had instructed, they'd used her initials. And not a single word had been altered.

He waited until six o'clock, then called the newsroom.

"Hello, this is the *North Kanto Times.*"

He'd assumed that his call would be answered by one of the first-year reporters working the night shift, but the voice in his ear was unmistakably Sayama's. Typical of Sayama to step up at a time like this, he thought. But this was no time to be sentimental.

"Have there been any complaints?"

"Five calls so far."

"What did they say?"

"Think how the bereaved families must be feeling—all of them like that."

After a beat, Yuuki asked the big question.

"Anything from the victims' family members?"

"Nothing."

They could hear each other let out a long breath.

"How many people are manning the phones?"

"We have four lined up. All people with a soothing manner."

"Got it. I'm going to come in early, too."

"Yuuki-san?" Sayama said hurriedly, just as Yuuki was about to hang up. "To be honest, I don't know whether it was the right decision to print that letter or not. I can't judge."

"Me neither."

"Yuuki-san!"

"Who can say? But, sometimes, you just have to do it."

"That's true, but this time it wasn't—"

"It was for me."

Yuuki's tone was harsh. He was irritated at himself for his clumsy attempt to make Sayama understand. He hung up the phone and, just as he was getting dressed, Yumiko came downstairs.

"Already?"

"Yeah."

"The crash again?"

"Yes."

Yuuki hurried out of the living room and was just slipping on his shoes at the *genkan* when he heard the tread of slippers behind him. He turned to speak.

"I might be leaving the paper."

Yumiko's sleepy face was suddenly wide-awake.

"No!"

"I don't know yet. But I just wanted you to be prepared for the possibility."

The wrinkles in her cheeks and eyes crumpled in a way he'd never seen before.

A strong magnetic force was trying to pull him back to the house, but he had to fight it. He realized that Yumiko's fear was very much his own, too.

## 52

The morning sun was just starting to shine in through the news-room windows.

Sayama was still there, tethered to the phone. The number of reinforcements had grown to seven. Inaoka from the Heartfelt column had come in early. He looked surprisingly lively. Chizuko Yorita was there, too, at the desk next to Sayama's: her long hair tied back, talking earnestly to whoever was on the other end of the line.

Yuuki caught Sayama's eye and raised a hand in greeting. He went over to him and checked out the cheat sheet he'd prepared.

*The* North Kanto Times *is open, impartial, and operates on a principle of fairness and neutrality. We print all views without prejudice. We respect all opinions, suppress none. It is our mission to inform the people of our prefecture in a well-rounded manner.*

It was Inaoka's hastily prepared statement. He'd made copies and distributed them to the whole phone team. In the corner, there was a box headed "tally." So far, Sayama alone had recorded eight protest calls.

He looked at Chizuko's sheet. She'd already answered six. Which meant that there must have been a total of around fifty calls so far.

How many had come from the victims' families? But before he could ask Sayama, the phone on the desk to his right began to ring.

Yuuki grabbed a ballpoint pen from his pocket and picked up.

"What the hell does the *NKT* think it's doing?"

The booming voice pierced his eardrum. This was the first time he'd ever had to deal with an angry customer, but he felt strangely calm.

"Which article is the problem?"

"It's obvious. Heartfelt, of course. How could you print something like that? It's disgusting. The poor families of the victims!"

"We decided that was one opinion. It's a sincere letter that encourages us to think about the topic of life and death."

"Then why didn't you print the author's name? All we know is that it was written by a twenty-year-old university student. It's clearly a bad joke. You think it's okay to print rubbish like that?"

"We know exactly who the author is, and the letter was written with perfectly serious intentions."

"You scum. The *North Kanto Times* is a local newspaper. Those bereaved family members have come here in pain and distress. You make me feel ashamed! I can't believe we've done this to them."

"It's because we're a local newspaper that we printed it. Please understand."

Sayama had a moment between calls and slipped a note to Yuuki. It read: "Victims' Families: 0."

Yuuki felt relieved, but the booming voice in his earpiece kept up to the end.

"Really? Then I'm not taking your newspaper anymore. In fact, I never want to set eyes on it again."

He was probably a perfectly well-intentioned person. And a regular reader. His declaration that he was going to unsubscribe was torture to Yuuki.

Every time they hung up the phone, it would ring again.

Tipped off that something big was going on, Kasuya, followed closely by Todoroki, showed up before eight o'clock. The two of them had spent the previous evening at a dinner put on by local business leaders and had been out of the office. Oimura had called to let them know that Yuuki had published a scandalous letter, but even with that advance notice its contents had still managed to shock them now. That had probably been Oimura's intention: to be deliberately vague about the subject matter so that they wouldn't realize, until they arrived, the severity of the situation.

Oimura showed his face briefly around nine o'clock but was soon gone again. Next, Kishi and Nozawa turned up, also earlier than normal. Apparently the managing director and the chairman were in, too. That was the rumor going around between calls.

It was past ten before the phones stopped ringing. Yuuki totaled up the number of protest calls: 283. It was the most they'd ever received, except for during the general election two years before, when they'd accidentally printed the wrong candidate's photo.

There hadn't been a single call from any of the victims' relatives. Of course, this wasn't something for Yuuki to rejoice about. The readers' anger was genuine. And while he listened over and over again to their reasonable arguments, he found it increasingly difficult to remember what he'd been thinking when he'd made the decision to print Ayako Mochizuki's letter.

"Yuuki!"

The hefty physique of editor in chief Kasuya approached.

Yuuki could see he was flustered.

"The chairman's here."

"I heard."

"Iikura's probably going to come storming in."

"I'll explain everything to him myself."

"You've gone too far this time."

What Yuuki heard was, *I'm not going to be able to protect you this time.*

"Well, it might be your salvation that there haven't been any protests from the victims' families. But there could still be some."

"I don't think there will be," said Yuuki. He could hear the hope in his own voice.

"Yuuki-san? Phone call for you."

He turned to see Chizuko Yorita holding the receiver close to her chest. She wore the exact same expression as yesterday when she'd come to tell him he had a visitor, so he guessed right away who it was. He hurried over to answer the call.

"This is Yuuki."

"Mochizuki here."

Ayako's voice was faint.

"What is it?"

"I read it. My letter . . . I . . . I've done a terrible thing to those families. It's inexcusable. I'm really, truly sorry."

She'd written that she wouldn't shed a tear for those bereaved family members, but now she was crying.

Yuuki felt as if he'd been woken from a deep sleep. Perhaps he had had to make Ayako say those words. He'd needed to hear the words that would break the spell, so he'd put that letter in. It hadn't been to ease Ayako's heart; it had been to save his own soul, which had driven Ryota Mochizuki to his death. That must have been his true motive for running it.

He stared up at the ceiling. The pain in his chest was greater than usual. He wanted to soothe Ayako's tears. That was all he could think about.

"Not a single one of the victims' family members has said anything to us."

There was no reply.

"I think they understood," Yuuki added.

"But . . . I . . . want to apologize. To the bereaved families."

"Then you should write another letter."

"What?"

"And if you do, I'll print that one, too."

"Really? Will you?"

"I promise. I'll make sure it gets in," he said confidently.

That was when it happened. Everyone in the newsroom turned around to face the entrance. Yuuki automatically followed their gaze.

A wheelchair rolled through the door.

It wasn't Iikura who'd come storming in. It was Chairman Shirakawa.

**5
3**

Everyone held their breath. One by one, each member of the staff was subjected to the glare of those bloodshot eyes. Nicknamed the "H-Bomb" back when he was editor in chief, Chairman Shirakawa had an intimidating presence that caused even Kasuya and Todoroki to stand to attention.

"Who did it?" he demanded, focusing his gaze on Kasuya.

"I'm s-sorry, when you say, 'Who did it?' you mean, er . . . ?" stammered Kasuya.

"Did you give the order?"

After a slight pause, Kasuya's mouth twisted.

"Er . . . no, I didn't."

The editor in chief had folded right away.

"So, who was it?"

The newsroom was hushed. Above Shirakawa's head was a second one—the beautiful face of his personal assistant, Manami Takagi, whose job it was to push his wheelchair. It was as if he'd brought a second pair of eyes with which to scan the room.

In his peripheral vision, Yuuki could sense the presence of Inaoka shifting uncomfortably in his chair. He realized he had to give himself up. He stepped forward stiffly. Just as he moved, a voice called out from behind him.

"We all did it."

It was Kamejima, though his usually cheerful tone was now absent.

Shirakawa stretched his wrinkly, blemish-covered neck.

"You *all* did it? This isn't junior high school."

"But that's what happened. The whole department decided to publish the letter."

"Nonsense!"

"It was me." Unable to stand it any longer, Yuuki had stepped forward. "I made the decision as JAL crash desk chief."

Shirakawa wore what could only be described as a satisfied smile.

"Of course. It would be you."

Yuuki nodded and steeled himself, but Shirakawa continued in a perfectly calm voice.

"Leave the *North Kanto Times*."

Yuuki raised his head. It was so abrupt that it lacked a sense of finality.

"You mean I'm fired?"

"Is that a problem for you?"

He wasn't sure how to respond.

"You pathetic little man! If you prefer, you can be transferred to one of our one-man branches deep in the mountains. Either way, I never want to see your face here at headquarters again. So, which is it? It's your choice."

Resignation, or a job in the middle of nowhere without any colleagues? Was he really supposed to make that decision right here and now? On the spot? This was deliberate torture.

Yuuki gritted his teeth. His fear subsided and was replaced by a wave of pure rage. He saw Ayako Mochizuki's weeping face. He'd made her cry. Without planning to, he'd used her innocent letter to cleanse his own soul. On the other hand . . .

The weight of a life. Its size. In the view of the *North Kanto Times*, in the view of that medium known as a newspaper, was it so wrong to have printed that letter? Was the letter worthless? Meaningless?

He had to speak up.

"I don't think I did anything wrong."

"Are you deaf? I asked you if you want to resign or go and live in the mountains."

He thought of Yumiko's terrified face, but he didn't lose any of his determination.

He felt a presence by his side. Todoroki had stepped up. The local news chief removed his dark, gold-framed glasses.

"Mr. Chairman, please give him some time to consider."

Shirakawa turned his attention to Todoroki.

"Give him time?"

"Yes. A day or two."

"I see. So you think the post of local news editor gives you some kind of power, do you?"

Todoroki's face turned instantly pale.

Shirakawa scanned the newsroom.

"Huh? Look at yourselves. You think I'm being unfair? Have you forgotten who you all work for?"

"Still, Mr. Chairman—"

But Todoroki was cut short by the explosion of the H-Bomb.

"Shut up! You editors, reporters, swagger around like you're untouchable. Just remember—without the name of the *North Kanto Times*, you'd be nothing! Don't think any of you are special. You are all expendable."

This time the hush that fell lasted much longer.

"Yuuki, tell General Affairs your decision by the end of the day. Let's go!"

The last two words were thrown over his shoulder at Manami. She immediately turned the wheelchair around.

"As a human being and an *NKT* employee, I have done nothing wrong," Yuuki yelled.

The wheelchair stopped. A head slowly turned back to look at him.

Yuuki locked on to those murky eyes. He had no intention of backing down. Chairman Shirakawa's dry lips parted. The second H-Bomb was about to drop. Or so everyone thought.

"Today. General Affairs."

And with this strangely gentle reminder, Shirakawa broke eye contact and rolled away. Manami closed the door behind them.

The tension in the room was broken. Slowly, people began to move. But Yuuki was left frozen to the spot. Kishi was by his side, looking closely into his face.

"I don't believe this!"

It was Kamejima who spoke. No one answered, but everyone wore the same grim expression.

Kasuya had disappeared. He must have slipped away quietly into his office. Todoroki was back at his desk by the wall, his dark lenses making his facial expression unreadable again. He hadn't actually gone so far as to defend Yuuki, but Yuuki knew he would never forget that simple "Still, Mr. Chairman—"

Nobody had realized that Oimura was in the room. There he was, standing by the door. His arms folded, he was staring coldly at Yuuki. Yuuki returned the glare. There was the face of a man who, back in his youth, Yuuki had once thought of as an older brother.

Yuuki couldn't make a decision. He had no particular feeling either way. He put his hand up to the collar of his suit jacket and began to take off his NKT pin. Kishi grabbed his wrist and tried to stop him.

"Get off!" Yuuki said, pulling his hand away. "Are you trying to make me into the chairman's puppy dog?"

"No, I was thinking more of a lone wolf."

"Enough!"

A voice rang out louder than Yuuki's.

"Stop fucking around, Yuuki!"

It was Nozawa.

"You're desk chief. Are you planning to abandon the JAL crash? If you're going to quit, then you'd better do a proper handover. For now, you're still responsible for today's layout."

Nozawa's voice was unusually high-pitched and, at the end, it began to crack.

Three-quarters of victims now identified
Voice recorder analysis; Captain: "All hydraulics lost"
Vivid picture of pilots' struggle
Compensation negotiations dragging on
Gunma police begin probe
Smiling again, appetite returned—three survivors at Tano
    Hospital
"I'm not going to let it stop me"—interview with surviving girl

Yuuki, with the help of the colleagues at the desk on either side of him, spent the rest of the day going through the wires and drafts with a red pen.

Kamejima came over to check on them.

"Ready soon?"

"We've got fifty percent of the local pages done."

"Got it. Thanks."

The atmosphere in the newsroom was the same as always. Everyone was behaving just as normal. Occasionally cold, but then warm again. For the moment, he was happy.

He felt calm. He knew it was because, deep down, he'd been ready to leave. He'd been given the chance now to break free from the spell this company had over him.

He couldn't forget Anzai's phrase.

*"I climb up to step down."*

Anzai must have felt the same way Yuuki did now. It had been a rite of passage, an untying of the ropes that bound him to this place—the ascent on Tsuitate.

*Climber's high.*

Anzai had been right. In his seventeen years at the company, Yuuki had plowed on down the reporter's road, elbowing people aside as he went. He'd never even thought about stepping down. But Anzai had been able to read his mind. He could see in Yuuki's heart that he was ready to call it quits. Or rather, that Yuuki was suffering from not being able to resign but not being able to stay on, either. Anzai had already made that decision for himself, and that was why he had invited Yuuki to join him to climb Tsuitate. He was going to push him to decide. Maybe ask him what kind of life he wanted for himself.

It was almost midnight. Most of the pages had been finalized. Yuuki was checking the proofs of the front page. He read through it twice, then looked up at Kamejima.

"Okay, Kaku-san. It can go down."

Kamejima made no response. He was staring so hard at Yuuki's face, Yuuki was afraid he'd burn a hole in it.

Yuuki stood up, took a deep breath, and laid his pin on the desk in front of him. Then he reached into his top pocket and took out his ballpoint and his red pen. He placed these on the desk beside the pin.

"How are you going to support your family?" asked Kishi, staring straight ahead.

"I'll find something."

"Sounds irresponsible."

"The economy's good. There's plenty of work out there."

"So, was it a lie?"

"What?"

"What you said the other day when we went drinking."

"What did I say?"

Kishi turned a stern eye on Yuuki.

"You said you loved this job. That you were going to keep writing your whole life."

"That was what I used to say when I was young."

"I heard it with my own ears."

"Things have changed."

"Nothing's changed at all!"

It wasn't only Kishi's voice that had turned fierce. He leapt up and grabbed Yuuki by the collar. He had surprising strength.

"Take the rural job or something! If you don't want to be the chairman's puppy dog, be a stray dog or a wild mountain dog instead. But keep writing. Write about the cherry blossoms or the summer festivals or stocking the rivers with ayu sweetfish, but just write something!"

"Let go."

"I'm not letting go!"

The shirt made a loud ripping noise.

"I'm begging you, Kishi. Please let me go."

"No way. You can't resign over something like this. If you're going to resign, then do it when you're ready to go."

He was shaken by Kishi's words.

*"When you're ready to go."*

"Didn't we start here at the same time? We're colleagues! Don't leave without me!"

Kishi was baring his teeth now. Yuuki was struck by his colleague's passion.

He hadn't noticed, but quite a crowd had formed around them. Kamejima was nodding in agreement. Yoshii was gripping his ruler. Inaoka was standing to attention.

Reporters from outside the office had come in to join the crowd. Sayama looked grave, Hanazawa, his eyes bright red. Chizuko Yorita had both hands over her face and was looking at Yuuki through her fingers. Wajima was there; Tamaki, too. And Nozawa's sulky face was peering through the gaps between everyone.

"Yuuki-san," began Sayama, stepping forward. "Whatever happens, you'll always be our JAL crash desk chief."

Yuuki began to cry. He brought both hands down hard on the desk and hid his face. Surely this was the meaning of happiness. There couldn't be anyone happier than him right now.

He heard a noise. It was the sound of the fax machine starting up. He stared at the paper coming out. He knew that handwriting.

*To Yuuki-san,*

*Thank you very much. I've decided to become a newspaper reporter.*

*Ayako Mochizuki*

**5**
**5**

September was on its way, and the record-breaking heat wave was finally starting to cool off.

Yuuki was about to leave for the tiny one-man branch office in Kusatsu up in the north of the prefecture. He would stay there alone during the week and return to his family on weekends. But before he left, he paid one more visit to Anzai. He asked Sayuri if she could give him five minutes alone with his friend, so she left the room.

Yuuki sat on the stool by Anzai's bedside.

"Hey! I thought I'd call in to see you."

It looked as if Anzai had gotten thinner. But the twinkle in his eyes was the same. In fact, Yuuki would have said they were sparkling today.

The night before, Yuuki had gone back to the Jotomachi entertainment district and revisited the Lonely Hearts bar. This time he had managed to get the whole story from Mina Kuroda. He found out that Anzai had indeed been ordered by his bosses to collect information on Chairman Shirakawa in order to create a scandal.

"So, Anzai, you were planning to leave the newspaper and go back to your climber's way of life.

"*I climb up to step down.* That's what it meant, right?

"But why did you ask me to go with you? Were you trying to tell me to step down, too?

"You're going to laugh. I couldn't step down. Looks like I'm going to have to keep on living this crappy life for a while.

"I'm leaving tomorrow, so we won't be able to get together for a while. I wish I could have heard your thoughts directly from your own mouth.

Perhaps if I climb Tsuitate I'll get it? But how am I going to do that now? You have to be there. There's no way I can climb something like that without you.

"Please wake up someday. Then we'll be able to climb Tsuitate together."

Then it happened. There was a change in Anzai's expression. Yuuki gasped.

He'd smiled. Just slightly, but he'd definitely smiled. His eyes, his mouth, his cheeks, they'd all—

"Anzai? Hey, Anzai! Can you hear me? Can you hear my voice? It's Yuuki. You remember? Yuuki from the NKT. Hey!"

He heard a noise behind him and turned. It was Rintaro who'd just come into the room, carrying a vase.

"Hey, Anzai just smiled! Your dad—he smiled!"

Rintaro smiled, too.

"Yes, I know. Dad's been smiling a lot recently."

"Oh. Oh, I see . . ."

Yuuki turned back to Anzai.

"You're going to get better. I know you're going to be out of that bed before long."

"Yes!" said Rintaro in agreement.

"He's definitely going to wake up. Because Anzai's immortal."

"Yes!"

Yuuki looked at Rintaro again. He looked very suntanned, and somehow a little stronger than before. His voice was also different. It would probably break before too long.

"So, do you want to go up to the mountains with me sometime?"

"The mountains?"

"Yes, with me and my son. I think you'd have fun."

"Yes, I'd like to."

"I'll be coming back most weekends to visit my family, so I'll give you a call, okay?"

"Yes, please."

"Right, then."

Yuuki stuck his hand in his pocket and pulled out a rubber ball.

"Let's play a bit of catch first, shall we?"

"Oh . . . Yes, please."

The two headed out.

In the corridor, they ran straight into Circulation Department chief Ito, apparently on his way to visit Anzai.

"So you're off to the Kusatsu branch."

"That's right."

"Lucky. All those hot springs."

It was strange, but Ito's oily voice didn't bother Yuuki anymore. And it even seemed possible that he might be a little envious of Yuuki being sent to the countryside.

"Pity, though. We all had great hopes for you."

"I haven't given up, you know."

"Huh?"

"You can't put out a newspaper with blank pages. I plan to fill them with articles from Kusatsu."

Yuuki looked Ito straight in his narrow eyes. He wasn't sure if he should say it, but then he decided he had nothing to lose.

"Ito-san, when you were a child, did you have a happy home?"

Ito went pale. He tried to laugh it off, but instead his face just twisted into an ugly, pained expression.

Of course. That was it. A father who is always out visiting prostitutes does not make for a happy family life. Ito's heart had its own dark storage shed of memories.

"Look after Anzai for me," Yuuki said, without bowing his head.

And with that, he hurried after Rintaro, who had gone on ahead.

## 5 6

He imagined himself plunged deep into the heart of Tsuitate.

He could see the way over the edge of the overhang. He grabbed the rock in front of him and pried himself up. His head moved above the "eaves" of the roof, and his field of vision opened up. Not the rock face, but bright, open sky. A blue sky with autumn clouds floating carelessly by. He pulled himself up a little farther and the rock face came into sight. And on that vertical wall, balanced on his aider, as he secured the rope, the figure of Rintaro. He was grinning.

"You made it, Yuuki-san!"

Yuuki was overcome with emotion. He'd climbed it. He'd crossed the first roof, the most difficult obstacle of the whole climb. He'd done it on his first try at the age of fifty-seven. And Jun had helped.

He pulled himself up to where Rintaro was waiting and checked his watch. He was surprised to see that it had been two hours since he had begun his assault on the overhang.

"The view is great from here," said Rintaro, as if he were showing off his private residence.

Yuuki followed his gaze. The clouds were floating across the Yubiso River and along the mountain ridge that ran from Shiragamon to Kasagatake. It was beautiful—enough to make him feel a little dizzy.

The events of the last seventeen years ran through his mind, all that it had taken for him to reach this point. All the faces, too.

This last spring, Sayama had been picked to be managing editor. He had experience, talent, popularity. It was a decision that everyone had supported.

Chizuko Yorita had become Chizuko Sayama and the couple had three sons. Chizuko would have liked to come back to her reporter's job after giving birth to the first, but it was too difficult to balance the life of a reporter with parenting. She'd made a rather sad goodbye speech at her farewell party. "There are as many job opportunities as there are stars in the sky, but I only have one family." It sounded as if she'd had to force herself to speak the words. Perhaps she'd made the speech in the hope that hearing the words coming from her own mouth would help her to believe them. Still, she seemed to be genuinely happy now. Sayama, too, was very comfortable in the role of father. The youngest boy was named Yuuzo, using the same character as Yuuki's name. Sayama and Chizuko had thought it would be fun to name him after "Yuu-san."

Hanazawa stuck with the Japan Airlines crash. He pulled one brilliant scoop after another: ANOTHER SEARCH OF JAPAN AIRLINES PREMISES TODAY or TWENTY EMPLOYEES OF THE MINISTRY OF TRANSPORT FACE CHARGES.

After the coverage of the crash was completely over, he took a recruitment test for Kyodo News Services and was offered a job. "I want to be able to write about world cases, worldwide," he used to say, shortly before leaving the North Kanto Times. He was usually blind drunk at the time. He was trying to fill the vacuum left in his life after the JAL crash was over. He was in Sapporo now. Still single, so he probably chased after news stories even in his sleep.

Three years after the crash, Ayako Mochizuki came to work at the North Kanto Times. Her attitude was exceptional from the start. She quickly grew into a highly competent reporter who could strike fear into the heart of the NKT's competition. She became the first-ever female lead police beat reporter at prefectural police headquarters. Although she was always extremely well-informed, she used to drop in occasionally at the Kusatsu branch office to ask Yuuki questions about working with the police. But her rather pure way of thinking never changed. Even now she was concerned about the gap between big lives and little ones.

There were major changes at the North Kanto Times. Shirakawa was deposed, and his successor, Iikura, also left the company, under a cloud of suspicion over misappropriation of construction funds for a new office building. And so it was Kasuya, the Conciliator, who quietly avoided all the infighting and was eventually rewarded with the top position. It was said that Oimura continued to strut arrogantly around the executive boardroom, but Todoroki went down a completely different path. He took a post as lecturer at Gunma Prefectural University. Kishi stepped into Kasuya's shoes as editor in chief; Nozawa, ironically, became head of General Affairs, spending every day dealing with personnel issues. Yuuki would receive letters from both of them at the change of every season: "Why don't you come back?"

Yuuki had spent the last seventeen years at the Kusatsu branch office. He put down roots in the region. After Yuka went off to university in Tokyo, they sold the house in Takasaki City and Yumiko moved up to Kusatsu permanently. She became a real country type. She also really liked the hot springs.

Next year, Yuuki would be eligible for early retirement. He thought he'd be happy to stay on part-time if it meant he could still be a reporter. He imagined growing his own vegetables while reporting from time to time on the daily events in the village.

*"I climb up to step down."*

He could still hear Anzai's words. But he also thought that the life he'd spent without stepping down had not been wasted. As long as you kept running from birth until death, falling down, getting hurt, no matter how many times you suffered defeat, you got up and started running again. Personal happiness came from all the things and people you came across, ran into by chance along the way. Climber's high. Climbing with all your might, concentrating completely on moving up, never being distracted by the meaningless stuff around you. He'd begun to think it was a fine way to lead a life.

The wind blew through his graying hair.

"You promised."

"Huh? What?" Rintaro answered.

"You promised, if we got to the top, you'd tell me something. Don't you remember?"

"Ah. You're right—I did. Okay, then. Next year, I'm going to climb Mount Everest."

Yuuki nodded. It wasn't surprising that a real climber would long to stand on the highest point on the planet.

"And?"

Yuuki hadn't missed the way Rintaro had blushed earlier, back at the Two-Person Terrace.

Now Rintaro's face turned just as red as before. In fact, redder—this time his ears and neck were crimson, too.

"When I get back from Everest, may I have your permission to marry Yuka?"

He'd already heard from Yumiko that Yuka was madly in love with Rintaro.

"Will you let me be the lead climber now?"

"What?"

"I'd really like to try. To climb lead."

"Ah . . . All right. That'll be fine, but . . ."

Yuuki grabbed the rope. He felt a new strength rush through him. *Anzai!* He called the name silently.

"So, let's go!"

As Yuuki reached up for the rock wall, Rintaro hurriedly cut him off.

"Yuuki-san? About Yuka . . . ?"

"I'll tell you when we reach the top."

It seized them both at the exact same time.

Peals of laughter carried on the pure, clear air and reverberated around the mountain peaks of Tanigawa.

A NOTE ABOUT THE AUTHOR

Born in 1957, Hideo Yokoyama worked for twelve years as an investigative reporter with a regional newspaper north of Tokyo before becoming one of Japan's most acclaimed and bestselling fiction writers. *Seventeen* is his second novel to be translated into English.

A NOTE ABOUT THE TRANSLATOR

Louise Heal Kawai was born in Manchester, England. She has spent the past twenty years in Japan. Her translations include Tamaki Daido's *Milk* and Shoko Tendo's bestselling autobiography, *Yakuza Moon*.